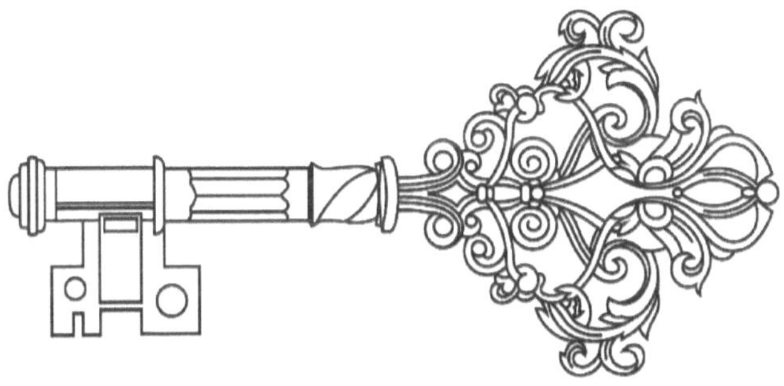

By Dana C Brentson

The Ambient Series: Sam
Salvation's Fall
Ambient Height
Desolate Seasons

The Ambience Series
Her Latent Charm

Short Stories
Grim Imperative
The Smile Before The Sword
Searching For Fortitude

Provenance of Power

The Ambience Series:

Book Two

Dana C Brentson

www.dcbrentson.com

For everyone who has ever had their power taken from them.
Take it back.

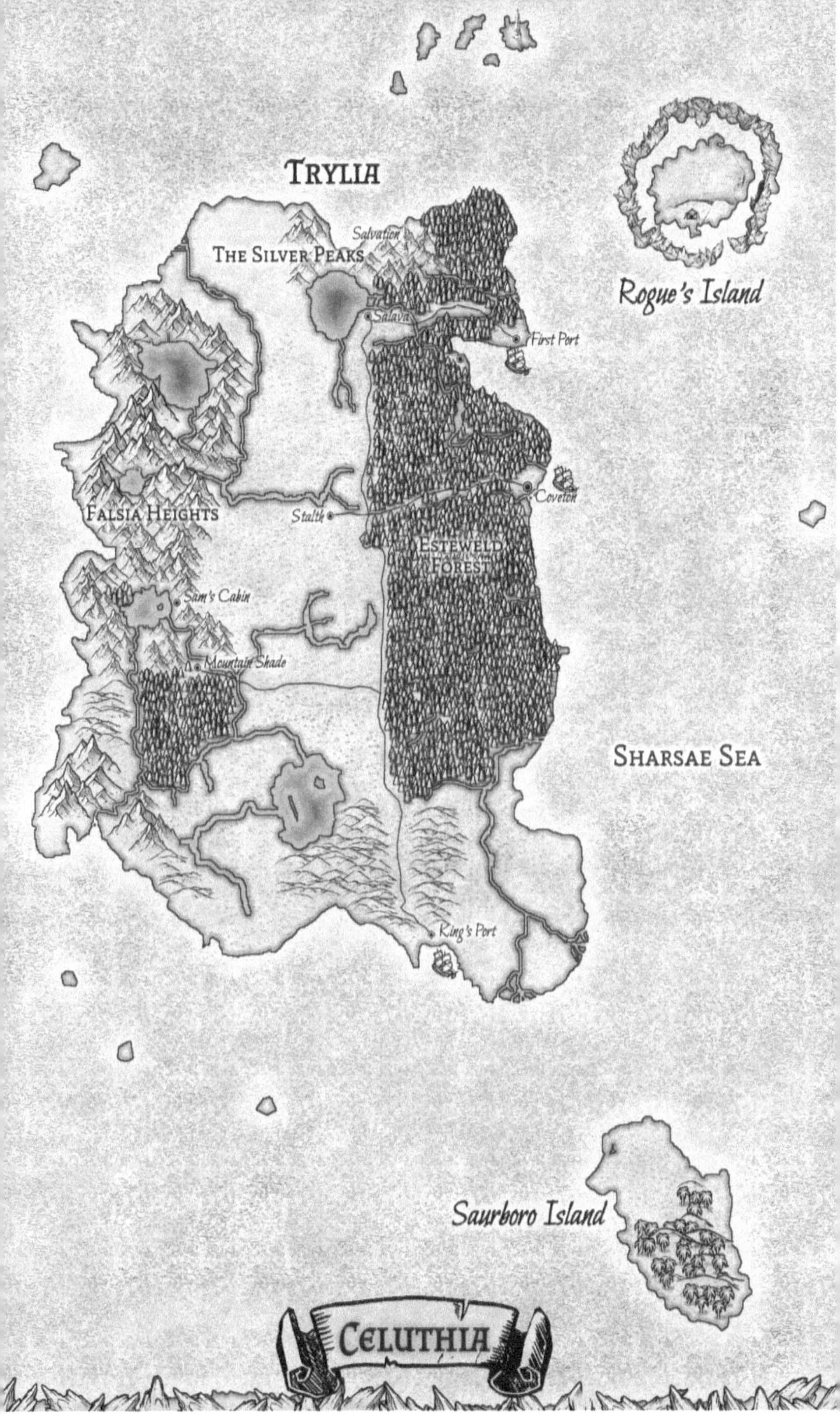

TRYLIA
The Silver Peaks
Salvation
Salava
First Port
Falsia Heights
Stalth
Coveton
Esteweld Forest
Sam's Cabin
Mountain Shade
Sharsae Sea
Rogue's Island
King's Port
Saurboro Island
Celuthia

PROLOGUE

Finally, after so much time alone, Cass had found love.

She hadn't expected it. Not after leaving the small town where she'd been born, a small port that never changed, reeked of fish, and had stopped feeling like home when she was old enough to wonder what else might be out there. Where sailors sailed in and sailed back out again, only interested in what was between her legs and on her chest, where the locals still treated her like the quiet mouse of a girl she'd worked so hard to put behind her. One man had caught her fancy, putting down roots to run the tavern where she worked, but he was too busy to notice her swoon when he spoke. It was the same when she moved inland; the big city may have moved faster, but the men acted the same as they did anywhere else. At least here, no one remembered who she'd been before.

But, on a beautiful spring morning with birdsong above and the breeze cool and crisp, *he* had walked into her tavern.

Cass hadn't thought much about him at first. He wasn't traditionally handsome and didn't have what she would call a welcoming demeanor. But he treated her like a queen, and when he spoke of his adventures, it was like waking up to find that her life had been a dream, and the real world was waiting.

Even now, out in the sunshine, she blushed, wondering what it would feel like when he finally put his hands on her, like he had in the dream she'd woken from, panting and yearning. He was such a gentleman, and she knew that it would be worth the wait, but her body wanted more.

The weather seemed to mirror her desire; spring had come in earnest, and she could feel the world coming alive in the warmth of the sun, and the smell of budding plants. It was like a lightning strike to her spirit. She felt strong, and full of energy.

Ready to take on anything.

She strolled to the healer's pretty cottage with its moss-covered roof, its dangling pots full of a multitude of healing herbs, and its large windows letting in the light. Lacy curtains embroidered with wildflowers were pushed to the side to let the sunlight in, and dust motes danced in the lazy air as Cass knocked on the door three times before she let herself in.

The elderly proprietor sat hunched over a far table, pounding something into fine dust in his mortar. The pestle slammed again and again with the *tink tink* of stone hitting stone.

"Teryl," Cass called above the noise, knowing that even if he weren't making such a racket he might not have heard her. But he turned and set the pestle down with a smile when he saw who it was.

"Cass, it's good to see you." His smile fell a bit as he looked her over.

Always the healer first, she thought.

"Don't worry, Teryl," she said with a reassuring smile. "I'm well."

His smile returned. "Then what can I do for you on this fine day?" he asked.

Cass walked nearer, running her hands over a bundle of dried herbs on the table by the door. She considered her words, not wanting to give away anything *he* didn't want her to.

"I have a customer," she said, "who was complaining about an injury on her leg. I was able to bind the wound, but I was wondering whether you have anything to keep infection at bay?"

Teryl turned back to his herbs and poured them onto a folded piece of parchment so he could tip it into a vial. "Send her my way and I'll take care of it for her," he said with a *think-nothing-of-it* wave.

"Well," Cass continued, lowering her voice conspiratorially, "she's a bit embarrassed about the wound. Doesn't want her husband to find out."

Teryl quirked his eyebrow in confusion as he corked the vial. "Why in the Elders' names would she be worried about her husband finding out?"

Cass grimaced, trying to look embarrassed. "She can't explain the wound without revealing... delicate information. Something that would put her marriage in jeopardy."

Teryl rolled his eyes and sighed. "Elders give me strength. I'll put something together for you, dear." He muttered a few choice curses about the folly of cheating spouses.

Cass relaxed, knowing she'd given nothing away. He'd be pleased. "Thank you, Teryl," she said. She waited for a minute or two while he shuffled back and forth, placing a few things into a bundle that he tied with string. He handed it to her, and patted her shoulder, sending her on her way.

Back to the inn as fast as she could. *He* was waiting.

She hustled past the tables full of travelers and regulars trying to flag her down. Ignoring them—and Falei's stare—she passed through the dining room, into the hallway, and to the foot of the stairs. She skipped steps in her haste, almost tumbled at the landing, but caught her footing at the last second.

To the end of the hall, with two quick raps on the door on the right. A pause, another two raps, and then she waited. A chair creaked, and footsteps shuffled forward. The lock clunked open, and the door swung inward.

Cass smiled and walked inside so that he could push the door closed and lock it again. Without a word, he shuffled back to the chair and sat while she prepared the herbs Teryl had given her. With anyone else she would have filled the empty space with chatter about anything that came to mind, uncomfortable with silence. But she knew he wouldn't like that, and for once, she didn't need it.

It was easy to be comfortable with him.

He shifted in his chair with a small grunt of pain as she rose, smiling into his pale blue eyes, waiting for him to roll up his right pant leg to reveal the wound. The large gash ran through the meat of his calf, the skin around it red and swollen, and she pressed the herbal compress over it to work the putrescence out as he'd taught her. He hissed, but she worked methodically, wiping away the discharge.

She wouldn't have imagined she could have the strength to do such a thing before. But *he* believed in her, and she wanted to live up to that. For him.

She wrapped the wound with a fresh bandage and gently pulled the pant leg down to cover it. He rose from the chair, holding an arm out to her for help, and she smiled, grateful for the chance to support him as he hobbled toward the bed. Cass washed her hands, and in moments, he was snoring.

Cautiously, she made her way across the room and out, down the stairs for food and tea that would be waiting for him when he woke.

The tavern was a mess of noise and movement; raucous patrons calling for fare and the other girls rushing back and forth to cover for Cass's absence. They looked so worried, and a small part of her wished she could help ease the burden, but she had a much more important job to do.

She passed behind the bar to the kitchen, and ducked out of the way of the cook as he brought a plate to the table by the door. Cass poured water from the boiling kettle into a smaller teapot and winced when she spotted Falei storming her way.

"Cass, what in the Elders' names are you doing? We have a full house and you're supposed to be down here, helping to feed them!"

Cass smiled over her shoulder, not bothering to stop. She grabbed a teacup and put it on the tray, and then a bowl and spoon. "Falei, you know I'm just upstairs. But I have my man to take care of."

"This isn't like you," she replied, a hint of worry coloring her agitation. Cass sidled around her to the big pot of lamb stew to fill the bowl on her tray. "Ever since that...*man*... came into town, you haven't been yourself."

Cass opened her mouth, ready to refute Falei's statement, but the words wouldn't come. She blinked once, Falei's words echoing through her head.

She's right, Cass thought.

She blinked again, and in that darkness that lasted a heartbeat, another voice drowned out her own.

No. The word was smooth and inviting, like a deep, dreamless sleep after a long day on her feet. She gave herself over to it, like she had before.

"I've never been in love before," she replied. "But he's paying enough for special treatment, don't you think?"

She tried to leave, but Falei blocked the door, shaking her head.

"Love shouldn't make you a different person. Not like this, not at the expense of all you are. You've abandoned everyone for him. You stole for him."

Cass rolled her eyes. *Not this again.* "It's hardly stealing, Falei."

"He hasn't paid nearly enough. Two days, all the food and drink he wants, and you serve him day and night. That's not how we do things."

"I love him," Cass argued. She looked up at the ceiling, wondering whether he'd woken yet. He never slept for long, and she couldn't let him wake up alone.

"He's only been here two days!" Falei roared. "And you were terrified of him when he showed up!"

"I didn't know him," Cass insisted. "Now I do."

Falei sighed. "I don't know what he's done to you, but if he hurts you, he'll spend the rest of his life in prison. You tell him that he owes me money, *and* I expect you to get back to work tonight. Or I'll involve the guard."

When she moved out of the way, red-faced but defeated, Cass walked out of the kitchen. Up the stairs without spilling a drop, back through the door to put the tray on the table. He was curled up on his side, and Cass crawled into the bed next to him and laid her hand across his chest. He felt too warm, but she would brew some herbs when he woke to help with the fever. She stared, amazed that he was hers. Amazed that in such a short time, she could come to love someone so much.

CHAPTER ONE

Wind buffeted my face as we surged forward, pulling strands of hair from my careful braid. One auburn lock whipped over my eyes, and I brushed it away. Ahead, the midday sun sparkled over a vast expanse of ocean, unbroken but for a solitary frigate with furled sails. But around the *Catherine's Revenge,* a large, three-masted beauty I called home, the water churned as we sped ahead.

This wind was *mine,* conjured in a concentrated, continuous gust out of nothing but my will and the strength of my power. I was a Conduit to the Ambience, the secret heart of the world of Celuthia, a birthright I hadn't understood until a year ago. Even now, with the spirits from the Ambient Pool surging around me and the utter certainty that I could do almost anything that sprang to mind, I could hardly believe that all the legends were true. The rest of the people living in Trylia certainly didn't, and while I'd spent my years traveling the length of that continent, nothing I'd seen had prepared me for the turn my life had taken.

The frigate's flag whipped in the mild natural wind—grey over blue—as we closed on it. The standard of the southern continent of Vortheim, an ominous place rumored to be the primary source of the slavers that plagued our waters. Rumored, because trade between our continents had dried up more than a generation ago, and no one I knew in Trylia knew much about Vortheim.

I hoped we wouldn't find that this vessel was part of the slave trade, but as the flagship of Trylia's new navy, we were prepared to act if necessary. Our patrol took us along the charted course between Vortheim and Rogue's Island, between the mysterious south and the lawless island northeast of Trylia. If slavers were out here, those were the most likely places to end up, and we were perfectly positioned to stop them.

This frigate seemed to be in some distress, however, which gave us the opportunity to offer aid rather than chase them down and demand to look at their cargo.

I released the wind, allowing our seasoned helmsperson Kai to take us alongside the frigate as we slowed. Captain Fallon Morrig—the man who'd taken me in as a small orphan and given me a home and a father—called to the crew, and the sails began to furl. The *Catherine's Revenge* slowed even more as we let the natural wind go.

Now that we were closer, I could see that their main mast had snapped near the top, with a shred of sail still attached to the bit of intact rigging. We approached, and a man with bushy gray beard and short gray hair stepped to the rail.

"Elders' blessings," he shouted, his high-pitched, musical voice carrying across the water. "What brings you from Trylia?"

Captain Morrig's deep voice boomed back. "Part of the king's navy, patrolling to keep the Sharsae Sea safe for travelers. Looks like you could use some help!"

The frigate captain nodded. "We could," he replied. "Went through a squall a few days back; must've done more damage than we thought, since the mast cracked in these winds."

"Permission to come alongside?" Captain Morrig asked. He smiled through his salt-and-pepper beard, lines crinkling the corners of his eyes.

The frigate captain nodded again. "Aye, and thanks."

Kai maneuvered us into the wind, the sailors letting out sail to keep us stationary as we came alongside. I descended from the nest, looking down at the much smaller ship in the shadow cast by our sails on this sunny day. As my feet hit the deck, Bryn strode to my side, one hand on the dirk hanging from a sheath on his belt, and the other snaking around my waist to pull me close. I leaned into his side until he released me.

"The captain wants a few of us to go over first, to look around while he talks about repairs. Since he's first mate, Hunter will do the talking." His cobalt-blue eyes narrowed, making them look darker and stormier as he surveyed the deck of the Vortheim frigate. His dark golden hair fell over his tanned face, and he raked his fingers through it impatiently. I fought the urge to run my fingers through it, too.

He glanced at me, and the seed of my power that I'd planted in his soul linked our minds. He poured desire through our bond to heat me from the inside, making it clear he'd noticed my attention.

My heart racing in reply, I squeezed my eyes shut and reveled in the feeling, and then pushed out a long breath to cool myself off. I needed to focus, and his self-satisfied lopsided grin didn't help matters. His next words were only audible in my head, another product of the bond I'd forged.

No Ambience for now, Lila. We don't want anyone bringing word back to Vortheim about you if we can help it.

Or Sam, I replied. I looked past Bryn to his friend, my mentor in the Ambience, his halo of white hair pulled into a severe bun behind his head as he gazed over the frigate next to the captain. He looked about the same age as Captain Morrig, though a few of us knew how old he really was. Sam had been alive at a time when the Ambient were prevalent in Trylia, almost four hundred years ago. Over the last year and a half, he'd taught me to embrace and control the wild power inside me as only someone with a few hundred years of experience and patience could have.

The lessons had been interesting, since he was a Tether, and his power—like most Ambient— manifested differently than mine. Tethers held an innate connection to the Ambient Pool, where the spirits of all living things were drawn after their death to replenish Celuthia's life force. To utilize this connection and manifest the Ambience to manipulate the elements, heal wounds, or a myriad of other uses, one of those spirits was drawn from the Pool in a Tethering ceremony. This bond between spirit and Ambient formed a bridge between the material world and the raw power of the Pool. As a Conduit, I had no Tethered spirit, because I was my own bridge. Each time I reached for my power, the spirits flooded to me, directed through my intent.

From what Roglin and Derth said, they're keen to have any *Ambient brought to Vortheim,* I thought.

Bryn nodded, both of us sobered by the thought. The wounds inflicted by his late uncle Roglin and Derth, the Ambient who had once imprisoned me within my own mind, were still raw for both of us. I had escaped with Bryn's help, but the horrors those men had put us through weren't likely to be forgotten. And it might have been much worse, if we hadn't broken free and killed Roglin, even though Derth *had* managed to escape.

Hunter led us over the rail and down the rope ladders to the other frigate, a few of our best fighters in tow. He smirked up at me, winked one emerald eye behind his curly brown hair whipped to frenzy by the wind, and turned to face the frigate's crew. I followed, taking my place at his side with Bryn at my back.

The crew certainly *looked* like they could use some help; a dozen haggard people stood watching us, grimy and exhausted, and I knew from experience that they'd been trying to repair their ship for days with little rest. The foresail was shredded, too, and what precious little of it they'd been able to patch wasn't likely to hold in wind like this.

Hunter approached the frigate captain and the two of them stepped around the repair supplies to point at what could be done out of port, and where our efforts could best be used. Bryn tried and failed to pull his too-long hair out of his face again, a sure sign that he expected trouble. I peered about, searching for the source of his instinctual unease, and found nothing amiss. But I trusted his instincts, and kept alert.

"Roy!" Hunter called to our ship, waving at our towering friend. Roy heaved himself over the rail, followed by one of our carpenters with a slew of tools slung in her belt.

Without taking my eyes from him, I thought to Bryn, *We'll let Hunter talk for a moment, and then we can head below. I want to get a look at their hold.*

I'm sure he'll bring it up before long.

As if on cue, Hunter clapped the frigate captain on the back with a smile. "We'd be happy to help and send you on your way, but it'll be a long journey with your mainsail gone. We can bring over a small spare sail, and we should make sure you have enough supplies to last." He gestured below, waiting for the captain to lead him. But the man hesitated, and I shared a knowing look with Bryn.

"We have enough," the man answered quickly. "And if we run low, we can stop at one of the island chains further south. Or we may meet another Vorthe vessel along the route." His face went blank, but his eyes were hard, challenging. My body tensed at the implied threat.

"Be that as it may," Hunter said, his smile harder in response, "as a representative of the king's navy—The Keepers—we have a duty to inspect your cargo, to ensure that no Trylian citizens are part of it."

The frigate captain's eyes widened for only an instant, but it was enough to let us know that Hunter's words resonated with him. My heartbeat quickened as I readied myself for a fight, itching to call the Ambience. Roy stepped across, and seeing the tension, put his rich obsidian hand to the axe in his belt.

"We don't recognize Trylian law on this vessel," the captain spat, his tone acidic. "If your inspection is the cost of your help, I'd rather we say good day to you."

Hunter chuckled without humor. "The inspection will occur with or without our help. Your vessel is in Trylian waters, and as such, is subject to Trylian laws. If you have nothing to hide, I'd suggest you let us go about our business." He addressed the rest of the crew, all of whom were watching the exchange intensely. "If you'd all step over to the rail and drop your tools and weapons, we can proceed."

Though Roy and our fighters stepped forward menacingly, the crew didn't comply with Hunter's instruction. Their eyes cut to their captain, their hands gripping their tools and daggers tight.

"Is anyone below?" I demanded.

He shook his head. "No."

I nodded to Bryn, who followed me to the hatch. A sailor stepped forward to stop me, and frowned down at the point of Bryn's blade that appeared before he stopped moving. I stared at the sailor whose mouth dropped open in confusion; I hadn't intended to change Bryn so much when I reinstated the bond between us, but I had to admit, in times like these, his increased strength and speed were impressive. The sailor looked up at me, and over my shoulder to where Bryn stood, and stepped back. More of our people stepped between me and the potential for violence, and I climbed below.

As soon as I broke the surface, I recognized a familiar smell. The smell of bodies packed close together, unwashed, reeking of desperation. A smell that I had experienced up close as a child, when I didn't know what it meant. My mouth turned down as disgust and anger turned my stomach.

"They have people down here," I called up to Bryn.

I made my way to the hold, where I knew I would find the source of the smell. There were the usual supplies for a long journey: barrels of fresh water, bags of assorted food, and, in the darkness at the fore of the hold, tucked behind a few large crates, a pen with metal bars. Hands reaching out through floor-to-ceiling bars stirred at the sound of approaching feet, attached to bodies packed tight inside the cage. I grasped the large iron lock on the door and stared at the dirty, sunken faces inside with my jaw clenched and my breath caught in my throat. Flashes of broken memory replaced the faces with those I'd seen as a child.

I knelt to grasp the nearest hand, which stirred an old woman with her face pressed against the door. "Hold on," I said. "We're here to help."

To Bryn, I thought, *Let Hunter know. I'll get them out.*
Understood.

I searched for a key to the lock, seething. From a cursory glance, I could tell that these people were sick, likely dehydrated, and pale, like they hadn't seen the sun for too long. Abducting people was abhorrent, but why go to all the trouble of abducting slaves if they were going to be neglected and die before reaching their destination? It was infuriating, and on top of that, there was no key to be found.

"Elders," I cursed, drawing on the Ambience rather than taking the time to search the cabins again or wrest a key away from whomever might have it. With a glance at the captives to ensure none of them could see me, I touched the lock, and the spirits touched it with me.

Ambient energy flowing through cold metal felt slower, less pliable than it did in the people before me, but it was there, and that was all I needed. The empty air outlined metal tumblers, and I flicked my finger to trip them, the lock opening with a satisfying *click*.

It fell to the floor, and I pulled open the door to crouch before the woman. "We're here on behalf of Trylia. We'll take you home," I told her.

The deck above me shuddered. *Bryn?* I thought.

They're attacking, he seethed.

I'm coming. I stood, calling over my shoulder to the people huddling toward the open door, helping the woman to a sitting position. "Stay here. We'll get you when it's safe."

A man's husky voice followed me as I rushed into the hall. "Thank you."

The deck shuddered above my head again, and I pushed myself to run faster. Bryn cursed loud enough to shout it through my head as well, just as sharp pain lanced through his jaw.

The ladder came into sight as a woman in bright blue, loose flowing clothes appeared from a doorway aft, her dark hair lined with lantern light, her gaze hard and angry. It flicked to the ladder between us, and then back to me.

The hair on the back of my neck stood on end as the moments passed and her arm drew back behind her. I crouched to pull the dagger from my boot. She thrust her arm forward, and the Ambience flashed between us, barreling down the hall toward me.

CHAPTER TWO

I barely got my hand up in time. A wall of Ambient force blocked the swipe of air—formed into a fine point like a needle—aiming for my neck. The blow reverberated through my arm as if I'd blocked it with a wooden shield. She moved again, and the lanterns hanging on the wall next to me glowed bright before the glass shattered outward, showering me with shards and licks of flames that burned through the sleeve covering the arm I thrust up to protect my eyes.

The fire flared white-hot as I moved my shield to block the heat. I realized my mistake when I heard something large thump nearby. Whipping my shield toward the hall, it deflected a heavy water barrel into the wall, shattering it and flooding the deck beneath my feet. The splinters scored my neck and cheek, and the water wrapped around my feet like the tentacle of a great sea beast.

I flung my shield of Ambience behind me to stay upright against the dragging force of the water and flung my dagger toward the woman. She darted to the side when the blade flashed, so I shoved against the air, using my hand to direct my focus, and the blade careened in her direction to slam into her shoulder the moment she reached the ladder's lowest rung.

She screamed in pain and the water splashed harmlessly to the deck, but she continued to scramble upward into the light of day.

"Elders," I cursed, touching my hand to my injured arm to seal the wound as I raced forward. The Ambient woman disappeared onto the upper deck when I started up after her, pausing to brush a hand over my stinging brow to staunch the trickle of blood running toward my eye.

My legs shook as the effort of my brief battle settled over my body. Sam's oft-repeated warning ran through my mind. *Never draw more Ambience than you have the strength to wield,* he'd told me in most of our lessons over the past year. *You direct the flow of the Ambient Pool itself, Celuthia's own power at your fingertips.*

My fingertips slipped from the top rung of the ladder, but the shield I hadn't realized I'd carried with me surged upward to keep me in place as if the spirits had sensed what I needed before I knew it myself, and I was flung onto the deck on my hands and knees.

Chaos erupted all around me. A tight cluster of arrows slammed into the deck near the rail, forcing the frigate's sailors back as more of our fighters climbed from our deck above. Roy had one muscled arm wrapped around the neck of a man almost as big as him. Bryn's face snapped back as another of the sailors punched him in the jaw at the center of the fray before a boot slammed down on my fingers, the corresponding leg blocking my view. I hissed through my teeth, and the foot stumbled away, into a blue-clad figure rushing for the frigate captain, who faced Hunter with his sword drawn.

They were close to the starboard rail, the woman bearing down on them. I had no desire to see Hunter thrown into the ocean again, so I got to my feet and took off after the woman. Leaping over bodies wrestling on the deck, I projected my shield between the woman and Hunter. She slammed into it and let out an agonized wail when the dagger shifted in her shoulder.

Her brown hair whipped around her face when she rounded on me, and the ocean to my right rose above the deck, the rogue wave like a hand poised to swat a fly.

"No," I said, too low for anyone to hear. My power exploded out to the water while my eyes stayed locked with hers. The ocean was teeming with energy, from the pull of the tides to the pulse of life in the smallest living thing, easy enough to redirect into encapsulating the wave and snuffing the woman's hold on it before she could wash me away.

Her eyes widened, her mouth forming words that I couldn't hear over the shouts of the battle, and slid to her knees. But Bryn's distress pulled my attention away from her, back to his reddened face, feeling his desperation for a breath as his vision went dark at the edges.

A growl of frustration ripped free from my chest, and I spread my shield out, around the Ambient woman to trap her inside. Leaving her behind, hoping she couldn't break free, I avoided one of my people falling to the deck, their sword wrenched from their grasp by a short, snarling man who lunged at me.

A quick pivot let him slip past me and I swung my arm around to slam my fist into his lower back, directly above his kidneys. When he crumpled, I slammed my boot down onto his hand, took the sword, and slammed the pommel into his temple. Without looking back, I ran toward Bryn, his hair tousled and eyes blazing, and he thrust his elbow back into his attacker's midsection. Bryn sucked in a much-needed breath while the man wheezed.

I stalked forward, sword ready, barely containing my anger and the spirits gathering the Ambience to rain destruction on the entire ship. A glance ensured me that the Ambient hadn't moved in the moments it had taken me to cross the deck, but when I turned back, Bryn's opponent had recovered and he punched Bryn in the gut, driving what little air he'd inhaled out again.

Bryn sank to his knees. The man above him smirked, grabbed a fistful of Bryn's hair, readying to knee him in the face. I bounded across the deck, sword pointed at his neck, the Ambience licking at my skin, begging for release. With my mental grip straining, I pushed the point of my blade until it rested against his skin.

He froze and moved his infuriated eyes to me.

"Let go," I growled. When he didn't immediately comply, I pushed the blade a bit harder to reinforce my command. I could have set him on fire, ripped him apart without touching him at all, and the only thing keeping me from doing so was the satisfying dribble of blood that ran below my blade. "Now."

His hands relaxed and Bryn straightened, coughing as he ran his hand through his hair. I glanced over my shoulder, toward the frigate captain standing at the point of Hunter's sword, and then to the Ambient. My heart dropped.

She was on her knees, blood pouring from her shoulder, but the shock on her face was gone. In its place was a bitter scowl and a scathing look my way. She bared her teeth and thrust her hands in the air, and the ship shuddered beneath us.

The Ambience glowed bright around her, spirits swarming to her like they did to me. But this was different. Hungrier. Overwhelming. It was the first fissure in a volcano before it erupts, the violence of it channeled through this woman who had reached too far into the Pool and found that she couldn't contain what she had wrought. The water rose around us, forcing our ships apart, the *Revenge* behind a wall of seawater that spiraled into the air from beneath the frigate.

We dropped into the vacuum left behind and the swirling wave rocked the *Revenge*. I thrust my hands out in front of me, palms touching. Ambience pulsed through the wave, vicious and desperate as the Ambient directing it. Spirits swarmed to the wave, becoming ethereal versions of my hands, interposed into the center to mirror my movements.

My physical body and spirit strained to keep hold of the energy in the water as I pulled my hands apart, and the wave split up the center. The effort drained my strength, and I let the shield flicker out to keep the other Ambient's will at bay so that inch by inch, the wave separated. The Ambience became a blaze inside me and panic clawed at me, a guttural scream tearing free. I wouldn't stop it in time, this magma in *my* veins. The Ambience wanted me to let it take over—I could feel it— to make me nothing more than its vessel. I wrenched my hands apart, flinging the remnants of the wave harmlessly to either side of the ship as I pulled away from the ravening power.

I collapsed onto the deck, panting and shaking, and Bryn slid on his knees to take me into his arms. He murmured into my ear, his hoarse voice lost in the roar of Ambience that wouldn't let me go, reminding me of another time not long ago when I'd lost control. I focused on his voice, connecting me to that memory, to myself, watching the spirits freed from their task bearing down on me as the Ambience clawed at my spirit.

I took one deep breath, and then another, focusing on the sound of Bryn's voice, the wood beneath me, the feet that rushed back and forth in front of me. *This* was what I wanted; to live in the world, to keep myself whole. Not to become a creature of the Ambience who endangered the people she loved. Another deep breath, and the Ambience retreated, like the spirits who now floated at the edge of my vision.

Bryn's concern echoed through my mind when he looked me over. My head felt like it was filled with rocks as I tried to turn to him, but I couldn't manage. Instead, I let my face fall against his chest.

I'll be okay, I told him through a garbled mess of fatigue.

For the love of the Elders, Bryn seethed. *You're going to kill yourself!*

The battle halted, everyone's eyes on the water falling back into the ocean, onto the deck of the frigate, until a woman's scream rent the air and a shockwave of Ambience knocked the breath out of my lungs. The woman dissolved in a flash of light, and a whirling mass of air and water and debris hurtled toward the *Revenge*. The light swirled with the cyclone, taller and taller until it dwarfed our ship, steeped in rage and desperation, bent on the destruction of my home and my crew.

Bryn!

I see it, he replied.

There was no time, and if I opened myself to that power tearing through the cyclone, I'd be lost like the Ambient that gave her life to end ours. Bryn hooked his finger under my chin to draw my exhausted gaze up to his.

We don't have a choice, he thought.

I can't lose them again. I followed the flow of my power to him across our bond, where a portion of me had melded with his spirit when I'd created this connection, to become something new. One person, one mind, with two bodies that moved in harmony, and a limitless expanse of possibility laid out before us. Our bodies tingled with Ambience, as if we'd become the Pool, the spirits swirling around us in a frenzied dance.

We gasped at the enormity of our combined strength.

We turned our attention to the cyclone that was nearly upon the *Revenge*, the water churning and roaring, flinging splinters of wood over both ships. Knowing we couldn't dismantle it in time, we cupped our hands and lifted them high into the air, diverting the cyclone over the mast.

The cyclone's will fought against ours, the Ambient's death throes echoing in our minds, their spirit binding to the maelstrom to force it back into line with the *Revenge*. The cyclone clipped the top of the main mast and the ship shuddered with a cacophonous *crack* that reverberated through our chest. The crew's horrified gasps were swallowed by the groan of wood bending. Once the cyclone cleared the ship, we dropped our hands and it splashed into the waves.

Before we could breathe a sigh of relief, there was another crack overhead. We looked up as the top of the mast broke free and toppled toward the deck. We threw our hands up, pushing a blast of air into the bulk of the wood and forcing it to fly out to sea. Much of the rigging went with it; what was left thumped onto the deck as the crew dove out of the way or splashed into the water between the two ships.

Stunned silence filled the air as everyone looked around. Hunter pushed through the crowd with the frigate captain in tow, his face filled with apprehension as he looked us over.

"Is everyone safe?" we asked, turning our heads to regard our friend.

Hunter's eyes narrowed. Our ship teetered on its axis, the remnants of the mast looming over the frigate as it swayed in that direction. We soothed the ocean's chaotic energy as the Ambient's spirit flowed with the others of its kind at our direction.

"Lila!" Captain Morrig and Sam stood at the rail of the *Catherine's Revenge*, peering down at us. Sam's warm umber complexion was wrinkled with fear. "Stop this, Lila," he commanded, his words infused with power, his spirit growing as it attempted to stifle the power emanating from us. We laughed, amused at the attempt to smother the Ambience within us, like throwing a rag on a bonfire. He was only a Tether, after all. No matter his skill, no matter how long he'd been alive, he couldn't hope to control us.

"Relax, Sam," we said, both smiling Bryn's lopsided grin. "We have it under control." Our eyes tracked the damage from the torn mast to the widening crack in the hull. "We need to get to port; we'll take care of it." The world seemed to crack open before us, trying to give us its power.

"No!" Sam shouted.

All we had to do was open a passage between where we were and where we wanted to be, and then push ourselves through it. As easy as opening a door and stepping through. We closed our eyes, thinking of King's Port. If we moved the entire ship and crew, we could be there in a moment.

We lifted our hands out to our sides, enshrouding both ships in spirits. They covered the broken mast down to the hull, and more wrapped around each member of the crew, each captive in the hold, and the frigate crew like cloaks. We pointed to a space before the bow and carved a wide circle in the air. More spirits flowed in that direction, mimicking our motion, and the sky in the center of the circle rippled.

Beyond that doorway, a wave of humid heat bathed us from clear water over the pale ocean floor. The crowd gasped, and Sam bellowed something we couldn't understand over the roar in our ears. The Ambience flooded through us in a torrent of light and heat, but we controlled it now. It wouldn't—couldn't—consume us. We were stronger together.

Sam was still shouting as we finished our preparation, and the hole in the world solidified. A shockwave erupted from the hole as we pushed the ship forward, and the crew reeled, set back onto their heels or flat on their backs. Everything passing through the doorway shimmered; the bow, the deck, the crew, and the air around all of us. The world spun, inverting and reverting maddeningly before it disappeared before our eyes where a gloomy, black mass of tendrils stretched out from within the hole. The *Revenge* glided through the center where silence enveloped us. The Ambience rose to meet us, its currents flowing around us, bathing everything in power.

We laughed, gleeful even as everyone around us screamed, the sound muffled in this strange space between the world we'd left behind and what was on the other side. Hunter fell to his knees, clutching his head as if to keep it in place.

And then we were through. The sky was bright, the ocean a clear, clean blue, and the air warm and humid and still. The hole closed behind us—a great sucking wound in the fabric of the world being sealed—and the crew staggered to their feet, shocked and disheveled.

We turned to smile at Sam, and everything went black.

CHAPTER THREE

My head screamed in protest as I woke, every part of my body aching as if I'd been broken and put back together several times. "Uhnh," I winced, wishing I could escape the pain. Instead, I grabbed the sides of my head to hold it together as it tried to rip itself apart.

"Good, you're awake." Sam's deep disapproval rumbled from somewhere nearby and I cracked one eye open. Sam was sitting in a chair placed by my bunk, deep frown lines suggesting he'd been scowling in preparation for this moment. "When I tell you that something is dangerous and possibly catastrophic, perhaps you'll be more inclined to listen now that you've experienced what it feels like."

We had little to show for all the months Sam and I had examined and researched the bond between Bryn and me. The first I'd inflicted upon Bryn when I was desperate and out of control before I knew anything about the Ambience, and the second I'd forged to replace what we'd lost. He no longer suffered from injuries that I sustained, and we'd retained the ability to share thoughts and feelings, as well as becoming this *other* being. Sam had assured me that there was no precedent for what I'd done. It was as if I had given Bryn a piece of my spirit, separated it from myself like a spirit vacating a dead Ambient to join the Pool.

I'd given myself to him in every other way. Why not a piece of my spirit?

"Not now, old man," Bryn grumbled. I rolled my head in his direction instinctively and groaned in instant regret. Lying next to me in the narrow cot in my cabin—there were my table and chairs, and the other cot I used for treating patients next to the chest with my surgeon's tools and remedies—he slung his arm across his eyes. "We understand that you need to scold us, but can it wait? My head is pounding."

I reached for the Ambience that was always slow to answer after we merged, but it slipped through my grasp. Sensing that, Bryn touched a hand to my chest, and the spark of my power inside him glowed. He shone with the prismatic light I saw every time I manifested Ambience. His grip tightened as the energy he expended flowed into me.

A restorative surge filled my body, and through our connection, the deep well of Bryn's stamina poured into me. I *wanted* it. I *needed* it. I knew that if I decided to, I could consume him as easily as the Ambience would consume me if I let it, and I recoiled from the impulse, cutting off the flow.

That's enough, Bryn, I thought. *Thank you.*

You're welcome, Love.

Sam sat silently, waiting as I used Bryn's energy to heal the pain in my head, and then reached over to Bryn to help him, too. The effort should have been minor considering what Bryn had just done, but it was almost more than I could bear. My stomach cramped the way it had when I was a prisoner on Roglin's ship.

But I didn't have time to dwell on the comparison, because Bryn sat up, folded his legs beneath him, and leaned against the hull facing Sam. "Scold away, old man," he sighed, running his hands through his hair.

Sam didn't hesitate. "What you two did was reckless! I've told you time and again that it's too much power for the two of you to wield, *especially* considering that you aren't even Ambient, *boy!*" He flung his hand in Bryn's direction, and Bryn had the good sense to look abashed. "And, as if that weren't enough, you ripped a hole in the world! What were you thinking?!"

Bryn glared at him. "We were thinking that Lila didn't have enough strength after the whirlpool to deal with that cyclone, Sam."

I touched his arm, shooting him a look to stop him from saying something he'd regret. *Sam's angry because he was worried,* I reminded him, but he shot me an exasperated glance.

"We didn't have a choice! We saved everyone's lives!" He turned back to Sam. "If you don't understand what we can do, fine. But that doesn't mean that we should be punished for what we did."

Sam matched Bryn's glare. "Perhaps since you're so determined to act like a child, you *should* be punished. What you two did... it didn't *feel* right. And everyone could see that it wasn't Bryn and Lila doing it; it was something *else*." Bryn opened his mouth to argue, but Sam cut him off with a brusque wave. "Don't argue with me, boy, you can't tell me it was just you. We don't know what the repercussions of your actions will be; not even the most learned Ambient from my time could have imagined what you could do..." He trailed off, and after a deep sigh, added, "I'm concerned about both of you, and I don't want to lose you."

His sorrowful declaration was the only thing that could be worse than his usual shouting. Now that I'd stopped worrying about the tirade we might have otherwise received, I noticed that his long white curls were loose, floating over his face rather than the tidy bun at the back of his head. He must have been sitting here, pulling at his hair while he waited for us to wake, wondering whether we would. Guilt mingled with the conviction of my response.

"I would have been lost either way without Bryn's help, Sam," I said. "The cyclone could have hit us, or I could have given everything to stop it. Instead, we did what we had to do. I realize that wasn't all we did, but we're in a much better position to get home now. If this is unprecedented," I continued, "don't you think we should learn what we can? Experiment with it in controlled environments, and record what we find?"

He nodded once. "Of course we should," he huffed. "But this is hardly a controlled environment. There are too many people, too many distractions, and there is no way of controlling you once you've started." He heaved a heavy sigh. "I'm trying to give you all the tools to avoid the worst outcome, but I don't even know if I'm pulling from the right set."

There was nothing I could say to give him comfort. *None* of us knew what we were doing, and I had to agree; there was something *different* about what we were when we became one.

Sam sighed again and ran his hands over his face. "The amount of power you command frightens me."

"Sam," Bryn said, "Lila's right. It's dangerous to have power like this and not know how to control it." He glanced at me, and I knew he was thinking of the way our time on his uncle's ship ended. In fire and death.

"What you did," Sam began, "was well beyond your capability. Separate, joined, it doesn't matter. You tore open the world, and I don't care how powerful you are, that's not how the Ambience *should* work. I had to watch as the Ambience burned you from the inside out, and when you fell, I thought that was the end. I didn't know if you'd ever wake to hear another lecture about why this is so dangerous. I'm grateful you both felt so awful this morning, because it means you survived."

Sam hung his head, releasing his worry and grief in a shuddering exhalation. I slid off the bed to embrace him, and he clutched me as if his life depended on never letting go.

"You haven't lost us yet, old man," Bryn said as he joined us. "We'll be more careful in the future, but you have to admit, we *did* save everyone's lives."

Sam lifted his head to glare at Bryn. "You did, boy. Almost at the cost of your own. Think about what you would have done if you had lost Lila." His words had a bitter bite to them; he hadn't shared it with us, but I knew he'd suffered loss as acute as either of ours.

Bryn *did* think about it. For a moment, his mind was awash in old grief and the deep-rooted fear he lived with as a result. It wasn't the first time he'd been terrified of losing me, and it wouldn't be the last, but Sam's words plucked at his insecurity as easily as a musician plucking the strings of their instrument. He and Sam stared at each other, resentful of the reminder of what they'd suffered, until Sam nodded at him.

"I see you understand now, Bryn. Let that be your lesson for the day." There was a knock on the door, and I opened it to find Captain Morrig and Hunter on the other side. Their shoulders dropped, anxiety giving way to relief when they saw that Bryn and I were awake.

"Thank the Elders," the captain sighed.

"You two look terrible," Hunter smirked, sliding past me. I made way for the captain and watched him take a seat, nodding to Sam as Hunter leaned on the wall next to where Bryn was still sitting on the bed.

I started to close the door, but it struck something hard. Roy smiled down at me when I looked up to figure out why, and I left him to close the door behind himself. There were too many bodies in here to move easily, so I wormed my way through to the bed so that I could sit and grab Bryn's hand in my lap. Bryn smiled at Hunter, even as his thoughts still lingered on what Sam had said.

Bryn, I'm alive, and I'm right here. Don't think about what could *have been.*

He let out a shuddering breath and squeezed my hand. *You're right,* he thought. *We're safe, but I guess I didn't realize how close we came. I won't lose you.*

You won't, I agreed. I placed my hand on his cheek; he sighed and closed his eyes for a moment.

"So," I said, glancing out the window. The sun was bright, and the sky clear. "Where are we?"

"About a day north of Saurboro Island," the captain replied. I blinked, surprised. "We're moving now with the sails we have left, but there was more damage than we realized. Sam thinks some of that is from what you two did to get us here."

"I guess that's what happens when you try to move two ships through a hole you tore in the sky," Hunter said. He grimaced like he had when we'd gone through. "I don't think I like that kind of travel, even if it saved us a few weeks."

The captain nodded. "I'll admit, it felt like my head was turning to mush. But we're here, and everyone is alive."

"Did we have any injuries? What about the captives and the crew of the frigate?" We were on the *Revenge,* but what had happened to the frigate?

"Odd cuts and bruises for our people, and all from the frigate are accounted for," the captain said. "Some of the captives are in bad shape; we've done what we can, but now that you're awake perhaps you can help." He glanced at Sam.

"I hesitate to use the Ambience to heal them, but I've done what I can surreptitiously."

"I'm sorry we couldn't do more," I grimaced, guilt twisting my stomach. I could still feel the reverberation of the mast cracking and hear the screams when we went through that void. I should have been there for the injured, for those slaves...

"Don't you dare apologize for not doing enough, dear one," the captain said. He shook his head and waved his hand as if to brush my guilt aside. "As I see it, you saved all of us. Each member of this crew knows that. Repairing the damage is nothing compared to what would have happened if you hadn't."

Hunter wiped a drop of sweat from his brow. "I didn't know you could do something like that. But let's not repeat it. My head felt like it was going to explode."

"What's the extent of the damage?" I asked.

Roy sighed and shifted his feet. "The mainmast's sails are all ruined. When the topgallant went, the rigging tangled up the others on the main and took a portion of the foresails and its rigging. The mizzen mast is still intact," he said in his musical, baritone voice. "We won't be going anywhere fast."

I groaned, already dreading how much work we had ahead of us.

"There are sections of the port hull above the water that tore free when we went through, but those will be easy enough to repair." He sighed. "Kai took a small crew to get the frigate back to King's Port for repair, so we'll have to make do with me at the helm."

Roy snorted, but his face was grim when I turned his way. "They had eleven souls in their hold."

"We should get the worst in here," I said, heaving myself off the bed. "Preferably one, so that I can do what I need to do."

"Understood," Captain Morrig replied. "Dismissed."

The others filed out of the cabin at the captain's order, leaving me alone with Bryn, who had moved to the edge of the bed to pull on his leather boots. He shoved his hair out of his face, flashing me a tired lopsided grin that made my heart flutter. I brushed it out of his eyes, the feel of his skin under my fingertips soothing the anxiety that had built over the length of the conversation.

"I had him, you know."

I frowned. "What?"

"That bastard that was choking me," he said. He laced his boots without looking away from me.

"Of course you did," I said as I looked him over. I hadn't healed the livid purple bruises on his swollen left cheek or the side of his mouth, but he seemed whole otherwise.

"But I enjoyed being rescued," he smirked.

Heat flooded my cheeks at the admiration on his face, but I turned away to ready the space for my incoming patients. I couldn't help but compare what I'd seen to my time in Roglin's cell. I'd been alone, left to wither away in darkness and filth. Bryn followed my train of thought, and moved behind me to snake his arms around my middle and pull me tight against him.

"Sometimes I can't believe we're here," I whispered. He'd been my jailor, but he'd been trapped as surely as I was. I turned to face him, gazing into his eyes the way I had the first time I'd come out of the foggy prison my mind had been in.

"I'm sorry I didn't help you sooner," he said. "A mistake I won't make with anyone else." He trailed his hand down my shoulder to my arm, sending a shiver of pleasure down my spine.

A shout from above broke our solitude, and we shared a tired glance before our footfalls joined the crashing thunder of our crew mobilizing from all over the ship.

I scrambled up the steep wooden steps and emerged to find the crew running to stations, stealing glances at something beyond the bow of the ship. I followed those glances and found another ship in the distance. Three masts held square sails pulled taut in the wind, its deep hull carved through the waves.

"They're raising colors," Captain Morrig announced, gazing through his spyglass. "She's from Vortheim."

CHAPTER FOUR

"They're changing course to intercept us," I said. Dread settled into the pit of my stomach. If they had another Ambient, I wasn't sure I would have the energy to counter them.

The captain shouted. "To your posts!" The crew exploded into motion, and all our months of training for a scenario like this came into focus. Captain Morrig divided his forces into small fighting groups with Hunter in charge of the hand-to-hand fighters, and Bryn in command of our archers.

Normally I'd be in the Bird's Nest, ready to maneuver us with wind and water and creating a shield large enough to encompass the ship. Without my normal perch, I stayed by the helm with the captain and took the proffered spyglass. The *Revenge* had taken too much damage for us to run. If it came to it, we'd need to fight.

"Can you do this?" Bryn demanded, concern twisting his mouth into a frown.

"I'll have to," I replied. My body screamed for rest, but if the worst came to pass, I'd need to be ready. I landed a peck on his cheek, stubble scraping against my lips. I climbed onto the rail of the quarter deck, hooked my arm through the mizzenmast rigging, and brought the spyglass to my eye.

I spotted the hurried movement of sailors taking *their* stations.

They swarmed around a ballista, I noticed with dismay, like ants over a piece of food, and ranks of archers lined up behind a line of pike wielders. This was no trading vessel. This ship was made for combat. But once they'd gotten into position, they didn't ready weapons, merely stood at alert. A white flag slowly rose below their Vorthe colors, signaling to request communication.

I snapped the spyglass closed and relayed what I'd seen to the captain. He called out to raise a white flag in response as Sam climbed the stairs to join us.

"I'll make a shield if necessary," he said after a long, considering look at me. I didn't argue with him; both of us knew how dangerous it would be for me to draw enough Ambience to do that in my state.

Bryn shot me a look filled with apprehension after that silent exchange between my mentor and me. *Please, don't push yourself if you don't need to.*

I'll be fine, I reassured him. *Get your archers ready.*

The archers in question chattered nervously as they fingered bowstrings and nocked arrows, watching Bryn descend to the main deck to join their ranks. Bryn silenced them with a gruff word, and then reassured them with a joke. They chuckled, more confident after seeing Bryn's ease.

An attitude that was *not* echoed by his thoughts.

I put the spyglass against my eye again in time to see a man with a short flop of white-blonde hair take a place on the forecastle. The wind whipped his hair around his face, but he stood steady as the ship crested a wave, with his hands clasped behind his back. His attire was immaculate, neat brown pants and billowing blue shirt noticeably tidy compared to the sailors that crossed behind him.

They let out their sails minutes later to slow their approach, and soon the Vortheim ship was close enough to make out words in the echoing shouts from their sailors. I didn't understand the words, musical despite the commanding tone from a figure near their helm. They took down their sails to all but stop. I didn't know whether to hope that this meant they wouldn't become aggressive, or to worry that they were confident in our destruction to negate the necessity for maneuvering.

The man smiled when they came alongside. "Elders' blessings," he said in perfect Trylian, with a lyrical, lilting accent. His deep tan arms gesticulated as he spoke. "We couldn't help but notice your apparent distress and thought we should offer our aid." He caught sight of me looking at him and smiled, nodding his head in a miniscule bow to me. Bryn seethed, though a glance his way showed me his face was still neutral.

"Thank you," Captain Morrig called, "but our destination isn't far, and we have enough of our sails left to make it there for repairs."

"Such an idyllic island," the man mused. "I see Trylian colors flying; what brings you to Saurboro in such treacherous waters?"

"We offered passage to some people looking to come home. Unfortunately," Captain Morrig gestured to the broken mast, "we caught a bit of ill fortune and a strong wind. We'll do what we can here, and then make full repairs once we're at home in King's Port."

"Ah!" the man exclaimed, his arms spread as wide as his smile. "Our very destination! What a coincidence!"

"What brings you to Trylia?" I asked.

He chuckled, and his eyes locked onto mine. There was something so alluring about his gaze, as if he could see through me, and he liked what he saw.

"I have been sent from Lacorsia, capital of Vortheim, at the behest of my superiors. My compatriots and I are searching for a dangerous criminal we fear has fled to your shores. I assume, as part of the Trylian Navy as your standard suggests, that I am speaking to someone with the king's authority to hunt criminals?"

He looked away, and relief swept through me, as if I'd been released from something tethering our gazes. "We are a Trylian naval vessel, a specialized branch known as The Keepers," Captain Morrig confirmed.

The man glanced my way again, and my heart fluttered. It wasn't a pleasant sensation, rather it was insistent, a twinge of intuition. Frowning, I concentrated on the feeling, Captain Morrig's next words lost as I realized that it was the Ambience trying to show me something. I opened myself to the energy surging around me like visible currents of air.

Distracted by the strength of those currents—vastly more vibrant and powerful than what I felt on Trylia—I almost missed the convergence of that energy on the man from Vortheim. An ethereal figure surrounding him like a cloak, the same as Sam as my eyes darted toward him to confirm what I was seeing. My breath caught in my throat, my anxiety spiking higher than before.

This man was a Tether.

"Then perhaps, when we meet in Trylia, you can introduce me to whomever I might need to speak with about the apprehension of this Vorthe criminal. And, when your ship has undergone repairs and is seaworthy again, if we have not reported his capture to your authorities, you might do us the honor of keeping your eyes open for him?"

I forced my face and shoulders to relax, desperate to keep my discovery off my traitorous face, even as Bryn tensed, feeling the shift in my demeanor. Hoping it looked as casual as I was trying to make it seem, I swept my gaze over the people behind this Tether.

One, an androgynous figure with long, curly hair and cool beige skin, another a woman with warm olive skin, muscles bulging under a tight shirt, pale green eyes narrowed at us, and a bald man with a smile on his plain face. None of them had the same aura of a spirit about them, not like their outspoken companion. Their immaculate clothes marked them as separate from the sailors, as well.

Captain Morrig nodded, charming despite the wariness underlying his outward presentation. "We will report to our superiors and ask them how they would like us to proceed, and we can leave your name as well as your ship's with them, to let them know you'll be coming." There was an edge to his assurance, a subtle declaration that we would be watching his movements in Trylia, and I could tell from the wry smile that this man had gotten the message. "I'm surprised a Vorthe crew would be so respectful of our laws. In my experience, Vortheim ships don't recognize Trylia's authority."

"Most ships and their crews aren't representatives of Lacorsia or the Malachi," the man replied. "But I am. My name is Colagh of Lacorsia, and my ship is the *Gloom Break*. I would be honored if you could mention our arrival to anyone with the authority to grant us access to your beautiful country, as it is the most fervent desire of the Blessed Malachi to extend a hand of friendship to your king."

His statement, and the apparent honesty with which he spoke, surprised me. I'd been under the impression that Vortheim had no intention of seeking peace with Trylia after continued aggression, especially considering the attack yesterday. Perhaps the situation was more complicated than I'd thought.

Captain Morrig pursed his lips, skeptical. "It's heartening to hear that the sovereign of your nation is willing to respect the sovereign of ours. I hope it's a sign of things to come."

Colagh nodded. "As do I," he said. "Our nations have been at odds too long. Let's hope that we can take the first step on the road to a successful relationship between our two nations. And, Elders willing, the capture of Derth."

"I knew we hadn't seen the last of him," I growled. Colagh had given us a thorough description of the man that haunted my nightmares while the *Gloom Break's* sails were readied. Once they'd moved far enough away that I assumed they wouldn't return, I'd gone below and screamed into my pillow to expel the rage, fear and frustration building in my chest.

Now, after designating two of the captives to be brought to my cabin for treatment, Bryn gripped and regripped the hilt of his dirk, watching Roy, Hunter, Sam, and Captain Morrig file into the cramped captain's cabin. My nerves had been frayed even *before* I'd had to endure us talking in circles for several minutes, and I needed to get to my patients. I didn't have time to go through it again. "If Vortheim is looking for him, we can't let them get their hands on him."

"Why not?" asked Roy, leaning next to the window, exasperation plain on his face. "If Vortheim wants him, let them take him. The man said he's a criminal, so let *them* punish him."

"Agreed," Hunter said. "He's dangerous. Let these people—with their own Ambient—make him *their* problem."

"And let him tell them about Lila?" Sam retorted. "He knows too much about us," he pointed at himself and me, "and we know he was supposed to capture Ambient. I can't imagine he'd have any qualms about handing us over."

Roy frowned, crossing his arms and leaning against the wall to peer out at the ocean again. The sun illuminated the scar on his forearm. A reminder of our battle with Roglin's crew outside King's Port.

"It's possible Vortheim knows about us already," I pointed out. The thought of being hunted again sent a shiver up my spine. I'd spent the first few months after our ordeal with Derth jumping at every unexpected noise, always looking over my shoulder, and it'd taken months after that to relax into my new life. To feel like I was finally free. But that fear was back, and I didn't know that I could get rid of it again. "Derth had plenty of time to alert them, even before Roglin died. I can't imagine someone like him would have worked so tirelessly to get me back if he didn't think he had to. He's a monster, but he's calculating, too. I don't think he'd chase me for the sport of it without anything else to gain."

I let out an exasperated sigh to blow my bedraggled hair out of my face. I hadn't realized I was running my hands through it. "*Someone* knows what I am, someone dangerous enough to scare Derth. If the Malachi has gone to this much trouble to find him, it must be connected."

"I'd rather we steer clear of Colagh so that we never find out," Bryn added, and then turned to Sam. "Could he already know that you're Ambient just from looking at you?"

"It's possible," Sam replied. "Tethers can utilize the Ambience to sense its use, but that's a skill that requires mastery to be reliable. People with an affinity for knowledge, like me, are capable of far greater sensitivity than most. Even after all my years of practice, I can only sense when it is being used, or in Lila's case, when a Conduit isn't in control of their natural connection, leaving it open because they are incapable of closing it. If any of them are Conduits, they are well-versed in their control of the Ambience. If there were more Tethers aboard, they were not using the Ambience as Colagh was."

He glanced at me with a wry smile. "Lila has learned to control her power, and no longer exudes Ambient energy. We can only hope that either Colagh of Lacorsia was using the Ambience for something else, or his ability to sense the energy around him is not as practiced as mine, or as sensitive as Lila's."

I recalled a conversation about this subject as he spoke, wherein he'd explained that I should be able to sense the Ambience because of my connection to it. *I need to work on that,* I scolded myself.

Sam continued. "Since he didn't show signs of recognizing us or our power, I think it likely he was using his for something different. Tracking, perhaps? I know it's possible to find people, animals, even objects and places, if there is some link to one's quarry. In theory, if you're close enough, there would be a trail to follow, visible to the person concentrating on the tracking."

"Or he's a very good liar," Hunter interjected. "But, unless we want to kill envoys of the Malachi, there's not much we can do about them. I can't imagine Derth would be happy to see them if they're set on bringing him to Vortheim. Imagine the damage he would do wherever he is. He'd have no problem destroying a city to escape."

"I don't know that I trust Colagh's intentions," I said. "Or the Malachi's. If I have the Elders' own luck, and Vortheim doesn't know enough about me to search me out for whatever reason they might want me, we can't let the Vorthes bring that knowledge home. Knowing that Derth can affect people's minds, if all they want is to bring him to justice, can we trust them to follow through? Will he take control of them?" I asked Sam, "Can normal Tethers overcome someone like him, like I did eventually, or is that only because I'm a Conduit?"

Sam shook his head and shrugged. No one spoke as they considered my questions, and I watched the last of Hunter and Roy's doubts about our involvement with Derth's capture falling away, so I continued. "Assuming they get him back to Lacorsia, how do we know the Malachi won't use him against us in the future? We don't know what they have planned for him, but I know that I need him to pay for what he did to me."

"We must find him first," Captain Morrig said. "Lila's right, he should face Trylian justice."

"We'll head to the palace as soon as we make landfall," Bryn said. "King Demetrius needs to know what's coming."

CHAPTER FIVE

With one hand on her back, I held the other beneath the old woman I'd first seen in the cage's frail, bony fingers clutching a clay cup as she lifted it to her mouth to take a drink. Her name was Sydah, and though she'd seemed to be in much worse condition, with a bit of care and adequate food and water, I'd discovered she should recover quickly. I smiled, letting a trickle of Ambience flow into her through my grip to help her body heal and strengthen a small degree as she sipped. Now that I had a job to do—and plenty of outrage about Derth to drive my exhaustion from my mind—my power had become the steady thrum that it usually was, waiting for me to call it. Or to let my control slip enough for it to come to the surface unbidden.

After a few more sips, her grip was stronger, and the cup shook a bit less. Her progress was encouraging, and I had every hope that she'd make a full recovery after the first few days of constant nursing, like most of the people we'd rescued.

"Where are you from?" I asked, easing Sydah onto the cot and placing the cup on the floor.

She cleared her throat. "A small fishing village on Trylia's southeast coast. You likely haven't heard of it." She smirked, and I grinned in reply. The wrinkles at the corners of her eyes deepened, a testament to a life lived smiling, and I was so grateful that it wasn't yet over.

My other patient coughed weakly, and Sydah cocked her head to peer around me. "Will he make it?"

I touched her shoulder, giving her a warm, reassuring smile when she looked up at me.

"I don't know, but I'm going to do everything I can." Her thin lashes fluttered. "You get some rest. We'll be at Saurboro tomorrow, and I'm sure you don't want to miss some time on dry land."

"Thank the Elders for you, miss." She smiled at me and let her eyes close.

My other patient was an older man named Eoutn, and though he'd taken small sips of water when he'd first arrived hours earlier, his breath had shallowed in the time I'd been tending to Sydah. I'd seen illness brought on by dehydration and malnutrition before, but never to this degree. His dark brown skin was ashen, his dark eyes sunken, open wide and unseeing.

"Eoutn?" I said, placing a hand softly on his chest. His lips were tinged blue, and with every rattling inhale his eyes widened, wild with panic. "Elders," I cursed, not sure whether I was beseeching their help or damning them for their negligence. *Did he inhale some of the water I've been dribbling in his mouth? Was he sick* before *he was taken?* It didn't matter; I could wonder at the cause for days, but I needed to act *now.*

After a glance over my shoulder to ensure that Sydah was already drowsing, I let the Ambience in. It was just below the surface, waiting for me to let it bubble up. It did now, and I willed it to help me understand what Eoutn was feeling, what was happening inside his body that wouldn't let him heal.

Everything in the world had an energy to it; from the slow steady thrum of mountains steadfast in the distance to the frenetic pulse of an insect, the Ambience was everywhere. In someone like me, it was a blinding, prismatic light eclipsing everything around it. In someone like Eoutn, it should have been a complex dance of muscles, blood, bone, and the spark that made him *Eoutn,* a small piece of the Pool that flowed so eagerly to me.

But what I found was sickly, feeble, and struggling to continue. Every heartbeat came slower than the last. The source was a mass of darkness in his lungs, draining the life out of him as it collected fluid and blood around it.

"Hold on," I whispered to him, focusing my intention and power on the damaged darkness. It extended further, exacerbated by his treatment, a fractured rib lodged next to the source, cutting him when he tried to draw breath. My light blotted out the darkness, easing the disease from his body while it knitted him back together. In moments, he was whole again, and I coaxed the fluid out of his lungs, holding a cloth to his mouth as he coughed it out.

He took a deep breath and settled, his eyes closing and his chest rising and falling evenly. The moment's tension eased, my fight to keep death at bay over, and exhaustion and satisfaction took equal hold of me. I pushed the Ambience away.

I waited for a time, watching my patients sleep, anxious for them to improve. But both seemed comfortable now, and I decided it was time to rest. I heaved myself out of the chair against the wall and walked out of my cabin, shutting the door behind me. I sighed, wondering what I'd missed the past few hours, eager to take a moment to sit without worrying about someone else.

The door to Captain Morrig's cabin swung inward on oiled hinges, and I poked my head around to make sure he was ready for me before barging in. Fading light streamed in through the window, limning the pine table and chairs, as well as Captain Morrig, in golden sunlight.

The dazzle blinded me for a moment. I blinked, and a spot at the corner of my eye persisted as I moved to his side, squinting at the charts laid out before him. He looked up with a smile when he noticed me.

"Come in, dear one." He rose from his chair and offered it to me, a concerned frown replacing his smile. "You look exhausted, please, sit. There's some food and a bit of water."

I plopped in the seat with a relieved huff and pulled the plate close. It wasn't anything special—a bit of hard cheese and a handful of grapes—but I would have sworn it was the most delicious meal I'd ever had. I wondered in a detached way when I'd last eaten as I looked at a chart of the channel and the area surrounding Rogue's Island.

Rogue's Island sat to the northeast, a haven for slavers, thieves, and murderers. A home for anyone who couldn't live within the bounds of society's laws, who would rather live out of the eyeline of the people who took offense at their way of life. None of the king's ships could bypass the reef of jagged rock and broken ships that surrounded it. And even if they found the single narrow channel that granted access, ballistae were mounted on the remnants of ship decks on either side, always armed to repel any ship without leave to enter.

I traced my finger along the other chart showing the most direct route between Vortheim and Trylia. The channel was the only opening for leagues between arms of coral, rock, and shallow sea, an easy place to monitor passage between the north and south of the Sharsae Sea for our ships *and* Vortheim's. Other passages existed, but they were perilous, winding journeys, made more treacherous by the bones of many sunken vessels reaching up from the depths to snag the hulls of passing ships.

"I'd planned to patrol the sea around the channel," Captain Morrig said. "It's our best chance to catch a single ship. Not many will risk traveling close enough together to pose a problem for us."

"As the best route between Vortheim and Trylia, it's a wonder that King Demetrius hasn't had ships patrolling this space before," I said. "He could have saved us all a lot of trouble," I grumbled, reaching for a bit of cheese. I rubbed my eye to clear it as I popped the cheese in my mouth.

"It's not as easy as that. Ours catch one or two of theirs, and then a large force from Vortheim retaliates. We may have set such a retaliation in motion with what we've been through the past couple of days. After seeing an Ambient on *both* Vorthe ships we've come across, we must operate as if there are enough Ambient in Vortheim to put one on every ship they send north. Even if they don't, if even *one* is sent against any ship but ours, they wouldn't stand a chance."

I fumed but didn't say anything. Every time I thought about being abducted when I was a little girl, and then my capture more than a decade later, all because no one had been there to stop Roglin's ship, it made me furious. But Captain Morrig was right, too. And the king of Trylia knew enough about the Ambient situation to understand the same.

Derth certainly wouldn't have let any Trylian ships interfere with his and Roglin's bustling slave trade and would likely have destroyed them without hesitation. And if someone had reported their presence, there wasn't anything they could have done to prevent their actions. I straightened, trying to shake my resentment, and looked out the window to the ocean and sky.

Derth. That quiet, sadistic Ambient that stripped my power and tried to kill me when I broke free of him. He was out there, doing Elders only knew what. Terrorizing someone, I had no doubt. I shuddered, angry that I hadn't been able to track him down months ago. His face haunted my nightmares. I hoped I could repay the favor for him, someday.

"At least we get to do something about it now," I sighed, forcibly removing Derth's face from my mind by staring at the chart as hard as I could.

Captain Morrig nodded. "Yes. Everyone acquitted themselves admirably, even in the face of such destruction. They work well together."

"They do," I said. "It's like seeing the old crew again."

Captain Morrig smiled sadly. "It's not *quite* like that, but I catch your meaning. After what you and Bryn did, I think it might be time to master your power, don't you?"

A lock of hair fell across my face as I shook my head in frustration. Sam's scolding—just this morning, though it felt like it'd been a week ago—ran through my head again. And if I had to admit it, the rational part of me tended to agree even as my spirit longed for that power. "No," I said. "Sam says that he doesn't want to risk a catastrophe. I told *him* that we'll be careful, that we need to explore it at some point. But he is one of the most stubborn men I've met. And knowing the men I've met, that's saying something."

Captain Morrig chuckled. "Well, he'll come around. What you did could have gone *very* badly, but you got us through. I trust you both."

"Thanks, sir. You should try telling Sam."

"I have, many times." He sighed. "Oh well. We'll arrive at Saurboro sometime tomorrow, Elders willing. At least we can return some of the people we rescued."

"I haven't seen Saurboro since our early trade days on the *Catherine*," I said. The small tropical island had felt like paradise in comparison to Trylia, like I'd come awake every time I stepped foot on its shore. I closed my eyes, luxuriating in how vibrant the Ambience felt all around me, and wondered whether *that* had been the reason for how I'd felt during my visits.

"We'll get our girl strong enough to get us home, and then we'll see what we can do to get to Derth before the Vorthes do. Now, you should get some rest." He gestured toward his neat berth, kissed the top of my head, and left the cabin.

Stifling a yawn, I shuffled to the bed and lay atop the blanket. My back spasmed before it relaxed, too cramped from hovering over my patients. My eyelids drooped while my mind cycled through all that I'd done, wondering whether I could have done more, knowing I'd done everything I could. It happened after every emergency, every prolonged illness. A way for my mind to process the stress of the situation and put my worries to rest. As I exhausted every possibility, I felt Bryn's comforting presence in my head, soothing my doubts, and my mind stilled. The sea rocked the ship up one side of a wave and down the other, lulling me to sleep.

CHAPTER SIX

The sun was setting when I finally awoke and went above deck. Its brilliant orange light stretched out in a line across the ocean from the blazing orb, like a finger pointing from a closed fist. With a hand blocking the bulk of the glare, I watched the sun disappear beyond the horizon, leaving a film of golden light to dance atop the blue waves.

I turned away as the last of the glow faded to a clamor of voices, searching the faces of the crew for Sam and Bryn. Instead, I found Bryn and Hunter sparring in the middle of a large circle as their blades flashed above the press, the screech of metal almost drowned by the shouts of the crew.

Weaving through the crowd with small touches on shoulders and a wide smile, I emerged to find two of my favorite men stripped to the waist, wearing ragged shorts, barefoot on the solid wood of the deck. They attacked without mercy, and I worried that the ferocity of their swings might lead to real injury until I spotted the shimmer of Ambience running along the blades. I whispered quiet thanks to Sam for the thin slivers of air cushioning their blades. It took much less energy to ease bruises than to reattach a limb.

I groaned and cheered along with the crowd; watching them spar was one of my greatest pleasures. After a few tense days between them—it'd taken time for Hunter to come to terms with finding me and realizing our romance wouldn't continue in the same day, even before learning that Bryn was Roglin's nephew—they'd fought some thugs in a brawl, and a fast friendship was born.

They were an equal match for one another; around the same height and build, both were very agile and quick. Bryn moved with the lethal grace of a mountain lion, stalking slowly, watching with unblinking eyes until he was ready to pounce. Hunter reminded me of a snake, always moving, seeming to slither in and out of Bryn's defenses.

They relished their battles, and the whole crew shared their delight. Tall, muscled sailors giggled like children when Hunter leaped back from Bryn's vicious lunge. Several of our archers groaned when Bryn brought his sword around in a flash, and Hunter blocked the blow.

The two men thrusted and parried, dancing around one another. A sudden flurry of activity brought Bryn swinging around to Hunter's side. Before Hunter could react, Bryn's dirk was at his throat. Both men stilled, chests heaving as they panted in the fading light, and we all cheered the victor.

Hunter smiled wide at Bryn, and Bryn started, looking down at a glint of light off a small knife at his belly. The crowd groaned, Bryn let out a bark of laughter, and my heart fluttered at his obvious glee.

"Where were you keeping that?" Bryn cried.

"You don't want to know," Hunter replied with an evil grin.

I smiled at a few of the faces that started to disperse, though there were too many to track at once. Roy was among their number, along with a handful of his fighters. I smiled at one of them, a petite female with a wild smile, before one of our sailors, a tall, barrel-chested man with long black hair wrapped his arm around her shoulders and escorted her to the hatch.

Hunter and Bryn stepped apart, and I stepped forward. "Well done," I said, smiling as I applauded. "I'm impressed that you're able to keep up with Bryn."

"I was holding back," Bryn said. He wiped his brow with the back of one hand, unable to hide the cocky grin peeking out beneath it. His mind was clearer now, some of his rage burned away from the exercise and violence. Perhaps I needed to spar as well, to release some of my own tension.

Hunter glanced sidelong at him. "You keep telling yourself that." He grabbed a shirt from where he'd stuffed it through a taut line and sauntered away.

Bryn replaced his sword and dirk in their scabbards and opened his arms to hug me. I grimaced, planting my palm on his chest to keep him at arm's length. Sweat slicked my hand and I recoiled, picked up his discarded shirt from the deck, and used it to wipe my hand clean.

"I can wait until you've had a chance to wash," I said, my words a denial even as the warmth of desire unfurled low in my belly. His eyes burned in response as he took a step closer. I put the shirt against his chest, a barrier against the lust that crackled between us, but it did nothing to keep the heat of his skin from sending tingles of anticipation up my arm. His thoughts flashed to memories of my bare skin, a sheen of sweat covering me for a very different reason. I took a deep breath, which did nothing to calm my racing heart.

Hunter winked at me as he crept up behind Bryn, bucket in hand, breaking me free from Bryn's hungry gaze. I smirked as I took a step back, and the bucket tipped over Bryn's head, cold water drenching him as he spluttered. He flipped his head back to shake the water off before he turned to glare at Hunter, and Hunter's eyes widened. Hunter dropped the bucket and ran aft. Bryn smiled and winked at me and took off in pursuit.

They ran a lap around the ship, dodging out of the way of the surprised crew before Bryn caught up. He tackled Hunter to the ground, the impact vibrating through the planks of the deck. A wrestling match began, and they rolled around amid shouts and laughter, finally coming to a stop at my feet.

"You're idiots," I sighed, but my heart warmed to see them acting like morons. Or puppies.

Bryn shoved, and Hunter rolled away. Bryn leaped to his feet and caught me in his arms. I screamed as he spun me around in the air, his wet skin soaking through my clothes. He set me on my feet as suddenly as he had lifted me, and I followed his gaze to find Captain Morrig staring at the three of us with a disapproving frown.

"All right, you three. If you have this much energy, perhaps you can put it to good use swabbing the deck!"

Hunter jumped to his feet to stand at attention next to Bryn, who mirrored Hunter's salute. "Aye, sir!" they shouted in unison. The captain pivoted, leaving us as I rolled my eyes at them and they walked away, still shoving at one another.

Since our cabin was still occupied, Bryn and I took berths with the rest of the crew. Both of my patients had recovered well, and I slept fitfully, though I knew Sam would care for Eoutn in my stead. So, despite the lulling sway of the hammock, I found myself at the bow of the ship before sunrise, waiting.

The sky lightened in a spray of hues; orange where the sun crept closer to the horizon, fading from yellow to white to clear blue. Each color reflected from the dancing ocean surface, moving with the current. When the sun made its appearance, I closed my eyes and basked in the warmth, trying to feel content like I had so many times over so many years in a similar position as this one.

The Ambience was everywhere, a loud thrum in the air, and water. It filled me with strength, easing some of my remaining exhaustion without the subtle insistence to unleash it.

The world was hushed, just the waves and the quiet movement of sailors around me. Bare feet approached from behind, and I glanced beside me when Hunter draped his arms over the rail next to mine. His curly brown hair draped over his face, each spiral outlined in gold from the sunrise. He chuckled under his breath.

"What?" I asked.

He swung his head between his arms and sighed. "It feels like such a long time since we stood here like this." He swung his head up to glance sidelong at me. "Everything looks different now."

I nodded slowly. "It does." Silence fell between us, and I recalled the words Hunter and I had shared at sunrise aboard our former ship before its destruction. Mostly, I remembered how terrified I'd been; of myself, of my power, and of letting my guard down enough to let Hunter in. And the heartbreak I'd caused him when our ship was destroyed, and then when he found me again only to realize I loved Bryn.

I couldn't face those feelings. "I still see their faces," I said instead. I didn't need to tell him I meant the crewmates we'd lost.

"So do I." He stood and rubbed his arms. "What has you awake this early? Do you miss your soft bed?"

I smirked. "A bit." I shook my head, and my smile dropped. "It was naïve and selfish of me to hope that Derth would disappear somewhere across the world and I'd never hear from him again. I should have gone after him sooner."

"You tried. We all did. He was gone. And you were half-dead from a head wound. You couldn't use the Ambience for a while after that; what do you think you could've done?" Hunter demanded.

"I could have done more."

"Not if you'd died. Now that you've spent the last year getting stronger?" He raised his eyebrows in question. "I think it's given you the chance to stop him."

"Maybe."

Hunter shoved himself upright, turned, and placed a hand on my shoulder. "We're with you, Lila. We'll see it done, no matter the cost."

With two masts gone and the air still, I spent the next few hours perched at the base of the mizzen mast to keep up a breeze strong enough for us to make progress toward Saurboro. The Vorthes were already ahead of us, and I couldn't abide our journey taking any longer than necessary. It felt good to flex my power without the fear of being overwhelmed.

A skeleton crew controlled our course and operated the sails while the rest began rudimentary repairs. I passed the time with my back against the aft side of the main mast, my legs propped up in front of me to hold my leather-bound journal. Called by my use of the Ambience, the spirits' ethereal forms passed in and out of my peripheral vision as my charcoal pencil raced across the open page.

A diagram of a wound I'd cleaned and stitched an hour earlier unfurled beneath my pencil, the tip scratching fine lines to indicate where the gash had been on the man's arm. I'd kept up the practice Smitts had taught me early in my tutelage, though our former surgeon's sketching skill had far surpassed my own.

I'd expanded upon the lesson by keeping a separate journal, bearing an engraving of my name, with my description of the healing process using the Ambience. Thankfully, there weren't many injuries that I had to treat this way. I'd finished Eoutn's entry already. I also cataloged my experience with Sam, the way I manifested what he taught me, and insights into my interactions with Ambience. I'd spent too long floundering for information; I wanted to leave a record for future generations of Conduits, so that they wouldn't be as lost as I was.

Bryn plunked beside me, leaning his head onto my shoulder to gaze at the last few lines as I finished.

"What have you been up to?" I asked. I'd been so absorbed in my work that I hadn't paid much attention to what he'd been doing, though his presence lingered in the back of my mind. I shut my journal with the pencil to mark my page, and he took my hand between his.

"I was below, talking to Sam and Hunter," he replied. "Eoutn is sleeping soundly, and Sydah felt strong enough to try some stew in the mess."

My stomach growled. "What were you talking to Sam and Hunter about?"

"The future, mostly," he said absently, frowning at my hand, tracing light circles on the back of it.

I brushed his knuckles with a light kiss, and then pulled our clasped hands into my lap, hoping to distract him from whatever was causing his frown. I could easily have pried into them directly, but we'd discovered that sometimes, being able to read each other's minds was detrimental to our relationship. Some things were better said after consideration. "That seems like a weighty subject. Do you want to talk about it?"

Rather than reply, he gazed out at the ocean. I followed his gaze, letting him sit in silence, and nodded to a group of sailors leaning against the rail nearby before I let the wind go. The natural breeze was calmer, and they scrambled to take in the sails to accommodate our new pace.

"I do want to talk to you about the future," Bryn finally said, his mouth set in a determined line. "I want to know what you want in yours."

It was my turn to sit in silence for a moment, staring at his profile. He wouldn't look at me, and something in his tone made me nervous. I pulled my mind away from his, rather than following my instinct to dive further in to find out what was wrong. If he was having second thoughts about being here, I wasn't sure I wanted to know.

"I feel like I'm home again," I started cautiously, "and I know it's going to be dangerous, but I believe that what we're doing is necessary. A beginning, maybe." I shrugged. "We won't stop the slave trade by waiting for it to come to us, but at least it's *something*. I learned a long time ago to live moment-to-moment because everything is so uncertain. And I haven't thought about much further than getting ready for what we're doing *now*." Steeling myself, I asked, "What do *you* want, Bryn?"

He took a deep breath and let it out slowly before finally looking at me. He looked like he'd been bracing himself for something, too. His gaze direct and piercing, and a hint of longing in his voice, he said, "I want you, Lila."

I let out the breath I'd been holding. "You *have* me." My distracted attempts at romance before I'd met Bryn hadn't prepared me for the depth of my love for him. Now that we had room to relax and explore our relationship without the threat we'd been under in the beginning, I couldn't imagine my life without him, and I knew that he felt the same.

"That's not exactly what I mean..." He trailed off before letting out an exasperated breath, and my mind raced, wondering what I'd do if he told me he wanted to leave the ship. Would I follow him, giving up everything I knew and the purpose I'd found? Could I give him up? "I want to have a life with you. I want us to..."

Hunter bounded forward with thunderous glee and squatted in front of us, cutting off whatever Bryn had been about to say. When he saw the look on Bryn's face, his smile faded.

"Did I interrupt something?" he asked.

I shrugged as Bryn brusquely said, "Yes." He scowled at Hunter, a

silent exchange happening between the two men as my anxiety reached
a fever pitch. *What is going* on? I thought. After a long, and tense
moment, Bryn sighed and stood, offering a hand to help me up. "You're
hungry. Will you eat with me?" I grasped his hand and let him hoist me
to my feet. He pressed a soft kiss to my temple and moved away,
leaving me standing with Hunter, staring at Bryn's hunched shoulders
as he stalked to the hatch and below.

Hunter grimaced at me. "What was that about?" I asked.

He shook his head. "I'm not entirely sure," he said. But he wouldn't
look at me, either; I'd seen that kind of evasion from him many times
over the years. He was hiding something.

"Bryn asked me about the future after he talked to you and Sam.
Should I be worried?"

Hunter sighed. "He'll have to talk to you about it himself."

"Okay," I drawled, trying to pull the information out of my friend.

Hunter patted my shoulder. "It's fine, Lila, nothing to worry about."

I grimaced. "Sure."

My stomach rumbled louder while I waited for a plate in the galley
with the smell of cooked beef lingering in the hall. Bryn waited for me
to claim my portion and led me to our cabin.

We ate without speaking; I stole covert looks at him from time to
time while he stared intently at his plate. Waves lapping against the
hull, occasional shouts from people above, and the scraping of forks
and knives across our plates broke the unusual silence.

When he was finished, he set down his fork and continued to stare
at his plate until I took the last bite of roasted potatoes. After a minute,
he nodded as if he had come to a decision, and then lifted his head to
stare at me as intently as he had at his plate of food.

"I want to spend the rest of my life with you, Lila," he announced.

Unsure of where his statement would lead, I took a moment to
reply while I studied his features. His lips were thinned in a firm line
and his blue eyes pierced mine with steadfast determination. His tone

brooked no argument, and his devotion was so apparent that a large part of the tension in my shoulders drained out of me. It didn't matter what else came; we would be together, and that was what mattered.

"I know, Bryn. And I want to spend the rest of mine with you. Why does it seem like there's a problem?"

"The problem is that we've been living together for almost a year, and we've never talked about what comes next."

"We love each other, we're together... What else is there?"

"*Land ho!*" The distant shout echoed from voice to voice, passed below to alert us all that we'd arrived at our destination. I glanced away for a moment, and when I turned back, Bryn's eyes were on his plate again, and his face was closed.

Before I could ask him about it, he stood and gathered our plates. With a kiss atop my head in farewell, he left me behind in the room to wonder what I'd missed.

CHAPTER SEVEN

Saurboro was beautiful. Bright, sandy beaches surrounded emerald hills covered with a riot of colorful flowers as far as I could see. At the shoreline, a small city opened to the wide docks, arranged in an arc facing the water. Today, every building was strung with colorful banners, laughter echoed throughout the town, and wide tables were laid out in the wide-open thoroughfare that welcomed visitors from docked ships such as ours.

A harvest festival was in full swing as we arrived, and we were greeted with hearty welcomes and wide smiles. The locals beckoned us into the celebration, and I followed Bryn and Hunter as they wound through the throng toward the wide tables that we found piled high with food. I found meat, sauce, and vegetables wrapped in flatbread, the spices inside making my eyes water when I came near enough to smell it. Another vendor offered a mixture of fruit and spices so sweet that my teeth ached while it set my mouth on fire. And my favorite, a stand of sweet rolls topped with minced fruit that I'd never tasted before.

None of the food was familiar, and though I had to keep a handkerchief ready to wipe my streaming eyes, I tried a bit of everything. Bryn and Hunter flitted from table to table too, asking for the hottest spices to see who could withstand them best. I watched as tears streamed down their bright red faces, and Roy walked by with the same dish, the picture of composure as he laughed.

Eoutn, his green eyes sparkling above a contented smile, wandered toward me with one hand on a dark wooden cane, and the other holding the arm of a slight man. His green eyes and wide mouth matched Eoutn's when he smiled as well. Eoutn looked at ease, though he coughed from time to time as he came to a stop in front of me. When he spoke, his voice was raspy and deep.

"This is the woman I told you about," he said to the man with him, who held a small basket draped with a cloth in his free hand. "She and the rest saved us all, but *she* kept me from the Elders. I didn't think I'd make it."

"Thank you so much for my grandfather's life," the man said, beaming with gratitude. "When he didn't make it back from Trylia, we feared the worst."

"It was my pleasure," I said, touched by their kind words. "I'm glad we could see you home safely."

"I could have sworn we were farther from the island," Eoutn said with his brows drawn close. "We made it back so quickly, we must have had the Elders' eyes on us." He motioned to the basket, and his grandson held it out to me.

I smiled as I accepted, my eyes fixed on the handle to hide my discomfort. "Strong winds, and a bit of the Elders' luck. I'm glad you found your family. If you need anything while I'm here, please let me know."

They walked away slowly, waylaid by a crowd of well-wishers and welcoming embraces. I smiled to myself, delighted to see that something good had come of our encounter. The people we'd rescued wandered through the festival, as well, and my heart filled with pride and purpose. Everyone was grateful to set foot on solid land, and I wondered how many of them would continue with us to Trylia, and how many would decide to stay here.

Lifting the cloth from the basket, I found several small tarts, soft dough surrounding an unfamiliar fruit filling with a drizzle of icing over the top. I beamed and lifted one to my mouth.

The tart fruit contrasted beautifully with the sweet icing,

complementing my surroundings—the smell of spices, the humid ocean breeze—as perfectly as a warm mug of tea on a cold morning. It was so delicious that I almost felt guilty, having grown up in Trylia, where the price of sugar was so high that most people couldn't afford it.

The locals pushed new clothes and plenty of food and drink into their hands. Our sailors paid for what they could, and Saurboro's citizens were grateful as they pulled more and more food out of their brick ovens to accommodate us. Several people made a point to tell us how relieved they were to sell the surplus of a bountiful harvest; with trade vessels few and far between, much of it would have gone to waste otherwise. We ate and drank as much as we wanted, glowing in the praise from our rescue of both their people and their economy.

My stomach bulged when I finally stopped eating, and I had to sit under the shade of a palm tree towering over the inn before I collapsed in a haze of heat and happy overindulgence. I fanned my face with my hand; this beautiful island was so *hot*, even in the shade.

I spotted Bryn and Hunter walking together, browsing wares, with drinks in one hand and sweet pastries in the other. Bryn said something to Hunter, who laughed, tossing his frizzed curls off his face as Bryn smirked at him.

Captain Morrig's voice carried across the open air, the familiar cadence of his negotiation bringing a nostalgic smile to my face. Charm oozed out of him, a big boom of laughter attracting more curious vendors. Once a merchant, always a merchant.

There were plenty of days when I missed the life we'd had. It'd been fraught, too, but it'd been simpler, somehow. The Ambience had been a nuisance, but not a daunting and awesome responsibility. I'd followed my captain's orders, with a clear path into a future where I took over for Smitts as the ship's surgeon, and perhaps would have followed Hunter's orders once Captain Morrig retired. I wouldn't have been the tip of a spear aimed at the Ambient of Vortheim, always waiting for a chance to right wrongs, waiting for a way to move toward the root of the problem.

But then Bryn caught my eye, smiling that brilliant smile that crinkled the corners of his eyes and lit his whole face. A happy, relaxed smile that drew out my own, only for me. As if I was the only person in the world that could ease the burdens he carried, which allowed me to put aside my own and exist in the moment with him, rather than dwelling on the pain of my past and uncertainty of my future.

Hunter nudged him, pulling his gaze to something lying on a table behind him. But the warmth of his affection stayed with me.

After our happy welcome, we got to work on repairs. The locals helped where they could, and the captain was only too happy to pay for the help of two master carpenters to speed things along. As the sun set, the *Catherine's Revenge* had a new patchy stripe on the side of her hull, just like her predecessor. I pictured the *Catherine* in pieces at the bottom of the Sharsae, a twinge of regret and sadness disturbing the peaceful moment. But with our crew back on shore to enjoy a well-earned respite, I shook off the melancholy to join in the festivities.

The day ended with a celebration around a huge bonfire at the edge of the beach. It crackled and spat sparks into the air, giving off enough heat to keep the chill of the night's ocean breeze at bay and people danced, drank, told stories, and enjoyed the autumn air. I caught snippets of stories—some familiar and some new—and even Sam joined in the revelry with 'myths' about the Gift long ago, surrounded by a gaggle of rapt children.

Bryn and I stood a little behind everyone else, watching the flames dance with our arms around each other's waists, and my head resting on his chest. I'd worked off the meals of the afternoon in time to indulge in a large slice of blueberry pie, and now I was replete and ready for sleep. My fatigue was contagious, it seemed, because Bryn yawned against the top of my head.

"Let's go to bed," I yawned. "I'm exhausted."

"Me too," Bryn replied, squeezing me tighter before he allowed me to pull away.

We stumbled and giggled back to the longboat with a few other sailors in similar states. Bryn helped me to the bow and took place at a set of oars. I watched the fire shrink behind us with my hand on him, feeling the muscles in his back move in time with the others. The boat thunked into the hull after no time at all, and I tied us off to the boat boom, climbing up once we were secure.

It was harder to haul my tired body up than it had been to disembark earlier in the day; Bryn had to brace me several times, his hand lingering on my backside longer than necessary, and I enjoyed it a bit too much, so I made sure to give him plenty of opportunities.

With so many people still on the island, the quiet peace of the ship was a stark contrast to the party we'd left behind. Bryn held his hand out and I laced my fingers through his and let him lead me below to our cabin. The door thumped shut behind us, and we were alone as we hadn't been in a very long time.

I stayed upright long enough to kick off my boots and shuck my cloak, and then I fell into bed and shuffled to the side to make room for Bryn. The bed shifted under his weight as I closed my eyes, and I scooted toward his open arms, knowing they'd be waiting for me. My mind wandering, focused on the feel of his embrace, a memory of an embrace surrounded by flames, and our first intimate encounter, just after I'd severed our bond to protect him from feeling my injuries in battle with his uncle and Derth.

The memory stirred that bone-deep need to feel his skin against mine, like it had the first time, and drove away my sleepy haze. I pressed a kiss to his neck, running my fingertips over the shirt covering his chest.

Bryn chuckled. *I thought you were asleep.*

Not yet, I replied. *I need you.*

He didn't require clarification; he felt my need, even as I wrapped my leg around his to pull him closer.

He rolled onto his back, pulling me bodily with him so that I was lying on top of him, straddling him, and rocked his hips upward. I ran my hands through his hair, closing my fingers to give it a gentle tug. He moaned and pushed his hips up again, letting me feel how much he wanted me, too. I brushed my lips against his, keeping a firm hold on his hair to hold him back when he tried to deepen the kiss, teasing him with a smile on my face as I squirmed against him.

"Lila." My name came out as a plea. His hands wrapped around my hips, and I ran my lips over his jaw, keeping his head still. "*Lila.*" This time a warning growl. But I just smiled down at him, and then ran my tongue up his neck. His hands wrapped around my backside as he thrust his hips upward, pushing his arousal against mine. I kissed him again, this time deeper, urgent, and hungry for more.

Releasing my grip, I sat up, relishing the lust in his eyes, and sat still while he unlaced my bodice, never taking his eyes from mine. I tossed it to the floor as he sat up to kiss my neck, and moaned as he nibbled my shoulder. His shirt came next, and then I pushed him flat on the bed and removed his pants while he watched, his eyes dark, his gaze like a predator waiting for the right time to pounce.

He did, just as I started to remove my shirt, and rolled on top of me, lifting my hands above my head to hold me in place to repay the maddening favor I'd given him. He slid down my body, kissing, licking, and nibbling each inch of bare skin that he exposed until I lost myself in the feel of his mouth, shivering with anticipation, naked beneath him. Bryn gazed at me from the foot of the bed. He kissed his way up my leg, smiling against my skin every time I squirmed, trying to get him to move higher.

Every kiss was agonizingly slow, his breath warm on my skin when he chuckled at my insistent moan. He paused to spread my legs and flick his tongue in my most sensitive area, and my back arched as a shockwave of pleasure ripped through me. Another moan escaped my lips as I pushed myself against his mouth instinctively, and his tongue moved again and again, my release building. His fingers closed on my nipple and I gasped, arching my back as I came undone. A frantic wave of desire coursed through him, heightening my pleasure as he continued, relentless, until I pulled him up.

I shivered, my body pulsing as I started to feel things external to that throbbing sensation. *I'm cold,* I informed him. He covered me with his body, warming me in more ways than one.

He smiled at me, kissed me again, and thrust forward. *Not for long.*

CHAPTER EIGHT

Our feet thumped onto the planks of the pier as the sun was rising a week later. The captain had given over the ship into the hands of one of the king's master shipwrights. The tall, older man stood scowling, visibly perturbed at the sight of the flagship ship of the navy in tatters.

The crew dispersed with orders to check in every other day to stay apprised of the ship's progress and help where they could, and the few we'd liberated that had sailed with us from Saurboro thanked us as they took their leave. Roy left to tell his mother Lottie that we were home, while the rest of us waited for the captain to finish so we could make our way to the palace.

I led us through the dock district, surrounded by the calls of gulls and sailors and the irate harbormaster who had already begun to bark orders at carpenters. I'd long since decided that my anger was useless without purpose, and resolved to lead the hunt for Derth no matter what the king thought, and my pace through the streets was brisk, eager as I was to begin. The surrounding city passed in a blur as I focused only on the path upward to the palace. Finally, with my legs screaming for a break after striding up the switchback road, we emerged onto the hilltop with the white marble wall of the palace sparkling ahead.

Bryn grasped my hand as we waited for the guards at the gate to allow us entry, his steady presence curbing some of my impatient energy as Hunter and Sam told them our business and Captain Morrig stood silently behind us. Finally, we were escorted across the grounds to the palace itself by the same taciturn guards we had seen on our previous visit. Leaves littered the grounds from the careful line of trees with the bare flower beds beneath them. Looking toward the palace, I squinted against the brilliance of morning sun glittering off the golden accents on the white marble façade.

We ascended the marble steps, passing between the large columns and in through double doors as another pair of guards swung them open before us. The warm air of the palace engulfed us as we stepped inside, and the smell of dried flowers filling the air from the ornate vases displayed along intricately carved tables lining the hall at intervals.

A stiff butler in his very neat livery bid us to follow him through the palace to the king's private sitting room. We passed through the main halls and turned down a hallway that led away from the throne room, and up a long staircase. We came out into a wide hall, where the simple décor was a stark contrast to the public rooms of the palace filled with rich color schemes and every surface dripping with extravagance.

There was something so familiar about this place, so comforting, like coming home. One small table looked like the table in my bedroom at Sam's cottage. The curtains covering a bedroom window through one of the open doors were almost the same as the curtains in Lottie's sitting room.

I could picture myself as a child, running through these halls. Bumping into that familiar table, looking out from behind those sheer, flower-embroidered curtains.

Finally, we came to a room furnished with comfortable chairs and sofas that faced one another near an open fireplace, reminding me of the sitting room in Sam's cottage where we'd spent a long winter honing my power. The room smelled of wood smoke and leather, with a faint hint of the ocean over everything as a breeze pushed curtains aside at the slightly open window.

The far end of the room held a large oak table, surrounded by chairs. Plain oak bookshelves lined one side of the room, with an armchair and small table nearby. Several books were laid open and stacked on the table, and one leather-bound volume sat alone on the red plush seat.

Through the door at the far end of the room I spied a large bedroom, also plainly furnished. Family portraits smiled from places of honor on the walls. These weren't the historical record of stone-faced monarchs lining the entrance hall; these paintings were mementos of a loving family. This was a home, rather than just the seat of power for the leaders of our monarchy.

The monarch in question emerged from the bedroom a moment later. He moved with peaceful grace, not the stiff, imperious strides of someone with utter authority over his subjects. He wore plain, comfortable clothes, not the grand uniform of his station. His silver-streaked black hair wasn't carefully slicked back, but tousled loosely around his shoulders. He looked like an entirely different man.

In a swirl of light blue, I caught my first glimpse of the queen, ushering three children just shy of their teens through the bedroom. I'd seen her from a distance before—during festivals, where her gowns and jewels sparkled as if she were a star plucked from the night sky—but never in the comfort of her private rooms, and never so close. Somehow, even in a plain linen dress with her hair in loose brown waves as she scurried after her children, she looked more elegant than I ever could. King Demetrius's smile was wide and genuine as he approached, and the door shut behind him, cutting off my view of his family.

"Welcome, my friends," he said. "I hope this isn't too informal for you, but we can speak freely here."

We'd had many meetings over the past few months to set our plans in motion, always accompanied by advisors and his general in some grand meeting room. I chose not to remark on the contrast between those meetings and this one when he gestured toward the group of chairs and sofas and took a seat in a large armchair. As we sat, a servant brought a tray with drinks to the table between us, and then departed, pausing long enough to close the door behind him.

"Thank you, Your Majesty," Captain Morrig said as he reached for a glass.

"Please, Fallon, call me Demetrius when we're in my home. You are all my guests here, and while I am still your king, I am also your host."

"That's kind of you, sire," Sam replied. "It's most welcome after all we've been through."

"Yes," the king replied as his mouth quirked into a wry grimace. "I heard about the damage. We'll see it repaired as quickly as possible. Tell me how it happened."

We took it in turns to tell our story. Not only the battle, but the months of training since we'd left port and how hopeful we were about the results. He asked a few questions about some of the things we'd seen, and informed us about some of the benign activity reported by the few other vessels patrolling between Trylia and Vortheim. In turn, we relayed our conversation with the Vorthe sailor. The conversation lasted long enough for another servant to bring a plate of meats, cheeses, and dried fruit that we finished.

"Your exploits on behalf of the people of Trylia have been impressive," the king said. "I'm glad you made it back in one piece, and am grateful that you were able to rescue a number of our citizens. The Vorthe sailor you encountered has been making inquiries around King's Port, having arrived a few days before you, and has requested an audience with me, presumably to discuss what he discussed with you."

"Has there been any trouble?" I asked anxiously. "Do you know if he's discovered anything?" I didn't want Colagh to get a head start.

The king shook his head. "No, there hasn't been any trouble reported, and we've kept a close watch on all members of the Vorthe ship. The sailors have stayed close to the docks, and Colagh and his three cohorts have been courteous and respectful as far as we've seen. His activities have been restricted to the docks, mostly, talking to sailors and mercenaries."

He paused and furrowed his brow. "What you've said about Derth, it makes me wonder if some of the reports from other cities across Trylia could be connected. To this point, it's only been odd behavior over the past six months—several smaller cities, as well as Stalth and Salava—but nothing warranting action. And my eager new guard captain in Stalth has her watchful eye on the situation."

Excited for a place to start, I leaned forward, even as my stomach dropped, suddenly heavy with dread as my body acknowledged the danger I was consciously ignoring. "Which cities?" I asked.

"I have a list," he reached out to the pile of open books and fished a worn piece of parchment from between the pages of one. After a glance at it, he held it out to me. *So many places.* There had to be a few dozen city names on the paper, each associated with several names or more, and a note of the incident reported. I read through a few, frowning as I did. "Acting out of character, a few thefts, a few brawls..." I looked up, handing the paper to Sam. "You're right, this isn't much to go on."

"But we know Derth can force people to do what he wants. Do we know when he was in each place?" Bryn asked. "Maybe we can track his movement, anticipate where he'll go next."

King Demetrius shook his head. "If there's any pattern to it, I haven't seen it. The smaller cities are scattered across the continent, but it seems the most activity was in Stalth and Salava. Both have been mentioned several times, like he's been going in and out of the cities over the past year. I've had a few reports from First Port as well."

"We could start in Stalth," Bryn suggested. "My friends may have heard something, and we can talk to your new guard captain."

"Since the *Revenge* is out of service," the king said, "perhaps your time would be better spent discovering whether Derth is truly behind these incidents. City guards would have no hope of subduing him if this is the case, and I don't appreciate the thought of such a man loose on the continent. Nor do I think that we would be best served by allowing agents of Vortheim to abscond with him. I can stall this Colagh for a time with the promise of a formal meeting, as he's requested, but there's more than one reason you should hurry. If Derth has taken control of our citizens, we should assume that he has spies, and the Vortheim agents' questions won't go unnoticed."

"In which case we likely won't find him," Hunter said. "He could leave Trylia altogether, maybe find a new home in Friga."

"He's probably worried about Vorthe ships finding him," Captain Morrig said. "He'd have nowhere to run."

I nodded. "And Ambient from Vortheim would eventually go looking for him no matter where he ended up. If the Malachi is using negotiations for peace as incentive to allow Colagh to operate in Trylia, they must have been behind his desperation to capture me. But I still don't understand what they had to gain by it."

"It's not the first time the Malachi has called for the abduction of Trylia's Ambient," Sam said. His frown deepened. "A long time ago the Malachi's daughter was sent here for that purpose, to take every Ambient—even the Hunters, which she called the Scourge—back to Vortheim, in an effort to draw the Ambience out of Trylia, to strengthen Vortheim. She claimed it would strengthen their defense against a great plague.

"But that would have destroyed us, and I couldn't allow it. I stopped her, after I rescued the heir to the throne from her clutches."

"We don't have many Ambient now," Hunter interjected, "and I don't think that's necessarily a bad thing. The Ambience seems to make everything more complicated."

Sam sighed. "When I was young, Trylia was a bountiful garden, so teeming with life that the very air hummed. Food was never scarce, there was joy in every season, everything felt... brighter, more hopeful."

I felt a pang of sympathy for the melancholy in Sam's eyes. Everyone was silent for a moment, possibly picturing our home in the light that Sam painted it as I was, until Bryn cleared his throat and spoke up. "I hope thwarting the Malachi's plans won't diminish any possible future peace," Bryn said. "*If* what the Vorthe said was true."

The king waved a dismissive hand at Bryn and smiled. "Let that be my worry," he said. "You have other things to deal with."

"Derth is dangerous," Sam said. "When we find him, we will need to be cautious."

Captain Morrig frowned. "Lila, do you think you've learned enough to stop him? Sam?"

I was already nodding. "I *have* to stop him," I said. "There's no one else who can."

"I admire your fervor," Sam said, "but that's precisely what I'm hoping to avoid. You *must* be in control of yourself, or he will have an advantage over you."

"If we get into trouble, we can use our power," Bryn added.

"And lose your lives in the process." Sam closed his eyes and pinched the bridge of his nose. "That is a discussion for another time. We won't get into it now." He turned back to the king. "We will seek him out, and do our best to apprehend him."

"With winter coming it'll be a hard journey," Bryn said. "We may have trouble trailing him if we're bogged down by snow."

Something tugged at the fringes of my mind. Like I was being watched, but the thought didn't inspire panic, the thrill that went up my spine when I felt eyes on me; it felt like the security inspired by knowing I had someone watching over me.

Like a spirit was calling to me.

Captain Morrig rubbed his hands together slowly, eyes unfocused as he plotted the logistics of this new venture. "Perhaps we can borrow a small ship to ferry you up the coast? It would cut your travel significantly if we took you to Coveton. From there you can take the road to Stalth, if you want to start your search there while I coordinate our forces' deployment."

"Excellent," King Demetrius said. He rose to his feet and held out a hand to Sam.

The watchfulness became more insistent. I searched the room for some sign of the spirit that wanted my attention; it felt so familiar.

We took it in turns to clasp the king's hand in farewell. "You will be provided with whatever provisions you may need for the journey," King Demetrius said. "And I'll draft a promissory note that will allow for food, board, and other supplies you may need in any town or city you stay in."

It was my turn, and when the king clasped my hand in his, whatever had been trying to reach out to me enveloped me in a wave of comfort that brought tears to my eyes. It was like every dream I'd had of my mother wrapping her arms around me, or my father tossing me in the air and catching me. I had no idea whether they'd happened, and I could never see their faces, even in dreams. But deep down I'd always known I'd been loved, even though I'd been lost.

The king released my hand as a flash of movement caught my eye, and touched the section of my shirt concealing the key dangling from a silver chain around my neck. But when I turned I found nothing, and the feeling faded, leaving me alone with its memory.

I glanced around the room as Hunter and Captain Morrig filed out. Sam had a faraway look in his eyes as he clutched the list. His thirst for knowledge was insatiable, fueled in part by the Ambience, and his kindred Tethered spirit.

King Demetrius walked us out. "Thank you. For all that you've done, and all that you intend to do."

Escorted through the halls, I frowned, thinking about the king's last words to us. In the months since Derth slipped away, I'd longed for this moment, when I would finally have some information that could lead me to him. I hungered for revenge, for justice, and for the opportunity to ensure that he couldn't hurt anyone else. But what did that mean? Was I qualified to make that decision?

The palace grounds passed in a blur as I wondered what, *exactly,* I intended to do about Derth.

CHAPTER NINE

Preoccupied as I was, the sight of Lottie's house didn't bring me the joy that it usually did. I followed Hunter inside, embraced by the homey smell of wood smoke and dried herbs. Lottie's strong, wiry arms wrapped around me as soon as I stepped over the threshold.

"Thank the Six you're all home," Lottie sighed as she released me. A broad smile split her small, elderly face, the same rich obsidian as Roy's, exuding maternal calm and joy. But then she planted her hands on her hips and narrowed her eyes, the picture of motherly disapproval. "Now, who wants to tell me what happened to our ship?"

I grimaced, more remorseful now than I had been with Sam, as she stretched on her toes to pinch Bryn's cheek in greeting. "I'm going to pack," I muttered, desperate for escape. I took the steps two at a time, the rush giving me the much-needed feel of moving forward, and shut the door behind me to block the nervous chuckles of the men and the disapproving cluck of Lottie's tongue.

For a moment, the sight of my room—mostly unchanged since I was a child—gave me comfort. The gauzy curtains fluttered at my entrance, blocking the brightest of the sun's rays while illuminating the light blue paint covering the walls. I ran my fingers over the small frame at waist-height next to the door. The one and only time I'd drawn on Lottie's wall, now a memento of my childhood, and my inadequate attempt to capture the likeness of a butterfly I'd seen on my windowsill.

Pushing away from the wall, I grabbed my pack from the dresser and plunked it onto the bed, realizing as I opened it that I had nothing to do here. It was still full, packed neatly, and my clothes freshly laundered. But I itched to do *something,* and my restlessness made me irritable, unsuitable for the company downstairs, even as I craved it.

Taking a few deep breaths, I paced to the window and pulled the curtain aside to watch as people walked through the cobbled streets below. Families strolling hand-in-hand, messengers set to deliver some missive or another, even a few people that looked as stressed as I felt. Just people going about their lives.

But watching them only emphasized that I *wasn't* calm. My mind ran in circles; *we have a place to start, we can't wait around while he goes Elders' know how far.* Agitated as I was, I jumped when someone knocked on the door, but once I disengaged from the self-absorption, I realized it was Bryn. Sensing my permission to enter, he opened the door, and then shut it gently behind him. "Lila, are you all right?" An unnecessary question, but a kind one, meant to give me space to work out the words I wanted to say, rather than taking them from my head. At any other moment, I would have appreciated it.

"No," I snapped. "I want to leave. I want this done." I paced back and forth at the foot of the bed. "I know it's idiotic to rush at him, especially in the middle of winter by the time we get as far north as Salava. And we have no idea what will happen when we do." I gestured wildly. "Can he get into my head? Can he take over my mind?" I shrugged so hard it was more of a roll. We wouldn't find answers to these questions until it was too late to do anything about it.

"Love, it's all going to be fine. You broke the connection." The end of the bed creaked as he sat to watch me pace. Bryn's calm patience was exactly what my frayed nerves needed in this moment, but I didn't want to give in to the balm he was to my spirit.

"I remember," I hissed. My words came faster and faster on the edge of panic. "But I couldn't stop him from doing it in the first place. We don't know if I can stop him now!"

I sucked in a breath to continue my panicked rant. "Even if he doesn't take control of me, or anyone else, he could be more trouble than we can handle."

Bryn remained silent as he waited for me to finish. When I had, I plunked down on the bed next to him, sending a puff of dust into the air.

"Feel any better?" Bryn asked.

I chuckled and shook my head. "No." But I did, slightly. Putting words to my inner maelstrom was a release of pressure that left me feeling more even-tempered.

"He's no match for us, Love. You need to believe that." He looped an arm around my waist. "Whether he's stronger than you, or Sam, it doesn't matter. You and me," he smiled and pulled me close, "we're stronger than everyone."

"Strong enough to kill ourselves and break the world," I muttered.

"We won't let that happen," he said. "Sam won't."

I took a deep breath and let myself relax into him. Derth needed to be dealt with, and my resolve hadn't wavered. But that didn't stop my worry over all that could go wrong.

"I'm sorry," I said. "It's one thing to think about how much I've wanted to hunt him down. It's another thing to have a way to do it. And I feel like every moment we sit here, getting ready, he's getting farther away."

"I feel it too," he said. He kissed the top of my head.

"Tomorrow morning is soon enough," I sighed. "We'll get everything ready and leave at first light."

"Good," he replied. "Because Lottie has a feast planned for tonight. And I wouldn't want to see how she would react if we left before she had a chance to serve it."

I spent the rest of the morning helping Lottie prepare for the feast, mincing herbs, kneading bread dough, and rubbing salt, pepper, and herbs into a large slab of beef that Lottie placed in an enormous clay pot before sliding it into the oven to cook for the rest of the day. It was nice having something to focus on, to do something with my hands to keep busy. And Lottie's constant chatter left little room for brooding and worry. When the persistent nagging thought about our trail going cold broke through, I reminded myself to unclench my jaw by taking sips of tea.

Sam and Captain Morrig sat at the table, heads close together as they talked after Captain Morrig's return from attending to his duties overseeing the Navy and recruiting a suitable vessel for us. I caught bits of their conversation in between Lottie's stories, and was thrilled to hear that we were commandeering the newest frigate, rumored to be the fastest in the fleet. Her name was the *Celerity*.

Hunter and Bryn joined us, having resolved to take on the chore of outfitting all of us for the journey ahead. "We should get horses in Coveton," Bryn told us as he plunked down at the table and the older men fell silent. He winked at me, and despite my mood, I felt an answering smile on my lips. "We'll move faster and be able to carry more supplies."

"All right," Hunter replied with a grimace, "but I'm not much of a horse person."

I shook my head, looking up from the sage and rosemary I was chopping. "Neither am I. I've never ridden one before."

"It's been a long time for me as well," Sam added. "But I'm sure we can figure it out. And I can teach you a few ways to make it easier," he told me.

"We can find some well-trained horses with the king's note," Bryn said. He waved the paper with the king's seal on it.

"And I can make sure we have everything we need if you all get me lists," Hunter said. "I'm not much help against that monster, but I can make sure we don't starve out there."

"Having someone for him to focus on will help," Bryn assured him, smirking. He swung an arm around Hunter's shoulders. "If he's trying to kill *you*, Lila and Sam can focus on *him*."

Hunter elbowed Bryn in the ribs. Bryn laughed through a grunt of pain. I rolled my eyes—a common reaction to their constant banter— and listened as they began to assemble a list of supplies.

Bryn and Sam had already mentioned food, cooking and camping gear, and other practical things. I needed warmer clothing if we were going to be riding across the country when winter hit. The rational part of me knew that setting out with winter on the way was a bad idea, but the rest of me knew that I couldn't wait any longer. Derth was out there.

I listed off a few things to Hunter, who wrote everything down with the rest. He snatched the king's letter from Bryn's grip, and scrambled out of his seat with Bryn in pursuit, both of them stumbling out the front door in a fit of grunts and laughter.

They were in and out throughout the day. The pile of supplies in the sitting area grew, ready to be sorted into individual bags. Sam portioned out what each of us needed, so that we could fill our packs to the brim when everything was ready, while Lottie, Roy, and I finished our meal prep and then lounged at the kitchen table with glasses of deep red wine in hand.

When the afternoon began its slow turn into evening, everyone gathered in the house again. Roy and Lottie volunteered to finish in the kitchen so that I could pack what Hunter had brought for me. After reorganizing several times I got everything inside; it was a tight fit, but I buckled the leather flap over the bulge, and ran my hand over the soft, worn surface. It had held up over months of running, a gift from Bryn's friends from Stalth, Arthur and Maude, and it was as precious to me now as it had been then. A reminder that someone had cared about us when we had little hope for a future free from the horrors that chased us.

The door opened as I reached for the handle, and I backed away so Bryn could enter. His hands were full of odds and ends—a small package in waxed paper that smelled of tallow, a new comb, and a small knife—which he dumped onto the bed, where his pack was still open. He meticulously found a place for each item, succeeding in closing his pack the first time. That done, he sat down and smiled up at me, but there was a cloud of uncertainty on his face, the same as I'd seen after our encounter with the Vorthe ships.

Unlike before, his mind was open to me, but there was some thought that he was holding back from me. Something that was feeding his uncertainty, something that he didn't want me to know. Which rekindled the anxiety that had ebbed as I'd packed, taking control of one small thing in a sea of uncontrollable events.

"How are you?" Bryn asked.

I studied him for a moment, still wondering what he was hiding. And *how* he was hiding it. "A bit better, now that I've done what I can do to get ready," I replied. My brow furrowed against my will. "But you have that look again, like there's something you want to tell me." I didn't have to add that I *knew* he was hiding something; we could both feel it. He pulled his mind from me, and my anxiety spiked.

"I'm wondering when this will end," he said. "When we find Derth— and we *will*—is that it? Can we get back to what passes as normal life for us, or will we have to deal with Vortheim next?" I said nothing, and he sighed, unburdening himself like he hadn't in a long time, his words pouring out of him in a rush. "I didn't have a lot of stability after my mother died, so I never looked much past the next hour, week, or day. Even with Maude and Arthur, even with Sam, I didn't stay in one place for long. I was so worried that they'd leave me like my parents that I bounced back and forth between them, or disappeared for a day or two, living moment to moment. But this past year, with you and all our friends, I wondered if it was possible to plan a future."

"Is that why you asked me what I wanted?" I asked, feeling the knot of tension caused by his mood ease a bit.

He nodded, so I sat next to him and slung my legs over his. One arm wrapped around my back to hold me close while the other draped over my skirt in his lap, and I waited for him to get whatever he needed to say off his chest. "When I was little, I had everything planned out. I wanted to go on adventures like my father, find a hoard of treasure, and build a farm, like my mother. I wanted to have a big family, so that none of my children would grow up without someone to play with." Tears filled his eyes, but he wiped them fiercely with the back of his hand, and my heart squeezed with grief for the loss of his dream.

"I started to think there could be more with Maggie, but you know how that turned out." He scoffed. I *did* know; she'd made promises she hadn't intended to keep, and their separation had been the catalyst for everything that he'd gone through since. "Being with you has given me hope," he said, turning his head to gaze at me. I cupped his cheek in my hand, his stubble scraping against my palm.

"I feel the same way," I replied.

"Have you ever thought about marriage?" he asked, and my heart skipped a beat.

My cheeks flushed, and I clenched my teeth. *Why is he asking?* I thought, safe in the confines of my own mind without Bryn there to hear me.

"Not really," I replied, my voice strained. Bryn nodded, looking away from my face. His was unreadable in a way that told me he was masking something from me. Was it regret about the way I was reacting? Relief that I wasn't yearning for a different commitment?

"I've never given it much thought," I continued honestly. "I know plenty of people who're married, met their partners, but I've also met plenty of people who were together without the Elders blessing their union, and I honestly couldn't tell the difference. My family has always been the captain and the crew."

"Did you and Hunter never talk about it?"

I shook my head firmly. "No. Most of the time we were together, I was so busy pulling away that we didn't have much time as a couple." I hesitated, my stomach churning as I considered whether to ask him why he wanted to know, until my curiosity won out. "Why do you ask?"

He didn't answer for a time, just held me, my body rocking slightly with each of his breaths. When he finally looked at me, it was with such passion that every inch of my body blazed.

"I grew up thinking that sharing my life with someone meant I had to declare it before the Elders, like Arthur and Maude, or my parents. I didn't realize it at the time, but that day on my uncle's ship, when you were covered in blood and I saw *you* for the first time through Derth's hold on you, I found the part of my spirit I hadn't known was missing. Even when my parents were alive, and I was safe and loved, I wasn't complete. Not until I found you. You are my heart, Lila. There's nothing I want more than to be at your side for the rest of our lives, and the rest of it," he shrugged, smilIng, "doesn't matter."

I struggled to put words to the feeling of my heart almost bursting with happiness, of the fluttering in my stomach, of falling more in love with this man than I already was. Everything he'd said about being part of his spirit, I felt it too. There had been so many pieces of my life missing—the details about my childhood and family, certainty about who I was and how I fit into the world around me—but I'd pushed through it all, feeling adrift. With Bryn, I felt whole, safe, and loved, in a way that I never had.

But there was something behind his words, as if he was resigning himself to a life that wasn't how he'd envisioned it, as if he wanted more than anything to ask me to marry him, but didn't want to push me in a direction I'd never considered my life might lead. I couldn't be sure because whatever it was was still locked deep in his mind. Instead of probing for more, I let the love wash over me and suppress the twinge of disquiet, and I leaned in to kiss him.

Everything else fell away, the two of us the only people in the world. His strong hands clutched the small of my back and the nape of my neck, anchoring me to him. I ran my hands through his hair, loving the shiver that passed through him, the feel of his skin prickling as I brushed my fingers against his neck.

He pulled away, his eyes boring into mine as we breathed heavily. I bit my bottom lip to keep myself from kissing him again. "I wish we could live a safer life, away from all this danger." A shudder ran through him, and he clutched me tight. "We're going to chase down the man that has hurt both of us the most, and I might not be able to feel your pain like I once did, but I would die if anything happened to you."

"I feel the same about you," I whispered, my voice trapped beneath the weight of emotion burdening us. "My spirit would crumble if I lost you."

"There's no one in the world stronger or more capable than you. With or *without* the Ambience." I closed my eyes when he pressed his forehead to mine, and took a deep breath of his smell of pine trees and leather. "It's the only reason I'm brave enough to do this."

"We can do it together," I whispered.

With our packs full and our hands clasped, we went downstairs to join the others. The smell of fresh bread mingled with the earthy herb scent that enveloped the tender beef, along with the aroma of butter and garlic, sweet potatoes, leeks, carrots, and beans. It was a stark contrast to Saurboro, with its citrus scent and the heat of the spices that I could taste in the open air. The island had felt like a volcano about to erupt. Here, it felt warm and comfortable, like a hearth fire.

My nose twitched as I smelled something sweet, something suspiciously like chocolate cake. I felt my first genuine smile borne of unburdened joy on my face, my worries forgotten in the face of my favorite dessert, a surprise all the sweeter for knowing how hard it was to come by. Everyone was seated around the table in the kitchen, and a chorus of happy voices beckoned us to our seats.

There were so many conversations at once that I had a hard time keeping track of who was talking to whom, and what was said. I focused on my meal, savoring every bite because I knew it would be a long time before I tasted Lottie's cooking again.

We laughed and ate, savoring the time to be a family, well into the evening. When the meal was finished, Hunter, Roy, and Bryn shooed the rest of us out of the dining room and washed the dishes while Sam served tea. I sat in my favorite armchair, listening to Lottie and Captain Morrig talk under the chatter of the men in the kitchen. I forcibly pushed away the troubles trying to reinsert themselves into my conscious mind, and relaxed into the soft cushions, letting the voice of two people that had given me refuge set me adrift in a sea of grateful nostalgia.

With fierce hugs and promises to be safe, we said our farewells to Lottie and headed upstairs. Lying in bed, I stared through the curtains into the dark night sky, wondering whether somewhere out there, Derth could be looking up at the same sky. Did he know that in the morning, I would hunt for him as he once had for me?

Bryn kissed my shoulder and snuggled close. I smiled and leaned against him.

At least we would hunt together.

CHAPTER TEN

The city was quiet as the dawn light brightened the sky, but the docks were already full of movement and noise when we arrived. We dodged through the crowd, following Captain Morrig's path to a pier in a different part of the harbor reserved for staging new vessels.

There was less bustle here, as the ships waited for a purpose to fulfill. The harbormaster appeared, scowling at Captain Morrig's approach, glancing at the maiden ship directly ahead of us, our crew preparing her to depart.

"I don't like this," the harbormaster grumbled as he fell into step by Captain Morrig. "You bring back one of these ladies in tatters, then turn around and take another the next day."

"We'll be cautious," Captain Morrig replied.

"You better be," the harbormaster growled.

Captain Morrig clapped the shorter man on the shoulder with a smile. The animosity was nothing new; the two of them had been friends a long time, and I knew Captain Morrig delighted in the sour disposition of the other. "I'm touched, as always, for your concern over my safety," he chuckled. "Sorry I couldn't meet you for that drink. First round's on me when we get back. And don't forget, Kai brought you a lovely new ship to tend to."

"At least *they* know how to care for a ship!" the man shouted.

"Unlike some old captains I could mention!"

Captain Morrig chuckled and looked down at me. "If anything happens to this ship, I think he might combust." I snorted out a laugh as I looked the *Celerity* over. It was much smaller than the *Revenge,* two masts to our three, with a streamlined hull and bow that looked sharp enough to pierce waves like a sword. She looked fast and lean, and I smiled as I tried to guess how long it would take to get north in such a sleek vessel.

Her sails were furled, anchor lowered as she sat still in the distance. A low fog surrounded her, obscuring the water below, making it seem as though she were floating on a cloud.

"She has a typical crew quarter assignment, with a small cabin for you to use as your surgery," Hunter said. "Sorry, no privacy for the young couple." He waggled his eyebrows at me, and I slugged him in the arm while Bryn chuckled.

"We'll be fine," I said. "We'll get to Coveton in no time. Look at her."

We rowed out to the ship, greeted by a jaunty melody led by Roy, a song of leave-taking and adventure. Bryn and I stowed our things in the surgery, which indeed had room for only a small cot and a desk, and then joined the rest on deck to ready the ship. With all of us working together, and Roy's driving baritone to keep a song on our lips, it didn't take long for the sails to unfurl and the anchor to rise, and we were off.

The cIty fell away behind us as the wind bit through my clothes, a hint of winter's chill settling over the world. Once we were clear of the harbor, I gathered the Ambience around me like a comforting blanket, frowning as I noted for the first time how threadbare it felt in comparison to the wellspring of energy surrounding Saurboro, and then pushed out a steady stream of wind that carried us faster and faster. The bow rose over the calm surface, and it felt like we were flying.

"We come," I whispered to myself, hoping somewhere, Derth felt a chill up his spine.

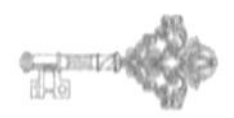

The lower marshland peninsula faded behind us after the first day, giving way to the thick forest that marked the east coastline. Grateful for the swell of waves beneath my feet instead of the rise and fall of the foothills, I watched the ocean sparkle in the distance.

That night, we devised a route to take through Trylia. We'd learn as much as we could in Coveton before taking the main road to Stalth. From there, we'd go to Salava, and then First Port, where we'd rejoin Captain Morrig on the *Celerity*. Either we'd find Derth along the way, or we'd continue our journey from there. Perhaps he'd taken refuge on Rogue's Island.

On the following day, when the sun was high in the sky behind wispy clouds that gave the sky a gray pallor, Sam approached me. "I think we need to go over a few things with regard to Derth," he said without preamble.

"Sure," I replied.

"What would you like the outcome to be?"

I'd spent so many nights envisioning what I'd do if I ever caught up to him, and I asked the first question that I'd mulled over. "Can we nullify his power?" I asked. We'd had a brief discussion about the subject before, but in the context of nullifying mine. Since that hadn't been an option, the subject hadn't been discussed much since.

"It's difficult," Sam sighed. "It takes a lot of concentration and power. And time," he added. His eyes darkened as he pursed his lips, his way of avoiding whatever reminiscence had overtaken him. He hadn't told us much about his life in all our time together, but the pain he carried was obvious in this expression alone, seen so many times during our lessons, in the middle of conversations, all too often as something seen or heard reminded him of something he wouldn't share. But I'd felt the spirit lingering in his family cabin in the mountains. He'd lost someone who had loved him so much that they hadn't returned to the Pool after their death.

But he didn't speak about that if he knew, nor did he talk about the centuries after the Hunters had almost culled the Ambient from Trylia. And I didn't want to force him to relive such painful memories for the sake of my curiosity. Now, though, it felt like there was more at stake. And I needed more information if we were going to survive.

"I did it, once," he said. He swallowed hard. "To someone dangerous. Someone I had thought of as a friend before she almost destroyed everything I loved." Anger, regret, and shame passed over his face in rapid succession. I knew them well; I'd seen them often enough in my reflection. "A long time ago, I studied how to do it. If I have enough time, I might be able to recall the process well enough to teach you." Sam took a shuddering breath. I could almost see him set aside his pain so that he could pull his knowledge around him like armor.

"Is it anything like what Derth did to me?"

Sam furrowed his brow as he considered. "It could be," he replied. "My studies didn't include the effects it had on Conduits, as they have always been rare. If I had access to Salvation's libraries, this would be a different conversation."

"We should go there and see what we can find," I said.

Sam shook his head. "I tried once, a long time ago, but the pass was covered with rock. Sealed, in fact. But I couldn't open it, and I almost died trying." He paused, and then looked at me with something like hope in his eyes. "I never went back because I didn't think I had the strength. That, maybe, Celuthia's strength had waned too much. You might be proof that it hasn't." He sighed, and gazed wistfully out at the water. "I would give almost anything to see it again."

I smiled, imagining myself pulling aside rocks to open the pass. Imagining the smile on his face as he laid eyes on Salvation again after hundreds of years. Something to look forward to after this ordeal with Derth was over. "I'll do everything I can to get you back to Salvation, Sam." But that brought my thoughts back to our original discussion, and my hope dimmed. We had too much to do to consider what might come after.

"What do *you* think we should do about Derth?" I asked, tucking a lock of hair behind my ear. "Every instinct I have tells me that he's too dangerous to be left alive."

Sam studied me for a long moment. It was a look I was familiar with, an analysis of my words and resolve. When he spoke, his voice was thick with worry and regret.

"Are you prepared to take his life, Lila?"

"Yes." I blinked, confused by the question. "I've killed people before, Sam. Everyone Roglin had is gone, mostly because of me, even his hired mercenaries."

"True," he replied. His eyes left mine for a moment, and I watched a cloud of some emotion I couldn't interpret travel across his face. When he looked back at me, his expression was hard. Closed off. "It's one thing to follow your instincts in the heat of battle, to react, rather than to consider your actions."

"I know. I hunted Roglin, remember?"

Sam shook his head. "That was as heated a battle as I've ever seen," he said. "We were trying to save Bryn's life, *reacting* to Roglin altering the plan we'd set."

I nodded, conceding to the truth in his words, and then decided to try my luck in pushing for more information. He'd raised the subject, after all. "You seem confident that you know the difference. Are you speaking from experience?"

"Yes."

"Then explain it to me, because from where I'm sitting, killing someone is horrible no matter the circumstance."

"Making the decision to track someone down with the intention of watching the life drain from their eyes needs a ruthless clarity that can eat away at your spirit. It can fundamentally change the person that you are, knowing that—even if your intentions are honorable, even if it will save lives in the end—you are capable of such a thing, and you follow through. It won't matter if they beg to live, it won't matter if they fight to survive, you are the harbinger of their doom, and it's only a matter of time."

I nodded, and though I hadn't experienced such a thing, I knew that I would go to the lengths that he described, possibly come out the other side of this with a stain on my spirit, to kill Derth. The idea of it gave me no pause; did that make me a monster?

"Did the people you hunted deserve it?" I asked.

Without hesitation, he said, "Yes."

"Would they have hurt people if you let them live?"

"Yes."

"Derth deserves it."

Sam stared at me for a moment longer, and then sighed as he rose to his feet. He turned quickly away, as if to keep me from spotting the moment that his intense stare caved to the sorrow behind it. I stayed where I was, squinting up to the sail as I pushed more wind into it.

He'd do worse to me if I gave him the chance, I thought.

"He would," Bryn called from across the deck. He strode toward me, sparing a glance full of indignation at Sam on my behalf. When he turned back, his eyes were stormy, his jaw clenched. But his anger wasn't entirely for Sam; he'd come to the same conclusion I had, but I realized now that he'd been holding onto this for much longer. While I'd spent time worrying about where Derth might be in the year following our last altercation, Bryn had spent that time privately plotting the best way to kill him if he ever crossed our path again.

The wind ruffled his hair and whipped his untucked shirt across his hips as he walked closer, his eyes never leaving mine. Finally, he reached me, and sat behind me, his legs wide so that he could pull my back against him and wrap his arms around me. "We'll get it done," he said. "If it takes both of us, we'll get it done."

With his arms wrapped around me, our hearts beating in time, our purpose and determination in sync, I felt safe. As if nothing had changed, that we were far from shore, not hunting the man that haunted both of us.

The wind's direction changed, bringing the scent of the trees from the coastline, and a gull cried out overhead. Tracking movement out of the corner of my eye, I didn't find the bird I'd expected to see. The spot was back, hovering at the corner of my vision. Leaning my head back against Bryn, I closed my eyes and took a deep breath, savoring the salt air while I could.

CHAPTER ELEVEN

Two days passed, and headaches plagued me, accompanied by the lingering spot at the corner of my eye that never faded. My eyes burned from trying to scrub it away.

My gaze skipped from tree to tree as I watched the shore drift behind us, and my mind drifted into memories of plunging through the forest as we fled from Derth and Roglin, recalling the mistrust between Bryn and myself in the early days of our acquaintance. My stomach soured as I recalled how much I'd hated him at first, how I'd assumed he was as bad as his uncle, and he'd assumed I would destroy us after my disastrous escape.

Don't punish yourself, Lila, Bryn thought. I saw through his eyes for a moment, to the cabin where he and Captain Morrig were discussing the journey we'd take with Hunter and Sam. *We were both being used; I just wish I'd been brave enough to do something about it. Like you.*

I snorted. *I wasn't brave, I was out of control. I put you through so much, and I'm grateful every day that things turned out the way they did.*

I'd go through it all again if it meant ending up with you, he replied. He flooded my senses with an outpouring of love so strong it took my breath away. I felt him smile to himself before he pulled away.

I rose to my feet, needing to see his face, feeling lonely up here when the others were below. And besides, if there was something to discuss about the path ahead, I wanted to be present for it. The door to the captain's cabin was ajar, and I walked inside to see Sam and Captain Morrig seated at the small table, Hunter and Bryn leaning against the hull on the other side of the room. Bryn's foot was braced on the hull behind him, and his eyes locked on mine as if he'd been staring at the spot where he knew I'd be.

Sam was leafing through notebooks, occasionally making a mark on the side of a page. I couldn't imagine where he found the space; every blank area was filled with his tiny handwriting and symbols that only he knew the meaning of.

"If you don't find him in one of the cities he's been, what then?" Captain Morrig asked. "I don't like the idea of you wandering the length of Trylia in the winter. You could get caught out in a storm, lose your way, or worse."

Bryn shook his head. "We may be stuck for a day or two, but until we get as far north as Salava, we won't have to worry much. Most of the continent doesn't freeze in the winter."

"Lila and Sam can keep us warm," Hunter grinned. "Or change the weather, or maybe Lila and Bryn can move us from place to place."

"That's out of the question," Sam snapped. "We will not tear the fabric of the world for our convenience."

"It was a joke," Hunter said. But he pulled the white stone he'd always carried from his pocket and turned it over in his hand. It was the only thing he had left of his mother, and he only brought it out when there was something troubling him. I hadn't realized he was feeling so insecure.

"I can make us a shelter," Bryn assured us. "Lila and Sam can help, but it shouldn't be necessary."

"If we don't find him anywhere, I'm hoping we can at least learn something about the path he's taking," I said, rubbing my eye to clear the incessant spot. "If there are reports reaching the king's ear, Derth isn't being very subtle. Someone *must* know something about where he's heading."

I snapped my mouth shut as the hair on the nape of my neck stood on end, a feeling of being watched, despite our isolation. The spot in my vision seemed to move, but when I blinked, it was gone. Instinct told me that there was *something here,* something that didn't feel like a spirit. It felt malicious and curious.

"Sam?" I called as I scanned the area. The conversation stopped. Bryn felt my anxiety, and the others rose to their feet, recognizing the urgency in my voice. The spirits swarmed around me, my unease a siren song of potential power.

We come.

What can't I see?

Again, I felt an intuitive tingle, something beyond my perception, something I might have noticed if I'd been open to it. The spirits nudged me in the direction of the door, and I stalked toward it, straining to see what I could only feel. Like the sensation of rain falling onto my head when there wasn't any.

Bryn appeared at my side and took my hand. With our hands joined, the Ambience welled up between us, a flood barely contained, and our eyes met.

Sam warned us not to, I thought.

I don't like being blind, Bryn replied, the connection between us open enough that he felt the same creeping sensation I did. *But I'll follow your lead.*

I hesitated. Sam's fears were valid, and I'd heeded the urging of spirits before, almost losing myself to the Ambience in the process. But the urge was so strong, and I wanted to feel the power flowing through us. I *needed* to see what was watching us.

Bryn felt me give in, and, with the sensation of consciously easing a muscle you hadn't realized you'd tensed, opened himself to me. Our minds joined, and the world came alive in currents of Ambient light. The flow of life was a tangible thing; if we wanted to, we could pluck a thread that would move mountains. But that wasn't our purpose, so our gaze moved to that place next to the door, where we found the source of Lila's unease.

A small orb, the size and shape of an eye, stared at us as it hovered above the door frame, swiveling back and forth as it surveyed the room and the people in it. Its hidden nature was clear now, the outer shell a null space that reflected the Ambience around it. In the center, like an iris in a void, it swirled pale blue.

The same pale blue that taunted us in our nightmares.

"Derth is watching us," we said. We looked at Sam, his tethered spirit surrounding him like an aura giving off the faint scent of old parchment. His fear floated on the air, tasting like a sour apple.

Hunter moved closer. The eye turned to look at him, and he groaned. The pain in his head was a twisted, confused thing that writhed like a worm. Was Derth harming him through this eye?

"Make it stop," he managed through gritted teeth.

Our arms lifted toward the eye, which rotated from Hunter to us, darting back and forth between Lila and Bryn. Our hands opened as if to grasp the orb, and the spirits rushed forward to surround it. But the Ambience diminished as they closed in, as if the energy holding them together was being siphoned into a nullifying void surrounding the eye, and through them, our own energy slipped away.

We crushed our fingers into our palm, and the spirits slammed into the orb like a tidal wave. We felt our strength being drawn into it, but we pushed harder, even as our power diminished. The void finally collapsed with an inaudible pop, and pain—Derth's pain—radiated outward, before it vanished, taking some of the Ambient light with it.

"It's done," we said. We unclasped our hands, letting the Ambience between us fade until—

I took a step back, and Bryn put a steadying hand on my shoulder as the ship rocked, slowing as the wind died suddenly. I groped for the nearest seat and sat down hard.

"What happened?" Hunter asked, his hand pressed to his head.

"Derth was watching us," Bryn said. "There was blackness, and an eye. *His* eye."

"Could he hear us, too?" Hunter asked.

Bryn nodded. "I think so. It felt that way."

"The feeling I had when he was watching." I said, "I've had it for days. He's been watching us this whole time."

"We have to assume he knows we're coming," Bryn said. "And that he's heard all of our plans."

A shiver ran along my spine. "This doesn't change anything. We still have to find him."

Bryn grasped my shoulder, and I clung to his hand. I needed an anchor against the lingering feeling of being drawn into the blackness. Hunter shuffled to us, and I grasped his arm. Another anchor.

"He did something to me," Hunter whispered.

"I know," I said. "I'm sorry."

"If he can do that from wherever he is, what's to stop him from killing us in our sleep?"

I had no idea how to answer his question, so I didn't.

CHAPTER TWELVE

Rough seas slowed our progress north, so it took the better part of a week before we approached Coveton. Trees gave way to the rock-strewn shore I recalled from the last time I'd visited, bedraggled and thirsty.

We anchored the *Celerity* in the harbor and rowed ashore in the pale afternoon sunlight, gliding between a fishing boat whose crew was hauling a net with a moderate amount of thrashing silver fish, and a vacant sloop.

"Like old times," Hunter grunted beside me. "I have to say, I didn't miss the blisters."

I chuckled. "I hate to admit it, but I did." I smiled at Bryn, whose hand was on the tiller. Hunter and I leaped out when our boat thunked against the dock, mooring us to it while the others stowed the oars. Captain Morrig and Bryn stepped out, with Bryn holding a hand to steady Sam as the water rocked him back and forth. After a wistful glance over my shoulder toward the *Celerity*, I followed the others off the pier.

A gaggle of curious fishers and townsfolk near the piers gawked at the ship and us, wondering aloud why we'd come so close to winter. The tall log walls that protected the city parted around the dock, and the smell of the harbor was replaced by the strong scent of the pines that had been felled to make the wall. As we walked inside, a familiar feeling settled over me, the walls looming like the walls of a prison. My eyes darted from corner to corner, waiting for someone to jump out at me. I shared a look with Bryn, knowing that he felt the same.

"We can start at the inn," Bryn suggested. "If the same man runs it, he'll remember Derth."

"A good place for gossip, too," Hunter added.

It was a short journey from the dock to the central city square, surrounded by squat buildings along the dirt ground. The familiar sign, with a mug and bed, waved back and forth in a steady breeze above our heads, as if asking me why I'd come back as we walked inside. Servers bustled between tables full of patrons, and I spotted the same man behind the bar, his black hair long and tied back now, his salt-and-pepper beard lighter, his frown lines a bit deeper. But the harried look on his face was the same as he rushed back and forth along a full bar.

"There he is," I said. Bryn looked where I did, pursing his lips in a momentary frown. "Why don't the rest of you get a table if you can? We'll go talk to him."

"Elders be with you," Hunter mumbled. He stepped to the side as a server swerved toward him.

I walked up to the bar, wedging myself between a man that smelled like fish and salt water and a woman that was leaning toward someone on her other side. Her laugh tittered above the rest of the din. I felt Bryn behind me, his hand on my waist as I waited for the bartender to notice me.

After a few minutes, his eyes darted to my face and he paused, his mouth drawing into a deeper frown.

He recognizes me, I thought to Bryn. The man took a deep breath before striding our way. *He doesn't look happy about it.*

"Don't want trouble," he said without preamble. His eyes darted to Bryn before settling back onto me. "Last time I saw you two, that's what you brought me."

"Stephen, right?" I asked. He gave me a curt nod. "We don't want to cause any trouble," I replied. "We're looking for a mutual acquaintance."

He shook his head angrily. "Trouble. I'll tell you the same as I told him; I'll not be in the middle of your conflict again. Last time, I had a new door to fix, a few bottles of my best liquor smashed, and my best girl left soon after. You can take your custom elsewhere."

"You saw Derth?" Bryn asked, leaning over my shoulder. "When?"

"The end of summer," he grumbled. "I ran him out as soon as I saw he was here."

"Do you know where he went?" I asked.

"No, and good riddance," he spat. "I watched the guards walk him out of town on the main road and haven't seen a hint of him since."

Why would Derth let himself be escorted out of town? I asked Bryn. *He could just as easily have killed the guards.*

That's a lot of trouble to go to for a place to stay, Bryn replied. *And would attract a lot more notice. That could bring Trylian guards here, not just the town guards.*

"Did anything unusual happen while he was here?" Bryn asked.

"No. Didn't give him the chance." Stephen scowled at us. "That one is cursed by the Elders, and I wouldn't go looking for someone with such darkness. Since you seem to be, you should be on your way."

He walked away without another glance in our direction to tend to his customers. Knowing we wouldn't get any more information from him, we left the bar, nodding to the rest of our group before leading them outside.

"I take it that didn't go well?" Hunter asked.

"No," Bryn said. "It seems our last stay here left him with a grudge. With Derth, mostly, but he made it clear that we aren't welcome here, either."

"If there's nothing to learn it would be best to leave, then," Sam said. He looked down the main street toward the gate on the west edge of town. "We can find horses and be on our way."

"This is where we part ways, it seems," Captain Morrig said, flashing a regretful smile. "As much as I wish I could go with you, I think it would be best to stay with the ship. I can meet you in First Port, where I need to coordinate the crews stationed in the north. When you need me, I'll be there."

"Thank you," I said. He wrapped his burly arms around me, and I breathed in the scent of ocean air permeating his clothes before giving him a quick peck on the cheek. "We'll see you soon."

"Elders' blessings on you, dear one," he whispered to me.

Another glance behind at Captain Morrig waving goodbye, and then I followed the others to the west gate. Bryn handed his pack to Hunter and disappeared inside the stable along the inner side of the wall.

I've been looking back too much, I thought. *I need to look forward.*

We waited for a while, watching the sun climb higher in the sky, pulling our cloaks close as a cold wind whistled through the streets. Bryn finally emerged from the wide doors ahead of a stablehand, four horses led between the two of them. They were much bigger up close, and I didn't know what to do with myself. Sam walked forward with a calm, confident smile, and I was surprised to see that despite his obvious nervousness, Hunter approached as well.

The stablehand explained that the four were named Whiskey, Badger, Dusty, and Raven, all gentle and trained to handle even novice riders for travel between cities. I marveled at the ease and gentility with which Sam and Bryn interacted with the horses they chose, and the genuine smile on Sam's face when his hand ran over the warm amber hair on Whiskey's neck. Even Hunter was getting along with his gray-brown horse named Dusty, after the stablehand pulled an apple out of the saddlebags and instructed Hunter to offer it.

I backed away when Badger stomped a hoof at Bryn, but the next moment Bryn was close, murmuring into the large, soft ear as he introduced himself. That left me with Raven, but I stared at her black body without approaching.

"Lila?" Bryn asked. He felt my trepidation as surely as the mare did. "It'll be all right," he said soothingly as he walked back to me. "You can do this. Just like Sam did. Don't be afraid," Bryn said, taking my hand in his. He led me forward to Raven's shoulder, murmuring to her as we walked. His calm demeanor helped me to feel the same, and more confident as the mare didn't turn away this time. Bryn placed my hand on her neck, and she nuzzled my arm with her soft nose. "Good," Bryn said. "I think she likes you, Love. Just stay calm."

Raven pushed her nose forward and let me rub the soft fur above it. I touched her soft ears and scratched her neck behind them. Bryn smiled at me, and then gathered everyone's packs to secure them to the saddlebags. He then secured Badger's lead to Raven's saddle and filed out behind Sam and Hunter as they led their horses through the gate.

Outside, he swung into Raven's saddle and held a hand out. "Grab my hand and swing your leg over when I lift you," he told me. "I'll ride with you until you get comfortable."

"All right," I replied, taking a deep breath to steel myself. "Like climbing into a boat." I gave him my right hand and let him pull me up. The saddle wasn't quite big enough for two; I had to squeeze between Bryn and the raised part in the front.

It was disconcerting to have such a large creature moving and breathing beneath me, and nothing like leaning too far in a boat. She shifted her leg to lean to one side as I settled into the saddle, and I swayed alarmingly before I gripped the saddle with both hands.

Bryn explained the basics of riding when we began, keeping my arms from rising in the air in front of me when he gave me the reins and scooted out of the saddle so I could place my feet in the stirrups to take control. He wrapped his arms around my waist and reminded me to relax my legs and stop leaning one way or another to keep Raven from moving in a direction I didn't intend her to go in. To move forward, I needed to squeeze my calves together, not jab her with my heels.

I started to relax when I didn't fall off, gaining confidence when I urged Raven to move around the bend in the road. I'd made the trip from Coveton to Stalth once before, and I had to admit, insecurities aside, this was much faster and easier. We'd get to Stalth in no time.

The road leading West from Coveton curved away from the delta, rising in a gentle slope as it was swallowed by trees. The path ahead was beautiful; light filtered through the canopy of evergreens towering above to give the road an idyllic air of nature's vibrancy, even this late in the season. Small madrone trees clung to the deepening rock walls of the river that emptied into the ocean, the occasional spark of red amidst the gray rock.

Every muscle in my legs and backside ached, as if I'd been in this Elders'-cursed saddle for days instead of hours. I shifted constantly, trying to relieve the ache as Bryn grunted behind me. Once my apologies numbered in the hundreds, he called for a break.

Bryn slid off behind me, and then offered his arms to help me down. It was a good thing he did, because I half-fell out of the saddle, landing awkwardly, with one foot stuck in the stirrup and my muscles screaming. Hunter doubled over in his saddle, laughing so hard that he could barely breathe. But I heard his groan when he shifted, and smiled grimly to myself. I managed to extricate myself from the stirrup with Bryn's help as Sam walked around Raven leading Whiskey.

"It's hardest at first," Sam said, "but you'll get used to it. Use your power to ease what pain you need to make it bearable, but leave what you can so you can get used to it." He waved a hand over his body and sighed, presumably taking his own advice.

I grumbled in response, doubting that I could get used to this sort of pain in any length of time, but decided to stretch and walk around. If I had any trouble when we rode again, I could take care of it later.

After too short a time to let the horses graze and drink and work out the worst of my aches, we set off again.

I rode on my own for the rest of the day. My muscles still hurt all over, and we took a few breaks throughout the afternoon to give me a chance to stretch and rest. To distract myself, I kept my senses open, hoping I might be able to feel whether Derth was watching again. Nothing came of it, but I was able to focus on something other than the pain for a time. And with Raven content to follow behind the other horses, it was easy to settle into rhythm with her now that I had the saddle to myself.

A frigid gust of wind cut through the trees and chilled me to the bone as the sun fell behind the towering canopy, casting us in darkness. "Winter's closing in fast," Hunter said. It wouldn't be long before snow fell.

"We'll get to Stalth before the first snow," Bryn said in response to my unvoiced thought. "I don't know how long it will take to find what we need there—if Derth isn't there—but no matter how long we take, it'll be an unpleasant journey north."

"Will we have to wait out the winter?" Hunter asked. Like me, he'd spent his winters at sea or in the southern reaches of Trylia, where we were subjected to a rainy season with only a few short-lived flurries.

"If we weren't worried about time, it would be the smart thing to do," Bryn replied. He looked up, as if he could see the weather changing through the trees. "I haven't been as far north as Salava, but around Stalth, even the harshest snowstorms didn't last more than a week. It will be slow and miserable, but we can get where we're going."

Hunter shivered. "I'm not looking forward to the cold. It's been a while since I've seen snow. I've never liked the stuff."

"Nor I," Sam grumbled.

Bryn chuckled. "It's not something I enjoy, either. But we're prepared. We'll be fine."

A strong breeze sent my cloak flying out behind me before I bundled it close. I could only hope Bryn was right.

The last vestiges of autumn faded into the bitter chill of winter as we rode west. The days became shorter, and we battled freezing rain that threatened to become snow the further we traveled. If everything went well, we should be to Stalth in a little over two weeks at a moderate pace.

Sam had been right; it wasn't long before I could ride for hours before needing a break, and I found that I enjoyed Raven's company almost as much as my traveling companions. She was calm and gentle, and helping Bryn take care of the animals at the beginning and end of every day became a welcome chore. There was something satisfying about picking debris from their hooves, removing stones before they could cause lameness, and seeing the horses' genuine pleasure when I gave them a treat or brushed them after a long day.

Now that we were alone and isolated by the late season and the barrier of the trees around us, Sam put me through my paces every time we stopped to water the horses, testing my defenses against any attack he could think of. What started as a clumsy effort to match his movements became an analysis of the feel of Ambience he conjured. The difference between the elements was tangible as they formed; it was amazing that I hadn't been able to feel it before, and it bled over into times when I wasn't open to the Ambience.

Sam had once told me that everything around us had its own

signature, its own flow in the Ambient currents of the world. I'd thought I understood it, but once I stopped focusing on Sam's actions during our sessions and more on my connection to the spirits and the Ambience, I realized that I'd only scratched the surface. Everything had its own frequency, a sound that I couldn't hear, but feel. Like the vibration of a heavy step, the feel of wind in my hair, or heat on my face from a fire.

The Ambience waned as the weather turned, as if it was beginning a deep slumber, waiting for a more vibrant time of year. Our bodies still hummed with power, connecting us to the slow hum of the earth, but we were bright spots in a dull landscape.

We'd been on the road for close to two weeks when the snow finally came. Each day we woke to a cold, white dusting over the campsite. The road froze over, making travel easier, if still miserable. Together, Sam and I created a perimeter of warm air that kept the snow off our faces and the wind from biting into our bones. When we made camp at night, we melted snowdrifts as water for the horses and ourselves.

Our progress was slowed, but not stopped, and over the next day the forest thinned, and then fell away to a vista of flat grasslands that eventually became barren farmland coated with ice and snow. As we approached the outskirts of Stalth's farms, Sam and I let the cold back in. We spent the last day in the open, shivering beneath our layers and wool cloaks as gray clouds closed in above us. Snow dropped from the sky like stark white sheets whipped by the wind. The city came into view through the blizzard, and I longed for a warm night's sleep even as I dreaded coming face-to-face with Derth.

Finally, we could finish what we'd left undone.

CHAPTER THIRTEEN

The wind howled, pushing us toward the city as snow and hail battered us relentlessly. The gates swung open as we approached, and the guards stared at us with wide eyes as we rode inside, the only part of their faces visible beneath heavy knit caps and scarves. They waved us toward a large stable nearby as they struggled to pull the heavy doors closed again.

A gust of wind nearly pulled me from the saddle when I tried to dismount, and Raven snorted when I ripped my foot from the stirrup and landed hard on the ground. Every step forward was a fight to keep my feet under me, but Raven pulled me forward into the still, hay-scented air of the stable with the others behind us. The horses' hooves clopped on the cobbled floor, and a few horses in pens further in nickered as we approached.

Several young stablehands took the reins from us as a woman appeared from a doorway to our right. She smiled even as her mouth opened in shock. "You poor dears, caught out in such a storm! What brings you to Stalth at this time of year?"

Bryn smiled back, shaking the snow from his cloak. "Left our travel a bit late," he replied vaguely.

"And how long will you be staying? We provide feed and board, and collect half the payment up front."

Bryn handed her the writ from King Demetrius without replying. Her brows shot up into her hairline when she spotted the seal. Once she'd read through the contents of the parchment, she handed it back to Bryn, even more curious about our sudden appearance.

"Well, if you're on the king's business, there's no need to worry about payment. I'll send a bill to the Bastion. What could the king have sent you *here* for?"

I smiled at her. "We're traveling through," I said. "We'll move on when the weather permits."

She nodded and smiled, but it wasn't as bright as before. "If there's anything we can do, let us know. We'll take good care of the horses, don't worry."

Hunter and Bryn gathered our belongings from the horses while I walked to Raven's stall. She poked her head out to nudge my shoulder, and I stroked the bridge of her nose. "Get some rest," I murmured. She nudged me again. "I'll come visit, I promise."

With our belongings slung over our shoulders, we raised our hoods again and followed Sam out into the snow. Flakes fell so fast and thick that I couldn't see the other side of the street, so I gripped Bryn's pack and relied on his send of direction through his hometown to guide me. We were at the edge of the circular city, the same ring as Sam's house, but I had no idea how close we were.

It felt like hours of leaning into the wind, trying to keep from slipping with the weight of the packs on my shoulders. Snow blew under my hood to slap me in the face. I squinted, trying to keep it out of my eyes, and looked up as we walked through the familiar leaning gate and onto the overgrown walkway. It hadn't changed in the months since we'd been here last. Under the slim cover of the awning over the door, I watched Sam flick his wrist to unlock it, and gratefully dove inside behind him.

Bryn shut the door on the blizzard, plunging us into darkness. It was almost as cold in here as it was outside; I shivered, my nose frozen and my fingers numb. A flame blossomed on a candlestick ahead of us, and then another beside it, revealing the same cluttered living room. Books teetered in piles around the overstuffed sofa and chair next to the fireplace, since the bookshelves lining the room had no space to hold them. The hallway that ran past the dining room to our right disappeared around a corner, leading to the bedrooms.

I slumped my shoulder to drop the heavy burden to the floor and rubbed my hands together. The others' packs slammed to the floor too, the floorboards creaking, and Bryn blew into his cupped hands as he strode across the room to the fireplace to arrange kindling for a fire. When he'd finished, Sam rubbed his hands together, creating friction that he could shape into a point of heat that became a spark. Before long, a log crackled, bringing light and warmth to the room.

Hunter sank onto the armchair, coughing from the cloud of dust he made, waving his hand around to disperse it. "I'm exhausted," he groaned. "And I'm glad to be inside. That was the most miserable trip I've ever taken."

Sam appeared at his side with a glass bottle filled with amber liquid and a few mismatched glasses. He handed one to each of us, cleaning his with the end of his sleeve before uncorking the bottle and pouring some of the liquid into it. "Wipe the dust out first," he said, "unless you like that sort of thing."

Following his suggestion, I took a sip that warmed my throat all the way to my belly, and I moved next to the fire to soak in the heat, spreading out my sodden cloak on the back of the sofa to dry. After a few moments for everyone to warm up, Hunter downed the rest of his drink and grimaced.

"We're here," Hunter said, "what next?"

"I suppose we can start asking around in the morning," I replied. "First, the woman at the tavern, since she was the one that drew the guards' attention. Maybe she has the information we need, and maybe she can point us in a direction where we can find more."

"Or we find Derth waiting for us," Hunter muttered.

"We'll find out tomorrow," Bryn said, setting his glass onto a table. "I need sleep first. And I'm sure our rooms have a nice layer of dust to clean before we can."

"Sam's houses always do," I smirked.

"Funny," Sam retorted. "You can always stay at the tavern in town. You know where it is."

Bryn chuckled. "I'll take my old room if that's all right. Lila?"

I nodded, putting my glass next to Bryn's. "Sure. I'll get my pack." Bryn plucked one of the lit candles from the hall and led the way, following plain wood walls around a corner to an even longer hall with several closed doors, ending in an open library. There were even more books back here, and each shelf was filled to bursting like the front room.

Bryn opened the door on the left to a small bedroom with a bed that almost filled it and a narrow chest of drawers wedged next to it. I set my pack on the floor and shut the door behind me as Bryn removed the dusty canvas cover and replaced it with clean sheets topped with a thick downy blanket. Every part of my body ached, and I couldn't wait to sleep in a bed again. I fumbled at the laces of my bodice, my thawed fingers clumsy, as Bryn deftly removed his shirt.

After a moment, a shirtless Bryn took pity on me, and finished unlacing it for me. I sighed, relieved, as the leather loosened and fell to the floor. It'd been too long since I'd taken it off, and I could finally breathe again. Bryn continued with the laces on my leather pants, and after he peeled me out of them, I stepped into Bryn's open arms. He smiled, and a warm thrill ran through my body to chase away the chill of the room.

"You are so beautiful," he breathed. One hand reached up to tuck a lock of auburn hair behind my ear. I opened my mouth to protest; my skin was grimy, my hair thick with dirt and grease. But, trapped in Bryn's cobalt gaze, I felt beautiful. I pulled his mouth to mine, and felt him smile through our kiss.

His other arm wrapped around my waist and pulled me close. The warmth of his skin burned through the thin fabric of my chemise, and I ran my hands over his shoulders and up through the hair on the back of his head, giving it a gentle tug. He growled and shivered, and I smiled as our tongues danced against each other, mine as playful and teasing as his was hungry.

He lifted me, and I wrapped my legs around his waist. With one hand cupped beneath my backside to hold me in place, he reached down behind me, and in one swift movement threw the blanket back and lowered us onto the soft mattress. He quirked an eyebrow at me, smiling that lopsided smile that made me fall in love a bit more every time I saw it.

"You're not too tired?" he asked. I closed my eyes, savoring the love and desire he poured into me through our bond.

"Not right now," I replied. He kissed my neck, and pulled away so that he could pull his pants down and throw them across the room, and stooped to press his lips to my thigh. I rolled my hips toward him as his hands trailed up my body, pushing my chemise over my hips to kiss his way up my legs.

I couldn't stand it anymore; I hooked my hands beneath his arms and pulled. "I need you," I moaned. He kissed me again, pulling my bottom lip between his teeth with a teasing smile, running his hands down my side and beneath me to lift my hips. I moaned again when he rocked forward, brushing against me.

He smirked when I leveled an impatient glare at him, and eased his hips forward, entering me so slowly I thought I might combust. He slowly rocked forward, the apex of the thrust sending shockwaves of pleasure through me, but he didn't pull away, just rocked deeper and held me there. When I couldn't stand it, I tried to pull away, but he held me in place and pushed a bit harder.

"Bryn," I whimpered, grasping the bed to squirm away from the overwhelming sensation, but he pinned my wrists at my side, chuckled his way up my neck, and rotated his hips. My back arched as I lost myself, and he nibbled my shoulder, making me gasp as my orgasm heightened.

My body relaxed slowly as he started to move again, and the pressure built once more. "Let's see how many more times I get to watch you come apart," he whispered.

CHAPTER FOURTEEN

The morning came slowly for all of us. Lethargy lingered after battling the weather on the road, and we snacked on some of the last of our road food until we couldn't stand it any more, and dressed in our warmest clean clothes to brave the cold day in search of something warm to eat.

The tavern was the same as it had been more than a year ago, down to the scent of stale beer over the smell of savory stew. I recognized the woman leaning against the bar, speaking to the bartender, as one of the servers from the last time we'd been in town. And, standing next to her, the petite blonde from the tavern in Coveton, who'd told Roglin where we were and started our flight across the continent.

"Bryn," I whispered, just loud enough to be heard over the noise of conversation and cutlery. "That woman there," I jutted my chin in the blonde woman's direction, "what was her name?"

He glanced her way and then back at me. "Cass."

The four of us sat around a table, and the bartender muttered a few words to the woman beside Cass, nodding in our direction. She walked our way, smiling at us as she came to a stop near our table.

"Welcome," she beamed. "Can I bring you some food, ale, or something else?"

We ordered breakfast, my stomach grumbling until it arrived and made my mouth water. Plates with eggs, bacon, and buttered bread seemed a feast after the fare of the past week, and we finished it off as another round arrived in the arms of our smiling server. I drank two mugs of hot tea, finally feeling all the way warm for the first time since we'd left King's Port.

Replete, I leaned back in my chair with the warm mug between my hands and let my gaze wander the room until they fell on Cass at the bar, and our eyes met. Her face went blank as her eyes darkened, and then she shook herself and flashed me a bland smile and turned away. I leaned forward with my brow furrowed, wondering whether she remembered us even as a tingle of Ambient intuition flared in her direction.

"Do you feel something?" Bryn asked me. Sam noticed the direction of my stare and peered at Cass, too. His Tether flared, his attention narrowing in on my vague sense of something *more*, but he shook his head when I cast him a questioning look. "I thought I saw a flash of something, but it was gone so fast that I'm not sure I didn't imagine it."

"She's not Ambient," I confirmed. "I can't tell you what it is, but there's something off."

"Do you think she knows anything?" Hunter asked through a mouthful of food. "Sure, she's here, and Derth was—or is—here," he glanced around the room as if Derth might show up any second, "but that doesn't mean she has anything to do with him."

"We know someone here was acting strange," Bryn reminded him. "And if Lila and Sam think there's something going on with her that we can't see, I think it's too big a coincidence to ignore."

"I think I should talk to her," I said.

Bryn pursed his lips; unease radiated from him. "I don't want you to be alone with her."

"Why?" Hunter asked.

Bryn shook his head with a frown. "I don't trust her. Last time we met she gave us up to Roglin. Now she may have a connection to Derth, and we don't know what to expect from her."

"I'll be fine," I assured him. "If something goes wrong, you'll know."

He didn't like it, but he nodded, trusting me to take care of myself. I waited for the bustle to die down a bit, for Cass and the other servers to take a moment to rest before I waved her over to our table. She frowned, but quickly replaced it with a smile. "Can I get you something else?" she asked.

"Actually, I was hoping I could speak with you." I smiled at her.

"I was afraid you might," she replied. She glanced back at Hunter and Sam, but resolutely avoided looking at Bryn.

"Cass?" I said, pulling her attention back to me. "I don't know if you remember, but we met once before, in Coveton." The twist of her mouth told me that she remembered perfectly well, so I continued. "We have no hard feelings, we're looking for someone, and I was hoping, since you see so many people pass through here, that you might have noticed them." She hesitated, considering my request. "It's a bit private, so is there somewhere we can go to talk?"

A long moment passed before she nodded, and then gestured for me to follow her toward the hall past the bar. She murmured a few words to the other server before she led me to the rooms in the back of the tavern. I turned to look at Bryn before the hallway swallowed me. His brow was furrowed, his eyes fixed on me.

Be careful, he thought.

I will, I replied. *I love you.*

Cass opened the first door on the left to a dim room, the only light peeking through the drawn curtains, and I waited in the hall with Bryn's warning ringing in my head. I couldn't sense anything Ambient inside, and was relieved to see that Derth wasn't sitting inside waiting for me when Cass drew the curtains to light the rest of the space.

Two beds flanked the center of the room where a beige rug sat. In the corner nearest the door was a small table and two chairs, one of which Cass took. She gestured for me to take the other.

"W-what do you want?" she asked, her voice small and frightened. I walked inside, my eyes darting to each corner to ensure we were alone before shutting the door behind me.

I sat in the offered chair. "Do you remember the men that were chasing us in Coveton?" She nodded. "Well, one of them is still out there somewhere, and we need to find him. We heard that there were some strange things happening in Stalth, and this seemed like the best place to start looking. Since you've seen him before and meet all kinds of people, I thought you might be the perfect person to ask. His name is Derth, the one with the hunched back that you saw in Coveton. He's very dangerous."

She put her hands flat on the table as she leaned forward, insistent and nervous. "I'm sorry I told that man where you were, I was so afraid that he would do something to Stephen." Her voice was thick with frightened tears. "He's so stubborn, and I knew he wouldn't listen, and I just wanted them to leave." A tear rolled down her cheek. I leaned forward to place a hand atop hers; she flinched, but didn't move away.

"I would have done the same," I said. "You were right to be afraid of them. I was for a long time." I was *still* frightened of Derth, but she didn't need to know that. I let go of her hands and clasped mine on the table. "If there's anything you can tell me about where Derth is, I would be so grateful."

She sat back in her chair, her eyes red-rimmed and wide. "He was here," a jolt of anticipation in my gut, "but he left." The expression on her face shifted, just for a moment, but I saw a glimmer of something wistful. "I was so afraid, but... he wasn't what I thought he was."

The fear on her face fell away all at once, leaving a beatific smile in its place. I couldn't help my furrowed brow as my mind wavered between worry and confusion at this sudden change, but whatever had stirred my intuition earlier grew. I still couldn't see anything, but the currents of Ambience shifted around her, something sickeningly familiar creeping over my skin. Bryn was halfway out of his chair before I gave him a mental shake of my head to stop him.

"How was he different?" I asked, forcing my face into a more neutral expression. When she looked up, she smiled and wiped her eyes. "How did you help him?"

"I gave him a place to stay, food to eat, and helped him heal his injured leg."

"That was kind of you," I replied, and her smile widened.

She nodded, as if excited to finally share something she was passionate about with a person who understood. "When he limped in the door I almost died of fright, but our eyes met, and I *knew* I had to help him." The more she talked, the brighter her smile became, as if talking about Derth energized her. "Falei—she owns the inn—wasn't happy about him taking the room, nor with me taking time to tend to him, but I had some Aelios set aside to pay his way."

"Did Derth ask you to do that?"

She shook her head, all trace of fear forgotten. "I needed to protect him, to make sure he wasn't disturbed. And the best way to do that was to make sure Falei has enough gold in hand to let him be."

Cass's eyes were wide, eager, and unblinking as she spoke. This was more than something that had happened to her. It looked like it was *still* happening, and as she continued to relate her time with Derth to me, an aura grew around her. It wasn't the aura of a spirit like I'd seen around Sam or Colagh, but a deeper connection to the Ambience than most non-Ambient I knew. But as that aura became too bright to look at, something dark siphoned it away. That darkness slithered across her eyes, around her head, into her ears, nose, and mouth. Not a full spirit, but a trace of Ambience that was twisted and shadowed.

It was the energy I'd seen as Derth watched us on the ship, and it was still holding on to Cass.

I cleared my throat and blinked, realizing that she'd stopped speaking and was waiting for me to respond to something. "What?" I said. "I'm sorry, I lost focus for a moment."

She finally blinked, but it was too slow to be normal. The darkness shivered. "I asked why you think Derth is dangerous. He was nothing but kind to me, and I want to know what you intend to do when you find him." She was still smiling, but it no longer touched her eyes, where her stare was too direct, too intense, for the woman I'd been speaking to.

"Oh," I began, sensing that I needed to be careful with my answer. "We want to find him before someone else does." A safe answer, considering Derth had presumably heard as much when he was watching us. "And we're worried about what he might be forced to do if those people find him first."

Cass nodded fervently, her blonde hair bouncing around her face. "I'm so glad you understand!" she said, beaming. "Derth told me everything that happened, but you need to know, he was *forced* to do those things."

I smiled at her, sitting back in my chair to get some space between us. I knew that if I tried to correct her, this discussion would not end well for me. "Why did he leave?" I asked instead. Her eyes flashed with anger, so I hastily added, "There must have been a very strong reason to pull him away from you."

Cass sighed, regretful now. The rapid changes to her demeanor were becoming maddening. "Falei started to make a fuss about Derth, said I wasn't myself, and threatened to call the guards. With the new guard captain in charge, I'm sure he would have been arrested."

"I understand," I replied. "Why didn't you go with him? Did he tell you where to find him?"

Shaking her head, she said, "I don't know where he is, but he said he'd come back for me once the trouble had gone. But it's been months. I miss him."

I nodded and smiled. "I'm sure you do. Being parted from someone you love is so hard." I stood, thinking of Bryn, wanting more than anything to be out of this room and in his arms. In my mind I watched him stand and move quickly toward the hall. "Thank you for speaking with me, Cass. I'm sorry you can't be with the person you love, but I'm glad to hear that he isn't the monster Roglin made him out to be." The words tasted like acid in my mouth.

As she stood, she wiped the tears from her eyes, and seemed to shrug off the darkness enshrouding her. She blinked once, a look of confusion crossing her face, and then she blinked that away, too. "I'm so glad to find someone who doesn't think I've lost my mind," she sighed.

I smiled again and opened the door, letting her trail behind me as I quickly walked to the main room, meeting Bryn at the hall entrance. I grasped his arm and pulled him with me, watching Cass return to the bar where a stern woman with black hair bundled high and tight on her head narrow her eyes at us with suspicion.

"Let's go," I said when I was close enough to Sam and Hunter for them to hear me. "We should talk."

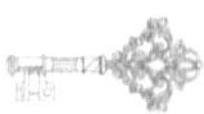

Back in Sam's musty house, after Hunter made a quick stop to buy enough food to make a few meals, we gathered around the dining table for me to recount my experience with Cass. Sam's frown deepened every moment as Hunter became more incredulous. When I'd finished, Hunter scoffed, and Sam remained silent and scowling.

"He must be here, right?" Hunter looked at Sam with no response, and then turned back to me. "He can't control someone without being close to them, *right?*" I shrugged, and disgust twisted his face. "Don't tell me he can control people from far away now, I don't want to hear that."

"I don't know," I admitted. "He's been watching us from Elders know where. We have no idea what he's capable of."

"We need to figure out whether he's still here," Bryn pointed out. "If we don't believe Cass because she's Derth's pawn, who can we ask? And is there some way we can help her?"

Sam looked up, drawn out of his thoughts. "It's possible, but I think we need more information before we proceed. Since she is a Still, a non-Ambient, it might damage her mind irreparably."

"We need to check in with the guard captain regardless, so we can ask them more about Derth," I said. "If they don't know where he is, maybe they have an idea of who else might have been affected in case they have more information. If it's possible, I'm going to help Cass. I don't want to leave her like this if we need to move on."

"Of course," Sam replied. "I wouldn't have it any other way." He smiled at me, but his eyes were still distant with an untold wealth of information swimming behind them.

"Hopefully, the king's writ will be enough to get some cooperation from the guard," Hunter said.

"If they want Derth stopped, they'll cooperate," I said. "And when we find him, we'll make sure he can't do this to anyone else."

CHAPTER FIFTEEN

The storm worsened throughout the day, and we were too tired to fight the snowfall, and so decided to enjoy a warm meal and an early night's sleep. I snuggled close to Bryn, listening to the wind howl outside, grateful for the walls that protected us. In the morning, after a leisurely breakfast and time for all of us to bathe thoroughly, we bundled ourselves and stepped outside again.

Thankfully the storm had abated and the sky was clear. The midday sun's cold rays sparkled on a fresh expanse of snow covering the city. It was beautiful, until we had to trudge ankle-deep through the street to get to the barracks.

The Bastion loomed above the surrounding buildings, sitting in the first ring outside the center of the city. I had expected an austere building, full of straight lines and gray stone, but the outer wall was a carved frieze depicting the lives of the citizens of Stalth. A farmer in a field of waving grain, a merchant handing a basket to a customer, a patrol of guards standing tall and proud atop a curved wall. It was beautiful.

Tucked next to it was another stone building with similar carvings, of six large figures in varying poses. I instantly recognized the Six Elders adorning the city's temple, and was surprised to see people walking out of the doors into the snowbank. In my experience, the

Elders were subjects of songs and fables, and something to curse when things went wrong.

Bryn grasped the iron handle on the thick oak door to the Bastion and pulled it open, standing aside for the rest of us to shuffle inside, stomping our feet to clear them of snow. A woman looked up from her desk, situated between two closed doors across from the entrance. She smiled at us, her eyes lingering on the mess we were making of the floor.

"How can I help you?" she asked.

Bryn stepped forward, pulling his hood back to flash an easy smile. "We would like to request a meeting with the guard captain," he said.

"On what business?" the woman asked. She clasped her hands together on the desk in front of her, a barrier between us and her captain.

"Business from King Demetrius," Bryn replied, offering the writ.

She narrowed her eyes when she spotted the seal and inspected it closely for a long moment before opening the parchment. After reading the writ she still seemed skeptical, but rose from the desk. "Wait here, please," she said, and walked through the door to our right.

We didn't wait long; the woman opened the door and gestured us inside with a too-bright smile. "The captain has some time now," she said, and turned to lead us through. Through the door was a short hallway lined with paintings of the landscape around Stalth hanging on the stone walls. We passed a closed door to our left as we headed toward one standing open at the end of the hall.

The office beyond was almost as large as the foyer, but there was nothing in here to distract from the stark stone walls but the two windows that let in the winter sunlight and the desk in the center of the room where a woman was awaiting our arrival.

It took me a moment to recognize her; our last meeting had been in the midst of running into Roglin as we fled the city. This was the guardswoman who had intervened, allowing us to slip away as they detained Roglin and Derth.

Without her helmet her hair was loose; bright copper with glints of gold, shaved on the left side and slicked back on the right, the short end tucked behind her ear. Her gaze was direct, piercing, and her posture rigid and upright. She emanated an attitude of someone waiting to correct me for saying something wrong.

"I understand you're here on business from the king," she said. Her voice rang out, as authoritative as her presentation suggested. "It's interesting that the lonely old man from the outskirts of town is back on business for the king, and in the company of the woman who caused such a fuss when she left Stalth, only to disappear before she could bear witness against the man who attacked her. A strange company of mercenaries. What *exactly* is your business for the king?"

Bryn and I shared a glance, both of us wondering how she could remember me after laying eyes on me once in such a tense situation. "We're looking for a criminal," I replied. "The king received your reports of strange behavior, and we think this man might have been involved. He was part of the incident you mentioned, and more dangerous than Roglin was."

"And why does the king think that you are more capable than his guards?" She cast a disdainful gaze over us, and I had to fight the impulse to wither like a child caught sneaking something sweet to hold her stare.

Hunter smiled, but she was unfazed. "We specialize in strange incidents," he said. "And the reports he's been receiving from your office made him think that we were the best qualified to investigate." The captain pursed her lips but didn't respond.

I jumped in. "Can we ask you some questions about what's been happening here? It may point us in the right direction."

"I suppose that's the least I can do, since you provided this writ." She lifted the parchment from her desk and set it down again. "Though I won't subvert the law at the behest of what amounts to a promissory note for any goods or lodging you might need." She held up a finger in our direction to emphasize her words. "I am in charge of this city's well-being now, and I won't see anyone, even those sent by the king himself, breaking our laws." She sat back in her chair and crossed her arms over her chest. "We just got out from under the thumb of corruption, and I'll not begin the descent back into it."

"Understood," Sam said. "We have no intention of breaking any laws, we can assure you."

"In that case, I will help any way I can. Ask your questions."

"How many complaints of odd behavior have you had?" I asked.

"Two that we investigated about six months ago, more that we could account to alcohol or any number of other causes. I still harbor doubts about the veracity of those conclusions as they coincided with the timeline for the other two," she replied. "I can get you a list of the reports I've seen, but most of the people named have fallen back into normal patterns of behavior, apart from the two mentioned in my report. Of those, one was the server at the Crossroads Inn in the city center. Her name is Cass, a young woman that put aside her duties and spent much of her own coin to pay for a stranger's room and board. Not something we would normally pay heed to—people can spend their earnings as they wish—but there was some concern for the woman's safety according to the owner of the inn, and her description of the stranger in question matched the man seen with Roglin. He fled before we could question him, but not before one of our guards helped him liberate my predecessor from our jail."

"Why?" Bryn asked.

She shook her head, holding up a worn piece of parchment, which Sam eagerly accepted. "Not an Elder-forsaken clue. My best guess is that it was repayment for *his* release from custody." She sneered. "To think that I could have kept this man safely behind bars and avoided all of this, if only I'd had witnesses to your assault to speak against them." She shot a pointed look at Bryn and me, and my cheeks reddened.

"I apologize for that," Bryn replied, "but considering the sum that Roglin was paying your predecessor to avoid consequences for any illegal actions he might have taken, our presence wouldn't have made a difference for your efforts. But our absence saved our lives."

She took a long moment to study Bryn's face, and I realized that she could likely read most people like open books, that she would recognize a lie when she heard one. But whatever she saw in Bryn's face seemed to satisfy her.

"My predecessor was as corrupt as they come," she admitted, "hence his subsequent arrest. If you're hunting Roglin's accomplice, I'm happy to provide what I can for that pursuit." She pointed at the parchment in Sam's hand. "I don't know that you will glean any more information from these people than we have, but as long as you refrain from harassing Stalth's citizens, you have my leave to try."

"Thank you," Sam said. "I find that the right context often leads to more helpful questions. May we speak with the guard that helped to release the former captain?"

"That can be arranged, under guard. And, since you won't provide any further details surrounding your presence here, I require that you keep me apprised of your progress and report any possible threat to the safety of Stalth's people directly to me."

"We agree to your terms," I told her, though I couldn't help but feel like there was something more to her terms than I was hearing. "If we find a threat to the city, you'll be the first to know."

She nodded. "Do you want to speak to him now?"

"If it's possible, yes."

"Follow me." She strode to the door and opened it, leading us back to the foyer.

I have a feeling that woman wouldn't react well if we told her the whole story, I thought to Bryn. *We need to make sure we don't say too much to this guard.*

We'll ask if he knows anything, he replied. *You and Sam can see if there's anything more going on, and we'll leave.*

The captain opened the door on the other side of the desk and waved at an armor-clad woman exiting a room mid-way down the hall.

"You can see the prisoner now," she told us, and the guard led us into the hallway on the left. Following the guard, we found a longer hallway with a few doors opening into dormitories, a kitchen, and a sitting room. Another door opened into a room only furnished with a table and chairs. But the hallway continued, and at the end, opened onto a large room separated into separate cells constructed of floor-to-ceiling iron bars.

Two were occupied when we entered. The closest to the door held an old woman in thick wool clothes, sprawled on a narrow bench with her arm slung over her head and gray, curly hair spilling out of the kerchief tied to her head. The other held a middle-aged man with long brown hair, wearing a guard's uniform. He sat on the bench, his legs apart and arms braced against them, tapping his feet. There were vivid bruises under his hooded eyes, as if he hadn't slept in a few days.

The guard led us to his cell, ignoring the woman as she snorted in her sleep. "Norin, you have visitors."

Norin stared at the guard, his eyes full of shame, but the guard frowned at him. She stepped away, taking a post at the open door as he watched her walk away before dropping his gaze to his feet. I took position at the door of the cell, out of arm's reach, and let the others arrange themselves around me.

"Norin?" I asked, feeling Sam's tethered spirit pulse, likely attempting to detect the Ambience as I was. I didn't sense anything, but if this man was like Cass, it might not be visible unless I triggered a change. "My name is Lila. May I ask you a few questions, please?" He nodded, his eyes not leaving the floor. "Can you tell me what happened with Derth?" I asked. When he didn't answer, I added, "The hunched man. Did he do something to you, or ask you to do something for him?"

He stopped tapping his feet, tensing his shoulders, and when he slowly lifted his head, I had to resist the urge to take a step back. This wasn't the same man I'd seen moments ago; the vacant stare was intense, the same as Cass. The others noticed too, and the same energy I'd seen in Cass appeared like a sudden gaping wound in the man's spirit, swirling around his head.

"He needed my help," Norin said, the gruff monotone sending a chill down my spine. The guard at the door took one step forward, her hand on the hilt of her sword, her eyes fixed and wide on the man behind the bars. I waved her back, but she stood coiled like a snake, ready to strike whatever had replaced the man she'd known. "He needed to leave the city, since the captain was coming for him. I couldn't let him rot in a cell."

"You took his place," Hunter muttered. Norin's eyes locked onto Hunter, who cleared his throat and shut his mouth.

"You helped him get the former captain out of prison," I continued. "Why? What did Derth want with him? Where did they go?"

Norin shook his head, still staring at Hunter as if he might leap across the cell and strangle him. "I can tell you." He turned his stare onto Hunter, then Sam, and finally Bryn, where it lingered long enough to send a shiver down my spine before returning to me as he spoke again. "If you're alone."

"Alone?" I asked. I couldn't help but retreat a step further.

Norin nodded slowly. "He's waiting for you, but I can't tell you where he is until you're alone."

I took a deep breath through my nose, hoping to conceal my fear from him, and looked at Bryn over my shoulder. "Maybe you should step outside—"

Norin interrupted me. "No." I turned back as he shook his head. "He knows they'll follow you. If you won't get rid of them, he will."

"Why?" Bryn demanded, stepping forward to shield me. "Why does he want her?"

Norin just stared at me. I glanced at Bryn, who shook his head. *I don't think he has more to tell us,* he thought.

I don't either, I replied. *If Derth is trying to unnerve me, he's succeeded. But I don't know what else to do. I can't tell where this power is coming from. Even if I did know what to do, I can't risk helping him here and now. Not after what Sam said about Cass. Or with the guard here.*

We'll figure something out before we leave Stalth, he thought. *We should go through as many names on the list Sam has as we can, to see whether Derth was involved in their reports, so that we don't miss anything while we're here.*

Good idea, I thought. I glanced at Norin, who was still staring intently at me. Turning away, I said aloud, "We can go."

Turning to the guard, Bryn said, "Thank you, we're done." Norin didn't move, but I felt his eyes on my back as I rushed out of the prison behind the guard, who shivered as we crossed the threshold to the foyer. It was a relief to escape back into the cold, away from the unnerving experience we'd left behind. Dark clouds heavy with snow had rolled through the clear sky, and I pulled my cloak close around me.

Sam held the captain's list out. "I agree with the captain that these are hardly indicators for Derth's presence. Drunken outbursts, young people's pranks... We could spend all winter tracking these people down and be no closer to Derth."

He paused, and the Ambience flared around him. It passed over me, trying to smooth the ragged edges made by the encounter with Norin, and I smiled my thanks to him.

"I don't sense anything in town that suggests an Ambient presence; if Derth is here, he's keeping a low profile," Sam continued. He glanced at me, his face drawn with worry, and looked at the list again "There must be something here," he said, nodding as if to reassure himself. "We don't have an alternative."

The wind picked up, snatching the parchment from Sam's hand as snow began to fall. Bryn stomped on it before it could flutter away, and gave it a quick look before he handed it back to Sam. A flurry became a storm in a matter of moments, and soon I couldn't see the end of the street where it opened onto the town center.

Bryn clutched my hand as if afraid to lose me, and I knew it was more than just the storm he was worried about. Derth was waiting for me, and had left these people broken, with instructions to give me direction if I left the people I loved behind.

Without that information, we were left with a list of names that might amount to nothing, or could be more people like Norin, which would put us right back here. Even if I abandoned my common sense and decided to go after Derth on my own, the only way to keep Bryn from finding me would be to break our bond again. And that was something I wouldn't do.

"No, you won't," Bryn shouted at me over the wind. "We'll go through the list, and if we find nothing, we move on when the weather clears. The stable owner we met is on the list," I looked up in surprise, "and we know where she is. I want to see if I can get some things from my mother's house, so we can talk to the owner when we head out."

"I'll ask around the tavern," Hunter offered. "Maybe Falei will know more about Cass and some of the drunks on the list."

I nodded and pulled my hood over my head to block the wind as I wondered how many people that'd seemed normal were secretly harboring Derth's foul imprint. I tugged on Bryn's hand.

"We need to visit Arthur and Maude before we leave town, or they'll never forgive us." I almost suggested we head there now, but a glance at the sky told me that we'd be buried in snow soon. Besides, if Derth planned on coming for my friends, I didn't want to lead them to the couple that had shown us such kindness when we were here last.

Hunter rolled his eyes. "I don't know what I want more, to find someone Derth has corrupted, or to head north, where it's even colder."

I snorted, feeling the same. "If no one else here looks at me the way Cass and Norin did, I'll be glad of it. Elders," I cursed, "they were unsettling."

"I miss King's Port," Hunter grumbled. "At least there, we'd be miserable and wet, instead of half-frozen from a walk across town. Prepare yourself because I think it's going to get much worse when we finally find Derth."

Bryn seethed beside me. "If he wants you," he told me, "he's going to have to come through me."

Sam was silent, the muscle in his jaw clenched, his nostrils wide. I opened my mouth to ask him what was wrong when I felt a flutter in my chest, so strong that it stole my breath. Someone was using Ambience, a lot of it. And they were coming closer.

I turned slowly, the feeling intensifying as I faced south. "Derth?" I asked. Feeling what I could, Bryn stood by my side, facing south with us. Hunter fell in on Sam's other side, confused as he took our cue.

"Perhaps he's returned," Sam replied. "Prepare yourselves."

Angling toward the south gate took us along the residential ring, and into an alley between houses. As we emerged, something slammed into my side, sending me sprawling to the cold stones. Hunter shouted, Bryn lunged, and I rolled aside as a blade flashed down at me.

CHAPTER SIXTEEN

My eyes swam as the hilt of a dagger slammed into the street. Bryn collided with the attached arm, and they smashed into me, elbows jamming into my side, leg, and temple. My head throbbed as the wind was knocked out of my lungs. Ears ringing, I sucked in air and coughed, trying to clear my eyes.

A fist rose next to me and came down hard. I couldn't tell who it belonged to, but I heard muffled shouts through the heartbeat thudding in my ears. The mass of limbs flailed as I sat up and scooted back, hands chafing and frigid. A leg kicked out at me again before it was snatched back when Bryn heaved whoever was in his grip away from me. Another flash of movement out of the corner of my eye made me jerk back, but when I looked for the source, there was nothing.

"Lila," Hunter called, his voice muffled, like I was hearing him through water. He helped haul me to my feet as I coughed again. "You all right?"

I shook my head, holding my pained side as spots danced in my vision. Bryn and the man who'd hit me were struggling, rolling back and forth, and it was hard to see what was happening. Hunter tried to wrench them apart, but his arm was slapped aside when Bryn was flung to the side.

Our attacker flew after him, knife flashing and eyes enshrouded by twisting darkness, and the Ambience screamed at me to unleash it. But the sound of voices behind us made me hold it back. Instead, I drew a knife from my boot.

I didn't get the chance to use it. Bryn planted his foot in the man's chest and shoved, sending him tumbling back up the nearby alley. As I stood, a wave of Ambience surged toward us from behind, and my heart nearly stopped. Was this man a distraction for Derth? I skidded to a stop and whirled around to find a figure standing at the mouth of the alley, backlit by a break in the clouds. Their arm was raised in our direction, their head cocked to one side. My instinct told me that this wasn't Derth—this person was too tall—but my fear demanded that I unleash the destructive fire I was holding at bay. I heard a loud crack from behind, Hunter cried out in surprise, and the man who'd attacked us landed with a thud at my feet. His head was wrenched too far to one side, his eyes wide and bulging, and he was still.

I looked up at the figure, who straightened as they walked forward. "Sam? Bryn?" I called, seeing neither of them in my peripheral vision as I stared at the shadowed person approaching. I pulled my sword, almost grunting with the effort it took to keep the Ambience from overwhelming me.

"Here," Bryn growled, pulling his sword and dirk so he could block Sam behind us. A long, dirty scrape marred his cheek, and blood dripped from his lip and nose.

Bootheels clicked on stone, and a voice called out, echoing in the alley. "It's so good to see you, my friends! I was hoping I'd find you here!" The voice was familiar, and the figure stepped out of the shadows. Gray eyes flecked with brown smiled at me over a satisfied grin, and the blood drained from my face. "It seems I have arrived just when I was needed most."

The Vorthe Tether had followed us to Stalth.

"How?" I blurted before I could stop myself. How was he here so quickly? How did he know to come here?

He chuckled as he came to a stop before us, glancing toward the dead man at my feet. He gestured to the figures resolving behind him, and the rest of the Vorthes appeared. As soon as his gaze was removed from me, I shut the Ambience away with a silent prayer to the Elders that I hadn't been displaying it strongly enough for Colagh to see. "A combination of luck, skill, and perseverance. But that is a tale for another time." He glanced past me, and I realized that I could hear people moving on the street behind us. "Pearl," he commanded. She stepped forward, waved a hand over the body, and it began to dissolve.

"Wait!" I shouted, but in moments, the body was gone. Rage clawed at my throat. "You can't just…"

"I already have, but there's no reason to be afraid, I will not hurt you," Colagh interrupted. More than *one* Vorthe Tether, then. "There is no turning back now." He rubbed his hands on his thick leather coat. "I can assure you, that man was not acting of his own free will."

"How do you know?" Hunter demanded.

The Ambience stirred again, barely contained as my anger grew. Colagh had just killed a man and ordered his remains scattered without hesitation. Was this something they did so often that he didn't feel any remorse? This man had been a puppet—a *victim*—not in control of his actions. He hadn't deserved to die.

The other Vorthes filed around us, disappearing in the night as I scowled at Colagh. "It's quite a coincidence that we have all braved the weather this time of year to come to this city. Especially after I divulged my purpose in visiting Trylia. Perhaps our goals are aligned, and you sought to reach Derth before we could?" Colagh pursed his lips as he studied each of us in turn. "Tell me, have you been sent to find the man we are seeking?"

When met with silence, he continued. "You see, I am Ambient, and I can see more than Stills like yourselves." He cast a glance at Sam and smiled at me. I couldn't tell from his expression whether he'd been able to sense my power, or he was still trying to figure me out. "There is an aura about the people Derth touches that lingers, and this man had it. It's possible there are people throughout the city who have been given orders to attack anyone asking too many questions. I encountered something similar in King's Port, which started me on the path that led me to you fine people. Now, I need to get out of the cold, and I hear there is a lovely establishment in the town center. Please, join me, and we can continue our discussion."

He turned and walked past us, back in the direction we'd come from. The flutter in my chest was gone; Sam had doused his power as I had, and Colagh was no longer emitting anything, either.

I stared at the others, Hunter shrugging and Bryn scowling as Sam sighed. "This man could have told us something, but that's impossible now." Sam's frown was deeper now, and he was becoming more withdrawn by the second. "We need to get out of the open. Now."

Colagh turned onto the main street, nodding and smiling to an elderly couple that passed him, before he ducked down another alley. We rounded the corner to find him waiting for us, and his eyes took a quick trip up and down my body. "It would be best if we put distance between ourselves and the attack as quickly as possible."

Bryn inhaled sharply at my side, and I grasped his hand. I didn't know which of us needed it more. There was something about Colagh that made me uneasy, more than the problem that he presented. Every time our eyes met, I could see the depth of knowledge that he held, and it was deeper than mine. His eyes told me that danger was looming for me. For us.

My mind flicked from thought to thought as we walked. Did he know that Sam and I were Ambient? Was he waiting to take this information back to Vortheim? Would he try to take *us* to Vortheim, like Roglin and Derth had?

I walked with my hand in Bryn's, letting him lead me. All I had to do was put one foot in front of the other. Keep moving, don't fall behind. Down another alley, out onto a street where the snow fell onto our heads, and then back into the shadows between two buildings.

A man stumbled into our path, swaying as if drunk. Bryn cut a path around him, but before we could move past, the man stumbled into me. His muttered apology died on his lips when he looked up at my face.

"You belong with him," he intoned. Before I could react, his hands flew to my throat and squeezed.

I couldn't breathe, and Bryn turned, grabbing the man's hands to pull him off me. But he took no more notice of Bryn than he would a gnat. He thrust me up against the nearest wall, one meaty hand crushing my neck to hold me in place as he pulled a club from his belt and swung.

The club connected with Bryn's shoulder with a sickening crunch. Hunter punched the man in the face, but it was as ineffective as Bryn's attempt to pull me free. The man swung again, narrowly missing Hunter's temple. Bryn grimaced through the agonizing pain, and I knew that if that club hit either of them in the head, they would be dead in moments.

As my vision blackened and my body began to slump, I reached out for Bryn on instinct. Our minds intertwined.

We gave Bryn's body more strength, and he wrenched the man's fingers back. First the left thumb, *snap,* and then the index finger, *snap.* This allowed enough air to enter Lila's body to prevent her death for a moment more. We looked over her shoulder, in the direction of the shadow at the edge of her vision that hadn't ceased, and found another sphere in the air.

Darkness twined around it, stretched out to the man holding Lila as the pale blue eye in the center darted back and forth between Bryn and her. Derth's presence was here, assuming direct control of this man. That darkness was focused on the man, and as we reached out, expecting to feel it sapping our strength as it had before, we found that the draw was so minimal that we could ignore it.

We reached up, calling a spirit to clasp the orb in its hand and crush it as our fists closed on air. It shattered, sending a ripple of air outward in a radius, and the man released Lila. He stepped back as we forcefully pushed the Ambience away, hearing shouts of outrage and a call for the guard.

I came back to myself, gasping for air and holding my abused throat. Each inhale burned as tears fell from my eyes and the world swayed. Bryn ignored the pain in his shoulder and swept me into his arms just before my legs gave out. The man was on his knees, but the Ambience had retreated, and I couldn't tell if the darkness still bound him. A guard appeared to haul my assailant further away, and a few more ran closer to help her.

Beyond the commotion, Colagh watched, his companions flanking him. The bald man spoke in his ear as he watched my assailant being dragged away, and Colagh gave a small shake of his head in response.

He noticed me watching, frowned, and glanced over his shoulder at the inn across the open space that marked the heart of the city.

The Vorthes melted into the growing crowd as another pair of guards pushed through them to restore order. Several citizens questioned them, gesturing angrily to the man being hauled off in the direction of the prison.

All I could do was huddle against Bryn's chest as he answered a few questions and promised to speak with the captain about the attack the next morning. When the guards let us leave, Bryn slid through the throng, sheltering me against his chest, away from the stares and questions of the onlookers. It seemed like everyone nearby had abandoned whatever had taken them from their homes, and the entire inn had emptied to gawk at us.

It felt like we were surrounded. We'd stumbled from one person to the next, marking ourselves as targets for Derth's assassins, hidden in plain sight. And that orb, that I had assumed he was using to watch us, gave him the ability to take control of the people he left behind, to kill us using someone else's hands.

How long would it take for one of them to succeed?

CHAPTER SEVENTEEN

The tavern was deserted apart from Falei and Cass at the bar, and a few cooks propping the door to the kitchen open. All were listening to Colagh's melodic voice as he relayed my attack to his audience, until the door slammed shut behind Hunter, and all eyes turned to us. Cass winced when she realized who she was looking at and muttered something to Falei before disappearing into the kitchen. The rest stared in confusion and concern as Bryn set me in the closest chair.

My throat burned when I swallowed. Bryn crouched in front of me, reaching out to touch me but stopping short, hesitant to cause me any more pain.

How do I help? he asked. *Tell me what to do.* His eyes were full of so much pain that for a moment I wondered whether he *could* feel it.

I glanced at Colagh, who was watching us with a frown of concern, and shook my head at Bryn. *You can't,* I told him, cold numbness settling over me. Shock, my healer's mind noted. *He'd see it.*

And we can deal with that later, after we heal the pain. He reached out to touch my neck, but I grabbed his hand.

He can't know about us, I insisted. *He might know about me, but he can't know what we can do together. Besides, there were too many witnesses. If the captain sees me without bruises, she'll be suspicious, too. Somehow, I'm just as afraid of what she'd do with someone like me as I am about Colagh and his people.*

Elders' eyes, Bryn cursed.

Bryn pursed his lips, angry and helpless as he watched me swallow and wince. But he let his arm fall, taking my hand instead. Colagh walked toward us, stopping to hand keys to his people standing nearby. They took one each, and then left in the direction of the inn's hallway of rooms. He smiled a pitying smile at me from behind Bryn.

"That looks painful, my dear. I'm so sorry I couldn't intervene this time. But as you saw, the city guard were so close…" He shrugged. "The situation is more dire than even I suspected. I hope you can all see now that it is in everyone's best interest to join our forces to stop this criminal before more are hurt."

"This isn't the time or place for this conversation," Bryn snarled, standing to glare at Colagh. I watched as if from a distance, my attention torn between the men in front of me, the screaming pain in my throat, and the numb dread gripping me.

Colagh retreated a step, holding his hands in front of him in surrender. "You are upset. It's reasonable, considering the situation. Perhaps we can retire to my room where we can speak more freely? Would that be acceptable?"

Bryn was unmoved, but the sound of people filing through the door—and the hushed conversation that followed—pulled his attention away. Hunter looked around and back at us, the question clear on his face. Should we leave, or stay and talk to Colagh?

The bald man accompanying him handed a key to Colagh, who held it up in invitation. After a curt nod from Bryn, we all followed him down the hall to the third door on the left, into a large room with a candelabra lit on a table large enough to seat four. The drab curtains were drawn against the cold outside, and Colagh strode across the circular brown rug to sit on the edge of the wide bed.

"I can't believe how *cold* your country gets." Colagh chuckled as he pulled his hair behind his head and plaited it with practiced movements. "I'm told this is normal weather this time of year. I cannot tell you how much I miss my country. Where it's warm all year, and not nearly so dark."

"No need to rub it in," Hunter grumbled as I sat, my weight supported by Bryn.

"Apologies," he said. "But that's enough talk of the weather. I informed you of my mission here, and now, I find that you are following the same path as my fellows and me. Unless you are some of the unluckiest people I've ever encountered, I assume you have been given a similar task to hunt down my dangerous criminal. Otherwise, why would you have run afoul of his victims?"

"We've been tasked with an investigation that we are not able to share," Sam replied, ignoring the question. "Orders from our king, you understand."

"I understand that you have reservations about our partnership." His musical accent rolled the words around as he said them. "But there is the order, and the intent *behind* the order. For my part, I'd like to accomplish what I've been sent to do, rather than follow the order to the letter.

"You have the advantage of knowing this country well, and the support of your king can open doors that would be closed to me. Being an Ambient, I have skills that we can use to locate and subdue this Derth criminal, provided we are close enough to get the chance." He cast a quizzical glance over our group. "You must know—by now at least, if you didn't before—that this man is too dangerous for a group of Stills to capture. What was your plan? Use your swords to threaten him?"

I took a deep breath and let it out slowly. Even my thoughts were monotone and numb. Too much like Cass and the others. There was no use denying what we were here for. If the Vorthes wanted to follow us around the city, there wouldn't be much we could do to stop them, short of using the Ambience. And, if we did that, Colagh would know what we were if he didn't already. There were no good options.

"How is it," Colagh drawled, "that you have been sent to hunt a man without knowing everything about him?" His scrutiny paused on me, and then his eyes locked on Sam's. "Perhaps you know more than you are willing to say to an untrustworthy Vorthe?" He clucked his tongue, shaking his head with a disappointed frown. "It seems that I must earn your trust, because I hope that we might work together, giving our shared endeavor a greater chance at success."

Bryn's hands on my shoulders tensed. "If you want to earn our trust, you can start by telling us everything you know, and *exactly* what your intentions are."

Colagh looked away, considering Bryn's demands, and then shrugged. "Very well. It took longer than I'd hoped to gain an audience with your king. While waiting to speak to him, we asked around, plied the locals and guards with alcohol and bribes to convince them to share some Trylian gossip. Just enough to give us an idea of a few places to search. As expected, we learned little from a formal request for information, and after an unfortunate incident wherein we were attacked by someone with the same trace of corruption we saw in your two attackers, we decided to leave with more haste than we otherwise would have. Thank the Malachi, we had the power to keep the horrid snow and rain at bay to move faster.

"As far as our intentions..." he waved a hand in a dismissive gesture, "they are as I've stated before. We wish to find and detain the criminal known as Derth and return him to Vortheim to face the Malachi's justice." He seemed open, as if he couldn't possibly be hiding anything behind his vague statement. I didn't trust it.

"I don't think there's any point in pretending we aren't here for the same person," Hunter said. "When we heard that you were looking for Derth, we brought that information to our king, as you requested. When we realized that he was still at large, after causing no small amount of harm over the years to Trylian citizens, the king sent us to bring him to face Trylian justice. I hope you know that no disrespect was meant to you and your crew. We were simply following orders." He smiled at Colagh, looking every bit as sincere as his tone suggested. But I knew better, and I hoped Colagh didn't.

"No offense has been taken," Colagh assured him, offering a slight bow.

"You're here now," Hunter continued. "So, assuming we were to agree to your suggestions, what do you expect from working with us?" His voice was calm, friendly, and generous, as if he was the kind of person you could tell your darkest secrets to without hesitation.

Colagh smiled—a typical response to Hunter's reassuring attitude—but I could tell he hadn't been swayed. "It's simple. Share what you find so that we may assist you and accompany you to find Derth. That way we can subdue him and prevent further abuses against your people. We stop him—together—and we take him back to King's Port to petition your king to release him to our custody."

I glanced at Bryn's scowl, Sam's closed expression, and Hunter's encouraging nod, and nodded for him to continue. No good options. "Very well, it seems we have an agreement. We would be grateful for any aid you can render, and we'll share all that we have learned."

Colagh sent for a cold compress for me, as well as some food and drink, while Sam and Hunter relayed everything we'd learned that didn't involve our Ambient nature or Derth's invitation for me. When the tray arrived, carried by Cass, I gratefully placed the cool, damp cloth on my swollen neck, watched her smile warmly at Colagh and stare cooly at me before she left the room.

"It's a shame that such a lovely creature could be used for such ugly purpose."

"What worries me," Bryn said, "is how much influence he still has over these people."

"The Ambience is an interesting force," Colagh told us. "It can do amazing things, and each one of us tends to have an affinity for specific manifestations of it. Derth must be very talented in the control of others to assert his dominance for such a long period of time, and from such a distance."

"You know so much about this, how do we stop it?" Hunter asked.

"*We* don't," Colagh said. "Only Derth can. Mind control is a tricky thing, or so I've heard."

"Had much experience with it?" Bryn asked.

Colagh met Bryn's glare with a smile. "No, that is not my specialty. It's always been a subject matter that made me uneasy. For obvious reasons."

"What happens to these people if we kill Derth?" Bryn asked.

Shaking his head, Colagh replied, "I don't know. It could be that they'll be freed, it could be that they will live forever with a shadow hanging over them. Or, they may go mad. There is no way we can know."

"That's comforting," Hunter huffed.

"If we can find a way to help these people, we will do so. But I fear it would be a waste of effort and ultimately useless, if not harmful. No one you've spoken to had any clue as to which direction he was headed?"

"No," Bryn replied. "He freed a guard before he left, and we have no way of knowing whether he's amassed more of a following."

"Stills do not worry me much," Colagh shrugged. "We have the numbers to overpower however many he might gather."

"That's reassuring," Hunter grumbled.

Sam looked up, steering the conversation in a different direction. "We have a list of people who might have been corrupted, if you'd like to accompany us as we talk to them."

"We would make quicker work of it if we split up," Colagh said.

"If you'd like, you and one of your companions could join Bryn and Lila, and the other two could follow Hunter and me," Sam replied. "As you pointed out, being sent by the king opens doors that might otherwise be closed to you."

Colagh chuckled; it was a delightful sound that made the corners of my mouth twitch up. "I can't ignore such wise words, especially when they were mine." He caught my gaze, pausing to scrutinize me as I watched the interaction. He gave me the impression that he was as good a judge of character as the guard captain, and much more dangerous. "Very well, we will accompany you. Perhaps first thing in the morning?"

"We are expected at the Bastion before anything else," Bryn said. "But afterward, we can stop here and collect you."

Hunter and I locked eyes, silent understanding passing between us. We'd seen enough negotiations in our trading days to know when we didn't have all the information, and I knew from the slight narrowing of his eyes and miniscule nod that he would be keeping an eye on these people, same as I would.

Colagh nodded and stood, heading to the door as we all stood as well. "I'm so pleased that we could speak honestly, and that you would consent to combine our forces. I'm looking forward to seeing what you Trylians can do."

CHAPTER EIGHTEEN

It was a long walk back to Sam's house. By the time we shut the door behind us, the shock had faded, and I was close to tears, both from the pain and the fear of discovery the Vorthes represented. The only way to watch for any more of Derth's orbs that might take control of people would be to share my mind with Bryn every waking moment. There was no way we could hide that from anyone.

If I wanted to break Derth's hold on Cass and the others, I'd need to think of a way to do that. Norin and the man that had assaulted me were both in the prison now, and to get to them I'd need to find a way inside unsupervised.

The more time we spent with the Vorthes, the more likely it would be for them to find us out, and I wasn't sure what that meant. Would they let us live our lives knowing what we were? Could we allow them to take Derth without knowing what they might want with him? I wished with every fiber of my being that I could go back into shock, to stop the overwhelming doubt from crushing me.

"Love," Bryn said, tossing his cloak aside so that he could grasp my arms. "Whatever he's planning, we won't let it happen." I stared at Bryn's chest, seeing only his rumpled shirt in front of me. Hooking a finger under my chin, he lifted it until I was looking into his earnest eyes, taking care to move slowly and avoid hurting my abused throat more. He was as worried as I was. But he was also convinced that we could handle Colagh, and made sure to project that over everything else. "No one is going to take you from me. I swear on the Elders."

I took a deep breath and let it out slowly, letting my shoulders fall as I tried to relax my tense muscles. "We won't let them," I croaked, but we both knew I didn't mean it. His face crumpled as he let go of my chin and kissed my forehead before pulling me into an embrace.

Heal yourself, Bryn thought. *I can't stand how much pain you're in.*

I can't show up to talk to the guard captain with no marks, I replied. *I'm fine.*

"You're not," Bryn replied out loud, his words full of the anguish we both felt. I flinched. "Please, you don't need to suffer."

The captain needs to see it, I said. *She'll notice if there's no marks, and then she'll suspect something.*

"I can take the pain away," Sam offered. "We can leave the marks until after our interview."

"All right," I replied. Sitting on his haunches next to my chair, Sam reached out and touched a finger to my throat and heat flashed through the swollen tissue. I winced, stifling a cry, but the heat faded until all that was left was a gentle, lingering warmth. I gave Bryn a weak smile, unable to do much else for now.

"Now Bryn," I said, pointing to his injured shoulder.

Hunter made us food while Sam healed Bryn. After a short time, we were seated before a delicious dinner, which I noticed in the back of my mind, through the thoughts revolving around how difficult a situation we were in.

"All right," Hunter said after we'd eaten in silence, "now that Lila's taken care of and we've had dinner, can we please talk about what we do next?"

"Talk to the guard captain," Bryn replied. "Stay out of jail long enough to help these people and leave when we can."

"There's a long time between now and then," Hunter said. "And how exactly do we help these people? Especially when they're coming out of nowhere to attack us?"

"Sam?" Bryn asked. "Do you have any idea what to do here?"

"My knowledge of the situation is no greater than yours. Derth is the one in control, and if Colagh is right, he is the one who can stop it. Lila may have a chance at it, *if* we can evade Colagh and the guards long enough."

"But we're still left with Lila feeling it out when the time comes," Hunter said. "There's nothing you can tell us about the subject in general? Controlling people has been done before, right?"

Sam muttered something to himself, but I couldn't make it out. "Of course it's been done before," he grumbled. "Ambient have attempted almost anything you could imagine, and much more besides. This is a specific situation that I don't have experience with, and it wasn't recommended study for us."

That was vague, Bryn thought, irritated. *He's not telling us something.*

He usually isn't, I replied.

"So, we find a way to make it work," Bryn insisted. He glanced out the window at the snowflakes falling so thick they blocked our view of the nearest house. "We stick to the plan that we gave Colagh." The name fell out of his mouth as if he were spitting something disgusting to the ground. "We'll talk to a few more people here, see if there's anyone else that might need our help, and leave for Salava when the storm breaks. If the Vorthes knew enough to come here, there's no reason they haven't learned about Salava."

Sam nodded. "This Colagh seems determined and intelligent, and I've no doubt that he will find anyone that we do. He is also Ambient, and may not share our reluctance to spare a victim's feelings, let alone their well-being."

"He could be as bad as Derth, for all we know," Hunter said. "Maybe he'll go around the city, taking control of people's minds to find the information he wants."

"Then we'll stop him," Bryn said.

"As long as we don't break any laws doing it," Hunter said. "Or we'll have Bestell's most devout disciple throw us in jail. That woman took that Elder's teachings a bit too much to heart if you ask me. Maybe she should give Elder Livette's forgiveness a try."

"Not likely," I scoffed.

"Watch your backs while you're wandering the city," Hunter added. "If Derth wants Lila on her own, who knows how many people might try to finish what those men started today. If we don't get out of here soon, we may be killed before we can."

"I'm sure nothing else will go wrong," Bryn said, rolling his eyes.

Hunter threw his hands into the air with a huff. "Now you've called Elter's chaos onto us. We're doomed."

The next morning, I headed to the Bastion with Bryn at my side. Sam and Hunter hadn't risen yet, but the two of us hadn't slept well. Every time I'd started to fall asleep, I felt hands at my throat, choking the life out of me, and startled awake. Bryn had held me and stroked my hair until I was finally able to close my eyes without the instinctual fear of being attacked. But old nightmares about the gray pall of Derth's control over my mind woke me before the sun started to rise.

After waiting for a short time in the entrance hall, I was escorted to the captain's office and asked to sit across from her, leaving Bryn in the foyer. "How are you?" she asked. Her stern expression softened as she looked at my neck. Livid bruises had appeared overnight, and I was grateful for Sam's intervention with the pain.

"In one piece," I replied, pulling my cloak tighter around my neck.

"Good," she said, "I'm glad your assailant wasn't successful, and I'd appreciate it if you could tell me what happened, in your words."

I recounted all the information I was comfortable giving, excluding the true reason for our presence, and Derth's influence over the man who'd attacked me. She seemed satisfied by my description of the event as she wrote it all down. When I'd finished, she stared up at me and thanked me, folding her hands over the paper.

"I'm concerned about the reason behind the attack. If the man had been paid to eliminate anyone getting too close to the criminal you are pursuing, that would make sense. But the man was relentless. It took four of my guards to restrain him, and he was muttering about you the entire way to the cell. It took several hours for him to calm down, and then he seemed to come out of a daze. He didn't remember his actions with any clarity and seems to have no motive for his crime after the fact. Almost as if he were a different person." Her eyes bored into mine. "What do you know about this strange shift in his demeanor?"

I hesitated, trying to think of a response that would appease her without giving any more information than I had. Her eyes narrowed, her suspicion rising with every moment that passed.

"Maybe he sobered up after the rush of the attack wore off?" I suggested. "I've seen people drink enough to forget where they'd been and what they'd done. That may have been what happened here." I paused, torn between the need to do what I came here for—to pry as much information as I could from the people Derth had touched—and the growing desire to run, to escape this woman's direct stare and suspicion, escape the city and the faces shrouded in darkness, to hide from the conflict that I'd so readily put myself in the middle of. In the end, I couldn't abandon what I'd promised to do.

"Perhaps I could speak to him while I'm here, to determine whether that's the case, or if he merely had too much to drink." A small part of me thought: maybe this could be my chance to help these people, to break their connection to Derth, even if I still had no clue how to do it.

"Our interrogation has yielded no evidence of a connection to your vague mission, unless you'd like to tell me more about it? Specifically, what questions you could ask that might give you more insight than we have." When I didn't answer, she shook her head. "I am under no obligation to give you unrestricted access to my jail, or the people held within. I hope this won't be an issue for you and your companions."

I had the distinct impression that it wouldn't matter if it *was* an issue for us. "I understand," I replied in a clipped tone.

"This is exactly the kind of behavior that I've been reporting to the king, and now you are at the center of it." She sat back in her chair and folded her arms across her chest, letting the façade of polite inquiry disappear. "I know you're hiding something crucial from me, but I can't fathom what it could be. I won't interfere, but if any of you gives me even the slightest justification, I will see all of you taking up residence in my prison. King Demetrius can read about it in my next report."

Several hours later, Bryn and I stood outside the Crossroads Inn with Colagh, having spent the intervening time speaking to the people on our portion of the list the captain had provided.

I was tired and hungry, and frustrated after finding no trace of Derth in anyone. Colagh's incessant smile didn't help.

"Do not despair, my friends," he said. "We will find what we're looking for, whether it's here or somewhere else. There are only so many places a man like Derth can hide."

Hunter and Sam exited the tavern as we took our leave. Bryn and Hunter left to buy more food from the grocer, but Sam and I elected to keep moving. I had no patience for shopping, and Sam was busy scribbling in one of his notebooks to veer from his habitual path home.

The storm was still raging, and it was an effort to climb through the inches of snow that had accumulated already. My cloak was soaked, and I was shivering by the time we got back to the house and I built a fire, leaving Sam to huddle next to a candle to continue with his notes.

Hunter and Bryn returned with bags covered with snow, full of yeast, flour, salt, onions, potatoes, and other food that wouldn't spoil quickly. As they tried to extricate themselves from their cloaks and hats and gloves, I emptied the bags, finding a pile of butter, and to my surprise, a small sack of sugar and another with chocolate. My mouth watered, and I gawked at Hunter's mischievous smile that appeared when he unwound the scarf from around his chapped face.

"What is this?" I asked.

"Amazing, isn't it?" He beamed, mistaking my exasperation for admiration. "No one else was buying it, so I thought I'd make us a treat."

"This must have cost a fortune!" I said. Bryn snorted a laugh, but wiped the smile from his face when I turned my wide eyes to him. "Where did you get the money?"

"Didn't need it," Hunter said slowly, like I was an idiot. "We have the writ from the king."

"That's to make sure we have what we need," I insisted, "not so you can buy whatever you want!"

"You may *want* chocolate cake," he sniffed, his tone dripping with mock superiority, "but I *need* a reward for all that we've been through. The weather alone is enough to warrant it, to say nothing of the impending doom that awaits us."

I cocked a questioning eyebrow at Bryn, and he threw his hands up in surrender. "Don't scold me, I tried to stop him." To Hunter, he said, "I told you she'd say that."

"She won't say anything but thank you after I've made her favorite dessert," Hunter said, gathering his prizes. He strolled into the kitchen, glancing back at me with a haughty expression, and I had to suppress a laugh.

The sound of bowls and utensils clinking came from the open door, and I had to admit that a treat sounded wonderful, though I felt a pang of guilt knowing that we were sitting here while Derth was loose. Instead of dwelling on it, I grabbed an armful of root vegetables and the bag of yeast to put away for Hunter.

"It's almost like being home at Lottie's," I told him as I placed everything on the counter. When he opened the bag of sugar, something like reverence passed over his face. He could likely count on one hand the number of times he'd handled it.

"Where do you think my recipe came from?" He wrapped the remaining sugar carefully after he measured it out.

"Thank you for feeding us," I said. "I still can't believe you know so much about cooking."

"You spent time with Smitts, I went to Drain. When you got past the ribald humor, he was a great teacher. Now, you can leave me in peace while I spend too much time ogling the chocolate." He shooed me out of the kitchen, and I snorted when he let out an exaggerated moan of pleasure.

"What is he doing in there?" Bryn asked.

"Having a tawdry affair with the chocolate. I hope the cake isn't ruined."

CHAPTER NINETEEN

After another wonderful meal with a chocolate cake as decadent as anything Lottie had ever made and an evening spent around the fire, we awoke the next morning to find the sun shining and sparkling snow brightening the world outside our windows. Hunter made pancakes fried in bacon grease, slathered with the butter he'd spent so much of the king's money on.

"I was thinking maybe we could ride out to my old house today." Bryn said while we washed the dishes.

I smiled, thinking of being out of the city for a while, away from everyone that Derth might send after us. "I'd like that," I said. "We can talk to the stable owner while we're there."

He flashed me a grin, though it faltered at the mention of the stable owner. "Of course," he said.

Hunter and Sam decided to meet the Vorthes again while we were gone, so Bryn and I set off alone for the southern gate along the arc of the circular street.

Every time we passed a corner, I watched for signs of an attack, my body tensing to draw my dagger or lunge out of the way of whatever might come. Bryn's concern for me was obvious through our bond, but he didn't try to reassure or comfort me. He knew there was no comfort to be had with the uncertainty we faced.

We passed spacious buildings with small orchards and garden plots covered with a thick layer of snow becoming more translucent as the day warmed. It would have been a magical sight if not for the sunlight reflecting from the thick banks like sparkling diamonds that made it harder to see what danger might lie around the next stretch of the city.

Finally, the large stable loomed ahead, and one of the young ladies darted out of the open door, bundled in a thick wool coat and hat, toward the city center as we arrived. Inside, the rest of the stablehands bustled about with bundles of hay, buckets of water, or carts of manure to dump outside the city gates. The stable owner noticed us and turned with a smile.

"Hello," she said. "Your horses are happy and healthy, despite being cooped up inside for a while. I'm sure they'd be happy to see you." Deep dimples appeared beside her wide mouth ringed with laugh lines.

I smiled in response. "We've been missing them."

Raven poked her head out of a stall with a happy whinny and tossed her head at me. I darted to the stall, her eager greeting breaking through the tension coursing through my body. I wiped a tear from my eye as I ran my hand over the bridge of her nose when she nudged me.

"Hello, Raven," I cooed. "How are you? I missed you." She nudged me again, resting her face on my shoulder.

The owner appeared at my shoulder with an apple in her hand, holding it out to me. "The fruit is starting to wilt, so we've been giving them a few more treats."

"That's wonderful," I replied, handing the apple to Raven. She took it with her soft lips and crunched it between her teeth as I turned back to the owner. She was still smiling as she scratched behind Raven's ear, but black energy swirled over her eyes when they caught mine. She was still there, not erased by the darkness like Norin and Cass, but her casual look became a hard stare. "Can I ask you a few questions? About a man that came through here about six months ago?"

"I suppose," she replied. "You are the king's agent, I guess that gives you the right."

"His name was Derth, a man with a hunch, greasy hair, blue eyes? He may have asked you for something?"

The shade shifted as I spoke, twisting first one way, and then another. The woman retreated, replaced by whatever Derth had left behind; her eyes widened and glazed over as her face slackened.

"I'm waiting for him to return, in case he needs anything," she said. Her words were flat and monotone, though not intense yet. The darkness flared as she spoke, drawing me in like the orb had, though the pull was weaker. Bryn tensed beside me, as if ready to throw himself between us. "I hope he's doing well."

"I'm sure he is," I replied, remembering how volatile Cass had been. I wanted to avoid that here. "Did he say where he was going?"

"They left the city on a pair of my best horses." The shade solidified, forming a barrier between us. "They left the city."

Not wanting to exacerbate whatever was happening to her, I smiled and turned back to Raven. After a few moments of silence, I saw her face change from the corner of my eye. She blinked a few times, looking around as if confused.

"I'm sorry, I seem to have gotten lost for a moment. What did you want to ask me?"

"Do you need anything for the horses? Has the city guard paid you?"

"Oh, they've taken care of things," she replied. "Thank you for asking."

Trotting out through the gates a short time later, I took a deep breath of cold air through a soft brown scarf drawn across my mouth and nose. Once the gates had fallen behind, I had to admit that it felt like a weight had lifted from my shoulders, as if we were leaving the danger behind. As soon as we lost sight of the city walls, the rest of the tension melted from my shoulders, and I let down my walls keeping the Ambience—which had been boiling beneath the surface, scratching at my walls—out, and unleashed it in a tunnel of wind that swept thick snowdrifts away, allowing the horses to step upon the frozen ground beneath.

"She didn't seem as bad as the others," I called, nodding in the direction of the city."

"No," Bryn replied.

"When was the last time you saw your house?" I asked to change the subject.

"After my mother died," he said, lapsing back into silence.

We rode north at a fast clip for some time, the sun not yet at its peak when we came upon a weather-worn wooden fence. A few hundred yards in the distance was a moderately sized farmhouse with an untouched expanse of snow between the two.

Bryn dismounted to open a gate in the waist-high fence, but when he yanked on the wood, the gate fell off its hinges to hit the ground with a thud. Bryn paused for a moment and stared at the gate, his mind awash in disappointment and grief, as if by watching it break, it had shattered the memory he'd kept of this place. It was a repeat of watching Sam find his cabin after years away, with all the grief and none of the muttering. My heart broke as I felt his stomach sink.

He swung himself back into Badger's saddle, and led the way across the expanse, telling me about the farm fields the horses were trampling beneath their hooves. Images of neat rows of vegetables and grain imprinted themselves on my mind, and I couldn't tell what was born of my imagination and what was Bryn's vague memory. "My mother was the one who kept the farm running," he finished. "My father, when he was around, was hopeless at tending the crops. He tried, but he wasn't a farmer. What I remember most was how he made us laugh."

Bryn smiled in reminiscence, but it quickly faded when we reined in next to the house. A dilapidated porch ran along the length of the front, where in many places the wood had fallen through to the ground below. The steps looked to have almost fully fallen apart as well; they leaned heavily to the right, and where the planks hadn't broken off, they were rotted through. It lent the house an air of hopelessness, as if it couldn't bear to hold itself up any longer.

Bryn and I dismounted and led the horses around to the back of the house, hoping that we would find a less dangerous way inside. We were rewarded by an intact door still hanging straight in the frame, with gaps at the top and sides of the door.

Bryn took Raven's reins with Badger's, tying them to a post nearby as I gingerly mounted the porch to wipe some grime from a window to the right of the door to peer through. I found a small kitchen with bare wooden countertops past the moth-eaten curtains, tidy if not for the thick layer of dust covering everything.

Bryn joined me at the window, taking a good look around before sighing again, resigned this time. The door was stuck when he tried it, and after much shoving and cursing, it finally swung free with a loud creak and groan, and Bryn went stumbling over the threshold.

I followed close behind as Bryn's shoulders sagged with grief. He moved throughout the house, touching the discolored walls and the faded portraits hanging there with fond melancholy. He stopped in the doorway of a small bedroom with a single bed and a shelf holding a handful of books and a few wooden toys, including a small sword that I recalled from previous conversations. He made no move to enter, so I ducked past him.

The walls were a dingy yellow and the curtains faded blue, but this was a haven for a child such as I'd always daydreamed I might have. I ran my fingers over the wooden sword, recalling the memory Bryn had shown me with a smile on my face.

Tilting my head to read the titles on the spines, I perused the books. He had a copy of my favorite book about the Ambience, and I lovingly rubbed the dust off the cover to reveal the rainbow ocean beneath. Tears filled my eyes, imagining my copy at the bottom of the sea.

"I'm taking a few of these," I told him, stashing the book in the pocket of my cloak as I turned to inspect the rest of the room. His eyes followed me, amused and vulnerable, as if I might expose some embarrassing secret he wasn't sure he wanted me to know.

I bent over a desk strewn with papers to peer at similar dark lines on every piece. Most of the pages were filled with drawings of a woman's face in different attitudes: smiling, laughing, and crying, as well as a few angry poses. The woman in all the drawings was the same, and the few that showed faded color gave an impression of long, wheat colored hair and kind blue eyes. The quality of the art was astonishing; I had seen only a few portraits hanging in the palace that rivaled the skill with which these were drawn.

I gathered some of the pages, choosing my favorites, and turned to Bryn. "Did you draw these?" I asked him, holding up the pages.

Bryn stepped forward and plucked one out of my hand. The woman in it was laughing, her hair spilled over her face and her nose crinkled as a tear fell down her cheek. He shook his head as he clutched the paper and stared. Tears filled his eyes as he beheld the face of the woman who had his eyes, his brow, the same lopsided smile.

I followed close behind as he turned his back on the room and purposefully walked through the hall to the back of the house, to a larger bedroom with a double bed. He stopped inside the door and fought the strong flood of grief that once again assailed him. Once he'd collected himself, he strolled over to the bed and pulled it to the side. A clear line of dust marked the bedposts' passage across the floor as Bryn knelt and swept his hand over the spot he'd cleared, revealing floorboards that were a few shades lighter than those around them. He wedged his dirk between the boards, levering it back and forth before the boards sprang free, revealing a large space beneath.

Bryn threw the boards to the side and reached into the space left behind. As he pulled his hand out of the hole, he heaved himself off the floor and placed a dusty bundle on a table by the window. He scrubbed his hands together to remove the grime as I untied the long-faded ribbon that held the bundle together. The whole thing was about the size of my pack, with thick canvas protecting it.

Bryn removed the ribbon and carefully pulled back the edges of the bundle, and then a second layer of thinner, waxed cloth to protect against the damp. A smaller package with similar wrapping fell out of a bundle of stretched canvas, and he set that aside to leaf through the rest.

They were smaller portraits of his family, complete with erstwhile father figure. One showed him smiling as he posed with Bryn's pregnant mother, and another depicted him holding an infant son while his wife beamed at him. His complexion was darker than hers, his eyes a dark grey beneath a wild mane of dark brown hair with the same texture as Bryn's.

"My mother was an artist. She loved painting our family." Bryn said.

I smiled up at him as he gazed wistfully at the portrait in my hands. "Your mother looks very happy in all of these," I said.

Bryn's smile vanished as he replied. "That's because she stopped having family portraits done when my father left."

"Your mother obviously loved you, Bryn," I said as I went through the rest of the paintings. There were a few landscapes, but most of them were of Bryn throughout the years.

Bryn's mother had captured him perfectly, especially his eyes, and I was enthralled by one painting of a very young Bryn sitting in a chair, smiling as he clutched a toy sword.

"I didn't know she kept all of these," he said wonderingly. He moved back to the table and unwrapped the smaller bundle as I finished perusing his mother's work.

I looked around the room, imagining the way it had looked when Bryn was a child. He was a mess of emotions; nostalgia, happiness, and safety, all beneath raw grief made worse for the comparison between his memory of the house and the house as it stood. What I saw, through his memories, was a family that loved and supported each other. That laughed and made each other whole. And for the first time in my life, it was something that I wanted.

Standing, I wandered back to Bryn's room, imagining what it would be like to live in a place like this, far from the conflict between Ambient and Still, between good and evil. A place where I could sleep in a bed that didn't rock back and forth, where I could use the Ambience to coax food from the land, with space enough to grow a family.

My heart ached as I considered the life he'd wanted, settling somewhere to raise a family, away from the danger and change the ocean represented. I wanted to give this to him. I was afraid that I could lose it before I'd been given the time to try. Most of all, I wanted to know what it would be like to live like a family with the man I loved.

"Bryn," I called as I walked back to the bedroom. He looked up as I entered, concerned by my wavering voice and the tear I swiped from my cheek.

"Love, are you all right?" He set something on the table and crossed the room in a hurry. On instinct, he searched for injury, wincing again when he looked at the bruises ringing my neck.

I took a breath to steady myself. There was nothing to fear; whether I'd waited too long or not, we could always continue as we were, and we would be happy together. But a small part of me wondered whether that was true, even as I assured myself that it was. "I didn't understand before, when you told me that you'd always wanted a big family, living in a place like this." I waved my hand at the house around us. "My home was the ship, and my family was the crew. But looking around here, feeling what you felt when you were young, it makes me realize that I want this. I want to know what it feels like to share my life with one person, someone I love, not a host in tight quarters."

Bryn's smile was sad but hopeful, and I hesitated, worried that speaking the next part aloud would make it true. "Please tell me I didn't miss my chance to live a life like this with you."

Ignoring his tumult of emotions and thoughts, too afraid to hear what he might say, I watched his face. A moment of confusion passed, and then he beamed with barely restrained joy. He took my hands in his and brushed a kiss across each one. "Are you sure?"

I nodded. "I love you more than anything, and I want you to have everything you dreamed for your life. Will you marry me, Bryn?"

Instead of answering, he reached into his pocket, pulled out a leather pouch, and produced a ring. A delicate, silver band with a large diamond in the center of a line of small emeralds. It was stunning, and excited fear flushed my cheeks with heat, and my skin prickled with chills. Light from the window sparkled off the diamond, reflecting in a burst of dazzling colors.

"This was my mother's," he said as he slid it on my finger, the perfect size. It was as though it had been made for me. Bryn grasped the nape of my neck to pull me forward.

Our kiss started as an expression of joy, filled with our hopes for a future beyond the dangerous task ahead. But it deepened as he pulled my body flush against his, both of us consumed by desire. Something change across our bond, as if a barrier between us had been washed away. My racing heart beat even faster.

"I love you," Bryn murmured against my mouth.

"I love you too," I said. I wrapped my arms around his neck and leaned back against the nearest wall. With a loud crack, I sank into the rotting wood as Bryn snatched me away. The wall crumbled, and I grimaced through my smile.

"Maybe this isn't the best place to celebrate," Bryn chuckled. His breath was short, his smile full of unspent desire. I kissed him again, running my hands down his back, loving the shiver down his spine and the grumble in his chest.

"Then we'll wait until we get to Sam's tonight." I pulled away, lifting my hand to admire the ring again. "It's beautiful," I said.

He pulled my hand to his mouth, kissing the ring and my finger beneath. "Not as beautiful as you. There's something else."

"Oh?" He pulled me in the direction of his mother's room, back to the bedside table where the small bundle was now open to display more gorgeous jewelry. Some of the pieces matched my engagement ring: a short silver chain with a teardrop diamond pendant and three small emeralds mounted to the top right of the tear, next to matching earrings that dangled from a chain with three small diamonds.

"Where did your mother get these?" I asked as I lifted the necklace. The chains alone would be worth a fortune. Far too much for a farmer to own.

"From my father," Bryn replied. "She said that he bought her these," he said as he gestured to the diamond and emerald set I was admiring, "right before I was born, and he gave them to her the day after."

I put the necklace down next to a delicate bracelet, made of small, irregularly shaped iridescent pearls studded with gold beads. What truly caught my eye, though, was a small and delicate silver locket.

The oval locket was the size of my thumb, and hung from a silver chain. The edges near the clasp were slightly tarnished, as if it had been opened many times. I didn't know what drew me to it, but for some reason it seemed more precious than the gems and pearls.

I picked it up and undid the clasp, and inside was a small piece of folded paper. I removed it while Bryn looked over my shoulder, curious about what I had found. Unfolding the paper, I noticed that the creases were worn almost through, as if Bryn's mother had folded and unfolded it a thousand times, and found a message written in small, slanted script.

"'Ella,'" I read aloud, "'you know why I had to leave, and I want you to know that you and Bryn mean more to me than the world. I will return for you both. All my love and more, B.' What was your father's name?" I asked.

"Bhalyn," he replied. "I wonder what he meant. I thought it was just another job that he never came back from." I folded the paper, replacing it in the locket.

"She wore that every day of her life," Bryn told me as I handed it to him. He placed it gently between the other pieces and looked up at me. "Would you wear these at our wedding?" he asked quietly, his voice full of nostalgia and hope as he handled the pearls. "My mother wore them at her wedding; they were a gift from her mother, they've been passed from mother to daughter for generations."

"I would love to wear your mother's jewelry, Bryn."

One of the horses whinnied, and Bryn went to the window and cursed at what he saw. I leaned around him for a look. A group of five men stood about ten feet from the back door in a small group with their heads together. A woman stood a short distance behind the group, watching the house intently. She turned toward the house, and we ducked away. When I dared peek through again, she smiled, noticing me. Bryn cursed again, louder this time, and paced away from the door.

"Who are they?" I asked.

"I don't know the rest, but the woman is Maggie." That explained the cursing; Bryn had been driven from Stalth after having his heart broken by the statuesque woman outside. His expression dour, he said, "I think we're in trouble."

CHAPTER TWENTY

Bryn threw open the door, drew his sword and dirk, and led the way outside as I drew my sword, *Desire*. The cluster of people stilled and turned as they saw us take a few cautious steps away from the door, but Maggie stood leaning on the fence inside the broken gate, her blonde hair in several braids trailing down her back, her curves accentuated by the tight leather armor she wore.

"Bryn," Maggie exclaimed, her cold stare belying her genial tone and wide smile. "I haven't seen you in a while. Where have you been?" she asked as her eyes roamed his frame. My grip on the hilt tightened as I seethed at her casual appraisal of him.

"Meglyn," Bryn replied easily, his arms relaxed at his sides even with his weapons grasped in his hands. "I see you've made a few new friends."

"And you've certainly made a lovely new friend, yourself," she replied, letting her eyes wash over *my* body, a mix of curiosity and appreciation. I flexed my fingers, wishing I could slap the look off her face. "What's your name, darling?"

"You keep your eyes on me," Bryn growled. Meglyn reluctantly slid her gaze back to Bryn, and her leer faded. "What are you doing all the way out here?" Bryn asked, his tone now friendly, but to my ears it dripped with veiled threat. I wasn't the only one who picked up on it;

the men in front of Meglyn re-gripped their weapons, shifting uneasily from foot to foot.

"We heard you were back in town, so we asked around and found out that you were staying with the old man, on the edge of town. But we saw you headed out in the direction of your old house, so I gathered a sort of... welcoming committee, you could say."

Bryn had loved her once, and she'd thrown his affection in his face. After hearing Bryn's stories about his time with Meglyn, I'd disliked her on principle. Interacting with her in person made my distaste for her much stronger. But it seemed she'd changed from the woman who only knew how to use her body as leverage for men's attention. Or rather, judging by her casual grace and the way she plucked a dagger from her belt to twirl it between her fingers, she'd learned how to leverage her body in deadlier ways.

Bryn bared his teeth, somewhere between a smile and a snarl. "Thank you, Meglyn, for the kind welcome. Now, if you would excuse us, we need to get back to town. The rest of our party will be missing us."

"Don't worry about that, my friend, there's no threat to your safety. At least, there *won't* be, as long as you hand over whatever valuables you came here to retrieve."

Bryn's brow furrowed in confusion. "You're working for Douglas now? Couldn't you seduce anyone with enough money to keep you happy?"

Maggie chuckled to herself as she shook her head. "You still don't know when to quit, do you, Bryn? So much has changed since we last spoke, but you're assuming I haven't. Is your view of the world still so narrow? Good and bad, right and wrong, and nothing in between." She chuckled again, crossing her arms over her chest. I scowled at her when she caught my eye. "I can't believe you were able to attract someone like her. She's far too lovely for the likes of *you*. Perhaps I should rescue her from your self-righteousness."

Bryn laughed, his brow nearing his hairline as he flashed an incredulous look at me, and then back to Meglyn.

She addressed me directly, saying "I know firsthand what it's like to bask in Bryn's affection. And I know how quickly it can sour when he sees what he thinks are flaws in your character." Meglyn's grin faltered, and she quirked an eyebrow as her men exchanged glances amongst themselves. Meglyn came back to herself and smirked. "Not that you've figured that out yet. But you strike me as someone who has experience in pushing a man past the limits of his tolerance, Lila."

I frowned, mentally speaking to Bryn as her eyes locked on mine like she could hold me in place with her stare alone.

I didn't tell her my name. Bryn tensed his grip on his sword as I lifted *Desire* and stepped in front of Bryn, instinctively shielding him from the pulse of Ambience even before my brain registered the change. "What do you mean, Meglyn?"

The expression on her face fell away, like petals from a wilting flower. "He gave you an easy choice. You leave your friends behind, and I can take you to him," she intoned in an all-too familiar way. "No one can follow. Since you won't listen..." With a wave of her hand, she sent her men in our direction, all armed with shortswords and shields. "Kill him, and try not to maim her."

I stood between the men and Bryn, and they hesitated, forming a loose half-circle around me. The Ambience strained for release as I reached behind me to pull Bryn's dirk from his grasp.

One man lunged forward, and I parried the blade aside with the dirk. Before he could pull back, I kicked the side of his knee, sending him crumpling to the ground, screaming in agony. Another took his place to bash me with his shield, and my feet slid on the icy dirt until I ducked to the side and the man tumbled toward Bryn. I slammed the pommel of the dirk into the base of the man's skull, and he didn't get up.

When I spun around, I saw the others staring at their fallen comrades in disbelief. I leveled a glare at Meglyn only to be greeted by the black aura swirling over dull, malevolent eyes. She stared at me as she pulled another long, slender dagger from her belt. I didn't need to tell Bryn that she was Derth's pawn.

Meglyn stalked forward, ducking past one of her people with such agility and speed that I lost track of her until she spoke again. "You belong to *him*," she said. She moved forward again, an arm's reach away, staring at me with fanatic zeal. Her daggers flashed up when a blade came down next to me, crossing to stop Bryn's sword before it could cut into her shoulder.

"*You* don't touch her!" Bryn snarled as he stepped forward, thrusting her back with his blade. I couldn't tell who he meant, Derth or Meglyn.

The man on my right tried to intercept Bryn, and I blocked his sword as he sent a wild, sweeping blow toward Bryn's shoulder. My arms reverberated with the shock of my blade colliding with his. With my side exposed, another lunged. At the last second, I firmed the air between us so that the second man slowed as he ran into it. He stared with wide eyes at the empty space he was caught in as his friend lurched free and swung again, this time at my legs. I threw myself back to avoid the tip of the blade and brought *Desire* up again.

Metal screeched as Bryn and Meglyn slashed and parried, and the two in front of me lunged in tandem at Bryn's exposed back. A blade stabbed forward, and I slapped it aside with the dirk. Another sword flashed, and I used my momentum to drive *Desire* along the blade to the hilt, spinning around to slash the first one's arm behind his shield as he turned back. He grunted in pain and stepped away, right into the second man's sword. The blade was withdrawn, leaving the first man panting as blood poured from the wound.

Our brief but violent battle halted as the last man dropped his sword and shield and rushed to the injured man's side. He looked terrified, a look I'd seen on Bryn's face when he'd almost lost me, and I felt a stab of sympathy even as I brought my blades into guard between us. The other two who were still conscious looked from their fallen companion to me, and then at Bryn and Meglyn. Their uncertainty was written across their faces, and I used that moment to wrap a current of air around their swords and shields and *yank*.

They stared open-mouthed at their weapons on the ground, and I held my sword out to keep them at bay as I glanced over my shoulder.

Bryn and Meglyn danced around one another with flurries of movement and a chorus of loud grunting whenever they crashed together. Bryn was a mess of confusion, regret, and rage, and he hesitated as she spun, leaving her side open. Rather than thrusting his sword into that vulnerable space, he readied himself to catch her daggers on the blade of his sword. He moved in a blur, faster than Meglyn could track, and it was clear the battle wouldn't last much longer despite her incredible skill.

Bryn swung his sword overhead, bringing it down with enough force to drive Meglyn to her knees when she blocked the blow. Bryn swung again, before Meglyn could move, and the daggers fell from her grip as her wrists cracked. She stared at me as Bryn kicked the daggers away.

Bryn stared at the woman kneeling before him, horrified. When Meglyn moved to stand, he shoved her down. She rolled to the side, using one hand bent the wrong way to prop herself up. Bryn kicked the arm out and put a knee in the middle of her back to keep Meglyn on the ground.

"Why did it have to be her?" Bryn shouted. "Lila, I need some rope!" Bryn grunted as Meglyn tried to roll again. I ran to the horses and pulled a length of rope from where it was attached to Badger's saddle while the men watched, stunned. When I gave it to Bryn, he wrapped it around Meglyn's wrists, heedless of the broken bones.

A cry of pain brought my attention back to the other men, and I thrust *Desire* into its scabbard as I ran to Raven to get my medical pack. The man with the stab wound was shaking as another held a blood-soaked scarf to his midsection. I knelt next to them, pulling some supplies out of the bag.

"Can I look?" I asked. At their nods, I lifted the torn leather armor to find the wound. It was deep, but the bleeding had slowed, and I thought he could recover if I closed it soon. I told them as much and pulled out my needle to stitch it closed.

When I finished, I found Bryn in a heated conversation with the rest of Meglyn's men. Meglyn was bound hand and foot on the ground, and by the way she was slumped, I thought Bryn might have knocked her unconscious. After packing my supplies away, I grabbed a handful of snow to wash the blood off my hands.

"We won't let you take her," one was saying, his fists clenched tight. By the looks on all their faces, they knew they might die if they tried to take her back, and Bryn was certainly poised to strike if they tried to get past him. Surprised, I looked at Meglyn, wondering how someone so awful could inspire such loyalty.

The darkness had faded with her consciousness, but I could see it like a vine, strangling her mind. The man on the ground called out, and when I looked his way, his eyes locked on mine, pleading. "She isn't right," he said, undeterred by the cries of protests from the others, "she hasn't been for a while now." He looked around at his fellows. "If they wanted us all dead, we would be! And they know what ails the boss." He looked at me again, pleading. "Save her."

Tense silence was broken by the sound of horses galloping toward us, and I saw Sam and Hunter heading our way. They dismounted, and Hunter glanced around with a frown.

"What happened here?"

CHAPTER TWENTY-ONE

The ragged gash was livid red against Bryn's tan skin as I wrapped a bandage around it, tucking the tail in to keep it snug. My fingers had thawed now that we were back inside Bryn's house with a fire crackling in the hearth. It didn't keep the chill from my veins when I glanced at Meglyn's unconscious body, lying on her side in the middle of the sitting room floor.

Meglyn's people were waiting outside after a tense negotiation for our help in 'fixing her,' still pacing when I turned my gaze to the window to check on them.

What a mess, I thought. If I didn't get this right, we would have to deal with them, and however many more of her people were in Stalth. It seemed a lifetime ago that I had assumed I was in control of my power, that with Bryn at my side we could conquer anything. Derth had taken that from me. Again.

"I'm glad we decided to come out here," Sam was saying when I looked up to find Bryn's piercing gaze read every thought in my head. I flashed him a weak smile. "I wasn't expecting to see her again." Meglyn stirred as Sam frowned at her.

Derth's black energy stirred as if it was coming awake with her. "I don't think we're going to have another chance like this to figure out how to get Derth out of someone's head," I said. "But first, I want to ask her a few questions."

As if on cue, Meglyn opened her eyes and rolled toward us. It wasn't the sensual, arrogant woman that had first greeted us; her arms were limp on the floor in front of her, her face devoid of emotion, and her voice a dull imitation of Derth's. She was a puppet now. The energy around her eyes swirled, and her stare focused on me. Her eyes were too wide, unblinking.

"Why did you come here, Meglyn?" I asked as everyone focused on her. Hunter and Bryn rested their hands on hilts, ready to strike.

"He needs you," she said, "and he wants your friends dead. He said you would come if he left you a trail to follow. I must bring him the one he needs."

"He's not here?" I asked. She shook her head with her eyes fixed on me. "Where did he go?" No reaction, just the blank stare through darkness. I turned away, too unsettled to match her stare, letting Hunter step between us as I turned to Sam. "Any ideas?"

Sam sighed. "It's so similar to what Avya did..." He shook his head and stared off as if seeing what he described unfold before his eyes. "I've seen something like this before, a long time ago. I can try to recreate what I did, to remove the Ambience and restore the person beneath, but I..." his eyes narrowed as he chose his words, "wasn't alone." Sam's eyes locked onto mine. "I admit I don't know if this is a similar situation, or whether Derth has left some nasty surprise for us inside her head."

I nodded, holding his gaze. "As far as I see it, we need to try. They're expecting it," I pointed toward the front of the house, "and even if they weren't, I can't stomach the thought that I could have helped someone going through what I did and didn't try." Sam nodded, and I knelt with him next to Meglyn, who watched us approach with no expression on her face.

Be careful, Bryn thought.

I will, I replied. *Be ready in case something goes wrong. I may need you.*

Sam reached out to touch the side of Meglyn's head. "It's been some time since I've seen you, Maggie," he said, flashing her a sad smile. "I'm sorry you found yourself in this situation. You don't deserve this."

I placed my hand on the other side of her head, watching as Sam's tethered spirit flared. Ambient light, a muted version of what made the Pool, mingled with the black tendrils over Meglyn's eyes. It squirmed, and she tried to move away, fear flashing across her face, but Bryn and Hunter grasped her bound arms to hold her in place.

"I'm going to try to get a better idea of what we're up against," Sam muttered with a glance in my direction. He tugged at the dark Ambience, and Meglyn screamed and writhed against her bonds.

"*No!*"

The darkness swirled, like fog rolling through Sam's light. It pulled at Sam and Meglyn, a devouring force bearing down on their spirits. A battle of wills, only visible to Sam and me, played out in front of us in an instant. And Sam was losing.

I recoiled as Derth's influence pawed at my mind, trying to overcome my defenses when I reached out to help.

Not again, I thought as I fought to keep my mind separate from the overwhelming darkness. Sam's light dimmed as the darkness grew, a familiar pall of apathy slithering over and into me, and I felt something beyond Derth's twisted intent in the black. It moved like a whisper barely audible beyond Derth's roar. I balked at its deep well of power, and then Sam grunted, and my perception of it passed, making me wonder if it had been there in the first place.

I let go of all trace of restraint on my power and fell into the space between the Ambience and myself, becoming the Conduit that I was, steeped in power and radiance, the entirety of the Ambient Pool at my fingertips. Surrounding that power was the cloying darkness, a swirling void that pulled at me like a vacuous whirlpool. It was transforming my connection with the Ambience into something sinister and suffocating.

My physical body tried to move away, but my hand wouldn't move as the dark wrapped around my wrist. Sam groaned next to me, still fighting to find a source, and his aura of power was dimming.

I tore at the darkness, shredding it mercilessly from my arms, from the air, and from Sam, leaving the tattered remnants fluttering behind me, unable to reform. Reaching out to clasp Sam's shoulder, his Tethered spirit flared at my touch, and the darkness receded enough for me to see my friend.

"Lila," Sam shouted, his voice reverberating through me, "I can't free her! It's more powerful than anything I've seen!" He and his spirit tried to pull the darkness away from something I couldn't feel, but it was wound too tight.

I placed my hand on Meglyn's head and felt what he was struggling against, what pulled at my power the moment I touched her. There was a small mass radiating the vile corruption I associated with Derth, and my skin crawled as I pushed my power forward to mingle with Sam's. Derth's cold, maniacal laughter echoed in our heads.

The void rose, engulfing us as it tried to sap our strength and rip us away from the mass consuming Meglyn's mind. Lethargy settled over me, and I had the overwhelming urge to give up, to lie down and let the darkness have me. The connection with the outside world was gone, our spirits separated from our bodies. We were locked inside our minds.

"Lila, you have the Ambience at your command, *use it!*" Sam used the last of his strength to pull at the mass, and it loosened enough to let me see the light beyond it. That light shot into me, and the lethargy faded.

I plunged into the light, finding the spirit beneath—Meglyn's spirit—subjugated by the darkness, used like fuel as wood consumed by a fire. The light inside me shone brighter in response, and spirits channeled Ambient energy through me to Meglyn.

She screamed, and I poured all my strength into rending the darkness apart. It clawed at me, dragging me down for every bit of progress I made, until the scraps I'd torn apart hugged me like a burial shroud. I pushed harder, my spirit flooded with the Ambience, threatening to ignite everything around me, until, with one final push, it broke free. It burned away as I fell, out of the darkness and into my body.

I opened my eyes a moment later to find Sam lying on the ground next to Meglyn, whose eyes were open and clear. The darkness was gone as she sat up and looked around, blinking as if she hadn't seen the sun in days. In a way, I supposed she hadn't.

"What?" Meglyn asked, her brow furrowed in confusion. "What did you do?"

Bryn released her and rushed to me. "She freed you," he said, running a hand over my cheek, peering into my eyes. "It's better than you deserve." Meglyn scowled at his back, but he didn't see it; his focus was on me.

"Freed me from what?" she asked. "Why am I tied up?"

"You've been under someone's control," I groaned. My entire body ached as if I hadn't slept in days, and though I could feel it, the Ambience was dimmer, as if by touching the darkness, it had diminished somehow. I put aside the thought for now. "Now you aren't." I looked past her to Sam, who was stirring and muttering to himself. "Sam, are you all right?"

"No," he replied with a grunt. "But I'll live. You?"

"Same," I replied.

"Will someone tell me what's going on?" Meglyn interrupted, pushing against the ropes around her wrist. She let out a screech of pain. Her wrists were still broken. "I... why am I here?"

"You don't remember?" I asked. I gave Bryn a small grimace to let him know I was in pain but otherwise intact, and he pushed his dark blonde mop of hair out of his forehead, closing his eyes in relief. I edged around him, back to Meglyn, to peer at her shocked face. No trace of darkness, though I couldn't feel much of anything Ambient right now. "What's the last thing you remember?" I ran my hand over her broken wrist—trying to force the Ambience to come to me felt like trying to grasp fog—and the bones reluctantly knitted back together. They felt as shaky as I did, but Meglyn's eyes went wide as she whipped around, trying to get away from me.

She shook her head, her face pained and angry. "I remember everything, but it's like I watched myself, like I wasn't me." She scowled at Bryn. "What did you do to me?"

Bryn scoffed and ran a hand over his face. "Elders help me, we *saved* you, you idiot."

"From *what*?" she shouted.

"The gift!" Bryn shouted, glaring at Meglyn. Sam winced, clutching his head. "The stories are true, and you got in the wrong person's way. It's my bad luck that he wasn't looking to kill you for it."

"Bryn," I murmured, putting my hand on his arm, "that's enough." He looked down at me, all the anger and resentment that lingered after this woman had used him plain on his face. "Meglyn has been through a lot, and we both know how hard it is to accept something like this."

We still need her, Bryn, I thought. *If you can't ease up for her—and your—sake, please ease up for the sake of getting information from her.*

Bryn released an angry breath as he gazed at me, and then nodded. *It felt like I was losing you to Derth. I heard his laugh, and you almost faded. If you hadn't come out when you did, I would have come in there after you.*

I grasped his hand to haul myself to my feet and reached up to run my fingers through his hair. The tension fell out of him all at once at my touch. *I know you would have. I was counting on it.*

"The gift is real," I said as I turned back to Meglyn. "There are people, like the man you met, that are dangerous, capable of things you've never imagined possible. You've been under his control since you met him, and you told us you were supposed to protect him, that no one could follow him. Do you know where he was going?"

Meglyn blinked a few times, and I couldn't tell whether she would answer. Bryn shifted, the impulse to hit Meglyn again rising, until she cleared her throat and looked at me. I'd witnessed several shifts in her demeanor since meeting her, but I hadn't seen this level of vulnerability and pain, and my heart sank as I recognized the horror in her eyes. It was the same horror I still felt.

"I remember all of it. Like a nightmare. Elders curse him, I couldn't stop myself." A tear fell from her cheek. "He made me kill my brother."

I couldn't think of anything to say. Bryn went still, shocked, I thought, even as a part of him felt a sick satisfaction, that they had suffered as he had when their actions had forced him to seek Roglin out. But then he thought of the friend Douglas had been before everything had changed, and he pushed that satisfied impulse away, disgusted by the thought.

"Why?" I asked.

She grimaced, trembling and staring at the ground as if she could see the events unfolding there. Her shoulders hunched forward as a tear ran down her cheek, though her expression was still hard and angry. For one brief moment, I saw the potential of a woman who was more than the villain of Bryn's story, someone who had lost as much as either of us. Bryn pulled the dirk from his belt and stepped forward, and my sympathy evaporated as I watched her jut her chin out as if daring him to slit her throat. She didn't need my sympathy, and she seemed like a person that wouldn't accept it.

Bryn sighed and reached behind her to cut her bindings, and she roughly wiped the tear away before she massaged her abused wrists. Hunter escorted Sam into the other room as Bryn cut the rope around Meglyn's ankles. She rose to her feet and stomped away a few paces, crossed her arms over her chest, and glared at Bryn's back as he walked away. I watched her, and when her glare transferred to me, I shook my head and followed Bryn over the threshold to the dining room.

Dust covered everything from the small dining table to the four chairs surrounding it, floating into the air in Hunter's wake. I pulled a chair out next to Sam, and Bryn circled around behind me, his eyes trained on Meglyn in the other room. She had turned away, pointedly ignoring us, and I wondered whether she would run out of the room to the men waiting for her outside. Part of me hoped she would, so that I wouldn't have to deal with her anymore.

Hunter handed me a waterskin, and I let the cool liquid slide down my throat. I lifted my arm to hand it to Sam, and my muscles shook as a cold sweat broke out on my forehead and neck. I hadn't felt this drained since I'd first escaped from Roglin's ship after months of neglect, and I didn't like the reminder of my helplessness, not in the wake of feeling Derth in my head again. Bryn placed a hand under my arm to steady me.

"I've got it, love," he said before he brushed a gentle kiss across my cheek. Sam accepted the waterskin but had to hold it with two hands to take a drink while Hunter hovered behind him, concern etched into his face.

After a short time, hesitant footsteps approached the dining room, and I looked up to see Meglyn standing at the threshold, her eyes red, her cheeks flushed, and the antagonistic glare back in her eyes. "Bryn," she began, "I..." She trailed off, cheeks flooding with color as her mouth twisted angrily, until she turned her gaze to me. The antagonism fell away, exposing the pain I'd seen before. "Thank you, miss, for what you did. And you, old man," she said as she looked to Sam. "I'm in your debt."

I glanced at Bryn, who narrowed his eyes at the last part, and nodded at Meglyn when our eyes met again. "You're welcome," I replied, "I wouldn't wish what happened to you on anyone. If you care to start repaying that debt now, you could tell us anything about where Derth—the man that did this to you—was heading. We're trying to find him."

"To stop him?" Meglyn asked. I nodded, and her mouth set in a firm, angry line. "Good. I hope you kill him." She walked to the table—Bryn stiffened when she walked in a direct line toward me—and pulled a chair across the room, setting herself against the wall next to the threshold to keep some distance between herself and the rest of us. "I can tell you what he told me."

"Anything might help," I said.

She nodded, and with a glance at Bryn, sat. "He was with the former captain of the guard," Meglyn said. "I figured he'd need plenty of resources to pull something like that off, so we stopped them outside the city, hoping for an easy score, and then my head went blank. It was like his voice was the only thought in my head. He was headed to Salava, and he wanted you to know, but only if you were on your own. "

"Did he say why?" Bryn demanded.

Meglyn scowled at Bryn. "No. Like I told you, my head was blank, and I didn't ask questions. I had my orders, and I followed them."

"Any idea why he took the captain?" Hunter asked. "Why go to the trouble of freeing him?"

"To have a guard," Meglyn shrugged.

Sam took another draught of water. "He could have taken more people along the way."

"That's not a comforting thought," Hunter grumbled. He glanced pointedly at Meglyn. "What do we do with *her*? Seems like trouble."

"We can give her to the guard," Bryn suggested, a wicked gleam in his eyes. "Where she can't harass anyone else."

"Now wait an Elders' cursed minute," Meglyn interjected. "I can be of more use if I'm free, I assure you." She smiled at me, ignoring Bryn's sneer as some of her arrogance settled over her shoulders again like armor. "I don't know what you have planned, but as long as you're in Stalth, you have a target on your back. Because I'm feeling so grateful, I'll personally guarantee you have our protection while you remain in the city."

Bryn scoffed. "There's no way we can trust her," he told me. Meglyn scowled at him again, and he turned his ire on her directly. "I have no reason to believe that you would follow through on what you're promising. More likely, you'd wait until the next best opportunity to rob or kill us."

Meglyn rolled her eyes at Bryn. "I don't care much about following rules, but Derth is evil, and I can see that you all are the best chance we have of stopping him." She turned away from him to look at me again, her face earnest, her gaze direct. "That would be enough on its own, but you and the old man freed me, and I don't know that I can ever repay that debt. For you, miss, I'll help."

I squeezed Bryn's hand, trying to get his focus to shift back to me.

We don't need her, Bryn thought, continuing to glare at Meglyn. *She'll only bring more trouble. Let me give her to the captain.*

If she's out on the streets looking to stop trouble before it finds us, we can focus on what we need to do. Maybe we'll be able to help the victims in the prison.

A thousand thoughts rushed through Bryn's mind; denial of my idea, fear of Meglyn's intentions, and above all, the urge to strangle the woman who turned a smirk his way. After a few moments of indecision, his thoughts cleared, and he murmured to me.

"Fine. But, if she does anything to threaten any of us, I'm hauling her to the captain myself."

CHAPTER TWENTY-TWO

I peered out the front window of Sam's squat house at the street beyond the leaning gate. Another storm had rolled in on our heels as we rode into Stalth last night, and it didn't show any signs of letting up this morning. I could just make out the armor-clad cloaked figures of two city guard bent forward into the wind as they patrolled the street. A new initiative by the captain to combat the rise of lawlessness in her city, according to the bold letters on the notice we'd seen on every lamppost we'd passed.

I rolled my head back and forth on my neck, trying to loosen the strain in my neck muscles adding to the dull ache behind my eyes. My focus wandered, my eyes blurring when a jolt of pain ran through my temple, until I realized that the pain hadn't originated from my head, but deeper, in my core. My power throbbed with a dull ache, as unfocused as my eyes. It was dimmer, slower to respond as I teased the Ambience out of the Pool, but I succeeded in using it to subdue the pain in my head and chase lingering exhaustion from my body. It left my spirit drained.

As I came back to myself a light flared in the manor house across the street. The front door opened, a silhouette stepped outside, and was swallowed by the snow. I was surprised to see that they resolved again, approaching our door with their hood pulled low.

I answered the knock on the door to find one of the men we'd seen with Meglyn yesterday. "Miss, we intercepted a letter addressed to you." He handed it to me, and then flashed me a quick smile. "And the crew wanted to make sure you knew we were grateful for what you did for the boss."

"Oh," I replied slowly, taken aback by his words, and the idea that they'd intercepted a letter before it could reach me. *Meglyn moves fast,* I thought. "Thank you." I looked past him to the manor he'd come from. "Do you live there?"

He shook his head, his cheeks and hands turning red in the cold. "No, the owner owed the boss a favor, so he let us set up there. The better to keep an eye on you, miss." With a deferential nod he turned and rushed back into the storm, leaving me to stand watching him, the cold air flaring my skirt around my legs until I noticed that I was freezing and shut the door.

"What was that?" Bryn asked, appearing from the hall.

I held up the letter and pointed over my shoulder with my free hand. "One of Meglyn's people is 'set up' across the street. He brought me this," I flapped the letter, "and said they're keeping an eye on us. What kind of favor does someone have to owe to let strangers into their house in the middle of a blizzard?"

"The useful kind," Hunter said. He reached past me to his cloak and slung it over his shoulders.

"I don't like the idea of Meglyn knowing what we're doing," Bryn complained.

"You wouldn't," Hunter smirked. "But if they're stopping *letters* from coming through, imagine how difficult it would be for someone to strangle Lila again." Bryn frowned at him while I turned the letter over and broke the seal. "There's enough to worry about already, Bryn. Take the win."

The handwriting on the letter was compact and simple, though the forward slant of the letters increased as the letter went on, and I could picture the author bent over a table as she wrote.

Dearest Lila and Bryn,

We heard from our neighbor that they'd seen you at the Crossroads and imagine my shock when I learned that this was not during your last visit to Stalth over a year ago, but just days ago! I am delighted that you have made it back home, Bryn, though I must wonder what could have possessed you to avoid Arthur and me for so many days since your arrival! I can only imagine that whatever your business, it must be terribly important, and so I must forgive you. Though my heart breaks to think that you may pass through without stopping to see us.

Lila, please tell Bryn what a mistake he is making, and force him to bring you for a visit, as I assume this oversight is entirely his doing, and not yours. I have been setting some things aside for you both in the event that just such a visit might occur, and I would hate to see them collect even more dust than they have already.

All our love and the Elders' Blessings,
Maude (And Arthur)

My stomach twisted with guilt even as I smiled at the love so evident in her scolding and held the letter out to Bryn.

"Maude and Arthur want to see us." The corner of his mouth turned up as he read.

He kissed my forehead. "With everything that's happening I wasn't sure we should risk them getting involved. But she's right, we *should* see them." His eyes softened when he pulled back to gaze at me, his smile filling his whole face. "We can tell them the news."

"What news?" Hunter asked.

I smiled over Bryn's shoulder and showed him the ring on my finger. His eyes went wide. "I asked Bryn to marry me," I said.

"Congratulations, you two," Sam said, shuffling out of the kitchen as the ring glittered in the candlelight. "I'm so happy for both of you. Especially you, boy." He smiled at Bryn, and I noticed that the wrinkles on his face were deeper, his hair thinner, the skin on his hands and neck looked a bit looser. I realized with a shock that our encounter with Meglyn had aged him considerably.

Hunter scoffed, and I pulled my worried stare from Sam's haggard face. "All that time practicing what you'd say, and *she* asked *you?*" He shook his head. "I feel used."

Bryn chuckled, and gently clapped Hunter on the shoulder. "I owe you, brother. I'll make it up to you."

"Yes, you will," he said, but he smiled at us, his ivy eyes bright with happiness. "You deserve each other. The good *and* the bad."

"Ha ha," I replied with an elbow to his ribs.

Bryn tugged my hand, and I looked up at him. "We should visit now. Everything else will keep while the storm is raging."

He held my face still as he dipped his head down, touching his lips to mine. It was a gentle kiss, but with all the uncertainty surrounding us, I needed the comfort only Bryn could give me. I wanted more than a gentle kiss. I pressed myself against him, and he wrapped his arms around me, holding me as close as I held him. Lost in his embrace, his hands crushing me against his chest as he sought the same comfort, I startled when Hunter cleared his throat.

"You have a room," Hunter said. "Let's not celebrate the impending wedding right here." I pulled away from Bryn to see Hunter's cloak in his hands.

Bryn asked, "Where are you going?"

"To the inn, so that I can keep Colagh at arm's length. Give him a bit of information, tell him we've hired some mercenaries to help us track down the names on the list, and maybe he doesn't look too closely at the rest of what you're doing." He swept out the door, and I caught a flash of light from across the street again as someone fell into step along with Hunter.

Bryn and I gathered our cloaks, bid Sam farewell, and plunged into the cold. As soon as we turned onto the street, the door across from ours opened to let two more cloaked figures out, and they fell in a few paces behind us.

The shutters were closed in Arthur and Maude's windows above, but the shades on the big shop windows were open, showing a shape moving within. Bryn opened the door, and with a glance over my shoulder, I watched our shadows disappear up the street to either side. I followed Bryn inside through the nearly bare shelves that held only a few winter cloaks and warm clothing in vibrant colors, pulling my hood back over my shoulders in a shower of snow.

Arthur appeared from the back of the shop, and a huge smile broke out on his face. "Bryn! Lila! You're here!"

"Arthur," Bryn said, striding forward to embrace the slight man in his arms so that the only thing visible was the wispy brown hair over Bryn's shoulder. "It's so good to see you!"

Maude appeared, satisfaction on her face until it gave way to a radiant smile. Her long blonde hair was loose over her shoulders, her lilac dress lying perfectly over plump shoulders, not a hair or thread out of place. She rushed forward, taking me in her arms for a hug as fond as Arthur's embrace with Bryn. It surprised me, since we'd only met once, briefly, and it'd been a rough start. Nonetheless, I was pleased, and hugged her just as hard. I'd had few maternal relationships in my life; it felt wonderful to have her inspect me head-to-toe with an appraising, proud expression.

"It's so wonderful to see you both again!" she said. "Pardon me for saying, but you look like you've been through the wringer. Though, still better than the last time we met. Not so hollow about the cheeks, and that lovely hair..." She ran her hand over my shoulder, picking up a long piece of auburn.

"We've certainly been through a lot recently," I replied.

"You're always beautiful, though." Arthur added. He and Maude swapped places and I hugged him tight, the wire frame of his spectacles pressed to my cheek. "Thank you for the letter," he said. "We were so worried when you left, after we heard about the struggle at the gate."

"Of course," Bryn said, extracting himself from Maude to wrap an arm around my waist. I tucked closer to him, clasping his hand in mine. Maude and Arthur beamed at us. "But we have some news."

"Oh?" Maude said.

Bryn held up my left hand, showing them the ring on my finger. Arthur clapped his hands together in front of his face, and Maude covered her mouth as if to hold in her delighted squeak.

"Your mother's ring!" Arthur said. Tears rimmed his eyes, and my eyes prickled with tears in response. "I'm so happy for you two!"

"It suits you," Maude said, pulling my hand forward to admire the ring's sparkle as she rotated it back and forth.

"We should go upstairs so we can celebrate this happy news!" Arthur said. He walked to the front door and locked it, pulling the shades closed.

We spent a few hours ensconced in their small, comfortable home, surrounded by beautiful paintings that brightened even this gloomy day. Embroidered pillows covered the chairs and sofa, something Maude confessed she did to keep her hands busy. I discovered Arthur was the painter, and I listened as he described the different landscapes he'd created from memory of youthful travels. I especially loved the view of Stalth from the rise of the edge of the Esteweld Forest to the east; I'd seen it myself, the first time we'd been here.

Maude hurried to the kitchen and reappeared holding plates laden with hefty slices of meat pie—lamb, peas, and onions spilling out from the crust—alongside a large piece of carrot cake. My mouth watered.

"A celebration for your happy news!" Maude announced. "We've done a good trade this winter, so we had a bit extra to buy sweets with."

"It smells amazing, Maude," I said.

"And when you're done, we'll take some measurements. Please, let me make your wedding dress!" She clapped her hands together, excited and imploring. "I have a few lovely pieces set aside—orders that weren't claimed over the years—and it would be wonderful to find a purpose for them."

"Oh, Maude, that would be wonderful!" I beamed. I hadn't thought about the logistics of the wedding itself, and I was so grateful for her enthusiasm. "I didn't know you made wedding dresses!"

She smiled. "It takes a good amount of time, especially considering how difficult it is to find the right materials, but they more than pay for themselves. And oh, how I love satin and silk and lace!"

My heart was full as I watched Bryn joke with Arthur, and listened to Maude spout ideas for ways she might alter the dresses she had. She waited on the edge of her seat for me to finish my food, and snatched my hand to pull me down the hall as soon as my plate touched the table.

"You'll love what I have set aside; Elders know I've been hoarding clothes for Bryn for years; it felt natural to do the same for you. He's always been so rough with everything. They're hanging from the door in Bryn's old room. Why don't you have a look?" She bounced on the balls of her feet, ushering me into the room, revealing the dresses hanging from a hook. Beaming, she added, "I'll get the gown I have in mind. You can try it on, and we'll see if it needs adjusting."

I gazed around at the room—so much more inviting than the house of Bryn's early years—and I pictured him as a child, warm and fed for the first time since his mother had passed. But I quickly focused on the pile of clothes that Maude had apparently been putting aside for us, determined not to let myself fall back into melancholy when I had a job to do.

There were a few more chemises, and I had to admit that mine were a little worse for wear, so I piled those on a chair by the door. A bodice and skirt hung from one peg, the color of the ocean, and I found my eyes drifting back to it wistfully as I tried everything on.

Everything fit well, and after a sharp rap on the door, Maude entered again holding a gown of ivy-green satin, accented with intricate ivory lace designs on the skirt. She held it up and slid it over my body, and I sighed as the cool fabric settled over me.

"Lovely," Maude said. She twirled her finger in the air. "Turn around so I can lace the bodice, and then we can see how it fits."

The gown had long embroidered sleeves that belled slightly at the elbow, coming to a tapered point just past my fingertips. The neckline was low and square, and as Maude laced the inner layer of fabric, the boning in the bodice pushed my breasts up. I was shocked at how much was visible at the neckline; I'd never owned anything like it, and I felt rather exposed.

Maude finished with the inner lacing, and then fastened the cloth-covered buttons in short, deft movements behind me. She turned me around to face her when she was done, admired her work with her hands clasped over her heart, and then stepped aside for me to see the results in the mirror.

I didn't recognize the woman staring back at me with wide, unbelieving eyes. Made of separate panels of fabric that followed the line of my body, it hid my flaws and accentuated my curves. The bodice showed off my waistline, and the color of the gown made the green in my hazel eyes more vibrant. The fabric around the bodice was a bit loose, but otherwise fit me as if it had been made for me. My hair gleamed like fire above the green, like the sea of trees below the rise near Sam's cabin, where Bryn and I had begun to open up to each other for the first time.

Maude clapped her hands in delight, tears rimming her eyes. "Beautiful," she said. "There's a few places where I'll have to make alterations, but they're easy to make." She smirked, full of pride. "I *knew* this was the one for you."

"I've never seen a dress so beautiful," I said. "Never thought I'd wear one."

"I suppose there's no call for something like this aboard a ship," Maude said. "Pity. But a wedding is the perfect excuse to dress like the queen herself."

"Thank you, Maude," I said, tears forming. I couldn't help but think of the mother I couldn't remember, and wonder whether she might be out there somewhere, wishing she could be here. But I smiled at Maude, so grateful for her kindness and care. "This is so much more than I deserve."

She waved a hand in dismissal. "Nonsense," she scoffed. "Bryn is the only son we've ever known, and that makes you our daughter."

I cried, her words touching a jagged hole in my heart that I hadn't felt in years. Hazy dreams of half-seen faces and impressions of unconditional love had faded, but in this moment, showered in motherly affection, I couldn't help the tears that came unbidden to my eyes as those old wounds opened anew.

"Oh, sweet Lila," Maude crooned, "I can see that you have a terrible weight on your shoulders. I can't pretend to imagine all that you've been through, all that you're going through. You don't have to put on a brave face for me."

Leaning down to rest my head on her shoulder, I let myself feel all the pain, fear, and loss that I kept bottled inside. I wept for the girl I'd been, before Derth and Roglin's attack, for the girl I'd been before I lost the family I couldn't remember. And I wept for the family I'd found, and how fortunate I felt to have people that cared for me.

It took some time for me to exhaust my tears, and I straightened to see Maude smiling up at me. "There," she said, "I've found it helps to let all of that out from time to time, or it eats me up."

"Thank you," I sniffed. I let out a shaky laugh. "I didn't know I needed that."

"That's how it works for me, as well," Maude said. "The times when I tell myself I don't have time to feel is when I need to take time for it the most."

"I hope I didn't ruin the dress," I said, looking down at the rumpled fabric.

"It's nothing a bit of ironing can't fix. I've got a few more little accents I'd like to add. Once you find a time and place for the wedding, we'll be there, and I'll have the dress ready."

"Thank you so much," I said. "I love it. And I appreciate you going to so much trouble for me."

"No trouble at all. I'm happy to do it, for both our sakes."

"Well, I insist on paying for everything. I've got some money saved from our work for King Demetrius, and I insist on paying for the gown. And the rest, we can use the writ he gave us for supplies. You've given us so much already; I can't expect you to give away so much more for free."

"It's no trouble, really," she hesitated, and gave me a conspiratorial wink, "but I won't turn down the extra Aelios." She helped me out of the dress, speaking absentmindedly as she arranged it on its hanger. "Fabrics are so expensive this time of year, but we could have stock ready before anyone else."

I put on my new blue dress, and a short time later Bryn and I stepped into the cold air, a grey, dark sky above and the snowy streets empty save for a distant pair of guards and the shadows that flanked us. The snow had lightened to a flurry, rather than a blizzard, but the clouds hung ominously above our heads, and I couldn't imagine we were through the worst of the storm yet.

"You were right," I said, glancing at Bryn.

"About what?" he asked.

"About taking time to visit. I feel better than I have in a while, like I slept for a day. And that cake!" I moaned. "I'm going to have dreams about that cake."

Bryn laughed, sounding as light-hearted as I felt. It was nice to hear. "How was the gown?"

"You didn't peek?" I asked. He shook his head. "Oh, it was beautiful. I've only ever seen dresses like that near the palace in King's Port, and I *never* thought I would have a reason to wear something so gorgeous. Somehow, the wedding feels more real after seeing myself in that dress."

"I can't wait to see it," he replied as he squeezed my fingers.

I felt restored, and hopeful for the first time in a while. With something to look forward to when this was finished, I felt more eager to return to our task.

CHAPTER TWENTY-THREE

I rode that wave of contented excitement straight into a surge of confidence, and I tugged Bryn's arm to direct him toward the edge of town rather than back to the house.

"Where are we going?" he asked.

"To the stables," I replied. "I want so badly for this to be done so that we can move forward, but since I can't get to Derth with this storm, I'll settle for the next best thing. We're going to get him out of another person's head." I didn't need to tell him who I meant; the only other people not already in custody were Cass and the stable owner, and of the two, I thought Cass might still be too difficult to help, especially surrounded by so many people.

Bryn squeezed my arm, beaming at me before he put his head down into a sudden gust of wind. The sky darkened above us, the flurry whipping against our faces, and I watched another cloaked figure step out into the road ahead of us. Another of Meglyn's people, I realized, and I let out the breath I'd held.

After a long and miserable walk, we finally arrived at the stables, grateful to step inside the warm, hay-scented space. Several horses with their noses out of their stalls looked our way, and Badger nickered in greeting. The owner stepped out of the nearest stall; her hair was in disarray, and she brushed a few long silver hairs away from her face as she smiled at us, and then frowned at the gale that battered the door we'd closed behind us.

"Are you heading out of the city again so soon? It seems an odd time to take your leave." She glanced at the snow behind us.

"Thank you, but we came to visit the horses," Bryn replied with a warm smile. "And perhaps to speak to you when you're available? We're planning on leaving when the storm breaks, but we'd appreciate your experience as we settle our plans."

She smiled. "I'd be happy to lend my assistance. We can talk in my office now if you'd like." We followed her to the end of the wide stable, through a small door leading to a stall that accommodated a table and chair. Atop the table were several wide leather-bound books, one of which she tucked a ribbon inside before closing it and setting it aside. "Apologies for the lack of seating, I don't usually entertain. Just need a place to keep my ledgers." She leaned back against the table. "Is there anything specific you'd like to ask?"

Despite its reluctance, I coaxed the Ambience out of its slumber so I could see the dull mask of darkness over her eyes. It was still for the moment, and I hoped that avoiding questions about Derth would let it remain that way. Perhaps that would give me an edge in ridding her of it. Bryn smiled as he answered her question. "I'd be glad to hear your opinion on the best routes we could take to make travel easier."

She pulled a map from between two ledger books. "Which direction?" she asked. She and Bryn began discussing the merits of different roads, and I took the opportunity to lean closer, ostensibly to peer at the map from her side as Bryn leaned over the opposite side of the table, and reached out to touch her left temple, my stomach in knots.

"What—" She broke off as I slid along the path the inert darkness took inside her mind. I lost sight of anything beyond the energy surrounding us, and the darkness flared as if alive, but not before I grasped its root. It tried to overwhelm me as it had before, but it wasn't as strong here, and I was ready. The woman's spirit was already clawing at the surface, so I pulled the root away and let her crawl out. It withered and crumbled, weakly trying to grasp onto my power, to siphon it away to keep itself alive. But I stamped it out with a flare of my own, the spirits dancing all around me.

She gasped as I let go, my eyes focusing on the world outside the Ambience, and blinked at me. I took a step back, toward Bryn, as my head pounded.

She shook her head as she squeezed her eyes shut. "What was that?"

"I was saying that we would love to buy our horses' supplies from you," Bryn replied. She opened her eyes to blink at Bryn as if confused. "And you've taken such good care of the horses, you should charge a bit more to the king's writ."

She looked back at me as I reached Bryn. He put an arm around my waist, letting me settle some of my weight on him as my energy waned. The Ambience fell out of me like water through a sieve, taking my strength to stand with it.

"I feel like I'm waking from a dream," she murmured, staring at me with wide eyes.

She frowned, and Bryn turned to leave. "We'll let you get back to work," he said, smiling as he helped me through the door. "Thank you so much for the advice."

"Y-you're welcome," she stammered.

I inhaled, held the breath for a moment, and let it out slowly. My knees buckled, so Bryn hooked an arm under mine to keep me upright. "You all right? That was faster than last time."

I nodded. "It wasn't as strong, and she wasn't expecting it. Maybe it's worse when Derth is in control? I don't know." Taking stock of myself, I realized that I was almost as drained as I'd been after freeing Meglyn. It didn't make any sense, but the Ambience was dimmer again, almost out of my grasp. As if in taking on the darkness, I was distancing myself from my own inner light a bit more each time. "It took a lot out of me."

"We'll say hi to the horses and then get you home," Bryn said. "I don't want to rush out of here after that, but I don't want to give her a chance to ask too many questions."

That evening, nestled in Sam's sitting room, I sat close to the fire with a blanket draped over my shoulders. After dozing through the afternoon, I still couldn't get warm. Violent shivers wracked my body and wouldn't stop, even with a bowl of Hunter's leftover soup warming me from the inside. I lifted another spoon of soaked bread ends, tomatoes, beans, and whatever else he found in the pantry to my mouth.

"I thought I'd gotten through to you about your recklessness. You haven't recovered from helping Meglyn!"

"I-I kn-kn-know," I chattered.

"You should get some sleep, Lila," Sam said. He rose to his feet slowly, groaning as he straightened his back. "We all should, and hopefully, you'll be recovered enough to deal with Cass soon. We may need to delay our departure if you want to accomplish that before we leave. But I'm ready to assist however I can."

I watched him go, my teeth rattling in my mouth, and exchanged a look with Hunter and Bryn seated on the sofa opposite mine. When Sam was out of earshot, Bryn sighed and ran a hand through his hair.

"It looks like his age has caught up with him," Bryn whispered. "He's always *looked* older, but now he's acting older."

"If he helps you, I think it might kill him," Hunter said without preamble. "Are we sure it's necessary to deal with these people before we leave?" He slid off the sofa to kneel in front of me, lowering his voice. "No one would blame you for saving your strength for Derth. We can come back to finish what you've started." There was a hint of pleading in his words, more than a hint of concern as I shivered.

"I can't leave them like this," I murmured.

Hunter's face twisted. "I hate what the Ambience is doing to you," he whispered. I touched his arm, and he rose and left the room, his shoulders hunched.

I watched him go, and then tried to set down my bowl. Bryn watched it rattle for a moment, and then gently took it for me. I was grateful when he ushered me to bed, tucking the comforter around me, still wrapped in the blanket. He kissed my forehead and tucked a strand of hair behind my ear.

"I'm going to talk to Hunter. Don't wait for me, you need sleep."

I love you, I thought, not trusting my words to make it past my chatter.

Bryn smiled. "I love you too."

I awoke from a dream where I walked in darkness, alone but for laughter that echoed from everywhere and nowhere. The room was as dark as my dream, and when I felt for Bryn, I found the bed still made. Rolling over to stand up, something stabbed into my stomach, and I screamed. I ripped the blanket from my shoulders and flicked my hand in the direction of the candle on the table across the room.

Light banished the dark when the wick caught flame, and I looked down, expecting to see a knife, blood, something. But my crumpled chemise was intact. Another flash of pain, and Bryn screamed across our bond.

"*Bryn!*" I screamed, launching myself from the bed. I threw the door open and skidded into the hall, just as something heavy *thudded* against the floor in the sitting room. Bryn cried out, and I pushed myself faster, faster, the Ambience pouring strength into my legs until I was a blur.

The sitting room was lit by the flickering fire, and the shadows were long and wavering. Bryn was curled on the rug with his arms wrapped around his middle, staring into the dining room in shock. I appeared at his side, my hands over his, clutching at his wound.

"Lila," he gasped, "she still has the knife!"

"You were supposed to come to me," a voice called from the darkness. My heart stopped as I recognized it. How was he *here*? "I'll take them all from you, one by one, until you submit."

"Derth?" I whispered, standing over Bryn, shielding him with my body. It killed me to leave him bleeding on the floor in agony, but if I left Derth alone, he would kill us both. An invisible shield surrounded us, fueled by the spirit-deep terror that voice instilled in me. I'd come so far, but that voice shattered all the walls I'd put up to keep the nightmares at bay. "You can't be here."

A figure stepped forward and I caught a flash of blonde hair. My stomach dropped, expecting to see the malicious pale blue eyes that haunted me. But Cass stepped forward, not Derth, holding a bloody knife, her face twisted into the same mask of delight that he always showed when witnessing someone's pain. The darkness surrounded her, not just her head, but stretching to reach her limbs, wrenching her arm out to invite me forward. Each step was halted, as if the darkness was acting as strings and she was its puppet. Revulsion ripped through me, ripped through my shield, leaving it in tatters.

"Let her go," I told him, but my words came out as a strangled gasp, and he laughed through her. Loud thumps carried from the back hall, and I could only hope that Sam and Hunter would come to help me. Trying to stall for their arrival, I spoke to the woman behind the shadows. "Cass, please, don't let him do this to you. If you kill us, you'll carry that the rest of your life."

She took a stuttering halt forward, lifting the knife to point at me, her voice lost behind Derth's. "Do you carry the weight of the people you've killed? All those sailors that were crushed, drowned, and torn apart, because of your rage?"

"I do." She moved forward again, and I threw a gust of air at her to push her back. Her hair blew back from her face, but the dark strings pulled taut, holding her in place.

Derth chuckled. "Your tricks won't work here," he said. "This woman is under my protection. Let's see how useful she can be."

Cass lunged, trying to move past me to Bryn, but her uncoordinated attack gave me plenty of space to move aside, knocking her arm away. Anyone else would have stumbled, but Derth's hold on her body kept her upright, and she swung the knife for Bryn again. I caught her wrist mid-swing and with my free hand, pulled her fingers free of the hilt, and one of them snapped in my grip, my strength intensified by the Ambience, as desperate for our survival as I was.

The knife fell to the ground, thumping onto the rug next to Bryn. Her free hand wrapped around my throat and squeezed, stronger than it should have been. I sucked in a breath before my throat closed.

"You sleep," Derth said through Cass. "When I've dealt with the rest of your friends, you'll be brought to me."

I kicked her knee, but she didn't flinch. I clawed at her hand but couldn't pull it free. I gouged at her eyes until blood ran beneath my fingers, but Derth laughed. Black spots danced in my eyes, but I wasn't helpless. I let the Ambience pour in, unrestrained and hungry, and my body filled with heat and light, my hair flew back from my face. The darkness in her—Derth's darkness—should have recoiled, but it grew in response, pulling the Ambience from me by fractions even as I became as strong as Bryn, and her fingers started to give. One tiny breath into my lungs—another finger snapped—and then a gasp of air. The first hint of fear shone in their eyes as a scream ripped out of my throat, and then a body with the outside chill clinging to its cloak slammed into us.

We crashed to the ground atop Bryn as hands grappled with Cass, and I wrenched at her hands to free myself. Bryn groaned as something inside him tore, and blood poured from his abdomen. I clamped my hand on the wound and looked up at the grimacing face of a man in a dark cloak with his arms wrapped around Cass. She struggled so hard, her eyes wild, that even his large, muscular frame couldn't hold her for long.

Another cloaked figure raced through the open front door past a third slumped inside the front door, and grabbed her feet, suspending her in the air as she thrashed. She made no noise, and those horrifying eyes were still fixed on me.

"Hunter! Sam!" I bellowed, just as the doors crashed open in the hall and they came running around the corner. I looked at Meglyn's people. "She's dangerous, make sure Meglyn knows," I told them as they moved slowly toward the door. Bryn took a shallow breath. "Hold on, I've got you," I whispered. Spirits surrounded us, my hands glowing with Ambient light as I sought the source of the bleeding. Bryn's energy was ragged, fading with every second that passed. Hunter barreled down the hall, paused to take in the scene, and then darted forward to help restrain Cass.

She must have twisted the knife, there was so much damage, and it took all my concentration and more stamina than I had to keep his spirit out of the Pool. I healed enough to ensure he would live, but when the Ambience sputtered out like a spent candle, much of the wound remained. It took a few moments to realize that Sam was next to me, speaking to me.

"Lila, wake up," Sam pleaded, terrified. I blinked slowly up at him.

"Bryn?" I asked, my words slurred with exhaustion.

"He'll live," Sam replied. "I'll help him as much as I can."

"Cass?" I asked.

"Gone," Hunter announced as he stepped through the front door, out of breath. "The guards have her."

"What? How?"

"We tried to get her into the alley, but she got loose and ran into some guards, bleeding and hysterical." He took a deep breath, still winded. "If we'd gone after her we would have seemed like we were the ones who'd *made* her hysterical and bleeding—which we were—and I didn't think getting arrested would be a good look for us. They were taking her in the direction of the Bastion."

"Elder's eyes," Bryn cursed. My eyes closed, wouldn't open, and I couldn't lift my head off the floor. "Derth was talking through her, Sam," Bryn grunted. "He had full control of her; who knows what he might do to them. We need to warn them." He shifted next to me.

"Lie down, boy," Sam grumbled. "You almost died. Hunter, help me get them to bed."

"I'm fine," Bryn said, just before he yelped in pain.

"Idiot boy, listen for once," Sam replied. I could hear the frown in his voice. "Let us help you. Hunter and I will find a way to figure out what's going on."

My body lifted from the ground, too tired to even shiver to warm itself, and I inhaled Hunter's scent. He still smelled like the sea, even after all this time away from it, even under the hint of spices.

"You get into the worst trouble, Lila," he murmured. "I don't know why I keep following you into it."

CHAPTER TWENTY-FOUR

Bright light danced across my eyelids, and I winced, wishing it would stop. Instead, it intensified, and I groaned as I rolled away.

"Cursed sun," Bryn grumbled, hissing in pain as he instinctively tried to roll toward me. My eyes shot open as I recalled the events of the night before.

"Bryn, are you..." I ran my hands over him. There'd been so much blood... The room was frigid, despite the early-morning sunlight streaming through the window. "Let me see." I pulled the blanket away to find his body wrapped in cloth, blood striking through the makeshift bandage.

"I'm all right, Love," he grunted. His hair was a mess, strewn over his pillow and glittering gold in the light over his pale face accentuated by the dark skin under his eyes. He flashed his lopsided grin up at me, and I grimaced back at him. "Don't look so worried, you got there in time."

"How did she get to you? How did *Derth* get to you? That was Derth!" Everything was coming back to me in confusing flashes; the glint of the knife blade, the hands around my throat, Derth's laugh...

Looping an arm around me, he ran his hand over my back in slow circles. "I fell asleep in the chair. Thank the Elders Sam never fixed that squeaky board, or I wouldn't have heard her coming. I think we should have a chat with Meglyn about how she got past the people she has watching us.”

“I need to make sure you’re all right,” I said, setting my hand onto the bandage.

He winced and grasped my hand, making me hesitate. “You need rest, Love. You almost killed yourself keeping me alive. I can heal the normal way.”

“And if we’re attacked again?” I asked. “What if you can’t defend yourself?”

“Then you’ll have to protect me. Again.” He smirked, his blue eyes flashing with amusement. “You do it often enough, what’s once more?”

I glared at him in reply, and then scooted under the blanket again, resting my head on his shoulder. His arm wrapped around me, holding me close without pulling at his wound. It felt like my heart would burst out of my chest.

“It seems like everywhere we go, someone wants us dead,” I whispered. “Do you think we’ll ever get to live normal lives? Build a cabin in the mountains, like Sam?”

“As long as we’re looking for it, I think we’ll find a fight,” he replied.

I sighed. “No one else was hurt last night?”

Bryn shook his head, his hair rustling against his pillow. “Everyone else was in bed. I was a convenient choice.”

“Cass—Derth—wanted to punish me.” I wanted to cry, or scream. “He’s not going to stop until all of you are dead. Because I won’t give him what he wants.”

“That won’t happen,” he said. He ran a hand through his hair. “Maybe Hunter’s right, and it’s time to move on. We can come back after we deal with Derth. With Cass in the Bastion, it’s unlikely we’ll be able to get to her. Who knows what she could have told the guards by now. And if she’s free, it’s a matter of time before she comes for us again.” I bit my lip, not sure whether I was more troubled by the thought of Cass being locked up for something that wasn’t her fault, or the idea that Derth’s puppet could be lurking anywhere in the street.

“Hunter’s right about something else,” he continued. “Breaking Derth’s hold is hurting you, and if we have any hope of stopping him, you’ll need the strength you still have. Think about leaving, at least.

Maybe we can force Derth to let these people go. Or we can hope that if we have to kill him, it will break."

"It could kill them," I argued. "Or leave them empty, or forever acting under his last instructions. We don't know." I took a deep breath and let it out in a huff. "I can't leave these people like this. They don't deserve what's happening to them."

"Let's get something to eat," Bryn hedged, pulling himself to a sitting position. "I'm starving, and I know you are too."

With thick wool socks inside my boots, my cloak pulled close around my shoulders, and an extra blanket draped over my cloak, I felt warm enough to leave the bed. The chills lessened as I walked down the hall, supporting Bryn's pained movements toward the sitting room.

Hunter surprised us with an early feast. "Both alive," he said when he spotted us. "Looking terrible, but alive. That's good."

He'd outdone himself; I saw apple butter and raspberry jam on toast, roast beef, carrots, and onions fried into a hash with potatoes, and fried eggs with deep orange, runny yolks over the top. With so much overwhelming me, I had to take a moment to appreciate the glow of pride on his face when Sam complimented the fare. It was heartening to have something small to appreciate, and the experience did more to rejuvenate my body and spirit than I'd thought possible.

"Sam's right," Bryn said through a mouthful a short time later. "This is your best meal yet." I smiled at our old friend, who, even though he seemed to be less exhausted, the morning light highlighted the deeper wrinkles set into skin that looked thinner, more fragile. He felt diminutive in comparison to the man he'd been before.

Hunter shrugged, but his smirk hid deep satisfaction. "Did you know your neighbor three houses down has laying hens? The eggs were laid fresh this morning." He paused to chew, and then added, "Meglyn came by before you were all awake with an update."

"What did she say?" Bryn asked. "Why did Cass get past her people?"

"She spiked their meals at the tavern with a massive amount of Valerian Root," Hunter said. "They were violently ill, and Cass slipped in while they were incapacitated. The next patrol found them after she got inside the house. Seems Cass is back to her normal self, now, and she's terrified that she's being held in the Bastion."

Concerned, I asked, "Why is she being held there? You said they thought she'd been attacked."

He nodded. "They did, but when the guards were helping her, she had that unsettling intensity that Norin did. The captain was already suspicious of her since her name was mentioned in those reports. They patched her up as best they could and stuck her in a cell to be safe."

"Of course they did." I dropped my fork and ran my hands over my face. *This is such a mess.* "I guess we don't need to worry about her running around the city, but how am I going to get to her now?"

"The Elders gave you a sign, Lila," Hunter said, staring at me over his plate. "Listen to it, for their sakes."

"I can't leave them like this, Hunter," I insisted, irritated. "You don't know what it's like to be his plaything. I *do*." I shook my head. "I can't leave them," I repeated, holding his stare.

"For *our* sakes, then."

My face crumpled under the weight of his worry, and the guilt that came with the knowledge that I couldn't give him what he wanted. Even if what he wanted was so much better for me than what I'd set myself up to do. All I could do was shake my head again, and his gaze released mine, disappointment etched on his face as he went back to his food.

We ate silently as the sun brightened—pale and frigid light from the sky reflected off the snow—until Sam broke the silence as what I imagined to be a near-constant stream of thought bubbled out of his mouth between bites.

"It's all happening again." His eyes were fixed on the far wall as he brought his fork to his mouth by rote.

"Sam?" Bryn asked with a hand on Sam's shoulder. The old man started, as if jerking awake from a bad dream, and turned his wide eyes on me.

"What Derth is doing... it reminds me of what was done all those years ago. Ellen twisted the spirits in Tethers like me, in the guise of helping them attain the power of Conduits, to create the first of her Hunters." Hunter, Bryn, and I went still, stunned by this sudden outpouring of information from our close-lipped friend. Had the encounter with Meglyn changed him *so* much? "When she was banished, she preyed upon more of us, until she was able to destroy Salvation and send the rest of us into hiding.

"It was the time that I found my wife, and we started a family, only for Ellen to take them from me in the end." For the first time in our friendship, I saw true rage in his eyes. Every time he'd scolded us when Bryn and I joined our spirits, I had seen a fraction of the anger he was capable of.

"I killed her," he whispered, his fury making the skin on the back of my neck crawl with fear. The Ambience flared around him, bright and terrible. "Not for my home, my parents, our entire society, or the wound her actions struck into the Ambience itself. For my wife, my son, and the baby I didn't get the chance to hold." Tears formed in my eyes, and I held back a sob of grief lest I interrupt him as he continued.

"I sent as many of her Hunters to the Pool as I could after that," he said. "It was my only purpose for a long time. Until I was given new purpose," his expression softened as he looked at me, the sob freed by that look. When he continued, the fury had faded. "That purpose sent me to wander over hundreds of years, searching for the one that would bring a new era of the Ambience to Trylia. I started to hope the Hunters had died out, and then I met a woman from Vortheim gathering Ambient and Hunters—she called them Scourge—so that she could bolster Vortheim's ranks. She also showed me how a Conduit like herself could save the Scourge from the dark spirits inside them that made them what they were."

"So," I said as he fell silent, "as a Conduit, I could help the Hunters, and I'm the only one that can help these people?"

Sam nodded. "I believe so. I thought I could; I thought the spirit holding these people hostage wouldn't be wound as tight around them as it would be around someone like us. It's not the first time I've been wrong."

"What happened with the woman from Vortheim?" Bryn asked.

Sam peered at him, his eyes hard again. "I killed her. She was taking control of people, abducting them. She tried to rip my tethered spirit from me, but the spirits of the elders who gave me long life came to me. They made me destroy her, and wanted to do the same to the

Scourge. But I used them, and the knowledge Avya had given me, to save the Scourge instead. I had a moment of feeling like a Conduit, like Ellen wanted, all because she tried to change the way the Ambience functioned. In a way, she got what she wanted."

Hunter asked, "Why not let her take the Scourge—I refuse to call them Hunters for obvious reasons—away from here so you didn't have to look over your shoulder?"

I interjected. "All of that power would be concentrated in Vortheim. I think of it like rain. If it rains in Vortheim, the crops in Trylia aren't watered unless it's also raining here." I paused, frowning as I recalled the difference between the vibrancy of the Ambience here in Trylia and in Saurboro. "Do you think the Ambience was stronger in Saurboro because we were closer to Vortheim?"

"It's possible," Sam muttered.

Sam grasped his notebook in his hands, as if it could protect him. My chest ached as his story ran through my mind again, finally understanding the pain Sam held just beneath the surface, something he'd lived with for hundreds of years. I had the intense urge to touch Bryn, to make sure he was safe, so I reached across the table to where he had placed his hand, waiting to clasp mine.

"The two people we've helped so far," I said, "you think we pulled a spirit away from them? I thought it was Derth's power. Something he did to these people, like he did to me. I've seen spirits, I've felt them." I shook my head. "This didn't feel like a spirit."

"My assumption is that he's done something to them, however many there are. It was like what I felt from the Scourge; Ellen altered their fundamental nature when she used them, but Derth has gone further."

"And," I added, "he's left something of himself behind. He controlled the man in the alley, and the orb was there. I didn't feel the same sort of presence with Cass. It felt like he *was* Cass."

Sam frowned, staring down at the leather cover in his tense hands. "Hundreds of years later, and people are still trying to change the way the Ambience works. I had hoped the mistakes made when I was young wouldn't come back to haunt me."

Bryn shook his head. "That's a lot to hold onto, old man."

Sam nodded. "There's a reason I don't talk about my life, boy. It fades if I leave it be. Otherwise, I have to live it over and over again." He lifted his eyes from his book, staring straight at Bryn, a mask of pain over his face, in the slump of his shoulders, and in the tremble of his voice. "Time doesn't heal all wounds, but, if you have enough of it, you can forget them."

CHAPTER TWENTY-FIVE

"If you intend to help Cass and the others, we need to formulate a plan," Sam said as we cleared breakfast. He'd shaken off the heavy emotional weight from his shoulders, and now his eyes pierced me with his usual directness.

"I do," I replied. "Whether or not it *can* be done, I have to try." I didn't tell him that I had serious doubts about my chances of success. I felt stronger, and my chills had stopped, but the Ambience felt further away than ever. The only comfort I had was that I had forcibly removed Derth twice now, and I had a reasonably good idea how to do it again. *If my power didn't fail altogether.*

"The spirits respond to you, Lila," Sam said, as if reading my mind. "It's in their nature to heed a Conduit's call, and what Derth has done subverts that nature. If this dark energy is indeed made of spirits, perhaps you can use that to your advantage."

"We'll need a way to get into the prison," Hunter said, an exasperated and resigned edge to his voice. "Maybe we can use Meglyn's people? Maybe they can keep our Vorthe friends out of the way, too."

Before I could respond, there was a knock at the door. Hunter motioned for Bryn to stay in his seat and walked toward the door. Bryn didn't listen, but rose gingerly, moving to where his sword hung from his belt on another chair. Sam followed close behind Hunter, putting himself in front of Bryn and me.

Hunter opened the door a crack and peeked out. When he opened it wide, I saw Meglyn standing on the path. Bryn remained tense, but I relaxed a bit when I saw who it was.

"Yes?" Hunter asked in a clipped tone. He was holding a grudge on Bryn's behalf, I knew, after Bryn had told him the history he had with her.

"I heard about the incident, and I thought I would check in." Bryn glared, suspicious, but she ignored him, though she took in the hunched, painful way he stood. "I thought the increased patrols were bad enough, but after last night, it's even worse."

"That's actually something we were hoping to talk to you about," I said.

"Of course." She slid past Hunter to stand in front of me, so close that I could smell the cold air on her leather coat. Hunter closed the door, and I retreated to a scowling Bryn, who wrapped his arm around my waist possessively. "What do you need?"

"A way into the prison," I said. "A distraction for the guards, and the captain."

Meglyn's eyes widened. "Why stop there? Why not take the garrison's stores, while we're at it?" She scoffed and rubbed her hands together. "You don't ask for small things."

"If what we needed was small, we'd take care of it ourselves," I retorted. Her arrogant attitude grated on my nerves, though not as much as it did to Bryn. "Can you help us? The people they're holding in those cells are like you. I don't want to leave them as they are."

She pursed her lips, slow to respond. "Knowing what they're going through, and how dangerous they are, I appreciate that," she finally replied, and then nodded to herself. "When do you want this grand distraction? I hope you realize that some of my people might join those poor souls in prison because of this. Maybe you can offer me some reassurance that they can be released?"

"We don't have that kind of authority. And the captain isn't fond of us, so I doubt our word will help."

Meglyn sighed. "As much as I owe you, *they* don't, and in case the worst happens, we'll need to negotiate some sort of compensation for their sacrifice."

"Typical," Bryn said.

Meglyn stared at him, all evidence of arrogance replaced with a stern glare. "It *is* typical for you, to think that there won't be consequences for your self-righteousness, Bryn."

"You and your people are criminals," Bryn spat. "If a few of them are taken off the street, at least there will be less of them to victimize the city."

Meglyn sneered at him and waved a hand in his direction, as if dismissing him from the conversation. "He still can't see beyond his opinions, and I have no use for that." She smiled at me. "You seem to have a more practical outlook, maybe you understand that sometimes your hands need to be dirty if you want to get things done."

"You don't know anything about her!" Bryn yelled.

"Stop!" I shouted. "We don't have time for this!" I let all my frustration and fear for the future of our task fill my words. "There are people that need us, and a man out there," I pointed toward the door and the world outside this conflict, "who will keep hurting people until he's stopped. You can work this out *after* Derth is dealt with." I glared at each of them to ensure their silence before I continued. "Can you both agree to put this aside until later? Our time here is short, and we need to use it wisely."

Meglyn nodded, followed by Bryn. Meglyn exhaled through her nose, her mouth in a thin, angry line. "What do you have in mind?"

An hour later we were all standing around Sam's dining table, a rudimentary overhead map of Stalth laid before us, and the beginning of a plan laid out. "Your people will stage a brawl here," Sam pointed at the street near the Bastion, "after Lila, Hunter, and I ask for an audience with the captain, Lila will give Bryn a signal for them to begin."

"I'll be there to sell what the rest are doing, to draw out the captain and her disciples of justice. They're stretched thin with the patrols they're working, so there won't be many inside. How long do you need?" Meglyn asked.

I shook my head slowly. "I'm not sure. I hope no more than a few minutes, but I can't predict that. If we can't get it done within ten minutes, we'll have to get out of there."

"My crew has enough experience causing trouble to get the job done." She looked up from the table to the two of her crew with us; she'd asked her lieutenants to join us so that they could disseminate whatever plan we'd come up with. I was glad to see one was the man I'd patched up outside Bryn's old home. He flashed me a brief smile when I caught his eye. "Get the word out, call in the favors you can. We're going to need all hands for this one." The lieutenants nodded and left the house in a sweep of cold air and a slamming door.

"How many people do you have working for you?" Bryn asked.

She gave him a long look. "More than you'd think, and enough to do what you need. And before you start, we are not the same crew my brother ran. Robbing caravans wasn't lucrative enough for me; my operation is widespread, from protection to information brokering to armed robbery, we do a bit of everything. If the stalwart captain of the guard gets too close to one outfit, we move on to another." She turned to me. "When do you want this to happen? I'll have my people ready, waiting to draw the guards out. And after it's done, we'll settle up."

"Dusk. We have a writ from the king to furnish us with whatever supplies we might need, on the crown. Get us a *reasonable* list of supplies we can provide you, and I'll look it over. We'll compensate you and your people as best we can."

She nodded and turned to leave. Before she shut the door, she turned back to me. "We'll get it done, miss."

"Thank you," I replied. The door closed, and Bryn let out a heavy sigh.

"It's possible that antagonizing the woman who controls whether we get caught by the guards isn't the best idea," Hunter told him. "Especially in your condition."

"Elders," Bryn cursed. "I feel like I'm the same idiot boy I used to be when I'm around her."

"You are," Sam chided.

"She's right, though," Bryn huffed, running both hands through his disheveled hair. He winced, and let his arms drop. "I've blamed her for so long that it's easy to put everything on her. But *I* made the choices that put me there, for them to drive me out of the city and into something worse. I could have left my uncle, but I was afraid."

"To be fair, he *was* terrifying," Hunter smirked.

Bryn lifted the corner of his mouth in an attempt at a smile. "He was. Derth was—is—worse. And my hands aren't clean, either."

Sam sat with a grunt. "Most peoples' aren't."

"We've all done things we aren't proud of, Bryn," I said, touching his cheek.

He put his hand over mine, his eyes blazing as he looked up at me. "I'd do anything to keep you safe."

"I know," I replied, leaning forward into his embrace. His mind was in turmoil as he reconsidered the events of his past, and the view of the world created in their aftermath. His arms tightened around me, our embrace a kind of anchor for him in this moment of upheaval.

All of it was worth it, because it brought me to you, he thought when he noticed me watching.

All of it, I replied, thinking of all the pain I'd endured on my own journey before it brought us together.

He held me tight against him as Hunter spoke. "So," Hunter drawled, "how *do* you plan on getting past the guards inside?"

"Bend the light around us," I replied. "They won't be able to see anything, like when we went after Roglin. I can unlock the door to the prison once we're there."

"If any of them get suspicious, I can try to pull their attention away from you," Hunter said. "Are we letting our Vorthe friends know what we're planning?"

"No," Bryn said. "I don't want them near this. The last thing we need is to showcase Lila using the Ambience. It'll be hard enough keeping Meglyn away from it without adding that complication."

Hunter nodded. "We haven't found anything suspicious, tracking down the rest of the names on the list, and they're eager to leave. I'll tell them we're getting ready to give them what they want."

"Let's get that wound seen to," Sam huffed, waving Bryn closer. "I'll need time to recover my strength before we tackle Derth's twisted power."

"I think this is my fight, Sam," I said gently. He narrowed his eyes at me. "You said it yourself; it took more than you had, and we both know how it felt with Meglyn. Think of how strong his hold is on Cass. He used her body, *talked* through her. If I need more power, it *needs* to come from us." I shot a pointed look at Bryn as he lifted his shirt. I winced with him when pain from his wound lanced through him.

"Fine," Sam grumbled. "But I'll be there in case anything goes wrong." The warning look in his gaze made it clear that he didn't just mean aiding us.

Hunter cleared his throat, uneasy. "I'll head to the inn. I'll meet you back here in a bit."

I nodded as light shone from Sam's hands, shadows growing on the walls surrounding us.

CHAPTER TWENTY-SIX

Tall buildings blocked the few rays of sunset shining between them as darkness descended on the city. Lamps provided small pockets of light in the deeper shadows like beacons drawing us toward the central lane. It felt like the city was escorting us to our destination, as if it could feel the corruption at its heart and knew we were the only hope of rescue. As the Bastion came into sight above the rest, passing a knot of winter-clad, cloaked figures with Meglyn at its center, I wondered whether I was up to the task.

Meglyn nodded when we passed—a flash of disheveled blonde hair, plain wool dress with a ragged hem and torn sleeve, and a swollen, torn lip—before we lost sight of her in the press. The group dissolved into the city and Meglyn was gone before a pair of guards rounded the corner, their eyes restlessly searching for any sign of trouble.

Another patrol passed us as Sam, Hunter, and I stepped over the threshold, past a pair of guards with stern gazes and rigid postures. Bryn waited outside, my link to the bodies standing in darkness with him, ready for my signal. I nodded to one of the guards, and the woman nodded down to me before disappearing into the dim light of dusk.

Inside, the desk guard pursed her lips as we stepped into her line of sight. "Is there something I can help you with?" she asked, irritated.

I flashed her my best smile. "I would like to speak to the captain, if I may."

She peered at me as if willing me to go away, and then, seeing that I wouldn't be deterred, let out a long-suffering sigh as she rose from her chair. "Wait here," she said. "I'll see if the captain has time. She usually leaves around this time of night, so you may have to wait until tomorrow."

"Tell her we're here to fulfill the terms of our investigation," I said. "I'm sure she'll want to see us." She gave me a mocking smile and left us waiting in the foyer. We didn't wait long. The captain walked out of her office, followed closely by Colagh. I groaned inwardly.

"So interesting that you both show up at the same time. You have something to report?" the captain asked. Colagh winked at me.

"We're leaving the city soon, and we're here to report what we've found, as agreed," I said.

The captain waved us into her office as she turned to Colagh. "Thank you for informing me of your departure. Elders' blessings for an easy journey."

"Thank you," Colagh replied. He quirked an inquisitive eyebrow my way, as if asking whether there was more to our visit than we'd said. I gave him a small shake of my head, and then the door closed behind us.

I felt Bryn waiting in the dark with bodies surrounding him. Both of our hearts pounded, anticipating our next move. *Now,* I thought, and Bryn whispered to the people around him. We relayed the story we'd concocted for the captain, namely that Derth had paid and threatened his way through the city before leaving for parts unknown, and that we anticipated the odd behavior would stop.

Hunter smiled his most charming smile, though it didn't inspire a similar response in the woman across the desk. "The most recent trouble was indeed inspired by our presence, we've learned. Allies of Derth, paid to stall or disable anyone that might come looking for him. We haven't found any others in our time here, and with us out of the way, you should have much less trouble in your city."

"Convenient," the captain said. "But I have a hard time believing it. Especially considering you didn't inform me of the Vortheim contingent searching for the same criminal."

There was a sharp knock, and a guard stepped into the office. "There's a brawl in the street. Should we dispatch a patrol to break it up?"

She sighed and nodded. "Yes, report in when it's taken care of, any instigators can cool off in the cells." The guard left, and she turned her attention back to us. "Is this connected to your criminal?"

I hesitated, feigning surprise as Hunter answered. "Not that we are aware of, but who can say?"

She narrowed her eyes, trying to see through his smooth lie. "And what of the Vorthes?"

"We were as surprised as you when they showed up," I replied. The truth. Before I was forced to say anything else, there was another sharp rap on the door, and the same guard's head ducked inside.

"There's a fire in the square, captain."

She rose from her chair in a huff and shooed the guard into the hall. I took the moment to check in with Bryn. *What's happening out there?*

The first group was chased off by the guards, then someone smashed a lantern in the square, catching some conveniently stacked kindling and wood next to one of the buildings. Are they sending more guards?

I don't know, the captain just stepped out.

She stepped back in, looking harried. "Our meeting will have to wait for another time. It seems I'm needed to coordinate my people." She grabbed her sword belt from a hook behind her desk and buckled it around her waist. "Perhaps we can continue this in the morning?"

We were ushered out of the office and walked down the hallway, the captain at our heels. In the foyer several patrols assembled, awaiting orders.

"Reinforce the squad nearby," the captain barked, "and cover the streets surrounding the square. Get that fire put out before it spreads and keep everyone in the square. There's no way these incidents aren't connected. I want everyone involved found. *Don't* let anyone slip through."

Guards filed out of the building, but the captain stayed put. As had Colagh, who smiled from his seat by a far window. Repressing a groan, I told Bryn, *She's still here, we need to give her a reason to leave.*

On cue, Bryn shouldered past the last guard to disappear, supporting Meglyn as she sobbed hysterically. "Help, please," Bryn called. The desk guard and captain stepped forward as Bryn deposited Meglyn on the closest bench.

"H-help," Meglyn whimpered. One trembling had clutched her torn dress to keep it from falling down her shoulder and exposing her chest, while the other covered her mouth and the livid gash on her lip. It was a convincing show; even the captain looked concerned.

"What happened, miss?" she asked.

"I was caught in the middle of a fight. I don't know who, b-but they were all around me." She cringed.

"Where? Close by?"

Meglyn shook her head, letting her hair fall over her face. "East side of the city, by the wall. I was walking home when it happened." Her eyes shot to the captain, wide with fear. "What about my family? I didn't see any guards out there, and if this is some kind of attack on the city…" She trailed off, overcome by tears.

The captain grunted. "I assure you, there is no attack. Please, tell us *exactly* where you were, miss." To the guard next to her, she said, "Assemble the rest of the garrison. If this is the start of a riot, I want all hands on deck."

Guards filed into the foyer moments later to assemble around their captain before she led them outside. Now, only the desk guard was left, staring intently out the window into the dark night.

Colagh turned a bright smile on us. "Friends, it's good to see you! It seems something strange is happening outside."

Sam stepped forward, offering a hand. Colagh clasped his forearm, brought his other hand down atop Sam's, and flipped his white-blonde hair out of his face, away from his gray eyes. "We look forward to our departure, and apologize for our lack of presence after all that's transpired. Perhaps we can meet you at the tavern later tonight, to discuss our plan?" Sam smiled, his brows high on his forehead.

"That sounds wonderful," Colagh replied, "though I feel it might be safer to remain here until the commotion is over."

They released each other's arms, and Colagh turned his smile on me. "You are looking lovely," he said. "I'm saddened to see the bruises remain, though you seem to have recovered from your ordeal."

"She has," Bryn said, stepping forward to wrap an arm around my waist. Our time here had brought out a possessive side of Bryn that I hadn't seen before. I glanced at the guard, wondering how we might be able to get past her to the prison.

Another flash from somewhere nearby, and she rose from her seat with her hands planted on the desk to peer out the window behind me. No way I'd be able to escape her notice now. Not that I wanted to try with Colagh standing next to me. So, I peered outside with the rest, unable to see anything but dark shapes beyond the lantern light. *Now what?* I thought.

Bryn shook his head so subtly that I wouldn't have noticed if I hadn't been able to feel it. *We need another distraction, one that won't rouse Colagh's suspicion.*

Glancing at Sam, I could see his thoughts churning, too. He had his old notebook in one hand, running his thumb over the cracked leather. His eyes flicked to the window on the opposite end of the room, and without moving, there was another, much closer, flash of light, and the building rumbled as if struck by something.

The guard darted from behind the desk and out the door. Sam turned to Colagh as Meglyn and Hunter stood, Meglyn clearly confused, and leaned over to whisper in the Vorthe's ear. Colagh grimaced, and then stood as well.

"Wait here," he told us, and sidled past Hunter and out the door. Sam moved to Bryn and me, waved his hand in our direction, and we vanished from sight.

"He's going to check that Derth hasn't returned," Sam whispered, "so you won't have much time. Get moving." Meglyn walked back in as Sam joined Hunter at the door, barring the way while we moved to the door leading to the prison. As we went through, Meglyn slipped into the office, closing the door behind her.

We should stop her, Bryn thought.

We don't have time, I replied, pulling him into the hallway. A few faces stared through our invisible bodies: guards left behind to watch the place were armed and armored, clearly waiting for orders to move out.

"What was that light?" one man asked. He was standing in the middle of the hall, blocking our path.

"Elders only know," another said. "Whole city's gone mad."

"Maybe we should go, back the captain up," the first suggested.

The other shook his head. "No, not without orders. I don't want to lose my job."

We don't have time for this, I fumed. I leaned forward, spotted the candle on a table near a rack now empty of the armor it had held, and coaxed the flame higher. With a flick of my finger, the candle toppled onto the floor, and the flames eagerly licked up a nearby curtain.

"Fire!" they shouted, and both disappeared inside. Another two came from across the hall to join their frantic comrades as they tore the curtain from the rod to stomp the flame out on the ground. As the flames sputtered out, Bryn closed the door behind them, and I touched the wood, swelling it in the frame to lock them in.

The door to the prison loomed at the end of the hallway, and I took a deep breath to focus as we reached it. Bryn turned the handle and pulled it open, revealing iron cells and the people within. The torches were unlit, and shadows reached out from the corners. It pulled at the Ambience surrounding us, and suddenly we were visible again.

Three heads snapped in our direction the moment we appeared. Cass's hair was dirty, matted with sweat and grime, more gray than blonde. So much like Derth's.

I felt the darkness swirling before I saw her. The other two, the guard and the man who'd assaulted me outside the inn, possessed the same aura that swarmed around Cass. With all of them here, the darkness stretched past their individual cells, giving the entire prison a pall of malice that pulled at the edges of my frayed nerves.

My sight blurred as I watched Cass rise from the bench against the far wall. I rubbed my eyes, and the blur moved to the corner of my eye, like every time Derth had watched us in the past. Bryn sensed my unease, and, understanding the sensation behind it, reached out with his spirit across our bond, joining it with mine.

The darkness materialized around us into fractured, tortured spirits. The spirits that had been with Lila her whole life had been ethereal, beautiful shapes that reminded her of something human, but felt like a smile from a friend, or a fear of the dark. It seemed so obvious that the darkness we'd been fighting against had been these beautiful spirits turned from their purpose, but there hadn't been enough of them to see the pattern in the dark. Now we were surrounded by pieces of such creatures, manifestations of arms connected to torsos by ribbons of pain and dark intent. They covered the prison, and Derth's influence surrounded us, taunted us.

We spotted an orb with Cass, and another with the guard. To our immediate right, next to the door, the same old woman we'd seen on our first visit cowered in the corner farthest from the others, sobbing to herself.

Sweeping our arms in the direction of the orb next to the guard, we swatted it against a wall, shattering it. A silent scream, pressure against our minds and power, and then Derth's oppression lessened a fraction. Derth's voice echoed from his three thralls in the cells.

"No more!" they screamed. The dark spirits reached out to us, interposing themselves between us to smother our shared spirits, tearing them away from each other as Lila had torn the others from Meglyn. Our connection cracked, as the surface of a frozen lake cracks under a boot, but it held. Ambient energy flared through us to patch the weak spots as we pushed back, and the pressure on our bond lessened.

We rushed to the nearest cell, where the man who'd attacked Lila lurked near the bars, and reached through to touch his chest. Feeling for the pieces of the shattered spirit restraining him, we used our strength to pluck each one from the place it was tethered to. The man's suppressed spirit barely stirred; part of him was gone, dissolved, absorbed, or eaten by the darkness imprisoning him. But together, *we* were stronger than Derth.

The strength of the Pool pulsed through us, and the space between it and our world,195here Lila retreated for strength and fought against the unseen forces Derth had conjured again and again, surrounded us. The spirits we called gathered the fragments of the tortured spirit and pulled it away from its tether.

Derth reached through the orb, and the darkness grew. It was alive, a writhing, wild version of the Ambience that we'd come to know. Devoid of the spirits that should have ushered it forth, it felt like it had been ripped from the Pool and was trying to take root here, with no guiding purpose.

Stop, we commanded the Ambience, and spirits flowed through us, trying to hold this wild force at bay. *It must go back.* One vibrant spirit rushed forward, taking the Ambience into itself, acting as a Conduit back to the Pool. We felt the energy of that spirit torn asunder as the Ambience was funneled away, the darkness receding so that the others could aid us in removing Derth from his thrall.

The fractured spirit came free, into the arms of the others who pieced it back together. The man's spirit was ushered into the arms of the myriad of others we'd conjured, and his body dropped to the floor of the cell, out of our grasp, while Derth surged forward again.

This time, we were completely smothered, and our connection broke... separating me from Bryn. A shockwave erupted from us, knocking Cass and Norin back a step, and I recoiled from the loneliness that overwhelmed me. It felt like my lungs wouldn't take in air without Bryn's help. It felt like the bond between us was weaker than before. Derth laughed, mocking us from two mouths instead of three.

"None of your tricks, little girl." Rage stirred inside me, Roglin's insults repeated by a man far more dangerous. "Leave my pets alone and face me yourself."

"Tell me where you are, you monster," I spat, struggling to my feet. Bryn was flat on his back next to me, his eyes staring at the ceiling, stunned. "After I help these *people*, I'll come for you."

His dark spirits surged forward, engulfing me, blinding me. They blotted out the world around me and forced images into my mind. Fog, city streets that I didn't recognize, and a tall, white tower shrouded in shadow. He grasped my spirit with so many broken, spectral hands, and hurtled it away from the rest of my body, my physical form crumpling next to Bryn as I was thrown into the confines of my head. Into the space he had made my prison.

One moment, we were in darkness, the screams of broken spirits deafening, maddening. The next, we were in an open, empty space, with a thick, misty gray curtain along one side. It fell away, revealing the shore that led to my version of the Ambient Pool. Radiant, prismatic spirits reached out to me to lend me their strength, and I reached for them, but my consciousness was yanked back to the darkness.

Claws sank into me, infusing me with all the terror, despair, longing, and rage of the spirits who yearned for freedom. There was no cohesion to their desires. They were a chaotic storm of emotion that battered my mind and my power, and I writhed in agony and madness, smothered by too many feelings, too many unrealized dreams, too many cloying nightmares.

Images flashed through my mind. Blue-gray eyes above a charming smile, a sweep of hair as black as the night sky. A man's voice, smooth and alluring, calling to Derth. Short, vibrant red hair angled toward a mass of dark auburn, two heads bent over something I couldn't see.

These were Derth's memories. "No!" Derth screeched, digging his claws deeper. They rent at my power, pulling me farther from my body, into darkness that swallowed my light. He cackled, triumphant, as I struggled. I felt my spirit diminishing.

But Derth didn't know how much I'd grown. He'd known a frightened young woman, someone with no direction, whose only purpose was survival. Now I had more to fight for, people to save, and I wouldn't let him take that from me again.

I turned on him, on the spirits that cried for release while obeying their corrupt master. Derth's malice couldn't dull their pain, and, as I fought for my life, I realized that I couldn't undo what Derth had done with more violence, tearing these remnants of the Ambient that came before me apart. They were broken, like I had been, and like me, they needed help to put themselves back together.

I stopped fighting, letting Derth drag me away from the light. But my power didn't rely on my proximity to that imagined space. I *was* the Ambience, born to be a Conduit between it and the world, and it existed within me to do what I asked of it. An instinct stronger than self-preservation, borne of long hours watching Smitts heal the crew of the *Catherine*, borne of the love that he'd had for all of us, rose above my panic. It was the love that I had for myself, and Ambient like me, that had long been absent in Trylia.

Rather than keep the Ambience from these broken creatures, I let it pour out of me and into them, filling the cracks in their fractured energy, their fractured intentions and desires, and they were made whole. They drifted like fog banks, ushered back to the Ambient Pool where they could heal, and add to the Ambience again. A place where they wouldn't be forced into service, to act against their nature. As they crossed that threshold the Pool rippled, and more spectral hands than I could count surged upward to touch the fog clouds, which trickled like raindrops sparkling in sunlight below the surface.

Derth's screams of rage faded as I came back to myself and heard bodies thump to the stone floor. A woman cried out in fear, and Bryn's voice coaxed me from the darkness.

"Lila, love, come back to me. Please." He pleaded, his fear palpable as he searched for my spirit through our bond. I opened my eyes, and his face flooded with relief. "Thank the Elders," he gasped, crushing me against him. His heart pounded against mine until they found the same rhythm, until they both calmed.

"Are they all right?" I asked as I sat up. The elderly woman was crying in her cell, clutching her head. Norin and Cass were sitting, but the other man was slumped on the floor. Cass blinked, and her face crumpled as she sobbed, too.

"That man hasn't moved. I don't know if he's alive." Bryn touched my face, as if to assure himself that I was whole.

I shook my head as I peered over Bryn's shoulder. "I think he was too far gone already. The others... Sam was right. Derth twisted spirits to hold these people, like the Scourge. They needed help, too. I wish I'd known sooner; I could have saved more. Did you feel what I felt? Like that darkness was something more than just Derth's doing. It felt—" My brow furrowed as I tried to find the words. "Wild... almost like the Ambience was being unleashed on its own."

"Interesting," A musical voice drawled from the doorway. Bryn and I whipped our heads in his direction as cold fear drenched me. Colagh. "There's so much more to you than I thought. Please, come with me. If you'd like to avoid joining these fine people, I suggest we leave before the stalwart captain of the guard returns."

CHAPTER TWENTY-SEVEN

We walked out of the Bastion as several rough-looking, beaten men were escorted inside by harried guards. No one paid us much attention as Bryn supported my weight, and we followed Colagh and the others down the street, in the opposite direction from the captain. I didn't see Meglyn anywhere, and I wondered whether she had escaped the office, or if she was waiting for her opportunity. The captain's eyes blazed inside her helmet as she gestured with her sword at guard and thug alike.

Colagh moved quickly, disappearing around a corner as the rest of us struggled to keep pace. Before the closest alley swallowed us, the captain called out. "I want patrols of four scouring the city for more of them! Form up!"

We moved from light to darkness between the Bastion's windows twice, three times, leaving me as disoriented as I'd been battling Derth's broken spirits. We came to a halt when Colagh held his arm out to stop us; a guard patrol passed through the courtyard, between us and the Crossroads Inn. Lanterns flanked the door, like beacons calling us home.

"Now," Colagh whispered. He strolled across the open space, his boots clicking on the stones beneath his feet, looking like he didn't have a care in the world.

"We should get you home," Bryn said, his voice low. I stumbled on a tall cobblestone, and he swept me into his arms. "You're exhausted."

"This is closer," I replied, letting my head droop against Bryn's chest. Hunter held Sam back behind us, letting a pair of guards rush past before they followed us. "After what he saw, I don't think we'll be able to put Colagh off."

"Fine," Bryn grumbled. My head bounced against his chest with every step, and my eyes drooped closed until I felt the warmth of the tavern surround me. Falei looked up from the bar and frowned at us as we approached. But Colagh was prepared, and smiled at the proprietor before she could open her mouth to speak.

"You look ravishing this evening! Would you do me the honor of providing me with something strong for my friend here?" He glanced over his shoulder at me as he leaned an elbow on the bar. "The poor thing twisted her ankle in the dark, and I think she could use some help with the pain."

Falei smiled at him and nodded, reaching below the counter for a bottle full of amber liquid and a small glass. I flinched when a table full of people started laughing at once, the boisterous sound overwhelming in its proximity. A moment later, glass in hand, Colagh ushered us into the hall full of wooden doors, toward his room.

The door shut with a click, and Bryn set me into a chair, but didn't take his hands off my shoulders. Colagh was grinning at me when I looked up, full of delight. "I see that I was right to share my task with you," he said.

I straightened, trying to exude anything but the helpless fatigue I felt. Colagh took one chair and pulled it close to me, clasping his hands together to prop on the table. He leaned forward, and Bryn shifted behind me.

"So, you have the power to free not one, but *all* of the enthralled. At once." He pursed his lips, raising one eyebrow. "I must say, I'm impressed. I know a few Conduits, but none so powerful as you seem to be."

I stared at him, at a loss for words. I wasn't naïve enough to think that my secret could be safe after he'd witnessed what I'd done. But saying it out loud made it real, and I knew I didn't have the strength to defend myself from him right now.

"Thank you for the compliment," I said icily. "What happens now?"

He blinked as if confused and sat up in his chair. "What do you mean?" he asked.

"You're from Vortheim," I replied. "Your country has a history of trying to take Ambient Trylians. And you're hunting a man that we suspect was fulfilling that role. I assume your task doesn't stop with Derth."

Understanding washed over his face. "So, *you* are the cargo he was unable to deliver. It all makes sense now," Colagh sighed.

"If you try to take Lila, we *will* stop you," Sam said. Hunter and Bryn nodded as Colagh looked at each of them in turn. When he looked back at me, shock was plain on his face.

"I have no intention of delivering anyone to Vortheim, except for the one I was sent to find. I must deliver Derth, or proof of his demise, to the Malachi upon my return." His face twisted in disgust. "I am no slaver."

When we continued to glare at him, Colagh sighed and flipped his long, pale hair out of his face. "Yes, slavery is a common practice." He wrinkled his nose in displeasure. The expression sent a pang of anger through me; if only the slaves abducted from their homes had the luxury of finding it mildly distasteful. "More common is the practice of indentured servitude, where people sell *themselves* into service. To pay off debts, provide more for their family than they could in a lifetime otherwise, or a myriad of other reasons. It is the practice of those less reputable to take people to sell. Nothing I endorse, I assure you."

"Speaking from experience," I said, "I can tell you that it's devastating for the people involved. How can your Malachi allow such a thing to happen?"

"How can your king?" Colagh demanded. "How can anyone? These things happen, there are laws against them, and enterprising individuals find ways to make money by taking things from those that cannot defend themselves. We have a specific branch of Tether authorities that are tasked with the capture of such individuals, of which I am one. It is why I'm here, hunting one that has proven more dangerous than originally anticipated."

I didn't answer as I considered his words. It seemed far-fetched to have an entire group of people dedicated to eradicating the slave trade, considering how much it flourished. If this was the result of such oversight, either these authorities were near-useless, or... I shuddered, considering how *terrifying* Vortheim must be.

"We are the beginning of such a branch for Trylia," Hunter said. He crossed his arms over his chest. "We liberated some abductees before some of us met you on Saurboro Island."

"And the crew of the ship?" Colagh asked. "I hope they are rotting in a Trylian prison."

"They are," Hunter replied. "It's gratifying to hear that not every citizen of Vortheim endorses slavery." He smiled, but I could see the antagonistic steel beneath it. He wanted to see how far he could push Colagh, to pull his patience taut and pluck it like the string of an instrument. He'd made many people sing before.

"I grew up in King's Port, hearing stories about the evil people of Vortheim who stole children from the water." Hunter leaned forward a bit, his brown curls bouncing when he chuckled. "My favorite story said you all were half people, half fish, said that you lived in houses on the ocean floor, and would creep into the harbor at night. Then, you'd transform your fish tails into legs, sneak through open windows on the ocean breeze, and snatch children that were awake too late to take home with you."

Colagh quirked an eyebrow and smiled back. "Interesting. But I think it would be much easier to take a child that was sleeping, don't you? Children are noisy, as a rule, but one that is asleep?" He shook his head. "Much quieter that way."

Hunter's smile widened when Colagh didn't take the bait. Bryn took a deep breath, containing his deepening well of distrust. I couldn't shake the indignation I felt at such a casual conversation about something that had changed the course of my life. Not once, but twice. They hadn't just been stories for me.

Colagh's expression changed again, following his mercurial moods. "But now, I have a much better chance of following through on what I must do. With a Conduit at my side, I cannot fail!"

"You're assuming we will help you," Sam said.

"That seems like a big assumption to make," Hunter added.

"I don't trust you," Bryn said.

Colagh protested, and the conversation between all of them revolved around and around, drowning out my thoughts. I tried to tamp down the anger that rose with the volume of these men discussing what *I* would or wouldn't do. And then it was too much.

"Elders!" I cursed, shouting above the noise. The men went silent and looked at me, and I glared back at all of them. "I'm tired of everyone arguing about me! *I* am the only person who can decide what actions I take. *I* am the only one in charge of what happens to me, and *I* can defend myself if I need to!" I shot a look at Bryn, and he had the good sense to look ashamed.

"I don't know if I can help you with Derth," I told Colagh. "Freeing those people, healing the spirits that bound them, it was one of the most exhausting, debilitating experiences of my life." Again, I felt the Ambience at a distance, like I'd delved too deep and exhausted even the Pool. I heaved in a breath, the air too thin in my lungs. "I don't know that I have enough in me to take on Derth himself."

"But you still plan on pursuing this man?" Colagh asked. I nodded. "As do I. After what I've seen here, I doubt that my people and I have the strength to subdue such a creature. If you say that you are not confident, that is troubling. Therefore, it makes the most sense to band together, to have the greatest chance of success. As I have said before."

"While I see the value of your suggestion," Sam said, "we don't trust your motives. Add to that the fact that once you return home and report our existence to your Malachi, our lives will be threatened."

"There is still the matter of surviving our encounter with Derth," Colagh said. "If we come out of this alive, we will discuss what comes next. I swear on the Elders, I will not send word of you before Derth is dealt with."

Bryn and Hunter glared at Colagh, but he held my gaze. I tried to look deeper, to discern what I could of his character from the look in his eyes. Was this a man we could trust to help us with Derth? Was it foolish to hope that he might keep our secret? I shook my head, breaking eye contact. All I could consider was the task ahead of us, and our chances of survival if we didn't accept his help.

"I don't think we have any good choices," I muttered. "Either we choose to go our own way, with Colagh and his people on our heels, or we join forces. Without them, we have another variable affecting the outcome. With them, the same, but hopefully a more favorable variation." I looked to Bryn, Sam, and Hunter in turn. "I think we need to accept their help for now." Looking at Colagh, I said, "I hope you understand that we will defend ourselves if we need to."

Colagh laughed, a throaty, heartfelt laugh that made me want to join in. It was infectious, though I was beyond laughter.

"Oh, to see what you are capable of!" He cleared his throat, and his smile now held an edge of menace. "That, my lady, is what I am counting on."

The next morning we gathered, discussing our impending departure, when a knock on the door interrupted our breakfast. The guard captain had come to call, one hand on the hilt of her sword and a strained smile on her face when she entered. There were dark circles under her eyes, and her hair was mussed, as if she'd spent all night running her hands through it.

"Good morning," she said. "I happened to be in the neighborhood, and wondered whether you might be willing to speak about what you saw last night?" She was putting considerable effort into putting forth a friendly demeanor, but I could feel her underlying current of suspicion.

I led her to the dining room as Bryn rose from his chair. "Of course."

She stood behind the chair at the head of the table as Hunter looked up with a mouth full of food and Bryn took his seat again. I noticed the tiniest grimace on his face; I'd need to make sure he was all right later. "I apologize for interrupting your meal," she said. Sam inclined his head from the opposite end of the table, placing his fork next to his plate and wrapping his hands around a mug of steaming tea with a mildly concerned frown on his face. "After an incident like the one we encountered last night, I feel it's important to gather as much information as soon as possible, so the details don't stale."

"We understand," Bryn murmured. He flashed me a wry grin, as if to tell me to stop worrying. I hadn't realized that I couldn't feel him this morning. "Please, have a seat," Bryn told her.

She pulled out the chair at the head of the table to sit. "As you are aware, there was some sort of attack in the city last night, though we have ruled out any outside influence in the matter. On the surface, it seems to have been a brawl between locals, and several fires caused by the fighting. The city is calm now, but we spent the night trying to track down the instigators with no luck. All we have to show for our efforts are a few drunks arrested at the scene. I wondered whether you saw anything unusual on your way to make your report last night." Her gaze penetrated each of us in turn. "Any hint of the chaos that ensued after you arrived?"

"I didn't see anything abnormal," I said.

"Nor did I," replied Sam. He took a long drink of his tea, and I envied his nonchalance.

"And when you left?" the captain asked. "Did you witness anything?"

"It was chaos, like you said," Hunter said after swallowing his food. "We saw flashes of light outside, heard someone scream about a fire inside, and thought the Bastion was under attack. When we got outside there were guards everywhere, and all we saw in the streets were people running like us."

She nodded, her gaze locked on Hunter. He shrugged, flashed her an apologetic smile, and took a bite of fried ham. She turned her attention to me with a wry smile, clasping her hands as she placed them on the table in front of her. "And you left the premises when the fire broke out in the armory?"

"If that's where it was," I said, my eyes flicking to Bryn. "We heard someone shout and left."

She didn't miss the movement, and her eyes narrowed. "Your friends were in the foyer when the fire happened, when my guards found the door closed behind them and jammed. Thankfully, the fire was put out before anyone was hurt. But you two," she glanced at Bryn, and then back at me, "were nowhere to be seen until you left with the others, including Colagh of Lacorsia."

I could see that there was nothing I could say to satisfy her suspicion, true or not. Before I could answer, she leaned back in her chair, fingers curling around the carved arm rests.

"All right, well, perhaps your investigation may have uncovered a reason for my prisoners' demeanor to change overnight? My former guard seems to have recovered his senses and claims that he has no memory of his actions. A woman who was found bleeding and hysterical in the street near here is now back to the sweet woman I've known, rather than the creature that was in my cell. She is also muddled about her actions and doesn't remember how she came to have such wounds. The man who attacked you," she nodded to me, "fell into a deep slumber that we can't rouse him from. What can you tell me about that?"

"It sounds like more of the same strange occurrences that brought us here in the first place," Sam replied, an edge to his voice. "Circumstances prevented our report last night, but we can make it now. The summary of which is that we believe that the strange behavior was indeed the result of the criminal we are pursuing."

The captain narrowed her eyes. "And have you uncovered the reason for this one man to cause so many different—and seemingly unconnected—disturbances?"

Sam sighed, his frown deepening. "That is something we are still trying to uncover. We know that he is *not* in the city and hasn't been for some months. We hope to find a more recent trail that we can follow, so that we might apprehend him and put a stop to all of it. Your vigilance in providing us with a list of potential victims—for the strange behavior and criminal acts were the result of coercion or threats—has helped us to spread word that this criminal is shortly to be brought to justice, and therefore has no further sway over the people he held under his thumb."

The captain's hard stare continued, stopping on each of us in turn. "I appreciate your report, but now I'd like to know what's happening here."

"What do you mean?" Hunter asked.

"Something is missing from your story, something that ties all of this together, something that makes all of this make sense. I *know* it, and I can't see it. But I have the distinct impression that you have that missing piece. I don't want to arrest you, but I can't let you leave knowing that you haven't shared all that you know with me. I can't leave the citizens and the city vulnerable because agents of the king withheld something vital."

"The only way to ensure that everyone is safe is to let us find him and stop him," Bryn said, his voice as hard as hers. "You said it yourself; we're agents for King Demetrius. This is bigger than one city. This is happening *throughout* Trylia, and we are the people who can stop it. We'll leave tomorrow morning, so you won't have long to worry about our presence."

"I still don't see—" she began, but I stood and slammed my hand onto the table. We couldn't afford to sit in prison while she decided our fate. I brought all the power and authority that I could muster to bear; I was a powerful Conduit, and likely the only person in Trylia who *could* stop Derth. I would not let this woman hinder me.

"You don't need to see the whole picture. You need to understand that we have it, and when we say that we will put a stop to all of this, we will. This is the purpose King Demetrius has given us, and we will see it through. Send word to the capitol, by all means, so that the king knows what happened here, and that we have moved on in our pursuit. Because I can guarantee you, if you lock us up to satisfy your curiosity, all of Trylia will regret it."

She stared at me, and for the first time, I didn't feel like *I* was the one being reprimanded. I could tell that she wanted to refute what I'd said, but she was hesitating, either from the truth of my statement or the power behind it. Instead, she rose from her seat, standing tall and stiff after my rebuke.

"Very well, then," she said. "I will make my report to the capitol and inform the king of all that transpired before you moved on. But," she held up a finger, "I will make it clear that I don't trust you, and you can be sure that I will be ready to arrest you on sight if my suspicions are confirmed in *any* way."

"I wouldn't expect any less," I replied. I watched as she stormed out of the dining room, Hunter on her heels until the front door slammed shut, and a worried Hunter came back to the table. All the tension rushed out of me, and I plopped onto my chair.

"You two can't help but poke at angry people, can you?" Hunter asked, flabbergasted.

"It's a talent," Bryn smirked.

"I need some air," I said, shoving away from the table. I was still so tired, but I needed to move, to work the stiffness out of my muscles. I didn't like the cavernous feeling between Bryn and me, and without being able to feel him, I didn't want to let him out of my sight. "Come with me?" I asked him.

"Of course."

Outside, the cold air lifted a few strands of hair off my face, though the sun was shining, and I closed my eyes to soak in its warmth. When I opened them, I noticed Colagh strolling toward the house, his wide smile greeting us as we joined him in the street.

"Well, friends, it seems you have escaped the stalwart captain unscathed." He glanced over his shoulder to a group of guards gathered around their captain at the main road. "No small feat, considering her penchant for arresting anyone who looks at her wrong. Will any of the captives be freed? The lovely Cass, perhaps?"

Intrigued, I tilted my head and cocked an eyebrow. "It may take some time, why do you ask? Worried about a few Trylians, or just one?"

He looked at his feet and smiled to himself. "She is a magnificent creature," he said. "To see her tainted like this," he shook his head, "it's monstrous. All of it has been, but this, especially, is an abomination."

"One more reason to stop him," I said. Colagh nodded. "Will you and your people be ready tomorrow morning?" I asked. "We want to leave at dawn."

He beamed. "Yes, of course! We are all eager to be on our way, after far too much time in dreary homes, speaking to nervous locals. My three companions were quite unhappy to miss the action last night, I can tell you. We are prepared for departure and will join you on the north road at dawn tomorrow." Bowing, he turned on his heel and walked away from us, in the direction of the inn.

I looped my arm through Bryn's. "I wish I could sleep for days, but I think we need to move on. Derth aside, the captain may arrest us if we stay longer."

"She may," Bryn said. "Especially if Cass or the others remember anything about last night."

"Tomorrow, then," I sighed. Derth's influence over the people here was broken, and a knot in the pit of my stomach loosened a bit as I realized that I had beaten him. After all that he'd put me through, I'd taken something from him. Those images I'd seen, perhaps there was something there that could help me find him. But the knot remained as I considered what was ahead of us. And wondered whether I'd be strong enough to finish this.

CHAPTER TWENTY-EIGHT

Raven's warmth kept the cold at bay as we rode northward, something I was grateful for as fat snowflakes drifted past my hood to land on my eyelashes from the gray clouds covering the sky. We'd been lucky the first week of travel, with the ground frozen enough to avoid sticky mud without snow to slow us. Now, it looked like our luck was running out.

Sam and Hunter rode in the lead with the Vorthes behind, and Bryn and me at the rear. Colagh was in the center of the group, one hand outstretched to the sky to keep the worsening snow from coating us. But I could see his body flagging as the storm picked up, already having spent most of the evening and dismal morning protecting us.

The horses nickered, throwing their heads to avoid the stinging snow. "If we want to keep moving, I need some help!" Colagh shouted. He glanced at the other Vorthes, but I felt the stirring of air and frost at Colagh's command, a subtle magnetism for the natural forces of the world, and it stirred the power that had been slumbering inside me since the jail. Relieved and elated, I reached out to it, coaxing it to shine again, and reached out to the violent energy of the storm.

And rather than fight it, I welcomed it in, turning that energy outward to repel the wind and snow, using its violence to create a peaceful haven. I let out a shuddering breath as even the bond between

Bryn and me flickered awake; it'd been so fragile after what we went through that I'd insisted we keep our minds shuttered, lest we snap that fragile bridge that I relied on so much. But it was strong again, and the wave of affection and pride that he sent my way felt like coming up for air.

Colagh whistled, impressed by my display. He shook his shoulders, like shaking off the burden of what he'd been doing, and the temperature rose inside the bubble, his spirit glowing like the heart of a fire. "Impressive, Conduit," he said, his lyrical words muffled in our enclosure.

Tanjiu muttered under their breath, and the horses calmed. I marveled at the way they spoke, moving their hands in the air as they told the horses a story, the Ambience flowing from their body to the animals, instilling them with peace.

I still couldn't quite grasp *how* their affinities worked. I'd seen it in Sam, the vault of knowledge and memories that he was, but it was such an intangible concept that I'd assumed all Tethers with affinities were the same. Watching the Vorthes, however, had opened my eyes to what it must have been like before the Scourge. Colagh's spirit was tied to the elements volatile as fire or lightning, and Tanjiu could sway even the most dangerous beast, their spirit soothing and gentle.

Pearl, in all her muscled, intimidating glory, channeled her power most easily into her combat prowess. Somewhat like Bryn, able to augment her strength or speed or agility, but with an eye for strategy and a sense for danger that lurked outside of what most could feel. But Paerna, the bald man with a constant smile and air of mischief about the eyes, remained a mystery. He was a Tether as well, and had utilized his power to aid Colagh many times over the past week when the former's strength waned. But if he had an affinity for anything, I hadn't seen it yet.

Hello beautiful, Bryn thought, interrupting my musings. I smiled inwardly, just for him. *I've missed you.*

Me too, I purred back. I felt wildly light-hearted, so light that I could throw myself into the storm and float away.

You're radiant, he told me. *The only light in the darkness.*

That's the Ambience. I rolled my eyes, though I appreciated his thoughts. And he knew it.

Not just *the Ambience.*

What do you think of our traveling companions? Without our mental dialogue, there had been precious few moments we could be sure we weren't overheard since leaving Stalth. And one of those had been a hushed meeting of lips and bodies in the forest. I blushed, recalling those stolen moments.

Bryn luxuriated in them with me, and then he locked them away, focusing on my question. He looked at the Vorthes, at the casual flick of Paerna's hand to hurl a large stone from our path, and Tanjiu's hushed murmur to Hunter's horse when he tossed his head at the sudden movement.

I feel surrounded again, he said simply.

Hunter glanced over his shoulder at Paerna, the same distrust plain in the scowl on his face.

It's unnerving, I admitted. But I also had to admit to myself that I was fascinated watching them. *I've wanted to meet people like me my whole life, but I never imagined it would be so dangerous.*

If they try anything, we'll stop them. Complete confidence. But it wasn't just confidence in himself, or in us together. It was a confidence in me, and all that I could do on my own. I flashed him a smile as the wind howled in muffled fury outside of our refuge.

The storm didn't abate, and even my strength began to wane, keeping such a large group shielded for so long, even using its own fury to fuel my efforts.

"I need to stop!" I called. Hail stones the size of cherries hammered into the shield, and I felt each one in the pit of my stomach.

"In the trees," Bryn said, pointing to the edge of the Esteweld to our right, off the main road. "We can take shelter in there."

Tanjiu whistled, and the horses trotted to the break that Bryn indicated in the tree line. The bubble flickered around us, a burst of cold air fluttering our cloaks in a mad dance before Colagh held a hand behind us to keep it back.

Bryn took the lead, guiding us between the trunks until the canopy was thick overhead. There wasn't much room to maneuver the horses, but Tanjiu kept them from panicking as we dismounted. Finally under cover, I pulled my power back, and the wind roared in my ears. The Ambience slid away, and I closed my eyes to keep a tear from shedding. Would it come back to me when I needed it?

Tanjiu tended the horses, our small herd following them further into the trees as the rest of us prepared tents, a fire, and a shelter above our heads of woven tree branches. The Vorthes followed suit, and soon there was a natural ceiling overhead that would keep the worst of the precipitation out of our camp. Indeed, the patter of hail stones continued throughout the meal that Hunter cooked, stopping only as he ladled hot stew—mushrooms, potatoes, and chicken with tomatoes and bay—into tin bowls.

Bryn and I sat on a log near the fire, trying to soak in the warmth. Colagh spread out a thick blanket on the ground next to us and groaned as he pulled his cloak tighter, sitting with his back to our log seat.

"How does anyone survive such infernal cold?" he demanded.

"Some don't," Bryn grumbled. "You could always keep yourself warm with your power."

"If I wasn't exhausted, I would," Colagh replied.

Dinner was a silent affair, and we were all too eager to find our bedrolls soon after. Pearl sat in the opening of the Vorthe tent, and Bryn guarded ours. None of us wanted to leave them unsupervised for long.

Sam was snoring when I climbed beneath my blankets with Bryn hugging his knees next to my head. Hunter paused next to him and stared at Pearl. She stared back, her face impassive and yet still mistrustful, before turning her watchful gaze to the forest around us.

"I still can't believe they're all Tethers," Hunter growled. I chuckled, but there was no humor in it. "How does this situation keep getting worse?" He scrubbed his hand over his face. "I should have stayed on the ship."

"Well, you're stuck with us now," Bryn said, and clapped a hand on Hunter's shoulder. "We'll watch them, and if they turn on us, they'll regret it."

"Any one of them could be Derth's spy," Hunter muttered. His face twisted into a snarl. "We should do this on our own. It would be better than watching our backs morning and night."

"We've been through this already," I whispered. They know where we're going."

After a glance Pearl's way to ensure we wouldn't be overheard, I leaned close to whisper to them. "I showed Bryn a few things I saw from Derth. At first, it felt like he put them there, and then..." I shook my head, "I don't think he wanted me to see. But, what's important are the things he *wanted* to show me." I described the images for Hunter, who frowned and shrugged, as lost as I was.

"I don't know anywhere like that," he said.

"Neither do we," I said with a glance at Bryn. "If he wants me to find him, he's going to have be more explicit." I snuggled deeper into my bedroll. "I'm going to sleep. Wake me for my watch," I reminded Bryn. "Don't let me sleep through the night, I feel just as tired if *you're* exhausted."

"Yes, love," he said. He leaned over to kiss my forehead and tuck my hair behind my ear. I leaned into his palm and kissed the heel of his hand.

Safe and warm, I drifted off, listening to Bryn and Hunter's whispering voices.

A gentle shake woke me some time later, and Hunter mumbled that it was my turn before plopping down next to Sam. I rubbed the sleep out of my eyes and scooted out of my bedroll, trying not to jostle a sleeping Bryn on my way out of the tent.

It was freezing outside, and I shivered as I pulled my wool gloves on and wrapped my cloak tight around me. Across the banked fire, Tanjiu sat at the opening of their tent, and nodded to me in greeting. I nodded back, yawning so wide my jaw cracked. I missed the warm confines of Sam's house in Stalth more and more.

Tanjiu rose and walked over to me, waving a hand around their body, ending with a gesture toward the embers in the fire pit. The embers flared to life, casting low, flickering light on the campsite. After placing a log on the fire, they moved next to the tent flap, and, after lifting a questioning brow at me and waiting for my nod of approval, enveloped me in the warmth they'd conjured for I "May I?" they asked, indicating the ground next to me.

"All right," I said, watching them warily as they sat. Their calming presence soothed the raw edges of that wariness, but I held it tight around me, lest they push me into complacency with their affinity. I had no idea how well it worked on humans.

"I don't think we'll ever get used to this weather," they sighed.

"I gathered as much, since it's all Colagh can talk about."

Tanjiu chuckled, their big white teeth flashing in the firelight. "Yes, he is the most sensitive to the cold, which is interesting, considering his affinity for the elements." They paused, and I could see them weighing their next words before they said, "I wonder if I might ask you something personal?"

"I suppose," I replied. I wasn't sure I wanted to say anything personal to them, fearing they might use it against me.

"When this is over, and we've either apprehended Derth or destroyed him, what comes next for you? Will you continue to guard the sea against my people's presence? Or is there something greater on your horizon?"

A test, or an honest question, I wondered. Was this a friendly attempt to elicit some information from me? I shook off their aura, and they blinked several times, as if they hadn't been aware they were exuding it. Or they weren't aware that I could refuse it. I was careful in my response. "As long as there is a threat to my people, I want to be there to help stop it."

Tanjiu smiled as if I'd given the right answer. "Such a large task for one ship, for one Conduit. The ocean is vast; how can you hope to cover every path between our two nations?"

"We can't," I said. My hackles rose at the question. Were they threatening us? Were they warning about something? "But I'll do what I can, and so will my crew."

"What if I told you that there is a much bigger threat than the slavers?" they asked. "A threat that hangs over us all, and has indeed been driving the efforts that you hope to thwart?"

Confused, I frowned. "What do you mean?"

"My home is riddled with pockets of Ambience with no direction, something we call the Gloom. Every year it spreads, and every year we lose people—entire cities—to its chaos. The slavers are a product of this chaos; as our leaders scramble to defend the continent, there are those that exploit their lack of attention."

I snorted. "You're telling me that Vortheim doesn't condone slavery, but I have a hard time believing that. Ships fly *your* colors, carrying people in cages like cargo. There has been nothing but conflict between Vortheim and Trylia for as long as most Trylians can remember, so why would I think the slavers are anything less than a way to slowly degrade my country? The only intention I can see from your leaders is to keep us living in fear, to weaken us so that we can't mount any kind of attack on Vortheim."

Tanjiu listened calmly while I spoke, a frown of concern wrinkling the skin on their cool beige forehead. I continued, the volume of my words rising as I became more agitated. "I don't understand why you haven't just destroyed us by now. It seems like you have plenty of Ambient, and plenty of ships that could bring you here. We would be helpless in the face of that. What are you waiting for?"

"If there is a plot to destroy Trylia, I don't know of it." Mild horror, open honesty. At least, that's what I read on their face.

I scoffed at them, shaking my head in disbelief. "That doesn't mean there *isn't* one."

"That's true, I suppose. I'm hardly in a position to know such things, if our leaders were plotting against yours. I *do* know that there is enough trouble at home that to think of invading another continent would be madness."

"And why the abductions of Ambient?" I demanded. "Derth chased me across Trylia, convinced that he had to capture or kill me, so that he could either deliver me somewhere or keep word of my existence from reaching someone. The Malachi? Someone with the position and power to inspire such fear in someone like Derth. Add to that the fact that the Malachi has sent all of you after him, and it feels like the pieces are coming together."

They stared at me for a long moment, and then sighed. "I don't know. What you say is true; the Malachi has a special interest in Derth. But we had no knowledge of his task here, only that he must be found." Their voice took on a hint of a pleading edge. "There have been Malachis in the past that believed they needed to concentrate the Ambience in Vortheim to combat the Gloom, and one of them sent agents here to do just that, long ago." I thought of Sam and worked very hard to keep myself from glancing into the tent where he slept. "Those agents never returned, and that theory died with them." They shook their head. "If that old theory has resurfaced, it is not common knowledge. But I can assure you, that is *not* what we were sent here to do."

"So why are you interested in my plans?" I asked. "Are you hoping to convince me to let your ships have free rein near our shores?"

They shook their head again, their tight curls springing around the crown of their head. "No. But I was wondering whether you might be persuaded to pursue the larger threat to us all."

"The Gloom?" I asked. Tanjiu nodded. "Why would I help Vortheim overcome something that is keeping its attention from us? Or Friga, or Saurboro? Why would I do anything to help when all I've known of Vortheim is violence?"

"Because the Gloom doesn't care where we hail from. It is indiscriminate in its destruction, and Colagh tells me that Derth is using it to control people."

A shiver ran up my spine as more pieces fell into place in my head. The unbridled Ambience I'd felt in the prison, that had destroyed the spirit funneling it back into the Pool, *that* was the Gloom? And Derth was unleashing it *here*?

"How?" I asked. "How do we stop it?"

Tanjiu turned to gaze into the fire, and I could see the fear and desperation plain on their face. "We don't know," they admitted. "And that is why we are afraid. Colagh told us that you are a Conduit, that you did...*something* in the prison to stop the Gloom before it truly condensed." They turned to face me, desperate and afraid. And...hopeful. "Would you at least consider the possibility that your destiny might reach beyond what you know? That you might have a greater purpose, to protect more than *your* people?"

I stared at them, unsure of what I should say, what I *could* say. The path they'd laid out before me was vast and unknown, leading directly to a place that I'd always associated with death and grief. After a time, they went back to their tent and curled up inside, leaving me to watch over the camp on my own. My instincts still screamed that I shouldn't trust Tanjiu and the others, that they were dangerous. But now there was another voice in the back of my head, asking whether it was instinct or prejudice.

The morning dawned cold and cloudy, but the blizzard had passed, leaving our patch of the forest closed off and serene compared to the maelstrom of the night before. We continued our journey, hoping we wouldn't be slowed again. If not, we should arrive at Salava within the week.

Anxiety blossomed in my stomach as I thought about what we might find there, after how difficult Stalth had proven to navigate. I hadn't been to the town, but Sam assured me that it was nowhere near the size of Stalth, and the number of people living there would be limited. Would he be there? If he'd moved on, would we find any indication of where he'd gone?

Add to that Tanjiu's words from the night before, and my mind was a mess of burgeoning possibility and a crushing weight of obligation. My lack of knowledge about what we might face irked me; this was too like my childhood, as I wrestled with my nature amid a world of ignorance on the subject. I knew I couldn't find the answers by playing the questions in my head again and again, but I didn't like feeling helpless.

One thing at a time, I decided. First, we would finish what had started the day the *Catherine* was lost. Then, I would pay back Derth for all the torment, for the months of running for my life.

And this time, *I* was hunting *him*.

CHAPTER TWENTY-NINE

I'd never felt so cold in my life. Every day we moved further north, and it felt like every step brought us closer to the heart of winter. We had thankfully avoided any more snowfall, but the frigid air cut through me like a knife, never relenting.

The land rose into the rocky foothills at the feet of the mountains that served as Trylia's northern border. Their silhouettes dotted the distance, the white snowcaps mimicking the clouds overhead. The trees of the Esteweld Forest that we camped in every night were older this far north, and I felt certain that there was something watching me from the depths of the shadows beneath the canopy. Whether it was the ghost of frantic flights through the trees, or the actual spirits of the forest itself, I couldn't tell.

We passed a few frozen farms, and Sam gazed ahead, the only one of us to have visited Salava before. "We'll arrive before nightfall," he announced on the morning of the sixth day after the blizzard. "Over the next rise, the land slopes into a valley where Salava Deep lies. So-named because it is the deepest body of fresh water on the continent; there are even fables that say it reaches all the way to the Ambient Pool. The town is at the southeast shore."

Hunter smirked at me as Sam droned on about the formation of the town. Always the teacher, waiting for the right moment to bestow some piece of knowledge onto us. But I smiled when Hunter turned back around; if Sam was feeling himself again, to the extent that he couldn't pass up the opportunity to teach us something new, I was grateful. He'd been too quiet for too long after Stalth.

"Elders," Colagh cursed, "it's like I've stepped foot on Friga again."

"You've been to Friga?" I asked. I'd only heard stories about the continent far to the north of Trylia, and only in the context of the most luxurious furs, beautiful gemstones, and little else. But the oceans that far north were often blocked by massive sheets of ice, making the passage dangerous and rare.

Colagh nodded with a frown. He shivered again, and this time his entire body looked like it was trying to shake off the memory of the cold. "I do *not* recommend it."

"Not everyone has the luxury of living in a tropical paradise," Hunter called.

Colagh looked over his shoulder and winked. "Perhaps you will grace us with your presence in the future, and I can show you around. One look at our crystal waters in the port of Lacorsia, and you'll never want to leave."

Cresting the rise a short time later, I looked down at the ice-covered body of water that gave the town its name in the distance. Running to the east and south were large, roaring rivers, wide enough to halt eastern travel if not for the rafts large enough to hold a horse and wagon. Huge wooden devices floated side-by-side on the eastern edge of the south river, and I could just make out the shape of another moored to the southern shore of the east river.

And nestled between the arms of the rivers, in an oblong oval that followed the curve of Salava Deep itself, was the town of Salava. Squat homesteads dotted the fields surrounding the city, and tall stone buildings rose from a wide space in the center of town.

We trotted down the slope to the wide riverbank where one of these rafts waited for anyone who needed to cross. No one was in attendance, and as we dismounted, looking around for some way to reach our destination, Hunter and I passed discerning eyes over the raft itself.

Our group was too large to take all of us at once, but wide enough to bring our horses along if we took it in turns to work along the river. Two long, thick cables of twisted rope as thick as my arm were anchored to long posts well back from the shore, and passed through steel loops atop pillars buried deep in the river's edge. They passed through similar loops attached to the raft at the forward and aft corners, and then disappeared beneath the water.

Hunter and I shared a look. "Pulleys on the riverbed?" I asked, excitement raising the corners of my mouth.

He nodded slowly, his own answering smile on his face. "I'm steering," he claimed.

I rolled my eyes. "I'm the better helm and you know it." I shoved my arm against his, smirking at his begrudging laugh as he pushed his curls off his face.

"Yeah," he said, "and you're probably not strong enough to pull us across anyway." My mouth dropped open in mock indignation. "Let the men handle it, little Lila."

This time I punched him for using my childhood nickname, the one only he had dared use. "Ass," I muttered.

"When you two have finished," Sam called, "I'd like to get across the river."

"Sorry Sam," we called together, and laughed aloud.

In the end it took three trips to get everyone across, because the Vorthes were useless when we tried to explain how to pull ourselves across the river and how to use the rudder to steer. Hunter and I took everyone across, with Tanjiu steadying the horses on each trip, leaving little space for the skittish beasts with so many people aboard.

The current was strong, but after much strain and no small amount of cursing, we were all safely on the other side of the river, able to continue on past the snow-covered fields toward the city proper. The mountains loomed beyond the town and the Deep, foreboding in their silent vigil, as if they had stood for centuries to guard something secret, safe within their roots of stone. Like the barrier that hid Sam's cabin from the rest of the continent, and I wondered what might be tucked away there, if anything.

The homesteads we passed were cheerful by comparison, even at this time of year. We didn't see anyone, but there was evidence of life in the flicker of candlelight beyond the windows, and the smell of woodsmoke rising from the chimneys. Cows, sheep, goats, and horses lowed at us from the safety of their barn when we passed, and our horses nickered back in greeting.

We arrived at the outskirts of Salava to a chorus of voices raised in agitation, bordering on outright anger. The sound carried throughout the town, along the ordered streets. The stables were deserted, aside from the horses that stuck their heads out of the stalls when Bryn called out. Their large ears flattened back onto their heads as the commotion rose to a new height.

"Let's tie the horses here," Bryn suggested as he dismounted. "Tanjiu, would you get them settled while we find out what's happening?"

Colagh made eye contact with all three of his companions, who nodded in reply as they dismounted. The creak of my leather saddle matched the creak in my back after fighting the current as I swung my leg over and dropped down, just as the commotion reached a fever pitch in the center of town. Tanjiu gathered the animals and walked them into the stable after a nervous glance over their shoulder.

Following Bryn and Hunter, I strained to see the crowd beyond them as we emerged from the street, into the square packed with bodies. People shouted and I tried to pick out individual words, but they were swallowed by the rest. All were clad in thick woolen cloaks, mittens, and hats, but most didn't seem to notice the cold; they were too busy shouting and crying. Until one woman ascended to a platform that displayed her above the throng. The crowd fell as silent as they could, considering they were on the verge of becoming an unruly mob.

Her black hair flowing around her in the steady wind, the woman spread her arms wide and waited for the voices to quiet. When she spoke, her voice was deep, husky, and authoritative. I felt an instant calming of my nerves as she projected an aura of control in this chaotic situation, though I sensed it wasn't the Ambience, just a natural ability to bring order to chaos. The effect must have been widespread, because even the most raucous voices silenced when she began to speak.

"We are all afraid, and angry," she said, "but now is the time that we need to come together. The infighting must stop. Even now, our fastest riders are on their way to Stalth and King's Port to ask for aid in our time of need. Rest assured; we *will* get our people back. We *will not rest* until the man who did this is found and brought to justice. And if any harm has come to the people he took, our justice will have no mercy."

"Harm?" a woman shouted, somewhere near the front of the crowd. "He took my *son*!"

"And my mother!" a younger voice called.

"There's been plenty of harm already!" the first woman shouted. "It's bad enough that we're suffering, not knowing what's happened to them. Now we have to wait for the crown to do something? You told us to be patient while you searched, but they've already been gone for *weeks!* It's time we went after them!"

A murmur of consensus drowned out the woman standing above the rest, who, despite her outward appearance of calm authority, had a bone-deep fatigue etched into her features when the chaos started again. She raised her arms, and that flash of weariness was gone. "I am meeting with the captain of the guard and the town council as soon as this crowd is dispersed, to decide what further action we will take now that the roads are clear enough to send riders out. Please, return to your homes, your places of business, and try to live your lives, so that we have a home to bring our people back to!"

Grumbles followed her words, but the fringes of the crowd began to disperse. Soon, the rest followed suit, as the woman watched on, her shoulders sagging a fraction with the relief I imagined she felt.

When all but a handful of people were left, our group approached the woman, who was now back on the ground, turning to address those that were left. She stood taller than me, her body thick with muscle beneath her heavy indigo wool dress. She looked in our direction with a wary, but curious expression.

She held her hand up to stall the words coming from a man much shorter than her, the top of his coppery head a bit lower than my shoulders, standing beside her. "Hello, travelers," the woman said. "It's a bit early in the season for anyone to visit. What brings you to Salava?"

Sam stepped forward with a smile. "We have been sent by the king to track down a dangerous criminal, who we heard may have come this way. I think we may be able to help you and your people."

The assembly around the woman all stopped their hushed conversation and stared at us, the shorter man sizing us up and not liking what he saw, if his sneer was any indication. The woman's features shifted slightly, still wary, but now full of hope kept under tight rein.

"I think you'd better come to my office," she said. She whispered something to the group, the short man scowled at us, and then she walked to the far end of the square, to the oak door in a wood-paneled building.

This wasn't an official office, like the Bastion in Stalth, but rather the foyer presented as a sitting room, complete with two small beige sofas and a hearth. We followed the woman past a young man who nodded at her with a small murmured, "Mayor," and then into a wooden staircase that angled up to a second floor. It opened onto a large room with a door at the far end.

Broad bay windows let the light into the open space, with a polished wooden desk to our left with a smaller window behind it. The mayor walked to the desk, gesturing to the chairs close to the window that faced the room. A cushioned chair sat on the side closest to us, positioned so that when the shades were drawn, the mayor could look out onto the square when she was at her desk.

"Please, take a seat."

"After being in the saddle for so long," Bryn said with a small smile, "I'd prefer to stand, if that's all right with you."

"Of course," she replied, making no move to take her own seat. "I'm feeling a bit too rattled to sit, anyway. Now, let's discuss your presence here."

We recounted the story as we'd told it to Stalth's captain, complete with writ to provide some proof of our claim. Colagh listened in silence, only interjecting that he'd been sent from Vortheim when questioned about his involvement. The mayor's eyes widened, the wrinkles in her brow deepening, ending with Derth's description.

Nodding, she said, "I believe the man you're after was here. The description is a match, and the way people have been behaving around him..." She trailed off, took a deep breath, and started again. "I'm sorry, I haven't introduced myself. I'm Laonin Zalkin, mayor of Salava. We will provide whatever help you need, but if I could ask one thing?" I nodded, flashing an encouraging smile. "Assuming you find this man, could you also keep an eye out for our people? I will have my assistant provide a list of names and descriptions. I hope you find them in one piece. I can't imagine what will happen if they don't come back."

"We'll do what we can," I said. "But please, it would help if we knew where he might have gone. Can you tell us where we might start asking around?"

"Of course," she replied. "Start with my assistant, Galin. He's been compiling reports for me and might have a better idea who to ask. He should be back any time now, and if you'll excuse me, I have a council meeting to begin."

She left us alone in the office, and I strolled to the window to gaze down at the town. It was a pretty place, with the lake glittering in the distance, reminding me of the ocean. I spotted the short, copper-haired man that had scowled at us earlier speaking to a group still lingering in the square. They nodded, and then the man turned and walked at a fast clip across the square. He took a few running steps, then collected himself and slowed his pace to a quick march before he disappeared into the door opening below us.

The mayor's voice drifted up the stairs, warning Galin of our presence and asking him to follow her once he finished with us. His high-pitched voice answered in the affirmative, and the door slammed shut as footsteps rushed up the stairs.

He was panting when he reached us, the scowl on his face again as he looked us over. "My name is Galin. The mayor has asked me to provide you with a list of our missing people and aid your search for more information." He pulled out a chair from the small table and took a seat, removing a piece of paper from the stack, along with a quill, which he dipped in an inkwell.

The quill scratched across the paper, stopping to dip into the ink after every few words, as Galin continued to speak. "About a dozen citizens left before the first snow fell, nearly two months ago. They took two wagons and a handful of horses, as well as a fair amount of provisions. They headed east, past the farmlands, and took the ferry to the eastern road." Every sentence was clipped, as if he'd recited these details before and had long since grown weary of them. "There are several families of the people taken from here, and they might have seen or heard something relevant."

Every word from his lips sounded like an accusation. I took an instant dislike to the man from the tone of his voice and the condescending looks he shot from the corner of his eye while he wrote. When the list was finished, he blotted the ink and held the paper out. Sam took it and scanned the list, pursing his lips in a way that told me he was impressed. If I never saw another list in my life after this, I'd thank the Elders for it. I dreaded the thought of repeating our actions in Stalth, only to strike out on our own again.

"This is thorough," he said. "Thank you for providing us with their locations, as well. That will help expedite our search."

"Of course," Galin said, giving Sam a simpering smile. "Unfortunately, I don't have much else to offer in the way of information. He came to town with a grizzled older gentleman and left with many more of our rougher sort. Looked like he was assembling quite the small army."

"Wonderful," Hunter grumbled.

"Indeed," Galin intoned. "If there is anything else you require, you may find me here during daylight hours. Any emergency you might have after the sun sets, you may direct it to the guards. Now," he said, rising from his chair, "if you'll excuse me, I need to get to the meeting as well. Good luck in your search." He pulled a few books into a satchel slung on the back of his chair, pulled the strap over his head to rest on his shoulder, and hustled downstairs.

I waited until I could see him on the street below before I let out an irritated breath. Turning to Hunter and Bryn, I said, "I'd rather not have to speak with him again."

"Must be hard to look down your nose at so many people that tower over you," Hunter chuckled. Bryn let out a bark of laughter, surprised by Hunter's joke. Sam scoffed as he continued to study the paper in his hands. "Looks like Derth's been busy."

"Wonderful," Hunter repeated in a grumble. "Just what we need, a madman with an army, and way too much power."

"Yes, it never ends well, in my experience," Colagh said. When everyone's eyes turned to him, he shrugged. "I've dealt with a few fanatics and demagogues in my time," he said. "True, the loyalty of their followers was their choice, but their influence drives people, and sometimes leads to violence. It ends poorly for the followers, while the leaders escape unscathed, and move onto the next group that they can manipulate."

"I hope that this time, it ends poorly for the leader," I said. "Let's go talk to some of the families."

Some of the locals were still clustered outside as we huddled around Sam to decide where to start. I caught a few glares leveled in our direction but thought nothing of it until the group came closer. Bryn looked up and straightened when he saw them. One burly woman clutched her fist to her chest in a sign to ward off evil, and more townsfolk appeared from the streets on either side of the square.

There had to be at least thirty people surrounding us now, armed with long knives, sticks, clubs, even rocks in their hands.

"Outsiders," a man called, stepping through the crowd to take a stand at the front. It was the same man who'd criticized the mayor. "We heard you're with that monster, that you're here to take more people away." He pointed at us. "We can't let that happen."

CHAPTER THIRTY

Hunter put himself in front of the rest of us, closest to the man who'd spoken. There was a loose circle formed around us now, with a few feet of space separating us from the angry mob.

"We're here to help," Hunter said, his most charming smile on his face. His eyes moved from person to person, trying to connect with someone, to have his voice heard. I'd seen him talk his way out of plenty of bar fights and street brawls, but this felt different. "We were sent by King Demetrius himself to stop the criminal that took your people. We have a writ to prove it, which we've shown to the mayor already."

The man leading the mob shook his head, a feral smile on his face. "Papers can be forged. And having the mayor's ear could make it easier to take our people. We need action, not more words."

Hunter didn't falter. "We feel the same way, but before we head off in a random direction past the river, we hoped to have more information. Someone here must know more than they've told us; about where the man was heading, where he was taking your family members." A bead of sweat trickled down the back of Hunter's neck as he spoke. He felt the malice surrounding us as well as I could, like we were in the eye of a hurricane, waiting for the storm to take us.

The Ambience roiled beneath the surface of my skin, and I said a silent thanks to the spirits for coming to me when I needed them. They'd been so quiet lately... The hatred of the gathered crowd rolled over us like a fog. It was the same blind hatred I'd felt from Cass, Norin, and the man in the street. But as I looked around, I saw no black tendrils on anyone, no sign of Derth on them.

"How can we trust anything you say, when you have Vorthe slavers with you? The whole country is filled with people like that monster," he pointed to the east, the vague direction we knew Derth had gone. "No," he shook his head, drawing his long knife from his belt, "you're just as guilty as he is."

He lunged forward, and Hunter darted to the side as he drew his short sword. In one last desperate attempt to avoid violence, he slapped the dagger aside and called out to the crowd. "If you kill us, your only chance to get your families back will be gone!"

"No more lies!" a woman screamed.

Chaos erupted around us as the people charged. I pulled *Desire* in time to deflect a club aimed at my face. Bryn brandished dirk and sword, and Colagh stood in the middle, the Ambience surrounding him.

"Colagh," I shouted, "don't!"

"I can't allow them to stop us, my dear," he replied, the face of calm in an angry sea. His arms raised on either side of him, palms outward, toward the surrounding crowd. I took a step back, out of reach of another knife blade, my back close to Colagh's side.

"They're just *people*," I urged. "And they don't know about us. Please!"

"In my home, we do not allow *Stills* to interfere with Ambient." He sneered the word Still. "They should be taught a lesson."

Wind kicked up in the square, a torrent of air that whipped my hair around my face. Colagh's spirit became the wind, an angry dark cloud. The people all around slowed, buffeted so that they couldn't move forward. Bryn and Hunter were caught in it, both yelling something I couldn't hear over the howl in my ears.

"Stop!" I shouted, but Colagh chuckled. "*Bryn!*" I screamed, in my head and my mind. *Help me, I can't stop him on my own!*

He didn't say anything, but his spirit reached out...

And we placed our hand on Colagh's outstretched arm. He glanced at us, tried to shrug our grasp off, but we clutched tighter. Spirits swarmed around us in a massive host, finally catching Colagh's attention.

"*Stop,*" we commanded, letting the spirits smother the influx of power Colagh drew. The wind died, and the crowd jerked forward. And then, in the glare of light that blazed in Lila's eyes, we saw an orb. Derth's dark aura poured from it, invisible tethers tying it to every person lifting weapons to strike us down.

We slapped our hands together in the direction of the orb, smashing it between hundreds of spirits' hands, and the tethers disappeared. Our bodies turned to face Colagh as one, and his eyes widened.

"What are you?" he asked, his eyes darting between our bodies.

"You must stop," we said. The Ambience drained out of us.

I blinked at Colagh, who looked terrified, before turning to the crowd. All of them stood, confused, as if they had no idea what they were doing. Their weapons fell to their sides as they looked around at us, and at each other.

Bryn stepped up to the leader and pulled the knife out of his hand. The man let him, looking at the knife like it would bite him if he moved too quickly. "Why did you come after us? Why did you think we were working with the monster?" His tone was firm but gentle, and the man gazed at him, his eyes pained and apprehensive.

"Galin told us you were part of it, that you'd take more people if we didn't stop you." His voice and posture were heavy, like he was trying to wake from a bad dream and hadn't quite managed yet. "I wanted to make you talk, to make you take us to him, but then I got so angry. I couldn't stop myself, I tried..." he shook his head, "I tried to kill you, and I brought all these people with me to do it. I'm so sorry."

"It's not your fault," Bryn said as he clapped a hand on the man's shoulder. He looked at me, and I nodded at him. "I think we'll speak with Galin."

"He was headed for home. I'll wring his neck when I see him."

"It would hurt more to tell the mayor what he's done," I told him. "But we'll make sure he gets what's coming to him. Can you tell us how to get there?" I asked. A nod.

The crowd dispersed, the man who'd led them speaking to small clusters before they wandered out of the square. Bryn walked to my side and grasped my hand, as Colagh looked on, his face still a mask of fear.

His house was near the dock, two stories tall, shadowing the houses around it. Wide windows looked over Salava Deep. The shingles on the roof were new, and the wooden siding had a fresh coat of white paint, much cleaner than the others in the neighborhood. Small things, but noticeable for the stark contrast between this home and the others. Salava wasn't the small town I'd imagined, a small village like Mountain's Shade, where the people did their best to maintain their homes, but didn't have a guild of carpenters and masons like King's Port that had trained all their lives to do so. So it was odd that this home in particular rivaled the grand homes I'd seen there.

Part of the house on the ground floor looked as if it had been added to the rest of the house, with fresh tool marks on the unpainted wall facing the neighboring house and large river rocks being fitted into mortar on the adjacent wall.

More suspicious looks followed us to the door, as the man and woman constructing the rock face watched us approach. Hunter flashed them a friendly smile, to which they nodded, but didn't return the expression. Bryn knocked on the door. After a few moments, scuffling footsteps approached, and Galin called out.

"What is it *now*?" he demanded, clearly irritated by the intrusion.

For a moment before the door opened, I wondered whether he'd seen us approaching. But the surprise on his face when he opened the door, followed immediately by the fear widening his eyes and making him take a step back, made me realize that we were the last people he'd expected.

He hadn't intended for us to survive, then. "Surprised to see us, Galin?" Hunter asked, a predator facing its prey. I glanced at the pair that had stopped working to watch our exchange intently, wondering whether they would defend him if it came to that. Bryn half-turned toward them, sensing my disquiet. "Perhaps that's because you sent an angry mob after us?" Despite the hard stare, Hunter still sounded like he was asking Galin if he'd like to join us for lunch.

"I-I..." Galin stammered. He swallowed hard, and then his mouth fell open as he began to panic, his eyes darting from Bryn's face to mine. They paused on Colagh, and then looked at the workers outside as if pleading for their help. "I... angry mob?" He shook his head, swallowing hard. "I don't know about an angry mob. But, if you'll just let me get dressed, I can speak to the mayor and we can sort this out."

He started to close the door, but Bryn slapped his palm against the heavy wood with a resounding thud. Galin looked at the tense muscles in the hand above his head, and then back at Bryn.

Bryn growled his words. "Those people thought we were with *Derth*. Because *you* told them we were. Why would you do that?"

"Why don't we take this conversation inside?" Colagh suggested in his musical accent. "Unless you would like to also explain to the people of this town why you are trying to keep us from our investigation." He swept his hand in the direction of more people walking down the street, casting curious glances our way.

Galin stepped away from the door and let us file inside. He closed the door behind us, and then disappeared through a doorway leading deeper into the house. Bryn and Colagh followed on his heels, and as I rounded the same corner, I watched the small man scurry into the bright kitchen, toward a door that opened onto the back of the house. Bryn leapt forward, his body blurring to interpose himself between Galin and the door.

Galin slammed into Bryn's chest, blinked in confusion, and tried to back away. Unfortunately for him, Colagh was behind him, and Galin stepped on the Vorthe man's leather boots. He squeaked, realizing that he was trapped.

"Please," he begged, trying to pivot in a different direction. "I didn't mean any harm." He came up short again, this time against his kitchen table. Unless he vaulted over or crawled under, he had nowhere to go.

Hunter stepped forward. "What did you do?" he asked. I watched him closely for a familiar slither of darkness, waiting for Derth to take control of him. But there was nothing; this man wasn't enthralled.

He hesitated, still looking for a way out. Hunter lazily pulled a knife from his belt and cleaned his fingernails with it. Galin's eyes widened at the implied threat, and squeaked again when Colagh clamped his hands on Galin's shoulders.

Tears fell from Galin's eyes. "I took some money to keep quiet," he sniffed. He sagged as if under the weight of terrible remorse. Bryn and Hunter narrowed their eyes, unconvinced. "It was either that, or he'd take me, too. I didn't report the complaints to the mayor, and when he left with everyone, I pointed everyone who went looking in the wrong direction. He told me he'd be watching me, to make sure I did what I was paid to do. That he would hurt me if I didn't."

That sounded like Derth, and he'd certainly been watching us. Maybe Galin *had* been forced to do what he did, the threats made to ensure that the sum he'd received was enough.

"Must have been a good amount of coin, judging by the state of your house," Hunter replied.

"Two hundred gold Aelios," Galin muttered. He hunched his shoulders, his hands in front of his chest as if to ward off an attack.

Hunter whistled, Bryn quirked an eyebrow, and even Colagh looked impressed. I couldn't believe how much money Derth had to give. But I realized that he could have compelled any or all of his followers to give him all the coin they had. Or steal what he wanted.

"That *is* a lot of coin," Hunter said. The corner of Galin's mouth quirked up in a small smile at their reaction. "I can see why a man might take that much for such a small job."

Galin nodded frantically. "Yes, that's more than I would see in twenty years in my position. And it wasn't such a bad thing that I did." His voice rose, as if he was trying to ask us whether his actions had been justified. "Those people left of their own free will. And I apologize for what happened today." He offered me a weak, pleading smile. "They were supposed to run you out of town. You were going to leave anyway, weren't you?" His shoulders rose to his ears in a shrug, his copper hairline damp from his nervous sweat.

"Sure," Hunter said. Understanding, consoling. But then his mask fell away to reveal the cold stare beneath. Galin blanched, and even I was taken aback. Wasn't this man a victim, of a sort? "Except for the fact that those people were set on killing us, not running us out of town. And the man you're helping, that you took a ridiculous amount of coin to assist, is probably going to kill the people he took." Galin's face fell. "And if he ever comes back here, there's no reason he wouldn't kill you, too."

Hunter scoffed. "You can stop acting like you're a victim. What I see is a man with a small amount of power, who wanted more. Derth couldn't hurt you if he wanted to use you to cover his tracks, but I'm sure he saw how easily you could be persuaded to do it."

Galin's entire demeanor changed; he straightened to full height, chin jutting forward and eyes hard above a fierce scowl. "I don't give information away for free," he snarled. Ever the expert in judging a person's character, Hunter flashed me a look that said, *I knew it.* "If you want to know where he was headed, it needs to be worth my while. Let's say fifty Aelios."

"What?" I asked, so angry that I almost forgot to keep a leash on the Ambience. My hands became blistering hot, and I shoved them behind my back to keep from raking them across his face.

But Hunter chuckled again. "What happened to being worried about retribution?" he asked. "If Derth was watching you to make sure you did as you were told." He glanced toward a window. "He could be watching right now."

Galin scoffed this time. "If he is, there's nothing he can do about it." Bryn and I shared a glance, but Galin didn't see it. "It's not like he left anyone behind, so the threat left with him. So," he said, a smug smile on his lips, "there's nothing stopping me from providing what you need. As long as the price is right."

"Elders curse you," I spat. "Is money all you care about? What about the people that were taken?"

"Like I said before, those people all left of their own free will. A bit of odd behavior doesn't change that. Maybe he paid them all to leave, if he was willing to give me so much to keep my mouth shut."

"Derth is not a normal criminal," Colagh added. "He is a master in the manipulation of people's minds. Capable of twisting anyone's thoughts to his will. Those people didn't leave because it was their choice. They left because it was *his* choice."

Galin's face twitched into a contrite frown. "I can see that I've not acted in the best interests of the citizens," Galin said, but his regretful tone was strained. "In light of that, perhaps we can settle on twenty Aelios, and call it even."

"Or," Bryn growled, "we can hand you over to the mayor and the guard, and ask you from a prison cell."

Galin looked at Bryn like he was a stupid child. I'd be impressed with his act if I didn't hate it so much. "Turn me in, and you'll never know where your criminal was headed."

Bryn stepped forward, hand on his dirk, but Hunter held him back. He pulled Bryn away, nodding for Colagh and me to follow. In a hushed voice, with his eye on Galin, he said, "We need to know what he knows. I believe him; if we turn him in, he'll never talk."

"Perhaps we can beat it out of him," Colagh suggested.

Bryn smiled, baring his teeth. But Hunter shook his head. "No, he'll just claim we had no cause, and *we'll* end up in prison. But maybe he'll see the wisdom in making a deal with us, to avoid prison so he can keep his gold."

"No," Bryn growled. "He can't get away with this."

Hunter clapped Bryn on the shoulder. "If we do it right, he won't."

Hunter turned back to Galin, whose arms were crossed over his chest as he watched us deliberate. "I can see that you're a shrewd negotiator, so I'd like to do you the courtesy of treating you as such. We can't move on in the most expeditious manner that we'd like unless you provide us the information you say you have. You can't afford to give that away for free, seeing as it's so important to us. And we can't waste time waiting for you to come to your senses in a prison cell."

Galin smiled like he'd already won as Hunter continued, pulling a few gold coins from his pocket. Not nearly twenty, but more than most people here would ever see at once. "An advance," Hunter said, holding his fist toward Galin as Bryn seethed, "and once you've told us what you know, you'll get the rest of your payment."

Galin considered him for a few long moments. Hunter wiggled his pocket, metal clinked on metal, and Galin nodded, smug. "I saw a map of the eastern cities and a chart of the coast. He only asked one other thing of me; he wanted a book of legends about the northern seas. With all the supplies they had, I'd say they're looking to settle on one of the larger islands off the northern coast. With that book in mind, I think I know which one. There's a legend about the haunted isle of the white spire, where the Gifted of old cursed the land and were banished from it. If anyone could brave such a thing, it would be him."

"And we're supposed to believe you?" I asked.

"You can believe me or not," Galin shrugged, "but it's what I saw. But a deal's a deal, and I don't want to see any retribution for my part. And to make sure you feel like I've held up my end, I'll give you one more thing. That criminal of yours didn't leave the same way he arrived. He lost a step while he was here. When he left, he was so weak, they had to help him into one of the wagons."

He held out a hand to Hunter, who smiled wide and reached into his pocket. But he paused before drawing anything out, and Galin's grin faltered. "Thank you, Galin, for that. As far as the rest of your payment is concerned, why don't we let you get a head start, and we'll call it even."

Galin lost his smile; first, replaced by a confused frown, and then red-faced rage. "We made a deal," he growled.

"It's a fair trade," Hunter insisted. "You see, the people that you tricked, that you've been lying to all this time, were on their way to the mayor to report what you'd done before we arrived. How long do you think it will take her to figure the rest out? You haven't been very subtle with your excess." He clicked his tongue, shaking his head in sad disapproval. Galin's face became so red that I thought he might faint.

"So you get to keep the gold that you earned by selling your people into slavery," Hunter spat, his mouth twisted with revulsion, "and you avoid prison here in Salava so that you can make whatever despicable life you can somewhere far from us. Because I promise you, as agents of King Demetrius, we will ensure that your name is spoken of in the same breath as the Vorthe slavers that plague us." Vicious pride filled me, watching Hunter spin his tale. And satisfaction at seeing this vile man realize he was in much more trouble than he'd thought.

Hunter leaned forward, and one word came out in a hiss. "*Run.*"

Galin stumbled when Colagh released him, and sprinted to the foyer and up the stairs. We waited for a few moments, listening to his thundering steps, slams and crashes of toppled furniture and décor, and then walked out of the house.

Bryn gave Hunter a nod, grim satisfaction plain on his face, too. But I let out a shaky breath, trying to rein in my outrage and a wave of relief. If we could believe Galin, this was finally information we could use to find Derth. And if he was going to an island, maybe he was still there. Maybe we had a chance to corner him. As angry as I was, I couldn't wait to tell Sam that we'd found him.

I couldn't wait to finally rid myself of Derth.

CHAPTER THIRTY-ONE

After braving another week of frigid wind and ever deepening snow, I smiled as First Port came into view through the trees. The entire city was built around the wide harbor; it wasn't enclosed like Stalth and King's Port, but rather sprawled along the coastline, only spreading inland when there was no more coastline to build upon.

The horses picked their way down the steep switchback road from the edge of the forest down to the edge of the city as Colagh removed the ice from their path to make the journey safer. I felt a momentary sense of vertigo as I looked down at the ocean.

"I hope the Lyrical Ship has clam chowder on the menu," Hunter said as his stomach rumbled. It was early afternoon, and we hadn't eaten much when we'd stopped to water the horses around midday. "They have the *best* chowder in Trylia, if Awnir is still the chef."

"Oh," I moaned, my mouth watering with even the pale memory of the taste. "Everything is better with bits of bacon in it. Maybe they'll have a fresh loaf of that crusty bread he bakes with garlic cloves."

"Yeah," Hunter said, leaning forward in his saddle. "And a few mugs of hot cider to go with it!"

"You two are making me hungry," Bryn grumbled. "That sounds too good to be true."

"It is," Hunter and I said at the same time. We laughed together, and it felt good. I felt optimistic as I gazed out at the ships anchored in the harbor, because I knew that it wouldn't be long before I felt the pitch of the ocean beneath my feet. Before we were one step closer to Derth.

"Perhaps we can discuss what you did in Salava's town square while we share a bowl." Colagh interjected, calling over his shoulder. My body tensed in response. We'd all been exhausted by our efforts to hold the cold and snow at bay so that we wouldn't waste any more time, and I'd always found a way to avoid Colagh until he was asleep for the night. To avoid exactly this conversation. "Both you *and* Bryn, in fact. Not many would have been able to command my power like that."

"What do you want to know?" I asked, trying to keep my tone even. "You know I'm a Conduit, sometimes I can do...interesting things."

Colagh turned a bit more in his saddle and narrowed his eyes. "Much of what you've done *should* be impossible. Being a Conduit explains some of that; you were able to undo what Derth did, at great cost to yourself, and I suppose it is *possible* that you could dampen a Tether's use of the Ambience. But, you should not be able to smother it completely, as if I were a novice child who had not undergone my Tethering ceremony. Bryn here should not be able to move as fast as he does without intervention by someone like us. And you should not be capable of tethering to another person. To share your power and be made more powerful because of it."

Sam stiffened in his saddle, and Bryn's hand went to the pommel of his dirk. My body tingled with fear and anticipation, and the spirits stirred around me.

We come.

I shook my head, trying to dispel the Ambience before it could overwhelm me, making me do something I might regret. There were too many of them to escape a confrontation unscathed. And, judging by the tension I felt in the air around me, the rest of the Vorthes were preparing themselves for a fight.

"What are you?" Colagh asked.

I shook my head again. "I don't know how to answer that question," I replied. "A Conduit, someone who doesn't know where she was born or who her people were. I don't *know* what that power is."

Colagh stared at me, his eyes still narrowed as he decided whether to trust me or not. He glanced at Bryn, at Bryn's hand grasping the hilt of his dirk, and then past me to the rest of his people riding behind us. When he turned around to face the direction we were heading, I let out a sigh of relief, released from his scrutinizing gaze.

"You are exactly the type of person—people—we are looking for in Vortheim." He held up a hand to forestall our predictable denial. "Before you start, I want you to know that we have no intention of abducting you. But the situation in Vortheim grows more dire by the day, and we could use all the help we can get. Tanjiu spoke to you of this."

"Even if what Lila encountered in the prison was something like the Gloom," Sam said, "It is not the same. You speak of great clouds that dwarf cities, that destroy everything in their paths."

Colagh smiled. "Yes, and Lila not only survived as one formed, she *stopped* it. Forced it back where it came from. Something that hasn't been seen in centuries. Long ago, when the Gloom first appeared, our Malachi was strong enough to keep it from spreading, to funnel some of the Ambience back to the Pool. But that ability was not passed down through the generations. He glanced over his shoulder at me. "People that can wield as much power as you would be an Elders-sent miracle."

"It seems like one person—no matter how powerful—wouldn't be able to do what hundreds or thousands of Ambient haven't," Hunter said. "Lila is great, but what can one person do against such a widespread problem?"

Tanjiu shrugged. "We don't know. But she brings hope we have been sorely missing," they said.

"Is that why slavers take people to Vortheim? In case you get lucky enough to find someone like Lila that you can force to fix Vortheim's problems?" Hunter snorted. "That seems like a complicated and unreliable system to me."

Colagh shook his head. "We have agents that search for Ambient all over Celuthia, but they are supposed to recruit them, to offer them incentives for joining us. And only if they prove themselves to be extraordinary in some way, as our Lila is."

He paused, his brow furrowed as he thought, oblivious to Bryn's scowl at the casual use of the phrase *our Lila*. When he looked back at me, I watched as some wall came down, exposing the pain beneath the confident façade he'd presented thus far. "As much as I hate to admit it, the same doubts that you have about the intentions of our leaders have gone through my head."

"So Derth *was* an agent for the Malachi," Bryn said.

"Yes," Colagh replied, "though his attachment to the slaver Roglin and his operation was not intended. I cannot share everything I know with you, but I can tell you this. We were told through the Malachi's representative that Derth was an asset for the Malachi. The hope was that with his affinity for influencing minds, Derth would be able to convince fellow Ambient to join our cause, even if they were reluctant to do so at first. We were sent to retrieve him because he sent word that he'd found someone powerful, someone he thought could help with the Gloom. But then he disappeared, and what little activity we heard about in Trylia suggested that he had no intention of delivering on his promise. And then he disappeared altogether, until our excursion here.

"I don't believe that we would have found him if we hadn't been following you, Lila. That he wouldn't have shown his hand without that enticement, mysterious as it still is to all of us." He chewed his lip, his eyes darting to me and away, like he was considering whether or not to tell me something.

Finally, he sighed. "The more I learn about Derth, the more I've wondered how such a monster came to work for us in the first place. The Malachi rules Vortheim, but each region is controlled by a Consul, an Ambient that reports directly to the Malachi and is charged with the welfare of the land and people in their region. They resolve disputes, they enforce the law, they combat threats caused by the Gloom. Each has their own agenda—what government official doesn't?—but until our visit here, I assumed that their pursuits were ultimately to the benefit of my country and its people. Now that we have seen some of the terrors visited upon a helpless Trylia for all this time, it makes me wonder whether the Consul did have our best interests at heart, or if they have become so corrupted by their own power that they sought to take more?"

The Vorthe's faces were grim as they listened to their leader talk, but they did not argue, and Colagh seemed confident in his assertions in front of them. Did that mean that they harbored similar doubts? I realized that I'd assumed speaking out against their superiors would be a punishable offense, something that might give a person pause before speaking such things aloud, but what did I really know about Vortheim?

"Perhaps it would be best if Derth never reaches Vortheim," Colagh said. He locked eyes with me, and then Bryn, who nodded.

We rode in silence after that, weighed down by our thoughts. The more I considered it, the more I wondered whether what I had thought was a simple matter of right versus wrong, Vortheim versus Trylia, was much more complicated than it seemed to be.

First Port was one of the oldest cities in Trylia, and I could see the history in the stones of the road, worn by countless feet, and in the creak of the wooden piers like a song over the waves crashing against the harbor wall. We passed through the newest construction at the outskirts of the town—including the stables where we left our tired horses to be pampered—and into the older sections of the city, where the stone buildings became more weathered and patinaed the further in we walked.

It wasn't long before we strolled through more familiar locales. Namely the long stretch of piers where boats were anchored for the winter, their sails furled like blankets tucked against the mast. Hunter and I had been through here many times aboard the *Catherine,* back when we were crewing a trading vessel. The city was the same, but so much had changed since I'd seen it last that it seemed like a lifetime ago.

Fortunately, the Lyrical Ship hadn't changed a bit; from the weather-beaten sign bearing a ship rocking back and forth in the wind like it would on the sea, to the broken lantern affixed to the right of the door frame. Even the clientele seated at the bar and the scarred tables were the same, including a broad-shouldered man with white-streaked black hair that looked up as the door opened to let the winter chill inside the warm confines.

Captain Morrig smiled as he stood, Kai and Roy flanking him with wide smiles. "Dear one!" he called before crossing the tavern floor in three long strides and gathering me into a firm embrace. "It warms my heart to see you! And so soon! It seems the winter cannot keep you from your path for long!"

"Kai!" Hunter smiled, clasping their shoulders before touching his forehead to theirs. "Back with us at last! I missed you, friend!"

The Vorthes filed in after us, and I shook my head, wishing I could keep my family separate from what we needed to do. Which was ridiculous, since they'd signed on to the Keepers, same as me. "You have no idea." I hugged Roy, and then turned to Colagh and the others, pointing them out as I introduced the two groups to each other. Tense handshakes were exchanged, Captain Morrig clearly concerned by their presence, as the others appeared confused. "Colagh and the rest are joining us in our search. They've come all the way from Vortheim on the Malachi's orders."

Before anyone asked any questions—or started throwing punches— Bryn intervened, exuding the calm reassurance that he was so good at. "We don't agree on much, but we agree that Derth is dangerous, and we can't do this without each other's assistance." It seemed to appease our friends, and then he turned to the Vorthes. "And we have their assurance that they don't intend to do anything more than collect Derth and leave, as King Demetrius allows."

Colagh smiled at him, bowed, greeted everyone warmly, and ushered his fellows toward a long table at the back of the tavern. After a few incredulous looks our way from Roy and Kai, we followed them. Hunter called for food and drink, and several of the servers winked at him in response.

Several rounds of ale, two bowls of delicious chowder, and two loaves of bread infused with rosemary and garlic later, and our entire journey from Coveton to First Port had been relayed. My head was swimming now, from exhaustion and alcohol, and I was ready to find a bed and sleep through the rest of the evening and the next day.

"So we're looking for an island that's not on the charts, that only exists in Trylian fables?" Captain Morrig asked.

"I think I've figured out which island we're looking for," Sam offered. "I can mark the charts once we're back on the ship, but I estimate it should take about three days to reach our destination barring any complications. That is assuming we are right about Derth's destination."

"If he's not where we think he is, we can search the other islands in the vicinity," Hunter replied. "Rogue's Island would be a good place for him." Bryn nodded in agreement.

"But how long will that take?" Colagh asked. "He could move on in the time it takes us to search. We know he can watch us from afar, he could know we're coming."

"We have to assume that he does," I said. "All of the thralls we've encountered have said the same thing. That they need to bring me to Derth. And if he knows we're coming, I expect him to stay put and prepare some sort of trap, rather than moving on."

Bryn shook his head, fear choking him at the thought of us walking into a trap. Of losing me. "Not going to happen."

"It won't," I replied, grasping Bryn's hand. I gave it a reassuring squeeze that did nothing to assuage his agitation. "Have you heard of anything strange while you've been here?" I asked the captain. "First Port was listed in the reports we thought pointed to Derth, but they happened more than six months ago. This was our best guess as to his destination, but we couldn't be sure he came this way."

"As a matter of fact," Kai said, "the ship that brought me here, one of the newest in our navy, was taken just after I got here a few weeks ago. It was slated to depart a few days after it did, so no one realized anything was amiss until the captain got here."

"The harbormaster recognized Derth from my description," Captain Morrig interjected, "said he got on with a group of civilians."

"An entire ship?" I asked. "Which one?"

"The *Bulwark*," he replied. My face paled, and Hunter let out a low groan.

Colagh glanced around the table. "What is the *Bulwark?*"

"*Bulwark* is our first man-of-war," Kai replied. "Two decks with ports made to function as arrow slits for archers—and a host of soldiers to use them—and two massive ballistae on deck that could pierce any hull and drag a ship under."

"We can take the *Celerity*," Hunter said, "but if the *Bulwark* is waiting for us, it might be a very brief trip."

"Elders' eyes," I cursed. "He has an entire warship now? *How* can he control so many people at once?" This was too much. It was too much *before* we faced the possibility of getting past such an obstacle.

"It seems his power was growing," Sam said.

"My fear is that he is harnessing the forces that created the Gloom," Colagh said. "And if he can do that, we need to figure out how." A fervor lit his eyes like nothing I'd seen in our months together. "Perhaps it's the key to the Gloom's destruction as well."

Tanjiu shot me a significant look. I sighed, exasperated and guilt-ridden. I empathized with their situation, but why did they have to pin their hopes on *me?* "I'll do what I can here, *if* it's the Gloom he's manifesting, but I'm not going to make any promises about the rest."

"Maybe it's not the best idea to involve us in Vortheim politics," Hunter suggested, a hard edge to his voice. Bryn's agitation had taken on a different focus; now, he was sizing up each of the Vorthes, ready to pounce if they so much as lifted a finger in my direction. I sent a soothing caress to him, but it came up against a hard wall of lethal intent. "You aren't even sure that *you* trust them, so why would we?"

"I trust the Malachi," Colagh countered. "And I know that even if the Consuls are corrupt—which I have no proof of, yet—most of my people are not. If there is *any* chance that you can help us, Lila..." He trailed off, his lips in a thin line. "You have my word that I will not try to force your hand, but if there is anything that you can do to help us, you would have an entire continent in your debt. Whether we could trust the Consulars with the knowledge that you exist..." He shook his head, his face full of bitter regret.

"I'll help you search for answers, Colagh," I said. "In whatever way we can that doesn't involve us going to Vortheim."

Colagh nodded, a look of gratitude in his eyes. "Let's get to the ship, then. We've kept Derth waiting long enough."

CHAPTER THIRTY-TWO

It'd been harder to say goodbye to Raven than I'd thought, leaving the horses at the stables with instructions to care for them until we—hopefully—returned. I couldn't deny how at home I felt with the ocean beneath me, the *Celerity* once again at our disposal, surging forward in the swift winter wind. As the sun rose in the sky and First Port shrank behind, I wondered whether I might see my hooved friend again.

But I had more important things to worry about as the knock on the door to the captain's cabin reminded me. Colagh entered with Bryn and Hunter, and Captain Morrig nodded to Sam to begin.

"The island Galin pointed us toward isn't on modern charts," he said, pointing at the captain's charts, "so I had to find something older before we left Salava. They didn't have much to work with, but their lack of current information worked in our favor." He indicated a large, unrolled parchment, brittle and yellowed with age. "An island can't be lost if it never existed."

The island he pointed to was the largest in an archipelago off Trylia's north coast. When I looked at the modern chart, it was omitted from the same archipelago, as Sam had said.

"I only wish we had the book Galin mentioned," Sam said. "So that we had some basis for whatever legend exists about this place."

"We don't need it," Colagh replied.

Fresh suspicion prickled the back of my neck. *What now?* I thought.

Bryn shot me a pointed look. Colagh took a deep breath, as if to steel himself for what he had to say. Or our reactions to it. "That island was an outpost for Vortheim, to monitor Trylia after the fall of their Ambient. They wanted to know whether it was an isolated incident, or something to worry about at home. It was lost because it was abandoned, and the legend of its being haunted isn't far off."

Everyone was silent. I automatically looked to Sam, thinking of his history with the fall and its cause. His face was blank, but his eyes were wide, and I realized that he'd spent centuries after the fall with no idea that Vortheim agents had been within spitting distance of Trylia. With even the little information Sam had given us about the Fall, I could understand why Vortheim would be wary of such a thing spreading. But I couldn't shake the feeling of violation that this revelation instilled in me. After all, they *had* attempted to forcibly remove the remaining Ambient from Trylia.

"Is that all it was?" Bryn asked, an edge to his voice. "A watchpost? Not a staging ground for an invasion? Because they *did* invade."

"Not an invasion," Colagh corrected, making Bryn sneer. "But I agree with your indignation, my people have earned it. It's not the point, though, the point is that I know what happened, and I know what we can expect. If you'd like to listen?" I nodded, and the rest did the same as Sam blinked, his eyes focusing on Colagh as he pulled a notebook and pencil out of his pocket.

"The island was an outpost to monitor the effects of the fall. Many of the Tethers living there were strategists, some of the most brilliant minds we could spare from the efforts to keep the Gloom contained, to assess this new threat. They moved their families, they built a repository of information that rivaled the palace libraries in Lacorsia. A haven against the proliferation of the Gloom and eventual destruction of Celuthia, and a sanctuary for the history and knowledge of our people, in the event that Vortheim was lost."

I watched Sam's face as Colagh spoke. His shock was gone, replaced by the same intensity and focus I'd seen whenever he studied his notebooks or taught me a new lesson. So much knowledge in one place; I couldn't imagine he'd seen anything like it since Salvation fell.

"But their zealotry and fear became their undoing. They built fortifications and defenses to keep the rest of the world out, to keep the Gloom out. The last message we received was of a breakthrough regarding the Gloom, and then they went silent. All methods of communication were severed, and the last team of Ambient sent to make contact returned with a handful of the island's inhabitants. Every Ambient, including the Malachi's own daughter, went insane, living in a state of constant terror for the rest of their lives. Now, a select few know of the island's existence, including my order, but only as a warning to keep our distance."

"And no one knew what happened? What put them in that state?" Sam demanded. I couldn't imagine anything powerful enough to drive an entire Ambient community of people like Sam to abandon the knowledge they'd hoarded.

A sad shake of Colagh's head. "No one that returned was capable of explaining what they went through. If we can discover anything about that breakthrough, it could save Vortheim. And Celuthia."

I'd been so confident that we would find Derth there, but if the island was as horrifying as Colagh said... "It doesn't seem likely that Derth would put himself through that," I said. My stomach churned with the thought that we'd have to start the search again.

"I think it sounds like the *most* likely place for someone like him to hole up," Hunter said. "An abandoned island that doesn't show up on Trylian charts, where Vorthes are afraid to go? If I were him, I'd find a way in and stay there the rest of my life."

"And if we can't get past the defenses?" I asked.

"Then we look somewhere else," Bryn replied. "The same if we don't find him there. If *we* can't do it, there's no way Derth can." He smirked at me, and I rolled my eyes. But I was grateful for his confidence; it gave me something to hold on to, one small shred of hope that we might be able to finish this.

"All right," I said, tapping the chart where the island was drawn. "We start here. I just hope it's not more than we can handle."

There was nothing to do but wait. Wait for our journey to reach its next destination, wait for whatever new trouble we would find, wait to see if we would be strong or clever enough to search the island. I didn't even have the task of propelling the ship now that Colagh was here, with his affinity for the wind and water. It contented him to help us move faster. But my lack of purpose felt like an itch I couldn't scratch.

As the first evening drew on, everyone not on duty gathered in the mess hall for dinner. Faces from the *Catherine's Revenge* crew surrounded us, and I smiled at a few before I gave up, still troubled by what might await us on the mysterious island.

Hunter sat with the Vorthes nearby, outwardly projecting his open and friendly demeanor to hide the vigilance in his eyes. Bryn and I sat nearby, bowls on the table in front of us, filled with steaming fish stew. I let the broth trickle out of my spoon, inhaling the scent of onion, garlic, oregano, and stewed tomatoes. The only indications that anything existed outside my focus were the sound of Sam rustling pages, Bryn's leg pressed against mine, and the voices and laughter of the crew chatting with the Vorthes further along the table.

I wanted to be alone, but I was starving, and I didn't have any food waiting for me in my hammock. I ate a spoonful, but the noise around me increased, and I couldn't enjoy it like I should have. Every time a voice rose above the rest, it felt like daggers in my ears. It felt too much like being surrounded by enemies, first in Stalth, where so many people had been turned against us, and then in Salava, narrowly avoiding being killed by an angry mob.

Sam grumbled something to himself, followed by a slurp of liquid from his spoon. The spoon clanked into his bowl as I gripped mine in my hands. More rustling pages grated on my nerves, and I hunched my shoulders as a chorus of laughter boomed in the close confines like a sudden peal of thunder.

"Lila," Bryn said, placing a hand on my shoulder. Concern, and a warning. The Ambience crackled beneath my skin like the embers of a wildfire. And they were catching.

I shrugged his hand off my shoulder. His touch irritated every nerve in my body, tense as it already was. Kindling to my flames. "Leave me alone," I snapped, glaring at another bout of laughter. How could anyone find something to joke about, and why did they need to be so *loud* about it? I rubbed at my tired eyes, one more irritation. Bryn tugged on my shoulder, and I rounded on him, giving my eye a rough wipe. "What?"

Bryn caught my hand, stopping me. My insides burned, as if my heart had caught flame. "Is something wrong with your eye? Like before?"

I snatched my hand from his grasp. Sam slammed his notebook shut and rummaged in his bag for another one. He pulled it out, flashing through the pages like an incessant fluttering of wings from a flock of birds. "They're *dry*, Bryn. Leave it alone." I turned to snarl at Sam. "Would you stop already? There's nothing there that you don't already know!"

Sam looked up from his notebook, and the rest of the mess fell silent as the crew, Hunter, and the Vorthes turned to stare at me. I glared at all of them. "Lila?" Sam asked. "Is something wrong?"

"Why does something have to be wrong with me? I'm worried, I'm overwhelmed, and it makes me angry! I'm allowed to be angry!"

"You are," Sam began slowly, "but it's unlike you to shout at us for being concerned about you." He let his notebook close and tapped it against his thigh as he peered at me. *Tap. Tap. Tap.* His eyes narrowed, his face contemplative. *Tap. Tap.* I flexed my fingers, wishing I could tear the notebook from his grasp. Wishing I could tear it apart.

That I could tear *him* apart.

"Elders, Lila," Bryn said. He squeezed my shoulder, but this time, it was a restraint. "Calm down."

My words came out as a growl. "Don't tell me to calm down, Bryn." Power pulsed from me as the spirits came, surrounding Sam as I prepared to do... *something* to him. My mind flashed through the possibilities in an instant. Set him and his precious notebooks on fire, pull the air from his lungs, rip him limb from limb...

Bryn grabbed my face in his hands and pulled my glare from Sam. Fear radiated from his deep blue eyes, and beyond my line of sight I heard the shuffle of bodies. Quickly.

Good, I thought. *They* should *be afraid.*

"Lila! Stop!" Bryn battered at the edge of my consciousness, trying to force himself to the fore. His body and his mind were barriers against the tempest of my sudden rage. But he was so small. Just a pest. "This isn't you!"

I scoffed at him. I felt more like myself than I'd ever felt in my life. There was nothing I couldn't do. Nothing I couldn't conquer. Nothing more in my way *if* I could just remove these last obstacles.

Lila! Bryn's voice in my head was like the whisper of my conscience, begging me not to act. He tried to push further in, to extend his spirit to mine. *STOP.* The command caught my attention, not because of its urgency, not because he'd convinced me to acquiesce, but because he was drawing on my power. *My* connection to the Ambience. I snarled at him, my muscles tensed to throw him away from me. He roared, with voice and thought. "*STOP!*"

My breath caught in my throat as his spirit interposed itself between the Ambience and me. The power drained from me, a reminder of the prison Derth had made in my own mind. I recoiled, but Bryn turned it back on me, plunging into me as he would into the ocean from the deck of the ship, taking control of the connection between us.

We turned to see the Vorthe group rising to their feet, Sam's eyes wide as he looked at our bodies. The radiant tether between Bryn and Lila trembled, held in place by Bryn's feeble grasp on the Ambience, fraying where his spirit clutched at the connection. It wouldn't hold for long.

We cast our eyes about, drawn by a familiar emptiness. And there, beyond Sam's shoulder, another orb, swirling with black malice. Whispers of Derth's voice stretched out like lazy fog, tickling Lila's face, slithering into her ears. Reaching across the tether, twining around Bryn's spirit. We swatted it from the air, the tendrils retreated, and a faint echoing scream filled the air for the space of a heartbeat. Hunter winced and cursed.

"What was that?" Tanjiu asked.

"Their eyes," Pearl whispered. "Why are their eyes like that?"

"Derth was watching again," we told everyone, raising our hands to point at the place it had been. "He was filling Lila with rage and hate, trying to force her to do something she'd regret."

Colagh cursed in Vorthe. "Derth is becoming more of a threat every moment."

"Elders curse him, *how* is he doing that?" Hunter growled. He rubbed the place between his eyebrows with his fingers.

Colagh scowled at us. "I asked you about this power before, and you said you didn't know. What *is* this?"

At that moment the air rippled, and we looked to the sky rather than answering him. Peering through the decks as if they were glass, we watched as the stars swirled and danced like they always did, but they seemed to tremble, too. Like they were fighting a great strain. Something in the world was changing, on a scale that we couldn't fathom.

"Stop," Sam said, rising to his feet as we looked down. He placed a hand on Bryn's shoulder, and then on Lila's. "The danger has passed, and you can stop."

"This isn't right," Tanjiu said, their eyes wide, their lip trembling. "Can you feel it? So many spirits..."

"Stop this, now," Colagh demanded. His spirit flared as he infused his words with power, like Sam had done when we discovered this strength. We chuckled, and Colagh frowned. He fished in the pouch at his waist. "Stop now, before I'm forced to stop you. No one can contain this much Ambience for long."

"You couldn't stop us," we said, "but there's nothing to fear from us." We began the process of separating our minds, like unraveling a thousand threads at once from the point that Bryn held, but then a hand clamped onto Lila's wrist, and the threads tore.

My eyes were already fixed on my wrist as Colagh pulled his hand away. On an innocuous braided leather band that seemed to have no end, the width of my finger, like a bracelet a child would make. It was all I could see as my vision darkened to a pinpoint of light, and my breath came out of me in a rush as my legs suddenly refused to hold me upright. My body crashed to the floor as all of its energy drained in the space of a heartbeat. I was alone in a void, and I couldn't feel the Pool, couldn't feel the Ambience. Without it, I couldn't draw a full breath, couldn't move my arms more than a twitch.

There were muffled shouts above me as my body stilled, and I was so weak, so tired, all I wanted was to shut my eyes. Part of me hoped they wouldn't open again. I was so *tired*. But the void brightened, and a warm presence caressed my cheek. A voice spoke in my head, reverberating through my dwindling spirit.

Little Flame, I'm here. The Ambience, the *voice*, was like the heat of a campfire in the cold night of this void. Like it was the only thing keeping the darkness at bay. I instinctually took a deep breath, but then the warmth and the voice were gone, and I was in darkness once more.

The world slammed back into focus, my heart began to beat a frantic rhythm—had it stopped? —and I gulped in lungsful of air.

"Keep him away from us, Sam," Bryn bellowed, "or I'll kill him!" Rage, terror, anguish. Was that me, or Bryn? "Lila, *Lila!* Talk to me!" I blinked, and Bryn's body sagged. Relief, gratitude, *rage*.

The emptiness lingered, a yawning chasm at the back of my mind like the memory of a nightmare, but my body finally caught on that I was still alive. I coughed. "What was that?"

"Thank the spirits," Bryn shuddered, his voice rumbling through me. A quick succession of thoughts; my body, the floor, eyes vacant and staring, the bond sputtering, Bryn's resolve to follow me, to drag me back from wherever I'd gone... "Colagh almost killed you." He glowered at someone; I assumed it was Colagh.

"How?" I asked, but my eyes flicked to my bare wrist. I made to stand, but Bryn held me tight, unwilling to let me go. Just as well, because I wasn't sure they'd support me. But I protested. "I'm fine," I murmured. I wasn't, and we both knew it. He lifted me to the bench that I'd fallen out of, careful to avoid the mess of stew I'd taken with me.

When I turned to Colagh, he was staring at us, poised to run, or pounce. Bryn practically vibrated with the effort of keeping himself still at my side when every instinct told him to lunge at Colagh for what he'd done. To shred him apart before anyone could blink. Tanjiu and Paerna were too still, like a deer scenting a predator on the wind, but Pearl stepped toward Bryn and me. She was a wall of menace between us and the other Vorthes, the Ambience ready to lash out, her fists clenched. "What did you do?" I asked Colagh. So quiet, Bryn's instincts adding to my own edge of menace.

He didn't take his eyes off me as he lifted the leather bracelet high enough for me to see it. I spared it a glance before I returned my cold stare to him. "This device suppresses the Ambience in the wearer, so that they can't use their power. Whatever you were doing, whatever you *became...* that was too much power. World-shattering power."

"It was *killing me.*" I blinked, and when my eyes opened, I was in a different position, standing above a head of auburn hair spilling from its plait. The room held a strange aura, as if Bryn's vision—*I'm in Bryn's head*—was blurring in his rage. *Spirits, those are spirits.*

I was back in my own head, though the path remained open behind me. Was this because Bryn had forced that joining? I glanced at him, at the spirits flocking to him, and my gut twisted with some heavy feeling I couldn't name when Sam growled, turning his wrath on Colagh. "Because your spirit is tied to the Ambience in a way that will not allow you to survive without it. Something that you are *well* aware of. What is that?"

"A Clinch. A device that nullifies the Ambience," he replied. He transferred it back and forth between his hands as he spoke, as if the leather burned. "It's a closely guarded secret amongst my order. The Malachi had them crafted for use in the capture of rogue Ambient. Only the artisan who created it or the person who placed it can remove it. I have not had occasion to use one on a Conduit."

Bryn took a step toward him, hand moving to his dirk. Roy moved in front of him as Pearl snarled. "You should have left it on," she said. "Whatever she is, whatever *they* are, they're more dangerous than the one we're after. How do we know they won't turn on us?" Roy had to restrain Bryn's hand before he could draw his weapon. His muscles bulged, shaking with the effort it took to keep Bryn at bay.

"Us, turn on *you?*" Bryn demanded. "You're the ones who attacked *her*! As I see it, you've already turned on us." Hunter stepped in to help Roy before he could break free.

"It was only a matter of time," Bryn growled. Hunter murmured urgently in Bryn's ear, but Bryn couldn't understand his words. His mind was consumed with getting past them, bringing his dirk across Colagh's throat, but they drifted to me through the bond. I couldn't shut it out; I didn't have any control over it. That rage boiled inside me, deeper than any I'd ever held, and the spirits striving toward him whirled toward me. The Ambience strained to be unleashed, and destructive flames pulsed along skin with the beat of Bryn's heart.

Lila's alive, Hunter implored, *look at her. Come on, brother, breathe,* think. *If you start this now, we'll all die. You'll kill Lila. Look at her. Look at her...*

Bryn *did* look then, turning his back on the Vorthes to lock his eyes onto mine, to the hand I reached out to him. A deep, shuddering breath, and then another, as Hunter continued his litany of encouragement, becoming the calming force that Bryn was for me. He crossed the space between us in a blur, dropped his dirk onto the table, and clutched his hand to my heart. The bond strained and fell away, and I let out the breath I'd been holding as Bryn's rage went with it.

Pearl hadn't retreated, but rather, had taken another step forward to glare up at Roy, who stood sentinel for us. And somehow, her presence towered over him. "Enough!" Sam shouted. "Stand down, *all of you.*"

Raising my voice, I didn't bother to try to hide my mistrust, my disgust. Bryn helped me to stand, but I couldn't see past Roy until I peered around him. "When this is done, we can talk about whether we have something we need to resolve."

Colagh narrowed his eyes, but Pearl remained where she was. Tanjiu put a hand on her shoulder, and her eyes darted to them, weighing her options, and then her stance relaxed, though she didn't take her eyes off Roy as she moved behind Colagh. "Until then, you keep that thing away from me so that I can stop Derth for you."

Colagh's nostrils flared, and then he gave me a slow nod. "Our goal remains, and I believe that Lila and Bryn are our best chance in achieving that goal. But before we continue, I need to know what you *are.*" His gaze was closed off, hostile, and I wondered whether we might ever see that friendly countenance again.

"I'm a Conduit," I replied. "But part of my spirit lives in Bryn."

Confusion replaced the open animosity on the Vorthe faces staring at us. "Our minds are linked, and we can join our spirits to become something more." I shook my head. "I don't know what it is, only that we think and act as one, and we are capable of so much more together than we are apart."

"Too much," Pearl muttered.

"Maybe," I snapped, "but I'm going after Derth, and the only way you're going to stop me from going after him is to use that bracelet to kill me."

Pearl looked me up and down, and something like begrudging acceptance crossed her face. But it was gone a second later. Roy finally stepped aside so that I could face them myself, Bryn's hand beneath my elbow in case I needed his support. I couldn't feel him, thank the Elders, but something had changed, something that we needed to figure out before we needed the bond again.

Colagh finally smiled again, but there was something different in the expression now. It was calculating, eager, almost zealous. And I didn't like being the subject of that attention. When he released my gaze, turning to take his place at the table again, I sagged into Bryn's grasp.

"Very well," Colagh said. "We will work together," he looked at his people, "to accomplish what neither can do alone."

CHAPTER THIRTY-THREE

Bryn and I hid in the captain's cabin the first day after that, ostensibly to let tempers cool between both sides, but also because we needed the time to sort through what had happened to *us*.

"You took control of me," I whispered, after hours of trying to start the conversation, only to fail because we were both still too raw. Bryn pictured my cold, limp body over and over, and the emptiness crawled out of the back of my mind where I'd tucked it away. We could only hold onto one another, to keep each other from losing ourselves in the horror of it all over again.

"I'm sorry," he whispered again. I didn't know how to tell him that I'd almost lost myself in him, that I couldn't separate my mind from his, that I'd been as consumed by his fury as he had. I didn't know how to tell him that I was terrified that it would happen again, and that the Ambience didn't feel like it was *mine* anymore. Not after he'd taken it.

At the end of the day, all we had to show for our efforts was a confession that we had no idea what had happened or what we should do.

But we agreed that whatever had happened, Bryn couldn't try to take control again.

Another day passed, and when I couldn't stand to be trapped in the confines of the cabin any longer, stares still followed me throughout the ship. I was that girl again, ignorant of her power, trying to hide it from superstitious crew mates. Bryn kept his distance, too, and I didn't know whether it was a relief or not.

I lowered the barrier I kept around the Ambience over and over, waiting for it to come, willing it to come, and finally trying to give myself over to it without regard to what it could do to me. But even then it was a pale comparison to the force that usually swam beneath the surface.

It was a relief when the lookout announced that he could see buildings rising above the thick fog that sat above the water, obscuring our view of the island. Before sunset we would be there, and I could focus on something outside of insecurities I thought I'd moved past and the new ones I now had to contend with. I put all of it aside and jogged to the helm. I kept my eyes away from Colagh at his side.

"We'll have to sail into the fog if we want to get close enough for the dinghies," the captain said. "And we'll need to do it slowly to avoid rocks tearing through our hull."

"I can help with that," Colagh offered. The wind picked up, trying to pull his white-blond hair out of its tight bun. He waved a hand in front of him, as if wiping dirt from a windowpane. Fog parted, giving us a path ahead free of dangerous shards of rock.

It receded further, revealing a large shadow in the fog. Longer than our ship, with tall shapes reaching into the sky, it took me a moment to realize what I was looking at. But as we moved closer, the shape resolved into something very familiar.

"The *Bulwark*," Captain Morrig breathed. "She's waiting for us."

She didn't wait long; her sails unfurled and she moved in our direction. The wind was in their favor, and she'd be in range to fire ballistae soon. The scout called down that they were loading bolts as they moved, and I looked to Captain Morrig.

"We can get around them," Colagh said. "I can push us faster so that we can get to shore. But that would leave you vulnerable out here."

"That might be a risk we must take," Captain Morrig replied. "Derth is the mission, this is a distraction."

"If the entire crew is under Derth's control, we can't leave you alone out here. If they've been ordered to destroy anyone who comes near, they won't stop until you're all dead. Without one of us to move the ship, you'll never outrun them." I finally glanced at Colagh. "But if we can get to shore, you and I can hold the ship long enough for the *Celerity* to escape." I looked at Captain Morrig. "We take dinghies, you retreat, and we can send a signal when we're ready to head home." I didn't need to mention that I had no idea whether we *would* head home. A muscle in his jaw twitched, a sure sign that he knew it.

Colagh was staring at the *Bulwark's* progress through the fog. "At least we know we're in the right place." He shrugged, and waved toward the fog again, letting it roll back in. "That won't obscure us for long," he said.

"Then we go straight through," Captain Morrig said. "We'll put more space between us to hopefully keep out of ballista range, and get you close enough to use the dinghies. If they attack, our Ambient will protect us as best they can. Let's make it fast."

He strode across the deck, barking orders as he went, sparking activity in his wake. My gaze lingered on Bryn, organizing the archers we'd brought with us, stringing longbows. Hunter helped to assemble swords and pikes to repel boarders as Colagh called the other Vorthes to his side. Sam joined Colagh and me as we discussed our strategy.

"I could use the current against them," I suggested.

"I'm not against capsizing the ship," Colagh replied, his mouth twisting into a rueful grin. "It would save us a lot of trouble and energy."

"I am," I shot back. "Those are our people, under Derth's control." I shook my head. "We need to find another way."

"You focus on the water, I'll take care of the wind," he said with a wink. Our sails filled, and the wind whipped my face as we lurched forward before I could brace.

I closed my eyes. *Please,* I called, reaching for the Ambience, letting every fear, every insecurity swell to entice it. In the times I'd needed it most, it had come, whether I wanted it to or not. *Please.* We wouldn't survive this if I couldn't deliver the power everyone expected. They needed me to be a Conduit.

We come, the spirits called, and I almost collapsed with relief. I felt Bryn's eyes on me, his attention drawn to the power that surged through me, but I grasped the current below with spiritual hands to turn it straight at the *Bulwark*. The wind shifted when Colagh felt the tide turn, and their sails buckled. Now sailing upwind, they tried to tack to starboard, but I redirected the current again, luxuriating in the flow of the Ambience around me. The *Bulwark* slowed to a halt. The massive ship tacked to port, but Colagh and I redirected again.

If they couldn't get in range, they couldn't destroy us. If *we* controlled their direction, we could slip past without a fight.

"Well done!" Colagh shouted, laughing.

"You too," I called, our triumph bolstering my confidence, helping me focus on the task over the rest.

"Keep it up!" Captain Morrig called. Kai whipped the wheel to starboard, away from the *Bulwark*. We cut a path through the fog, Sam and Tanjiu parting it for us so that Colagh and I could concentrate. Kai swung to starboard again, back in line with the island.

The *Bulwark* couldn't move forward, but they'd pivoted just enough for our hulls to be parallel to one another as we gained speed. "What's the range on those ballistae?" I shouted to Captain Morrig, my triumph fading as I noticed movement toward the hulking contraptions.

He shook his head. "I don't know," he admitted. "Elders," he cursed as one of them angled in our direction. "To port, Kai!" he shouted. "I want more distance between us!"

I knew how hard a normal ballista bolt could hit—I'd never forget the way it'd punched the breath from my lungs when it hit my shield—and the *Bulwark's* ballistae we scaled to fit the size of the warship. I couldn't take any chances. I looked beyond the stern. *Push,* I commanded, and the water behind us rose, shoving us further along our path, away from theirs. The bowsprit tipped too far, slicing through the water, and I pulled the current back, just enough to keep us going.

"Bolt incoming!" Hunter shouted.

"And another!" Bryn called.

"Sam!" I shouted. Maybe he could deflect one, and the other... The first soared in a perfect arc, and then slammed into an invisible wall. Sam and Tanjiu grunted, both of their tethered spirits flaring from the force it took to stop the wicked barbed hook.

Pearl and Paerna shouted, and the second bolt crashed into the deck point-first between our masts. Bryn jumped aside before his leg was impaled, and the rest of the crew scattered as the bolt began to drag backward, the thick line attached to its haft pulled taut. The barbs scored the deck, and then the *Celerity* was brought to a shuddering halt as they dug into the rail, sending me crashing painfully onto my side.

"*Crew overboard!*" Hunter bellowed a heartbeat before a few splashes and cries. The hull groaned as the grapple dug deeper, lurching us closer to the *Bulwark*.

"Cut that line!" Captain Morrig ordered.

"It's too far, sir!" Roy called. "We can't reach past the haft!"

"Ambient!" Captain Morrig ordered, "Cut that line!"

Paerna scrambled to the rail and sliced his hand through the air like a sword. The thick line unraveled, but one small section remained. Our ship lurched to starboard again, and the tension snapped the line the rest of the way.

"Another volley!" Sam shouted as he held his hands up. Tanjiu and Paerna joined him, and together they stopped two more massive bolts, sending them splashing harmlessly into the ocean. All three of them slumped against the rail, exhausted from the force it took to stop the momentum of the bolts.

"I don't know if we can stop another one, sir," I told the captain. "I might be able to do it if I let them move."

"Do it," he ordered. "If any get through, then we'll keep cutting the lines," Captain Morrig said.

"Colagh," I called, "I'm going to shield us. Do whatever you can to get us moving!"

He gave me a curt nod in reply, and wind shot into the sails. I widened my stance, ready to hold my balance against waves and the fight against a ballista bolt.

"Another volley incoming!" Captain Morrig shouted. The crew braced for impact, and I braced myself for the drain I knew was coming.

The heavy bolts fired in unison and flew straight toward us. A small part of my mind marveled at the might they displayed, at what our shipwrights and artillerists had accomplished. But the rest of my mind was running through a litany of curses in the seconds it took for the shining metal tips to approach.

We come, the spirits intoned in my head as they swarmed again, creating a barrier of pure Ambience between us and the bolts. It felt like a piece of myself floating in the air, and when the bolts struck, it felt like they had struck me. They hit with such force that my feet skid across the wood, the shield transferring some of the impact to me in place of letting them through. The breath left my body in a huff as if I'd been punched in the gut, and I gasped as the bolts fell into the water, their sharp tips blunted against my shield.

I fell to my knees as I gasped, and felt the captain's hands on my shoulders. "Dear one, are you all right?"

I couldn't form words yet, so I nodded, staring up at him with my eyes wide as I clutched my middle. Boots thundered up the steps to the helm, and Bryn was there, on his knees next to me. I patted his arm to let him know I was all right, and he helped me to my feet.

The *Bulwark* picked up speed, no longer hampered by our efforts. They came about, following us on our path to shore, trying to close the distance between us. We had the wind that Colagh provided, but they had a longer hull and larger sails built for power and speed. If we stopped to lower the boats, they'd have us.

The ocean churned all around them, and they slowed again. I looked at Colagh, who winked through the strain evident on his face.

"I can't hold this for long," he grunted. The wind in our sails flagged as he focused on the water. "Whatever we're going to do, it needs to be soon."

"We can look for another way into the island," I suggested. "We'll retreat and search for somewhere else to land."

"No good," Colagh replied. "I feel a sandbar stretching around the island to our right, beyond my senses. And rocky stacks surrounding the island. This is the clearest approach on this side, and I have no reason to believe that they don't stretch completely around it. They feel..." he squinted, like he was trying to work out the words, "unnatural. Like they were put there all at once, rather than eroding over time. Another defense."

I sighed, exasperated. "Of course they did." I pushed the wind into the sails, and we lurched forward again. "We keep going and hope you can hold them."

We pulled away as Colagh and I gritted our teeth, straining against exhaustion and the natural forces of the elements working against us. *Just a bit further,* I thought. *"Bryn!"* A shout, not a thought. Though I felt him look at me. "Ready the boats! We'll have seconds!"

He moved, dragging Hunter with him, yelling for our archers to ready themselves while Hunter gathered sailors to help them. The boats lifted off the deck beneath the stay tackles, Colagh let out a rough breath, and I turned to see that he was slumped against the rail. In the seconds that it took my brain to recognize that he wasn't holding the *Bulwark* any longer, they swung about, much closer now, and brought their ballistae to bear.

"*Brace!*" Captain Morrig shouted as I dropped the wind and tried to raise the same shield as before. But I could feel how weak it was in comparison, and as the bolts fired, their momentum was only slowed, not stopped. They ripped through the shield, landed on the port side seconds apart, and dragged across the deck until they embedded into the rail with a thunderous crack.

The *Celerity* jerked to starboard, all of us scrambling to stay upright. The lines went taut, reeling us in like fish. Targeting the line, my desperation came out as a burst of flames that burned through some of the strands. I lashed out again, so tired that my legs shook, but unwilling to give in and let them take us without a fight.

Bryn's strength poured into me, and my legs stopped shaking, the flames grew hotter, and the closest line snapped. He was there, his presence at once bolstering and overwhelming, and I fought to keep my concentration, to stay rooted in my own mind. But I couldn't pull away when he was the only thing between me and collapse, between cutting the lines and remaining in the *Bulwark's* grasp. Both ships lurched as one tether was lost, but the other was still in place, and Paerna and Tanjiu stumbled closer.

Like the faint scent of smoke on the wind, I sensed Derth's darkness reaching out from the *Bulwark*, as if it had caught *my* scent and was searching for me. My body shivered in revulsion as I felt him. I turned to look across the water, and found the *Bulwark's* crew staring at me. Even the sailors loading new bolts into the terrifying ballistae, every glance they could spare was in my direction. The entire ship was coated with Derth's swarming darkness, like shadowy snakes searching for their next meal.

"We won't make it to shore if I don't stop them," I muttered to myself. Bryn's attention focused on me as he caught my train of thought. I opened myself to the creeping influence reaching out to me. It darted forward, toward its prey, and as it tried to embed itself in my mind and spirit, I used the connection to follow it back to its source on the other ship.

Bryn shouted my name at the edges of my hearing as my focus was drawn to the captain of the *Bulwark*. I'd met her once at the King's Port docks, when Captain Morrig had helped her put together the crew that surrounded her like bees waiting for their queen's instructions. Derth's darkness flared out from the captain, touching every one of her crews' spirits. She was serving as Derth's anchor, tethered more strongly to the darkness than anyone in Stalth had been, so that she could affect everyone like the orbs that had been following us had created a mob in Salava.

"Lila," Bryn said, touching my shoulder. I shook my head, knowing what he was suggesting without having to read his mind. But it was too dangerous, the bond too fragile, and I was so afraid that I wouldn't come out the other side the same. All of this passed through my mind in the blink of an eye, and when I turned to Bryn, love and understanding in his cobalt eyes, I knew that we didn't have another choice.

Bryn nodded, hearing my acceptance as our spirits reached toward each other, our minds and thoughts mingling. "We do this together," he said, grasping my hand.

I took a deep breath, the darkness like Derth's clammy fingers sliding over my skull. It wormed between Bryn and me, trying to block my mind as it reached for his. Our bond trembled, but Bryn waited, until I had no choice but to plunge my spirit into his.

We watched with trepidation as the full scope of Derth's depravity was revealed. The *Bulwark's* captain was indeed an anchor for the darkness, a nexus of tortured spirits that screamed in pain and horror, rent asunder and put back together in a mockery of a Conduit's connection to the Ambience. And the Pool itself was tainted by the corruption, as if by inverting the nature of the spirits—the life force of Celuthia, bridges between the natural power of the world and its mortal inhabitants—the Ambience was tearing the world apart.

We followed the beckoning darkness of fractured spirits, gathering more from the Pool to surround and heal as we had in Stalth. But the moment they answered our call, they were pulled into the darkness, absorbed and ripped apart like the others, increasing the pull of Derth's influence. It spread to our ship, and our crew clutched their heads, screaming as the darkness rolled over them in a torturous wave.

A volley of arrows loosed from the *Bulwark* to rain down onto our deck. Tanjiu, Sam, and Paerna threw their arms up to shield at the last moment. An arrow penetrated the shield to impale Roy's shoulder, and another skimmed along Tanjiu's thigh. Several more found their targets in other crew members, their screams echoing over the water.

Our presence lured more spirits from the Pool, and they were lost in the fractured maelstrom. The *Bulwark's* captain pointed at Lila, and several of her sailors climbed onto the line holding the ballista bolt still attached to our hull to shimmy over the churning ocean toward us.

We tried to turn, to sever the line, but our power was now locked in a struggle with the darkness, drawn to the void like spirits. Paerna cut the line free in one motion, and the sailors fell into the ocean.

"Archers!" Hunter shouted, standing near us. "Loose!" A volley of our own flew through the air. The arrows found their marks, dropping soldiers all around the captain, but the captain was unscathed despite standing in the center of the volley. The remaining sailors stepped closer to their captain as one.

Sam appeared next to Bryn, a gash on his forehead oozing blood down his cheek. "Is something wrong?" he asked us.

"There are too many spirits tied to the captain, and the crew are Derth's puppets," we replied. "Derth has subverted the Ambience here; it's tearing the Pool—and the world—apart. When we try to undo his work, our power and the spirits we summon fuel it instead. Our only choice may be to destroy them and the captain tethering them here."

A cacophonous *thunk* heralded another ballista bolt. With a miniscule gesture the bolt disintegrated in mid-air, but the spirits channeling the Ambience at our behest were engulfed in darkness. It pulsed outward, the spirits screaming so loudly that we gritted our teeth in pain.

We focused on the captain as the power she embodied focused on us. It tried to draw us in again, hungry for our power. But we grasped the darkness with the light of the Ambience manifesting from our bodies, and it writhed as it failed to escape. The torn spirits clawed at our power, trying to shatter our bond. A shift, and Lila stumbled forward a step, out of sync with Bryn. Another shift and the claws dug deeper. Bryn's head turned away as Lila stared forward. The Ambience flourished, driving the darkness back, away from the groaning strain on the bond.

The last time we encountered these broken spirits we embraced them, healed them, and welcomed their power back to the Ambient Pool. This time, we obliterated them one-by-one, tearing them out of the captain by the root before they crumbled like dry leaves in our grasp.

We heard another loud *thunk* and felt a warm spray on our faces, screams all around us as the shattered spirits reeled. Someone near Lila and Bryn collapsed, a dark shape protruding from the deck outside their lines of sight. The captain of the *Bulwark* fell to one knee as her crew clutched their heads and cried out in pain when the dark tendrils emanating from their captain tore free.

The world twisted around us, our companions oblivious to the tumult beyond the bounds of their mortal ears. With one last wrench that tore her head from her shoulders, the darkness tore free of the captain, and the world went mad. The void collapsed in on itself as the spirits were destroyed, sending a shockwave of Ambience and darkness outward that rocked both ships.

I fell to my knees next to Bryn as we were jettisoned apart, the Ambience ripped from my body with such ferocity that it felt like my heart went with it, leaving a void in its place. I couldn't hear the spirits, but the screaming didn't stop. The world was grey, swallowed by fog so that I could only see the ship around me and nothing beyond it. Warm liquid tickled my ears, and when I wiped at it, my fingers came away coated in blood. A wave of dizziness washed over me, and I put my head in my hands to hold it still.

"Lila," Bryn groaned. I opened my eyes, and my breath caught in my chest. His clothes dripped crimson, his face a mask of blood.

CHAPTER THIRTY-FOUR

"Whose blood is this?" I shouted, struggling to my feet. I slipped in a puddle of crimson liquid, and realized that my clothes were soaked, too. After a quick scan to assure myself it wasn't Bryn's, I cast about in a panic, my healer's mind knowing that this was too much blood for anyone to have survived. "What happened?"

A man screamed in pain, and my heart stopped. Not that voice... The captain roared. "*Lila!*"

I launched myself down the stairs, feet barely touching long enough to slide, and landed on the deck next to two bodies. Pearl, propped up by the ballista bolt protruding from her torso, was taking shallow breaths, blood bubbling out of her mouth. Hunter was suspended, too, his arm attached to one of the barbs as Roy and Captain Morrig held the rest of his body up to keep pressure off his arm.

I ignored Hunter's scream of pain and the resulting twist of pain in my heart as I approached. The barb had somehow torn through his lower arm, shattering the bone and sundering the skin and muscles all around it. Blood poured from the wound, and Hunter's skin was waxy and pale. Blood gurgled out of Pearl's mouth with every rasping breath.

Tanjiu approached, tears running down their face. "W-we need to get her down. I can break the bolt, can you heal her? Any of you?"

"I don't feel the Ambience," Colagh said.

"Neither do I," Paerna replied. "Tanjiu?"

They shook their head. "No. Lila," they begged, "you're a Conduit. You can help her."

On instinct I reached out for the Ambience, knowing there was nothing I could do for Pearl without it, but there was nothing there to grasp. If I couldn't see and smell and hear it, I wouldn't believe there was *anything* around me. The world had gone still, my senses told me, the hum of energy muted. The spark was still there, I had a connection to *something*, but the Pool couldn't reach me through the stillness.

"It's gone," I muttered. Tanjiu sobbed again, and Hunter screamed through gritted teeth. My eyes went wide as I grasped the consequences. "The Ambience is gone."

All around us, the fog darkened. It roiled like a storm cloud that blocked out the sun and crackled with chaotic flashes of light. With each flash I felt the Ambience, but it was raw, primordial, feral. There were no spirits to direct it. Bone-deep fear gripped me.

The Vorthes stared at the shadowy cloud in terror. I looked again at the blood trailing from Pearl's mouth, her skin losing its color with every heartbeat, and knew there was nothing I could do.

Tanjiu appeared opposite me to cup Pearl's cheek and whisper into her ear. A faint smile, one long, shuddering breath, and Pearl was gone. I swallowed my own sob of grief as I stepped around them to Hunter's side.

In the mere moments that had passed since discovering the Ambience was gone, Hunter had gone quiet. Without my power, I relied on the training Smitts had given me. "Bryn, give me your belt," I ordered. "Roy, captain, hold him up, he can't do it himself. He's lost too much blood." Bryn's belt slapped into my palm, and I wound it around Hunter's arm above his elbow. "Another belt, piece of wood, *anything. Now!*" I barked. Understanding my intent, a crewmate stepped forward with a small bit of wood whittled into a flat relief of a bird and put it between Hunter's teeth.

I looked at the men holding Hunter. "Get ready." The belt cinched onto his arm, jarring what was connected to the barb, and Hunter's eyes went wild, his guttural scream muffled by the wood held in his mouth. "Bryn, get my pack. I need my tools."

"Already here," he said when Kai appeared with said tools in their hands. I grasped the large kit and unwrapped it, removing the wire saw within. My stomach twisted and I swallowed a sob of horror and sorrow as I thought through what I needed to do. I focused on my training, trying to lock away the fact that Hunter would be under the saw. I couldn't afford to hesitate.

"Kai, get us out of this fog!" Captain Morrig shouted. "I want to see land by the time we're done here!"

"Aye!" they called, bounding away through the crowd gathered around us.

"The rest of you, sail the Elders' damned ship!" Captain Morrig's voice cracked through the tenuous hold he had on his emotions. But he stood strong, holding Hunter's torso as my friend drooped against him. "Do it, Lila," he commanded. I stared into his eyes, every bit the little girl he'd rescued, worried about my friend. But the steel in his eyes hardened my resolve, and I gripped the handles of the saw in either hand.

"Bryn," I said, "hold the barb and his arm when I tell you. I can't save his arm; my power is gone. So I'll do what I can to save his life. But it might not be enough. And it's going to hurt." Hunter mumbled something, his eyes pleading, sweat and gore dripping from his sodden curls. Tears streamed down his face. I cupped his cheek, and he gave me a tiny shake of his head. "I've got you."

"Now." Bryn took hold as I brought the wire down. I detached from the part of myself that suffered along with Hunter so that I could focus on the task. There was no sound but the sound of the wire cutting through, no reality beyond the wound in my hands. Minutes passed, my hands numbing from the effort. The arm came free, and they placed Hunter on the deck while I looked for my kit so that I could stop the bleeding, tie off the huge vessels that only oozed with the tourniquet placed above. The light changed, and I could see the sky again.

We drifted through the edge of the fog, leaving behind a perfect dome over the water that didn't move despite the wind that filled our sails. The energy of life all around us sparked through me like lightning. I gasped in a breath, the Ambience filling my chest with the ocean air, and the white-hot glow of my desperate sorrow filled my hands.

My hand hovered above the remnant of Hunter's arm, where I felt his weakening spirit slip toward the Pool. The spirits created a bridge of radiant Ambience, calling him home.

But my call was louder.

"Hunter," I shouted, glancing at his still, ashen face, "stay with us!" His heart beat too slowly, his breaths came in shallow, uneven gasps. Vessels, tendons, ligaments, and skin came together in a blink, seamless in a way that I couldn't have accomplished with my healer's kit. I flushed Ambience through him to replenish what had been lost and to ease his pain.

With my hand and my power, I felt the thud of his heart steady and his chest rise and fall in deeper, more even breaths. His eyes fluttered, and I looked up to see Captain Morrig bent over him next to me. When Hunter woke, ours were the first faces he saw.

"My arm," he groaned. Fresh tears slid down his gore-stained cheek. He reached with his left arm to feel for the right, and his fingers flinched when they came to the end of the stump. Another groan and fresh tears, and he buried his face in the captain's shirt.

"I'm so sorry," I whispered. To give him a moment, I turned to the captain. "What happened?"

"The bolt flew toward Pearl, too close to you and Bryn. Hunter tried to pull her free, and got caught when the line went taut."

I put a hand on Captain Morrig's shoulder and stood, turning to the Vorthes who'd gathered around Pearl. They'd removed her from the bolt so that she could rest on the deck. Her arms were crossed over her chest with her sword clutched in her hands. The others sat with their legs crossed, one hand in a fist against their chests and the other resting on Pearl's body. I waited while Colagh muttered in Vorthe until they finished. When Colagh glanced at me, his eyes were filled with pain.

"I'm so sorry. I wish I could have done something to help her." Grief overwhelmed me, but I had no more tears to shed.

"There was nothing to do," he replied. "Even the Ambience has its limits. We were all beyond them already. Will Hunter survive?" I nodded, and Colagh's mouth twitched in a sad smile. "I'm glad to hear it." He held out a hand to me, and we leaned on each other to stand so he could gaze out at the fog. "I never expected to witness the birth of a new Gloom, let alone survive it."

"I wish we *all* had survived it intact," I sighed, turning to look at Hunter now sitting up with the captain's help. Bryn was on his knees and touched his forehead to Hunter's. They sobbed together as Bryn spoke softly, as Hunter had done for him when he'd been past the point of hearing.

The *Bulwark* sailed ahead, into our path, and my body tensed with fear. But as they came about to run parallel to us, they were no longer moving in unison, nor were they projecting the same ominous darkness through the Ambience that they had before. This was a crew of frightened sailors and soldiers who'd just lost their captain.

"Sir," I called, "the *Bulwark*."

"Are they clear?" he asked. Hunter slid away from him so he could stand, though he clutched the captain's hand for a long, fraught moment before letting go. Captain Morrig nodded to Bryn, who clasped Hunter's shoulder, before he turned to the warship.

"I think so," I replied. My eyes strayed to the Gloom behind us. I couldn't feel the darkness in that, either, because I couldn't feel *anything* from it.

"Good. We'll reach out, and then we'll get you to that island. Kai, set anchor when we're close enough for the dinghies, and bring us close enough to board the *Bulwark*."

"Aye, captain," they called from the helm.

We moved in tandem with the *Bulwark*, both of us slowing as we approached the shallows close to shore. We set anchor, and they lowered a boat into the water. A group rowed over to us as our crew dismantled the bolt, the Vorthes having moved Pearl's body to the forecastle deck. Hunter and Bryn stood, and Hunter nodded to something I couldn't hear as I approached them.

I placed a hand on his uninjured left arm but removed it when he flinched. "Hunter..." I shook my head slightly, at a loss for words, "I... I'm sorry," I finished.

He flashed me a pained smile as he shrugged, and I could see how hard he was trying to put on a brave face. My heart twisted. "It could have been worse," he said. "I wish you could have put it back together."

"I'm so sorry," I said again, guilt like a weight in my heart.

"Hey," he tried to smile, but it couldn't get past the grief, "don't apologize for saving my life. I might start to think you regret it." His chuckle came out as a sob, and I wrapped my arms around his neck, pulling his head to my shoulder so that we could cry together.

We looked up when the first mate of the *Bulwark* climbed over the rail and strode straight to Captain Morrig. "Sir, I cannot express the depth of my regret for our actions. Apologies cannot suffice for what we've done—"

The captain took the man by the shoulders, cutting him off. "You were not yourselves, and you were following your captain's orders." The first mate took in the bolt, the pools of blood, Pearl's body, and the haggard state of our crew, and shook his head in denial. Captain Morrig didn't let him voice it. "Your captain was under duress when she ordered you to leave port, and you followed her orders. Now, you'll follow mine when I tell you that is all you need to know."

The first mate hesitated, licked his pallid lips, and then nodded. His cheeks were too hollow, his eyes sunken. A quick glance at the rest of the crew that had boarded confirmed that they were the same. Why did they look half-starved? "Aye, captain. Tell us how we can help."

"We need to get our people to that island," Captain Morrig said. "Ready one of your boats." He pointed to Bryn and me, Sam, and the Vorthes. "Once they make landfall, we'll pull our boats back and monitor for their signal to return."

"I'm going," Hunter said.

"No," I said, my healer's authoritative tone emerging. "You need time to recover."

"I don't," he insisted. "You fixed that. And I can use a sword with my left hand just as well as I can with my right." His breath hitched, but his stony expression didn't waver. "I'm seeing this through."

"Hunter," Bryn said, "you need time to adjust. You're more skilled with your off hand than most people with their dominant side, but we don't know that another sword will do any good, anyway."

Hunter glared at him. "You don't know that it won't. I'm going. I want to see that monster pay for everything he's done."

I knew the look in his eyes; there wouldn't be any swaying him from his decision. He might well jump in after us if we tried to leave him behind, and he would suffer more if we refused to support him. I exhaled hard, and then nodded. "Fine, but don't take unnecessary risks."

"When do I ever?"

Less than an hour later I stood on the shore, watching the boats recede on their way back to the ships. The cold wind chapped my face, my hair in tangles as it whipped free of my braid. Colagh and Paerna were ahead of me, with Tanjiu tucked close behind; Tanjiu hadn't stopped trembling since Pearl. Sam's eyes were wide, committing everything to memory, no doubt, with Bryn and Hunter flanking him, wary eyes relentless in their search for any sign of danger.

Ancient stone piers reached from the shoreline like elderly fingers, their edges dulled by constant buffeting of the waves. Several dinghies like ours were drawn onto the shore, but there was no one in sight.

The piers led to a wall made of stones like those littered around the landing site; it was about ten feet tall and ran as far as I could see in either direction. It enclosed the entire island. Only one small entrance, wide enough for one person to pass through, broke the stone façade in front of us, and I could see little else of the island from where we currently stood.

Clover filled the space between the edge of the island and the wall poking up between the uneven, flat stones that formed a path from our pier to the solitary opening. Two more wound from the other piers aside our landing site.

Tanjiu stepped ahead of the rest of us, and we waited while they inspected the arch, back and forth, several times before they turned to us.

"Nothing here, and I don't feel anything inside. I think we're safe." They walked forward, beneath the arch, and disappeared. I didn't hear a struggle, or an alarm, so I walked past the others to follow.

Bryn nodded to me, pulling his sword and dirk as he looked at the hilt of *Desire* jutting from my sword belt. I followed his clear suggestion, drawing my sword before walking beneath the arch after Tanjiu. The weak warmth of the sun was swallowed by the cool shadows cast by the tall stone above me, forming a narrow passage that turned to the right a few yards from the entrance. Tanjiu was nowhere to be seen.

I paused, letting my senses reach beyond my body, trying to feel the energy of the place. I felt the air around me, the heat of the sun a few feet above me, and the slow, steady hum the stones exuded. But nothing else. Not the thrum I should feel from the bodies of my companions, and nothing beyond the stone walls. Was this part of the defense that the Vorthes had unleashed? To nullify the Ambience beyond a certain perimeter?

I continued forward, trying to suppress the fear of having my power stripped from me again, and peered around the corner before I stepped further into the passage. Still no sign of Tanjiu, but I felt Bryn's presence appear behind me, though I couldn't hear his footfalls. He'd always been able to move like a silent spirit when he wanted to.

I let my eyes linger on his face for a moment, his wary expression softening when he saw me watching him. I flashed him a wan smile, wishing I could hear him while fearing to reach out again, and then turned back to the only path I could follow. Inching forward, I walked as quietly as I could. I came to another corner, and sidled up to peek with one eye to ensure the way was clear.

A sense that I'd done this before, that I'd lurked through narrow passages, waiting for an attack that never came, settled over me. Like glimpsing a familiar port as we sailed into it through a fog, a memory almost came to mind. Tall walls, halls that twisted back and forth, searching for something or someone who was hiding. Someone who might jump out to scare me at any moment.

I blinked, and the memory was gone, replaced by the relief that washed over me as I spotted Tanjiu at the end of another long stretch, waiting for the rest of us. My pace quickened until I stood behind them. They held up a hand to stop me in my tracks, and then peered over my shoulder to watch for the others.

"We're nearing the end," they whispered. Bryn brushed my hand when he arrived, a simple gesture with so many meanings behind it. I clutched his fingers in mine. "I can see buildings in the distance, and there's a ward just outside the arch." They pointed at an arch identical to the one that had led us in here. I felt it too; there was a vibration to the air that felt like it was searching, watching for intruders.

"I can disable it," I offered, but Tanjiu shook their head.

"No, leave that to me. There may be other dangers beyond that." We waited for the rest of the group to catch up, their presences masked until they rounded the final corner between us and them. Tanjiu briefed the rest of the group as they had with Bryn and me, and then turned toward the arch.

They held their hands out, cupping them as if holding a large sphere between their palms. Tanjiu's arms shook, Ambient energy pouring through them, into the sizzling ward, and back out into the world. A wave of hot air buffeted my face as an inferno erupted between their hands, contained in an invisible sphere.

The inferno shot downward, into the stones at their feet, cracking them in a circular pattern before dissipating. Tanjiu stood panting, their hands on their knees, until Paerna walked forward to place his hand on their shoulder. Tanjiu murmured a few words to him that I couldn't make out. Paerna nodded, and after a moment, Tanjiu stood again and turned to face us. New tears rimmed their eyes, though they seemed to be trying hard to swallow the grief they felt.

"That was placed recently, full of so much energy that I almost couldn't contain it." They blew air out of their nose forcefully, their eyebrows raised in amazement. "We should take some precautions now."

The Vorthes nodded, and began to erect shields of Ambience around themselves. Something to ward off the energy another Ambient could hurl their way, nothing that would stop a sword or an arrow. I did the same to Bryn, Hunter, and myself, as Sam took care of his own.

And then, cautiously, we stepped through the arch.

CHAPTER THIRTY-FIVE

The heart of the island, hidden from view by the monstrous walls those brilliant, paranoid Ambient had constructed long ago, was a city. The buildings were untouched by the ravages of time, the streets an orderly grid spread out below. Pristine tile roofs reflected the glow of the afternoon sun, and the air was warm. In the heart of winter, far to the north, the air was warm.

In the center of it all, reaching toward the sky like a finger pointing at the sun, was a tall, white spire that sparkled and reflected prismatic light, as if filtering the sun through a diamond. The tower Derth had shown me in Stalth.

"It looks so much like Salvation," Sam murmured. He looked around in awe. "What is this place?"

I took in the tall pines in a cluster off to our left along the south wall, the sea glittering beyond the furthest reaches of stone, no sign of the fog that we'd passed through to get here. As amazed as I was, it was nothing compared to the pall of dread hanging over the city, as if something ominous was waiting for us to step onto the streets, to trap us within.

"Do you feel that?" I asked Tanjiu.

"Yes," they replied. "I feel it. This place doesn't want us to be here." Their head rotated slowly, from one end of the city to the other, as they scanned for danger. I did the same, finding nothing but a peaceful, empty city. But my body screamed that something was very wrong.

My heart raced, beads of sweat breaking out on the back of my neck and forehead. Hunter and Bryn appeared at my side, but as I watched, their faces blurred. I rubbed my eyes, trying to clear them. When I looked at Bryn again, he was gone, replaced by the maniacal glee on Derth's face as he tortured me on the deck of Roglin's ship. Startled, I stepped back into something solid, rounding on Hunter. He slapped my sword with his before I could slash his chest open. Bryn reached out to grasp my wrist before I could lift it again.

"Lila, what happened?" he asked.

Looking around, I found no sign of Derth, the ship, or anything else that shouldn't be there. "I saw Derth," I said, breathless.

Bryn scanned our surroundings, his hand tightening on his sword until his knuckles were white. "Where?" he demanded.

I shook my head. "No, I saw a vision of him. Or a memory. I'm not sure what it was. Did any of you see anything?"

Hunter and Sam shook their heads. Paerna did too, but Colagh and Tanjiu looked as startled as I felt.

"I was transported back to one of my more frightening memories," Tanjiu said as they ran their hand over their face. "It was only a moment, but…"

"The same for me," Colagh affirmed, wiping a tear from his cheek. "Either our criminal is getting into our heads, or the city's defenses are." He closed his eyes, his aura flaring, touching the strange energy surrounding us. He gasped, and his aura snapped back into place, hard as a shield. "The defenses, they're…alive, like predators stalking through the streets for prey. But they weren't meant to bring our nightmares to life. That's the monster's doing."

"How do you know?" Hunter asked.

Colagh's eyes found mine, and my blood ran cold from the terror staring out from the depths of his gaze. "They told me."

Hunter shook his head, pursing his lips into a frown. "No." It was a denial of everything around us, a refusal to listen to one more piece of insanity.

A scream echoed through the streets. Many screams, from familiar voices. Before I realized it, I was running. Something was drawing me forward, drawing my breaths into ragged gasps. "No," I whispered, with no idea what I was denying. "I can't let it happen again."

I turned a corner, and I was on the *Catherine,* surrounded by my crew as they lay dead and dying. Roglin stood over it all, laughing as he thrust his sword through Captain Morrig, his dark hair blazing like fire in the setting sun. Smitts stared up at me from the ground, Marl cradled Roy's shattered body in his arms. Walter rushed forward with a shortsword in his hands, the blade longer than his small torso.

"No!" I screamed, pulling a sword from a cold hand at my feet. "I'll kill you!" I stabbed, the tip of my sword aimed at Roglin's evil heart, but Walter was there first, and the steel slid into his small back, blood staining his white shirt. Sweat darkened his blonde mop of hair, and I dropped the hilt in horror.

Roglin sneered down at me and opened his mouth to speak. But it was Derth's voice that I heard. "You shouldn't have done that," he scolded. Shame stirred in my chest. "They're going to be so mad at you."

Confused, I looked up, but Roglin's eyes were pale blue, his hair such a light blonde that it looked white. "They?" I asked, my voice smaller, scared.

"They said you would break it if you weren't careful," he said. He was younger, less like the terrifying maniac that haunted my dreams, and more like an older sibling scolding a younger one. Like Hunter had when I'd broken Captain Morrig's compass when we were children. But it wasn't broken glass at my feet, it was blood. Walter's blood.

"Lila!" Someone was shouting my name. Who needed my help? Who could I save? There had to be someone left. Hands grasped me from behind, and I whirled around to face my attacker.

"Lila!" Hunter shouted. "Snap out of it!" He shook my shoulder, and I could see the city behind him, Bryn and Sam on the ground, writhing in pain, Colagh bent over Paerna, who seemed to be unconscious. "It's not real!"

"W-what?" I stammered, trying to make sense of what I was seeing. Bryn groaned, and my head cleared. "Bryn?"

Hunter released me, and I fell to my knees next to Bryn. Pain coursed through his body, and I knew immediately what he was experiencing. "Bryn!" I shouted. "I'm here, we're okay. He's not here, he's not hurting us anymore." Sweat soaked his head, and he thrashed against me, against Derth's torture, his consciousness back on the deck of Roglin's ship before it exploded.

"Don't touch her!" he screamed.

"Bryn, I'm here!" I yelled, my face inches from his. My lips crashed down onto his cheek, his forehead, trying to wake him from his vision. I slammed my fist against his chest. "It's not real!" I pleaded, echoing Hunter's words as he did the same with Sam.

Bryn, please, I thought, throwing caution to the wind. If I couldn't get him back, it wouldn't matter if I didn't come out of this unscathed. If he went insane, would I go with him? The bond felt like a tightrope strung between us, a gaping cavern with no end below me. I ignored the fear of falling, and plunged ahead to a mind in turmoil, convinced that we were dying, that the ship was breaking apart around us, but Derth continued, unfazed. *I love you, I'm here.*

Lila? His eyes opened as he finally heard me, and I exhaled in relief, even as I scrambled back from the connection, slamming a wall between us. A flash of pain in his eyes as he felt it go up, and then, "You're all right?"

I nodded, kissing his forehead again. "I had another terrible vision, but I'm all right. Hunter woke me up. Sam?" I called. "Hunter, is he…"

"I'm fine," Sam croaked. "The others?"

"Paerna is coming around," Colagh replied. "We need to stop this. Our wards are doing nothing against these attacks."

"They're slowing us down," Bryn said, standing.

The dread was a palpable thing, intentional and searching, seeking out the Ambience reaching out from me, sensing the energy all around us. Tendrils of darkness languished in the streets, a plague of Derth's twisted power, branches meeting in the streets, touching spots along the walls, following a path further into the city. With a glance at everyone, I followed along the path that they led, stopping to peer

around every corner I approached, listening so hard for signs of life
ahead that the silence roared in my ears. As we approached the spire
along a wide street, I looked up, and realized with a shock that we were
surrounded.

Set into the walls of the buildings, built into wooden cages atop tall,
slender poles, were orbs. Hundreds of them, the same size and shape as
those that Derth had been using to watch us for months. A cloud passed
overhead, and in the dim light, one of them illuminated with a soft
white glow. A source of light in the darkness, but the tendrils clung to
them, refracting from within the orb, as if projecting Derth's will
throughout the city. Was this how he'd been watching us? Was *this* how
he'd altered the city's defenses?

The darkness stirred as we approached the courtyard between
where we were and the spire, so I paused two streets away, holding my
hands up to stall the others. But we'd awoken something, and those
tendrils snapped out, and we moved too late.

The blast hit Paerna, Hunter, and Sam. They doubled over, Hunter
cried out in pain as the darkness swirled around his head, inserting
itself into his eyes and ears. The others grunted, and the aura of their
tethered spirits fought against the darkness trying to drag them down,
into the madness that awaited. In moments, I knew, they would
succumb.

Hunter lunged at me, his sword level with my midsection, and Bryn
tackled him to the side, onto the stump of his missing arm. Hunter
thrashed in his grasp, but Bryn held firm, his Ambient-granted strength
making his arms a cage that Hunter couldn't escape. Blood trickled
from Hunter's nose as Bryn caught my gaze.

This wasn't the same orb he'd used before, but if he was projecting
through this one, maybe I could smash it on my own? I flung a hard
plane of air against the wall, and the orb shattered. The darkness
receded, and the oppressive presence lessened. Paerna and Sam sagged,
their eyes clearing from whatever they'd witnessed, and Hunter rolled
onto his side when Bryn released him, panting as blood poured from his
nose.

"What are these things?" Hunter growled. He looked up at an orb
affixed to a building. "What was that?"

"These orbs are everywhere," I told him. "I can feel Derth everywhere, and he's using these somehow, to come after us. To turn the city against us."

"It's not the city defending itself?" Bryn asked.

Colagh answered. "The defenses were meant to work slowly, to protect the secrets held here by seeding a fear of leaving into the residents. It became too much for them, something awful happened, but..." He closed his eyes as if to shut out everything but whatever he was listening to. "They weren't meant to be a weapon like this."

"And the orbs?" Hunter asked.

"We use these in Vortheim, some are meant as simple illumination, some are used to communicate over long distances. But Derth has taken control of the whole network, and he might not stop at giving us nightmares. It may only be a matter of time before he takes control of one or more of us, and we turn on each other." He glanced at me.

"Then smash them," Hunter said.

Bryn and Hunter crouched to find loose stones at their feet, and the rest of us struck with the Ambience, smashing the orbs lining the streets, illuminating intersections, anything within our eye line. For every one that shattered, a flare of darkness shot into the sky, and a silent scream that I could feel in my gut echoed through the Ambience like a beacon.

If Derth hadn't known where we were before, he did now.

We waited in silence as loud as the noise had been. One heartbeat, two, three, and then the rumble of feet slamming into the ground, thundering in our direction. Figures filed out from the streets, sprinting straight toward us. Paerna stepped forward, holding his hands out in front of him. He turned to us and winked. When he spoke, we could feel it in our bones, as if his very words had power over us.

"Now I get to have some fun."

CHAPTER THIRTY-SIX

There were at least a dozen of them; some matched portraits the Salavans had shown us of their missing, others wore Trylian naval leather armor, and all brandished swords or clubs, all their eyes fixed on us as they ran forward.

"Stop."

We could feel the power radiating from Paerna, and knew that if he'd directed that word at us, we would have a hard time fighting his order. The wave of bodies ground to a halt before us; they had no choice but to obey. The darkness wrapped around them, filling their heads, pulling their limbs like strings pulled a marionette.

One second passed, and then another, and then they began to twitch. A finger here, an arm there, and then a foot slid forward. Paerna glanced over his shoulder at Colagh standing next to us, and there was uncertainty in his eyes.

"They shouldn't be able to do that," Colagh said, his face pale.

"Lila!" Sam shouted. "Free them before they do it themselves!"

I stepped forward with Bryn at my heels, between Paerna and the bodies moving closer. The disjointed spirits screamed in anguish as they smothered these people. But they turned to me as I opened myself to their energy, their pain like a knife in my heart. But I was a healer, and I could wield the Ambience as well as anything else in my kit. And I let down every wall I'd put up to keep it out.

Ambience soared from the Pool, flooding my body, *becoming* my body, my mind, my spirit. I floated up as my skin illuminated, a beacon of Ambience for the spirits to follow. *"Be at Peace,"* I told the spirits. They twitched, much like the people they controlled twitched against Paerna's demands. They wanted to come home, I could feel it, but they had been hurt for so long, they had forgotten their purpose. They had forgotten that they weren't Derth's creatures. As I burned from within with the force of the Pool flowing through me, they lashed out.

Darkness curled out of the collected thralls before us, a visible cloud that roiled with Ambient fury. It tugged at the Ambience I unleashed, trying to contain it, the darkness within lit by flashes of Ambient light. Colagh and Tanjiu recoiled. Paerna, however, was stuck, holding the thralls in place as long as he could. He couldn't escape the fury unleashed in his direction.

"The Gloom!" Tanjiu shrieked. They turned and ran as the slim hold on their terror slipped, and disappeared between two buildings. Colagh stood frozen, muttering to himself as tears streaked down his face.

I wouldn't be enough to hold it at bay. I glanced to Bryn, who had been reaching for me already, something in his spirit calling to mine. It was laid before me, as vibrant as any Ambient's, the mirror of my own, flawed and generous and beautiful. Our spirits snapped together. The Ambience surged through both of us now, and Bryn's body lifted from the ground to float next to Lila's, their hands clasped together.

Spirits overflowed from the Pool to contain the fractured spirits that swarmed over Paerna, the leading edge of that dark cloud. He twisted away, screaming, and then fell thrashing to the ground as the thralls were released.

Come, we called. More spirits rushed from the Pool, and the area surrounding us became blinding. Sam and Hunter shied away, Colagh shut his eyes, and Paerna continued to writhe. But the darkness shied away from the spirits that surrounded them to coax them back into the light. The spirits were ours to command, the Pool was ours to control, and there was nothing Derth could do to stop us.

A vacuum of pressure, a tug from the Pool, anchored in the spirits—

fractured and whole—and we tumbled forward as the world shifted. Not toward a void to destroy and consume, but toward the essence of life and light, back to the Pool at the heart of Celuthia.

The cloud funneled through us, the link to the Pool, and was gone. The spirits rushed through us, a cacophony of memories, affinities, voices of those that had come before. It was too much for us to contain. Our power strained and the link swelled, ready to burst. So we dug our fingers into the face of the world, and opened a direct path to the Pool.

The spirits left us, drawn by the ancient energy that called them home from the other side. We were left weightless, serene. It would be so easy to join the spirits as they floated through the rent in the world, beneath the surface of the Pool. To become one with the light, to let the Ambience take us. What remained for us that could compare to the bliss we would feel? Why would we stay in a place where we had experienced so much hurt, had lost so many people?

We turned to say goodbye to our friends, but when our eyes landed on Sam, struggling to stay on his feet, and Hunter, whose nose was still bleeding, who was shielding his eyes with his remaining arm as he gazed through the rent, we faltered.

The outstretched hands of so many spirits urged us to follow. But one large figure stepped forward, their arm outstretched to hold us at bay.

No, it said. *Not yet.*

Lila's body turned back, reaching out to Hunter, and her desire to help him seeped into our minds. Bryn took a step toward Sam, and the pull faded as we let the spirits slip away. The rent closed behind us as we descended to the ground.

The power rushed out of me all at once, and I swayed on my feet. Bryn did as well, and we clung together to stay upright. Paerna lay motionless on the ground, and Colagh knelt next to him, sobbing. The thralls twitched, prone. Sam rushed to Hunter as I stumbled in his direction and laid my hands on his head.

"Hunter, can you hear me?" I asked. There was so much blood, dripping in a steady patter from the tip of his nose. I tried to heal him, but the Ambience wouldn't come. I panicked, seeing events unfolding in the same way again, powerless to help Hunter when he needed me most. But part of me was relieved; I'd given myself over to the entirety of the Ambience, to Bryn, and *I'd* come out the other side.

Sam took my place as my hands fell from Hunter's face. The bleeding slowed, and then came to a stop. But the pain was still evident in his grimace, and in his fingers tightly grasping his curly hair.

"Twice now!" Colagh shouted, closing his friend's eyes. He rounded on us, tears streaming from his eyes. "How can he so easily conjure Vortheim's plague?"

I shook my head, unable to form words around the lump in my throat. We weren't prepared for this. We never could have prepared for *this*.

Colagh stood, his fists clenched at his sides. "The only justice is death," he said. He stalked forward, his strides became a jog, and then he sprinted away from us in the direction of the spire. He cut to the right and was lost behind a building.

"Wait!" Bryn called, but Colagh was gone. I looked down at Hunter, who was rising to his feet with Sam's help. And back in the direction where Colagh had disappeared. My instinct told me to follow him, that he would be killed if he went after Derth alone. But the rest of us weren't ready, and Tanjiu was missing.

Another figure stepped out from behind an adjacent building, shrouded in darkness, a huge sword held in one hand. "Bryn," I said, pointing toward the new threat.

Bryn drew his weapons and raced toward the figure as it glided closer. I drew *Desire*, and stalked forward, too. We couldn't let this thing get near the others, especially all the helpless Salavans lying on the ground. I couldn't make out any features beyond its shroud, and as the first tendril of dark energy slid over my boot, a chill ran up my spine.

Bryn darted forward, sword point lunging for the middle of the figure. The darkness swirled around his blade, swallowing it to the hilt before Bryn was wrenched to the side. Ice crystals spread across his hand, so cold it burned; he winced in pain and backed away.

"Be careful, its touch is freezing!" he shouted. The large shadow blade arced toward him, and he parried it aside with his dirk, wincing again.

The Ambience was a distant shadow when I reached for it, so I swung my sword low, but the figure was already moving in Bryn's direction. I gave chase, swinging my sword upward to slice across its back. Bryn had warned me, but I wasn't ready for the frigid pain that radiated from my sword when it made contact. It stumbled into the path of Bryn's lunge, and the shadow receded from a wound in his arm where the blade penetrated it.

I shouted in pain, trying to regain control of my frozen fingers. Bryn wrenched his dirk free as the darkness tried to coalesce around the wound again. A tendril shot out in Bryn's direction as he ducked aside. Knowing I couldn't put much power into my next strike, I brought the hilt up near my chest. With one palm on the pommel, I used my body to push the blade forward, into his shadowed shoulder. The longer the blade stayed in, the more the cold burned, and I screamed against the pain so that I could hold him in place. "*Bryn! Now!*"

Bryn lunged again, catching the larger blade against the guard of his longsword. Their entangled swords wound around each other, and Bryn shoved it aside before plunging his dirk deep into the thing's chest. He pulled back, and then stabbed his sword alongside the dirk.

I pulled *Desire* free, and the burning faded. My arms and hands were bright red, numb, and the skin beneath my fingernails darkened as I watched. Bryn released his weapons as a man fell from the shadows that slithered away, disappearing into the city like snakes fleeing a larger predator.

Bryn staggered close to me, holding his hands against his chest. The skin was black up to his wrists. "Lila, your hands…"

"Yours are worse," I said, but I couldn't feel my fingertips, and a distant part of my brain realized how bad that was. "Sam! We need help!" Sam was there in an instant, trying to take my hands in his while I tried to push him toward Bryn. "He's worse," I insisted. "I can wait."

"No," Bryn shook his head. But Sam hissed when he grasped Bryn's hands. If not for the Ambience, there would have been no way to heal the damage done. But Sam poured healing energy into both of Bryn's hands, and the black coloration faded, leaving healthy—if red and painful—skin behind. Sam turned to me, and though I was grateful to keep my fingers, I longed for the numbness that gave way to the burning when I could feel them again.

Several people stirred, groaning where they had dropped. I started, having forgotten about them for the moment, but now my instinct propelled me forward, toward people that might need help.

I crouched to help a woman sit up, clearly confused. "Where am I?" she asked. "Where is my daughter?" She turned too quickly, suddenly panicked, searching among the rest of the stirring faces for a daughter that wasn't there.

"She's safe," I said in the soothing voice I reserved for my patients. "In Salava, looking forward to seeing you again." I had no idea whether that was true, but I needed her calm.

"How did I get here? *Why* am I here?" Her face clouded, as if lost in memory.

I shook my head and grimaced. "It's hard to explain, but I promise we'll get you home. For now, I think we should get all of you inside. Bryn," I called, "can we find a safe place for everyone to wait for us? So that we can get them back to the mainland?"

"The mainland?" the woman asked.

I nodded at her, but spoke to Bryn. "Maybe one of the larger buildings? Can you get one open?"

"Yes," he replied. He touched my hair, letting his hand linger for a moment. I closed my eyes, savoring the feel of his fingertips as they trailed through my hair, and then he was gone, his footsteps diminishing as he jogged away.

Taking a deep breath, I opened my eyes, seeing all the people gather into a cluster, helping each other to stand. My eyes moved past them, to Paerna, where he'd been abandoned when Colagh left. I stood, having to push myself off the stone ground with my hands, drained and empty. But I moved forward, wondering how I would move his body so that we wouldn't have to leave him in the open street. I'd have to wait for Bryn to come back, because I didn't want Hunter to strain himself, and I was too afraid to face the emptiness to try the Ambience again.

I sank to my knees and froze. His arms and legs were longer, sticking out from sleeves. His fingernails looked like claws, now, and the skin on his head was covered in gray scales. *What is this?* I thought.

How could he have changed them so much? Is this what it's like in Vortheim? Colagh had told us the Gloom manifested in different ways. Was this what he meant?

I shook my head in disbelief as I placed a hand on Paerna's chest. When I moved to take it away, I felt a faint thump, so I left it where it was and held my breath. Could that be a heartbeat? Seconds passed, too many to let my spark of hope grow. But, as I nearly gave up, I felt it again.

"Paerna?" I asked. I waited again, my eyes wide as I tried to will his heart to beat again, for him to take a breath and open his eyes. "Please, Paerna," I pleaded. Another thump. His finger twitched, and I let out a sigh of relief. Another thump, faster this time, and then his chest rose as he took a breath.

"Sam," I called over my shoulder, feeling his chest rise again, and his heart beat a bit faster. "Paerna is alive." Sam grunted as I looked back at Paerna, and then Sam was with me. He frowned when he saw how he'd changed.

"How did this happen?"

"The Gloom?"

"If Derth can conjure it at will..." He didn't finish his sentence, and I didn't need to. I was already aware of how dangerous Derth had become.

I lifted a scaled eyelid, and Paerna's slitted pupil contracted against the light. My skin prickled at the sight, at how *much* he had changed. But he didn't stir, and I gently let his eye close again. "I think we should get him inside with the others. I don't want to leave him exposed." Sam followed my gaze, his mouth tightening. "How is Hunter?"

Sam grimaced. "Pounding headache, blurry vision. I think Derth is affecting him more than us because he isn't Ambient. Bryn has your power to protect him, but Hunter doesn't. I did what I could to help him, but he's in a lot of pain. I think he should stay with the townspeople."

"I'll try to convince him," I said. "Will you stay with Paerna while I talk to him?" Sam nodded, so I stood and shuffled my way to Hunter. He was sitting up now, his elbow propped on his knee and his face in his hand. He squinted at me when he heard me coming, and tried to smile.

"Hey, Lila," he said, his voice weak. "Is he dead?" he asked, looking past me.

"He's still alive. Derth… did something to him. He looks different. Not entirely human."

"Elders' eyes," he cursed. "Is that going to happen to me, too?"

"Let me take a look." I inspected his face, his hand, his shoulders, even lifted the back of his shirt to see the strained muscles in his back. But I found nothing like the other two. "I think you're still you," I told him. "How are your eyes?"

He tried to open them, but closed them before I could see more than a flash of green. "Sorry, the light hurts."

I sighed. "I think you should stay with the people, with Paerna. To keep an eye on them."

He was already shaking his head before I could finish. "No, I'm with you. I just need a minute to clear my head. Maybe you can help with the pain?"

It was my turn to grimace. "I'm a bit worn out after…" I gestured to the place where Bryn and I had been, but let my arm drop when I remembered he couldn't see it. "I'll try after we get everyone situated. Seems like I need a minute, too."

He chuckled at that. "Alright, Lila."

Bryn arrived and placed his hand on the small of my back. I leaned against it. "I found a house on the next street. Are you all right? I can't feel you."

I tried to smile, but there was too much weighing me down to pretend. "I'm not," I admitted. "Paerna is alive, but he's not the same, and we need to protect these people, find Derth, stop the Gloom he keeps throwing at us, and risk ourselves over and over every time we join our spirits…" I trailed off, my mouth opening and closing as I struggled to put how overwhelmed I was into words. "I don't know if we can do this."

He pulled me closer and wrapped his arms around me. "We'll find a way," he murmured.

"How?" I asked his chest. "He's so powerful, and I feel like we've already pushed ourselves too far. Tell me you didn't feel it. The

Ambience, trying to take us?"

It took a few seconds for him to answer. "I felt it," he replied.

"We came so close to being consumed, like Sam's always warning us about, and we haven't even *seen* Derth yet. What do we do when we find him? How can we stop him *without* using the Ambience, and how can we use it without being consumed? How can we avoid being consumed by the darkness that keeps trying to swallow us when the Pool isn't?"

"We work together," he said. I started to protest, but he pulled away and stopped me with a finger on my lips. "I don't mean what we did here. I mean, you do what you do best, and I support you. If you need my strength, you have it. You always have it. Plus, we have more than Derth has. We got rid of his army of thralls. We have our friends, and we have each other."

I tried to take heart from his words, to take a fraction of his confidence. But I couldn't. There was an empty pit in my stomach, the pall of dread still hanging like a cloud above my head. Instead, I decided to focus on what was in front of me. There were people to help here, and we needed to follow Colagh.

"We work together," I told Bryn. "Let's start by getting these people safe."

CHAPTER THIRTY-SEVEN

The city was quiet, and Bryn found no sign of Colagh in the time we gave him to track the Vorthe down. The people we'd freed were emaciated and dehydrated—their supplies had run out a week ago—and I hoped they were heeding my advice to ration the food and water we'd left so that they wouldn't bring it all back up. That, along with the fact that Hunter wouldn't stay behind, had my stomach in anxious knots when we set off again.

"I'm fine," Hunter hissed for the hundredth time, waving my concern away with his remaining hand. He glared at me, which was at least a sign that he could see again. "Stop looking at me like that, Lila."

We didn't know where to go, so Bryn had suggested we move toward the white spire at the city's center. It seemed like the most logical place for Derth to hide, and if he wasn't there, it could give us a vantage point from which to determine where we should head next. With weapons drawn, we walked as quietly as we could, letting Bryn take the lead so he could scout ahead, and Sam followed behind, a shield at the ready.

My eyes moved constantly, looking ahead, behind, around corners, hoping to find Colagh, hoping we might encounter Derth so that we could end this, while dreading the same.

Bryn slowed, turning his head to the side to listen to something the rest of us couldn't hear. The three of us slowed as well, and as our footfalls stopped, I made out something like distant thunder. The ground rumbled beneath us, like the tremor of an earthquake from a vast distance. A shout, and then a familiar laugh echoed through the city.

Derth.

A thrill ran through my body—fear, anticipation—as Bryn took off at a run, and we followed close behind. A right turn past a house, a left between two barren garden beds, and another right. I lost sight of him for a heartbeat, lunged past a tendril flaring from an orb on the wall next to me, and then we emerged from the alley. They opened onto a large square, the spire looming above, casting a shadow over the cobblestones. There Derth stood, laughing as Colagh hurled stones and fire and air at him with little effect.

"I *thought* I felt you!" Derth screamed over the noise of a boulder crashing into an invisible barrier in front of him. Seeing him, his greasy blonde hair blown back by a gust of air from Colagh, his ice-blue eyes seeming to shine with a strength of madness I'd not seen before, washed away every other emotion warring for dominance in my heart. In their place, rage burned like an inferno.

Derth's clothes were ragged and filthy, his patchy gray beard long and scraggly, and darkness swirled around him. Tortured spirits writhed and screamed in silent agony along with it. "Our connection runs deep, something that cannot be broken, even with the strange power you have. The power that you steal from the one you've enslaved."

He glared at Bryn, who was sheathing his blades and reaching for his bow. "We have that talent," Derth continued. "To control people, to bend them to our wills. I felt it in you when I took your power away. I fought against it, denied the truth of it, and convinced myself that I needed to give you to the Malachi. But now that I see you there, throwing your thralls at me as I did at you, I know that we are the same."

Revulsion joined the rage burning through me. That he could think I could do to anyone what he'd done to me... I snarled at him as Bryn nocked an arrow.

"I'm nothing like you!" I shouted.

"You could decide to join me," he said. "If you knew what I did about the Malachi, you would *want* to help me." Derth extended his arms, and darkness shot forth, wrapping its tendrils around Colagh, restraining him. Bryn loosed his arrow, aimed straight at Derth's chest, but it clattered against a barrier and ricocheted to the side.

Derth laughed, and the darkness tightened around Colagh's throat. I ran forward, and the Ambience came back to me in my desperate rage. I gestured at him, trying to wrench the tendrils away, to bring Ambient light to push back the darkness, but it retracted, pulling Colagh with it.

He was dragged back, closer to Derth. He tried to scream, but had no breath to do it. His mouth opened and closed, his eyes wild and desperate, rolling in his head. They flicked up and down, up and down, and stayed down. Looking at something, I realized. At his hand, where he was clutching something.

The bracelet. It was in his hand, held against his side by the darkness. Sam rushed forward with Hunter on his heels, and Bryn loosed another arrow. And another, knowing it wouldn't get to Derth, but trying to distract him long enough to get Colagh released. I did the same, grasping some loose stones to hurl at Derth as he laughed behind his barrier, impervious to our attacks.

"We need to get closer!" I called to Sam. Bryn dropped his bow and drew his sword, running so fast that he passed the other two in moments, and slammed against the barrier himself. He slashed it again and again, pouring all of his fury, all the strength he possessed, into the blows. Sam placed a barrier of his own, stopping the tendrils from retracting any further with Colagh, but his body was being crushed by the opposing forces.

Hunter leapt forward, his blade sliding through the tendrils without severing them. Seeing that he couldn't help, he dropped his sword and grabbed the bracelet from Colagh, whose face crumpled with relief and pain.

I caught up with Hunter, who palmed the bracelet into my hand. But I had no idea how to get it around Derth's wrist. He'd spent all that energy, all those people, trying to get me here. If I obliged him, he would let me through, right? Bone snapped, and Colagh gurgled. "I'll stop him," I said, and ran toward the darkness. It retreated from me, confirming my suspicion, to form a path that I could walk through safely even as it began to wind around Bryn, who was still slashing at the barrier.

"Derth!" I shouted, the Clinch enclosed in my fist, numbing my skin. "Let Colagh go, leave the others, and I'll come to you."

Derth paused, shuffling to the side to get in his eyeline. I held my empty hand out and touched the barrier, a cool, solid surface beneath my palm. Bryn stopped his attack and stood panting from the effort, shaking his head in denial. "No," he choked. "I won't let you go with him."

"I have to, Bryn." Tendrils writhed up Bryn's legs, over his torso. "Stop, Derth! If you want me, leave them all alone!" I turned from Bryn with an effort that took my breath away. "*Just* me."

Derth bared his teeth in a feral smile. "Come through, and then I let them go."

My heart raced and every instinct told me to run. My rage and resentment propelled me forward against those instincts.

I pushed against the barrier, where a tingle of Ambience slid over my skin like rancid oil that made my gorge rise. Bryn called my name in terror, and then I was inside. The dread was more oppressive here, malignant. Every instinct I had told me to turn and run. But I couldn't. Not until this was done.

Colagh and Bryn were released, and Colagh crumpled to the ground, his body contorted. Bryn slammed against the barrier again and again, screaming my name. Derth held his hand out to me, beckoning me forward. It couldn't be that easy, could it?

"All that power," he said. A shiver passed over him.

Was that delight? Anticipation? My stomach flipped sickeningly.

His voice became a whisper of anticipation. "It should have been mine from the start."

Reaching out the hand with the bracelet tucked inside, I watched him reciprocate, reaching toward me, his eyes flitting back and forth from my fist to my face, eager to be near me again. I kept my face blank, hoping that it wouldn't betray me now, when I needed to keep my thoughts hidden. His hand was so close, and my fist opened to hold the bracelet out. Gnarled fingers slid through the leather, tightening around his wrist as I let go.

The barrier fell away in a rush, the darkness disappeared, and Derth stood with his mouth agape, staring at the bracelet. His manic glee was gone, replaced by disbelief. His eyes found mine, and I smiled, knowing he could do nothing to hurt me. Not anymore.

He smiled back, and then his face dissolved before my eyes, leaving me alone in the street. I whirled around, and they were all gone.

Where are they? I thought. *Was any of it real?* The Clinch was in my hand. How?

Desperate, I reached out with my mind again. *Bryn?* Silence. I couldn't even feel him. Fog rolled in, choking the rest of the city from view, leaving me with nothing but gray. I heard nothing but the sound of my ragged gasps. Panic rose within me as I recognized this fog; it was the same dull gray that had imprisoned me before.

I screamed.

CHAPTER THIRTY-EIGHT

I ran, not sure where it would take me, just knowing that I had to try to escape this gray hell before it claimed my emotions again. As I hurtled through the fog, nothing changed, though I darted left and right with abandon, trying to escape. There was no way out, and every moment I spent in here, I could feel my essence bleeding away. Any moment I would cease to be me, my emotions and the very core of my being locked behind some wall in my head. *Again.*

I clenched my fists and screamed again, trying to burn my fear away with white-hot rage. "*DERTH!* Come out and face me!" There was no answer. "I've escaped before," I shouted, looking up to see nothing but gray fog. "I escaped when I had no idea what I was doing." I lowered my gaze, staring ahead as I began to move again, letting my power radiate out from me. Derth's chuckle echoed through the fog, coming from everywhere and nowhere. It receded from me as spirits began to circle me, creating a barrier of my own against the effects of the fog, leaving me a small space in the infinite gray.

Snarling, I said, "You don't understand how much trouble you're in."

"Lila!" Bryn screamed, her name tearing out of his throat like a knife. She'd been behind him a moment before, but when he felt that emptiness inside him again, like those agonizing moments with the Clinch on her wrist, he'd whirled to find that no one was there. Frozen, like when his mother had died, and he'd had nowhere to go. He'd stayed in that house until the flies came, her body decaying before he knew what that meant, and he'd finally realized that she wouldn't wake again. Everything he'd done to keep Lila safe was colored by the fear created then. And here he was, just as powerless as he'd been as a child.

The city was empty, and he found no trace of where the others had gone. No imprints of their boots in the dirt between the stones, no sounds beyond his pained, panicked gasps. "Where *are you?*"

He dashed down one street, turning north, the spire appearing through gaps between buildings. He found the place he'd put the people they'd rescued, but it was closed, empty. There was no one left.

Thrusting his blades into their sheaths, he ran his hands through his hair as he cast about, looking for a direction she might have gone. His fingers wound around clumps of hair and pulled, the pain distracting him from the gnawing panic in his gut and the hole in his heart. Where could she be? Why couldn't he feel her?

His eyes locked on the spire, the white gleaming beacon at the heart of the city. If Lila was lost, she would go there. If he didn't find her there, he could see more of the city from that height. It was still the best option, so he ran.

It was still a surprise to move so fast, to see the streets blur around him. All because Lila had given part of herself to him, because she trusted him so much that she'd made him part of her. There was nothing more important than finding her.

And if Derth hurt her, there was nothing that could stop him from ripping the man apart.

Lila's voice rang out from somewhere nearby, a scream of pain that chilled his blood as he skid to a halt. He could feel her again, and her agony tore the breath from his lungs. Bryn turned, following the sound, away from the spire, toward the outskirts of the city.

"*I'm coming,*" he said, to himself and to her, hoping she could hear his thoughts even though he couldn't hear her. "*Fight.*"

Sam ran through his cabin, yelling his wife's name as he searched every room. When no reply came, he bolted through the kitchen and out the back door. Looking around, he could find no trace of Penelope or Sammy, until he saw a few drops of blood on the ground by his feet.

Frantic, he searched the ground nearby, sobbing when he saw more blood a few feet away, in the direction of the forest. He sprinted, following the trail of blood, hoping against hope that Penelope had somehow harmed Ellen and not the other way around.

He reached the line of trees and saw a clear path had been forged through the fallen pine needles. It wasn't a clean line of footprints, but a haphazard scattering of needles, as if someone had been thrashing as they were dragged.

He continued despite the knowledge that he could be too late, not willing to give up the hope that he might still save his family. He raced over the hills, until he emerged on the hilltop clear of trees where Ellen stood over his pregnant wife and young son.

Penelope's face was marred by a large gash on one cheek and Sammy's innocent face was already bruising from whatever assault he had endured.

When his family spotted him, Sammy cried out for him, and Ellen turned to face him. Penelope thrust her hand out, hurling a gout of flame in Ellen's direction. But the gaunt woman, her blonde hair wild, swatted the fire aside with a casual sweep of her hand. Another sweep, and blood gushed from a rent in Penelope's neck. When Sammy screamed and lunged, Ellen repeated the same gesture, slashing his throat.

"NO!" Sam screamed. He flew forward, trying to get to his family. But Ellen held him at bay, his arms and legs locked in place. He couldn't turn his head when he heard Bryn shout from behind, nor when Lila crested the hill with her sword drawn. He couldn't move as the two of them were engulfed in flames as Ellen cackled with delight. All he could do was stand and watch as his family bled to death, and his new family screamed in agony.

Tears rolled down Sam's cheeks. Ellen sneered as she raised her hands to him. "It's your turn."

I gasped as I came back to myself, the images of Bryn and me burning and Sam's family bleeding and blinking out of existence. First Bryn, and now Sam. Both suffering, living through their worst fears. They were as helpless as me. I tucked the bracelet into my bodice and started to jog, trying to find my way out of the haze.

Hunter stood surrounded by cloaked figures, their faces shrouded in darkness, only their hands visible as they pointed at him. "There's no escape for you, Hunter." He couldn't tell who'd spoken, or *if* anyone had spoken. But the ground began to rumble beneath his feet, and pain exploded in his head.

The circle blasted apart as Lila came charging into the fray. Hunter dove to the side, landing on his arm as Lila threw her hand out, a thunderous boom sounding as the figures were thrown back. He groaned as Lila stopped next to him, her long red hair falling in a curtain over her face before she impatiently threw it over her shoulder.

"Are you all right?" she asked him, her face contorted with anxiety.

"I'll live," Hunter replied as he tried to stand. The motion jarred his head, and he clutched it, feeling as though if he didn't, his brain would burst through his skull.

"Barely," Lila replied with a smirk on her face. But she crouched in front of him and put her warm hand against his cheek before helping him to sit upright.

"Thanks," he said as he regained his feet. He looked around, noticing that the figures were gone. "Where did they go?"

"They took off when I got here," she replied. "I guess I was too much for them."

Hunter rolled his eyes at her to hide the dread that twisted in his gut whenever she used her power. It was the same around all of them. Sam, the Vorthes, Lila, even Bryn, when he did something inhuman because of how Lila had changed him.

He sighed. At least Bryn wasn't here to do their creepy 'we' thing. Whenever they did that near him, the urge to run in the opposite direction was so strong that resisting it made his stomach churn.

"You think I don't see the way you react to me now, but I do," Lila whispered.

Before he could wrap his mind around the implications of what she had said, she casually flicked her hand to the right, and the world fell away. He crashed into a nearby building, all the air forced from his lungs before he crumpled to the ground. He gasped and watched Lila slowly stalk toward him.

"You could never understand how much *someone like you* disgusts me." She was a predator, staring at him with wide eyes. Savoring the hunt before the kill.

"Someone like me?" he croaked, her words tearing into him, ripping his heart to shreds.

"You don't know?" she laughed, her mouth twisted into a sneer. "How pathetic!"

Her fingers curled like claws, she swiped her hand in his direction again. Deep gashes opened in his chest to pour blood onto the ground as he screamed in agony. Hunter curled into a ball as she did it again, leaving cuts in his side.

He lunged at her feet, but she threw him as easily as he would throw a twig, and he went sprawling across the stones, his head cracking against a rock. All the pain in his head intensified, and when he touched it, his fingers came away bloody. Lila stood over him, a look of disgust on her face as she peered at him.

"This time, I'll make sure you *stay* dead."

Bryn felt like he'd been running for hours, and all he'd found was more empty streets. His lungs ached from all the running, his muscles protesting the abuse as he pushed them harder, to move faster.

He turned back toward the spire, the air rushing past his face and pulling his clothes out behind him. It had been too long since he'd heard Lila scream. If it had been real, she might be dead by now. He couldn't lose her, not after all he'd already lost. His father, his mother, his home... The ache in his chest told him that he couldn't survive if he lost her, too. So he ran faster, even though his legs threatened to give out with every step.

When he emerged from the city at the base of the spire, he ground to a halt in its shadow. Standing at the base, next to a wooden door that opened into a dark room, stood Derth. He smiled as Bryn appeared, and held up his hands. As he did, Bryn heard a choked sob, and looked behind Derth to find Lila on the ground, writhing in agony.

"Don't *touch her!*" Bryn screamed, drawing his sword and tensing to spring at Derth. But Derth twitched a finger, and Lila screamed.

"I don't have to *touch* her," Derth said. His murmured words were like a shout for Bryn, worming their way into his head, squeezing his heart. Lila's hair was matted with dirt and sweat, her head thrashing as she curled to the side, facing the spire with her back to Bryn. "I'm having some fun. But, if you come near us, I will make her suffer so much more."

Derth crooked a twisted finger at Lila, and her body rotated so that Bryn could see her face. Dirt marred across her cheeks and nose, as if she'd been writhing in the dirt for a while, the only clean spots the trails left by her tears. Her eyes were wild and unseeing, entirely focused on her pain. It was a sight that would haunt his dreams for as long as he lived, the same look of terror on her face as she'd had the last time Derth tortured her.

He ached to rush to her, took a step forward, but Derth saw it. "Do you need me to demonstrate how serious I am?" His fingers closed into a fist, and Lila's arm snapped up at the wrong angle, the sound of her bone breaking like the shattering of Bryn's heart.

"Stop!" he screamed. "Take me, but spare her!"

"What makes you think I want you?" Derth spat. "You're useless.

The only reason you think you are important is because she *made* you. Without her, you'd be nothing."

Derth's hand opened, and Lila stilled. Bryn couldn't tell whether she was breathing or not, and he couldn't think, couldn't breathe. But his body moved, and he sprang forward faster than he thought possible.

But it wasn't fast enough.

Derth held his hands up as if to ward off Bryn's attack, but Bryn felt thousands of cuts opening all over his body. Blood soaked through his clothes, and still he moved. Plunging his sword into Derth, satisfaction bubbled up in his throat as he coughed, and blood spattered on the ground.

His sword snagged on Derth's ribcage, and the weight of his body pulled Bryn off-balance, sending him toppling to the ground with his face right next to Lila. Bryn lifted his hand to touch her cheek, but it was cold. Blood mixed with the tears that fell.

She stirred, and his heart leaped into his chest. "Lila? Love, can you hear me?"

Her head turned, and her eyes were black. Darkness oozed out of them, caressing his skin as she smiled. Bryn screamed.

"BRYN!" My scream exploded in a wave of spirits that blew the fog apart. The spire loomed above me, sparkling in the setting sun. At its base was the wooden door I'd seen as Bryn's tortured body fell in front of it, but there was no blood, there were no bodies. I sank to my knees, to run my hand across the stones and assure myself that he wasn't there. That the empty street wasn't the illusion, the blood had been.

What happened to them? I wondered, tears falling from my eyes to land on the back of my hand.

My vision blurred, and I watched Bryn battling some opponent, though the image was hazy. He screamed my name, looking past the woman thrusting a sword as he spun to the side and used his dirk to wrench her blade from her hand. Leaving the woman behind, he ran toward something I couldn't see, shouting my name over and over again. But there were more opponents, more blades, all slicing into him as he ducked past one, and skirted another. Every time his vision changed, so did his wounds.

Not real, I assured myself. But he slowed more and more each time, the phantom wounds taking a physical toll. He slammed his dirk into a man's ribs, pulled it free as he spun to slash another, and slammed the pommel of his dirk into someone's face. He fell to one knee, but pushed against the ground and rose. Before anyone could stop him, he ran.

The vision of him running with blood streaming behind faded, and I was on the ground in front of the spire. I saw something move from the corner of my eye, and whipped my head in that direction to see Bryn standing in the middle of the street. He was panting with his weapons in his hands and wounds all over his body. Blood flowed freely from a gash on his forehead, and he briskly wiped it away with the back of his hand as I fully turned to face him.

"Bryn!" I cried as I stood and ran in his direction. How had I not heard him fighting when he was so close? I dismissed the thought as he turned to me, his body sagging with relief, and a wide smile on his face.

I was about twenty feet from him when a hulking man stepped out from behind a building to his right, a claymore gripped between both hands. He snarled at Bryn through perfectly white teeth, a sharp contrast to the shadows that seemed to surround his frame.

"Behind you!" The smile disappeared as Bryn turned, but I knew that he would be too late to block the blow. I gathered and solidified the air around me and unleashed it at the man with fierce abandon—*too slow too slow*—but he just smiled as the sword came down.

"No!" I screeched. Blood spurted from Bryn's shoulder. His arm dangled from a strand of muscle after one forceful blow.

Bryn sank to his knees as I continued to rush headlong at him. But I drew no closer as the man pulled back, preparing to swipe Bryn's head from his shoulders. My throat was raw from so much screaming, but I couldn't help another one from tearing free when that bastard looked up and smiled at me before bringing his weapon around viciously. A sickening crunch, and then a thud from Bryn's head where it hit the stones, tumbling free.

I screamed again and pushed myself even harder to move forward,

to run with all the speed that I possessed, and still, I couldn't get any
closer. The man retrieved Bryn's head, dragged his lifeless body behind
him by the foot and out of sight around the corner of a building, and
only then was I able to move forward.

When I rounded the corner, they were gone. The only evidence that
they had been there at all was the trail of blood smeared on the ground,
so I followed as fast as I could as it turned around corner after corner,
finally ending up at the base of the spire and disappearing through the
wooden door.

I continued my headlong sprint, crashing through the door hard
enough to make my arm go numb with the impact. The trail led me
through another door to my right, and I only paused long enough to
draw my sword before throwing it open. I was greeted by the sight of
Hunter and Sam on their knees before the same man that had killed
Bryn. Before I could take a step inside, the man thrust long daggers
through each of their backs with enough force to push completely
through their bodies.

I shrieked, and hungry flames licked up *Desire's* blade as I charged
forward. Hunter and Sam slumped to the side when the daggers were
pulled free, and the hulking man stood from his crouch to face me. I
swept aside both of his arms with one forceful swing to my left, and he
staggered, trying to keep his balance.

Before he could recover, I thrust *Desire*, flames and all, into his
side. I wrenched the blade to my left, cutting through his middle as
easily as I would slice an apple, and then pulled it free. He fell silently
to his knees, and then his head hit the floor.

I stood still for a moment, panting from the effort of sprinting
through the streets and nearly slicing this man in half, before I
remembered that I might still be able to save my friends. I dropped my
sword and nearly fell to the ground next to Hunter, but he was already
gone.

A ragged breath drew me to Sam's side. *Please*, I begged. But when
I reached for that thread tying me to the Ambience, I found nothing,
like it had never existed. Sam's eyes closed, and there was nothing I
could do as he slipped away.

"No," I cried, trembling where I knelt on the cold stone floor. And then, a spark. That Ambient thread flared bright and vengeful, igniting the walls around me. The flames blazed orange, and then white. Glancing at the inferno hot enough to crack the stone wall, I knew that I would be killed if I didn't move. But I caught sight of Bryn's headless body nearby and the flame grew brighter. There was no reason to save myself. Not anymore.

Instead, I dragged myself over to his body to rest my head on his still chest. But my hands passed through him, and when I blinked, he was gone. Sam and Hunter, too, though the flames licked higher. The room was empty, just the conflagration covering the curved white wall of the spire spreading to the wall flanking the wooden door.

I let the flames have me.

CHAPTER THIRTY-NINE

The flames burned bright, and every moment I expected to feel the fire consume me. Instead, there was an impact against the back of my head, and then the red light behind my closed eyelids disappeared. Confused, I opened my eyes, and the fire was gone.

A single candle illuminated an unfamiliar room, and I gasped in ragged breaths, trying to reach my pounding head. But my hands were bound behind me, painfully taut, and when I tried to stand I felt the ropes binding my ankles, too.

My neck screamed when I lifted my head, as my skull crashed against the high back of the wooden chair I'd been propped in. My head was pounding, my skin raw, and the world slammed back into me.

"Head injuries are dangerous things," Derth said. My mind went blank, my body stilled, and I couldn't help but look in the direction of that rasping voice. I could feel him, bathed in shadows that obscured everything but the gleam in his icy eyes. "I can fix that for you, if you'd like?"

"No," I grumbled. "But if you'd like to free me, I can take care of it myself."

He chuckled at that, and the hair on the back of my neck stood on end. There was something *else* laughing with him. Or through him. "It's interesting to me that you need to have your hands free to use your power. Either you're lying, trying to give yourself room to escape, or you're more incompetent than I'd imagined, despite your assertions to the contrary. Which is it?"

I thought of the vision, knowing that it was just another fabrication, and wishing it hadn't been. But I arranged my features into a defiant sneer. "If this is your idea of torture, you're doing an awful job of it so far."

He didn't answer, and I could feel him watching me, waiting for...something. I took a deep breath and willed the pain in my head to subside. To my surprise, I felt the ethereal, comforting hands of the spirits on me, and the throbbing faded. The Ambience was laid out before me, and all I had to do was take my wall down, and I could obliterate Derth before this went any further.

But that thought gave me pause, and I kept that wall in place. I peered at the shadows, wondering why he wouldn't have done something to cut me off yet, why I could feel the Clinch tucked into my bodice. *Does he not know about the bracelet? Does he* need *a bracelet to sever my tie to the Ambience?*

"I can see the strain thinking is causing you," he said. "Be careful, or you'll undo your hard work."

He's toying with me, I realized. And I couldn't stop myself from asking, "Why?" He waited for me to say more, as if he could feel the questions trying to break free. "You got away, you had the entire world to run to, but you stayed. *Why?* Why make yourself a nuisance in so many places, why *enslave* so many people along the way?"

"To lure you in," he replied, and I could feel the curious tilt of his head as he regarded me. "Haven't you figured that out yet?"

I shook my head, ignoring the bait. *"Why?"*

He laughed, and beneath his throaty rasp, a deep rumble tore free. I flexed my wrists against the unyielding rope, but there was more than hemp holding me fast. Even as I let the Ambience seep over the knots, looking for a weakness, a place to burn through, my power recoiled as if stung. Derth's darkness was infused in the rope, a barrier to keep my light at bay.

I'd broken it before, and I could do it again. I just hoped I'd have enough time to do it. Because there was no one coming to help me.

A flicker of power escaped me, seeping into the rope, seeding itself into the darkness. If he'd harnessed more spirits to break them to his will and fuel the darkness, I just needed to find the source, to heal it and usher it back to the Pool.

"I'm done running," he replied. "And I need to take what you have, so that I have the power to rival the Malachi, to usurp him."

"You're insane," I hissed. "The Malachi controls Vortheim; do you really think you can just walk up to him?"

He stepped out of the shadows, then, though they clung to him like an aura, like a tethered spirit so far descended into the darkness that it had become a void in the Ambience. Like the spying orbs he'd sent to harry us. And he did nothing to dispel my assertion of his mental state when he smiled at me.

"You'd be surprised by what's possible. Especially with the collective knowledge of Vortheim at your fingertips. It took me months to find what I was looking for, after our little spat a year ago. But I came back to Trylia to leave enticing clues for you to follow whenever you came home from your new *mission*." He pursed his lips as he said the word, as if he found it amusing. "I knew you wouldn't be able to resist."

It made sense, I realized as I thought back to the trail we'd followed. The wide-spread net that he'd cast, ensuring that wherever I went, there would be some hint of his presence. Because he knew that I'd be looking for them.

He'd never caused so much trouble that he would risk being caught, or that the people he'd enthralled would. When his invitation had failed, he'd tried to destroy everyone around me, to control me, so that I would have nothing left but to find him.

My mouth went dry. He nodded, watching the pieces of the puzzle come together in my mind. "But... you can't take my power," I breathed, my conviction as weak as it sounded.

Bryn rounded a corner, and the spire finally came into view. The fact that he'd rounded this same corner before didn't fill him with confidence. There had been a moment when he'd felt Lila, a surge of Ambience that tugged him in the direction he'd been heading, unmistakably hers. It felt like sunshine and smelled like the ocean. He desperately needed to feel it again.

Looking down, he spotted a boot print in a patch of dirt. It could have been Lila's, but he had no idea whether this was real. With nothing else to go on, he shook his head and stood. Another print in the dirt between the stones, and then a smudge on a window led him on a meandering path through the streets, until he came upon the main thoroughfare at the foot of the spire.

He shuddered as he found evidence of her passage here, deeper tracks left behind fast, heavy footfalls. Was she running from something, or toward it? He rushed down the street, turning this way and that, following a shred of her cloak snagged on the wood siding of one building, and a handprint smudged on a dust-covered door of another.

Bryn looked up from the tracks as he emerged from between two buildings to find that he was once again at the foot of the spire. He rushed through the open door, terrified at the thought of what he might find, and stuck his head into the small room on the right. The walls were scorched, and the room was still smoking in the aftereffects of Lila's power.

Is this where that surge came from? he wondered. The room was empty, so he darted back to the main chamber. Finding nowhere to go but up the spiral staircase, he climbed. His heart beat faster with every step, and he couldn't tell how much was exertion and how much was the mounting dread that settled in his stomach like a weight.

One floor up, he found a door across from the stairs, and opened it. He stopped short as his stomach lurched. Lila was lying on the floor, her hands and feet bound in chains, her clothes in tatters, just as she had been the first time he had set eyes on her. She turned at the sound of his entrance, and stared at him with blank eyes as he fell to his knees at her side.

"I'll get you out of here," he told her, caressing her head. He scanned her body for injuries while he fumbled with the chains.

"Why?" she asked, her voice monotone. His heart twisted as he realized that his nightmares had come true. Searching her face for some sign that she was still in there, hoping Derth hadn't done this again, his face crumpled when he saw the blank stare that he feared most.

"Love, I'm going to let you out of these chains," he told her gently as he fought back tears. "We're getting out of here."

"He told me to stay here," she replied, turning her head to stare at the ceiling.

Bryn stood and moved around the room, looking for a key and finding nothing. Frustration tore out of him as a guttural scream. He knelt by Lila again and asked, "Do you know where the key is?"

"Yes," she replied flatly.

"Where is it?" Bryn asked.

"Around your neck," she said, still not looking at him.

His brow furrowed, but he looked down to see that she was right; the key was hanging from his neck. He touched it tentatively, wishing it wasn't real, denying the implications behind it. He pulled the leather tie from around his neck and unlocked her chains. When she didn't move, he asked her to stand.

She obeyed immediately, and he put his arms around her. Lila didn't return the embrace, didn't even acknowledge that he was touching her. He pulled back and looked down at her face. Her eyes still stared straight ahead, and her face was smeared with blood and gore. Her beautiful auburn hair was matted and filthy.

"Let's get you out of here, love," Bryn said. He tried to lead her by the hand from the room, but she planted her feet.

"I'm to stay here," she said. "He said that I'm not supposed to leave here alive unless he tells me otherwise."

"He told me to fetch you," Bryn pleaded.

"I'm not to leave unless he fetches me himself."

"Enough," Bryn said, lifting her into his arms and cradling her against his chest. "We're leaving."

He moved to the door and back into the hall, holding her tight. He didn't know how, but he would save her from this. He could set it right this time, and leave the regret for his previous inaction in the past.

Before he could move more than a few feet from the doorway, Lila pulled the dirk from his belt. He shouted, but she plunged it into her midsection in a blur of movement. He rushed to place her on the floor without jostling the dirk, but she twisted and wrenched it to the side, opening her belly.

"No!" Bryn cried as the dirk fell from her bloody grasp onto the floor. He tried to draw on her power, but it wouldn't come. As she lay bleeding on the ground with her head cradled in his lap, her eyes cleared, and she gasped. She looked at herself, her face a mask of pain and horror, and then she looked up at Bryn.

"What..." she asked, offering her blood-soaked hands to him.

"You need to heal yourself, Lila," he begged. "I tried, but I can't do it." He pushed her hands to the wound, willing her to save herself. She'd done it before; she could do it again.

Her face paled with every passing second, and when it relaxed, a sob tore out of his throat. She was beyond pain now. Lila smiled up at him as her eyes closed. "I love you," she whispered, and then she was gone.

Bryn screamed and clutched the love of his life to his chest, rocking her back and forth in his agony.

"Bryn!" I screamed, but his pain overwhelmed all my senses, and wouldn't let me shut him out. He was so lost in his vision that he couldn't feel me, couldn't feel that he was dragging me with him. Derth's eyes gleamed, black as the void surrounding him.

"How is our young hero doing?" he asked. "Has he given up yet?"

"Stop this," I demanded through my tears. I shoved more power into the ropes around my wrists, but the darkness rose in response, draining that power away from me. Another sob tore free from my chest; I couldn't force my way out of this problem, I needed patience. And that was in very short supply right now. "I'll give you what you want if you just...*stop*."

His smile widened, and my eyelids began to droop. I lost my grip on the Ambience, on the ropes, on my mind. "That's not how this works."

CHAPTER FORTY

I watched Bryn, Hunter, Sam, and even the Vorthes stumble through horror after horror, seeing their worst fears play out in their minds. Their minds and bodies were breaking, and I could feel every crack as it appeared. They wouldn't last long like this, and I couldn't shake their terror from my heart. I couldn't save them.

I blinked, and I was back in the room, Derth's malicious grin widening as he realized I could see him. My screams still tore out of my raw throat like claws as tears poured from my eyes.

"You monster! How can you do this to them?"

"You're the one who came up with the fear of losing everyone you love," he replied. "All I did was give it substance." He looked up toward the ceiling, lost in his musings. "The Ambient who lived here were quite powerful. They had so many secrets to protect, and so much fear. It was an inspiration for the defenses they set up, to inspire fear in anyone who came unbidden to their shores, to ensure that the residents were too fearful of the consequences to try to leave.

"I don't think they truly understood the pervasive nature of fear, or they wouldn't have given it so much power over this place." He smiled, flashing his yellowed teeth at me. "It tends to spread, as you well know. The perfect catalyst for my affinity. And with a network of projectors at my disposal, there's *nowhere* that I can't send it."

I blinked, and Derth was standing in the confines of his cabin aboard Roglin's ship, and then at the grassy base of the foothills, smiling behind a shield engulfed in flames.

I'm losing my mind, I thought. There was something comforting in the thought. Maybe I wouldn't have to feel this pain anymore if I couldn't tell what was real. A wicked voice—Derth's voice—hissed from the back of my mind. *You'll have nothing* but *pain.*

I longed to hear Bryn, to feel his hands in mine, to know that he was all right, to have something real to hold. But he couldn't save me from this. I had to save myself or let my mind fracture.

"Was any of it real?" I asked. Derth smirked, but his eyelids drooped, his hunched frame heavy with fatigue. I laughed. *He's so tired,* I thought. *Maybe he should lie down.* "Are they alive?"

"For now," he replied. He took a deep breath and exhaled, trembling.

I giggled, imagining him in a fluffy bed, tucked in tight. *Say goodnight.* But I latched onto the image, part of my mind focusing on the hilarity of it while the other recognized the weakness it created. *He's overexerting himself.* The thought was crystal-clear, and I used it to pull myself out of the mire of madness.

"There's so much trauma in all of them, it's easy to keep them busy while I focus on you."

"Keep pushing yourself like this, and I won't have to worry about stopping you," I told him. "You'll do that yourself."

"I have more strength than you realize."

I shifted my hands, and the pain woke me the rest of the way, the visions retreating from the sensation of something biting and *real.* I fed a trickle of Ambience into the ropes again, fraying the threads while I picked at the darkness, searching for the source again. Derth prowled around the room like a predator waiting for the perfect time to pounce. When he circled behind me, it took every ounce of my willpower not to crane my neck to watch his progress, and to keep the Ambience still. The visions crept back in, and I twisted my wrist to keep them from overwhelming me.

There. Blood dripped—*pat, pat, pat*—onto the floor. And the essence of the spirit touched the edge of my power. It screamed in my mind, through my power, once more in a sea of pain and screaming that echoed through my head. I slammed my wall down to let the Ambience in, and the spirit surged along a bridge of ethereal hands that fit its pieces back in place, healing it before it was swallowed into the Pool. Derth growled from somewhere nearby, and the shadows snapped into place around him.

The rope was just a rope again.

"My power can't be so easily destroyed," Derth snarled. "You'll lose your mind long before you can make a dent."

Flames scorched the rope at my wrists, and I smiled.

CHAPTER FORTY-ONE

I snapped my wrists and ankles from the chair, the rope turning to ash, and leaped to my feet as I thrust the flames out, directly at Derth. He cried out as it engulfed him. For a moment, I felt a sense of wicked triumph. I needed to watch him *burn*.

But even as I unleashed the entirety of the Ambient Pool in a blazing torrent of white flame, it fell away from my control, like a handful of sand in my grasp. Derth's shadows grew and swarmed like a cloak flaring in a sudden gust of wind, more than darkness. They formed a void in the world where no light or heat could exist. Where everything was consumed and pulled into his orbit.

I ripped the Ambience back, away from that pull that I'd felt in Derth's orbs and the spirits he'd twisted to make his thralls. Because that pull was from something older than Derth, something hungry.

Derth's filthy presence struck at my mind as I gathered the spirits around me in a shield, and then the void descended to consume me, forcing me to pour Ambient light into the shield, to keep the darkness back, to burn it away. Derth's whispers ceased, but the void grew, seeping into my shield like a pervasive fog. It drew the breath from my lungs as it ate away at my shield, looking for a way to burrow deeper.

It broke through and wrapped around my arms and legs, holding me in place. I thrashed against the restraint, clutching the edges of my shield closer, but it was too late. The darkness had me. Its tendrils wrapped around my legs, and then my arms, and then pinned them to my side as it wound around my torso. It slithered up my chest and around my neck, then closed over my mouth. I couldn't scream, couldn't breathe. It was like drowning all over again, and my frayed mind pictured the ocean surrounding me. And reminded me that Bryn wasn't coming to save me. Derth stepped inside the shroud and placed his hands on either side of my head. I couldn't pull away, forced to watch his black eyes widen with anticipation and listen to the whispers tearing at my sanity to push me over the edge.

My heart felt like it would burst from my chest, my lungs ached for air, and I didn't hold back when the Ambience flared out without direction. It became a shockwave that should have knocked Derth off his feet, should have crushed his body against a wall. But there he stood, his smile widening as his black eyes fixed on mine.

"Your outbursts may have worked in the past, but there are so many things you don't know." His mouth turned down and his brows furrowed. "You don't deserve this power. It never should have been yours."

He squeezed, and my agonized scream was swallowed by the darkness as he pushed deeper and deeper. My vision darkened, and the color faded from the room. This was my nightmare, coming to life before my eyes. Not just inside my head, where I could feel the Ambience being taken from me, but in the world itself.

WE COME.

A blast of Ambience stronger than anything I'd ever summoned slammed into Derth, but the void consumed it, growing exponentially. Derth's features slithered with shadows; he was becoming the void, with a direct line to the Ambient Pool, through me. And the more power I used, trying to stop him, the more he consumed.

The spirits screamed, tearing through me as they had in Stalth when I'd realized that I could *heal them*...I sent the Ambience out, searching for the spirits that fueled the darkness, separate from the void. It drew that energy into itself, but I sent more, only to find that there was nothing to heal. No spirits remained within the void, and I'd just given it more fuel.

"*More,*" the void rumbled. So I gave it more. I gave it *me.*

My body went numb as it crept over my face, into my ears, my eyes, my nose, and there was nothing but darkness, chilling me all the way through. But Derth was there, clinging to my mind like a stubborn child, keeping the void from taking hold of my connection to the Ambience. And to keep that tenuous hold on the void, I let him in, exposing my mind and my spirit like I had to Bryn. That connection still held, like a small flame in the void that couldn't be snuffed out. But the rest... the rest was Derth, and the hole in the world that he was creating.

"There's so much," he whispered. He pursued the spark that connected me to the Pool. To find the source of my power—Celuthia's power—so that he could take it all for himself. And I let him, gathering that void, absorbing it, looking for a way to channel it in the same way that I could channel the Ambience.

This *was* just the Ambience, after all, broken as it was. And I was a Conduit.

The room emerged from the darkness when all of it had funneled into me, releasing my limbs. I let it wash through me, luxuriating in the power *he* held, as he'd coveted mine. A tether tied us together, light and dark mingling together, Ambience and void waiting to see which of us would triumph.

The Ambience beckoned me as the void waited, fed by the light of the Pool. For a moment that seemed to stretch out into eternity, a choice laid before me. If I wanted it, all Celuthia's power could be mine. The world was laid bare; the Gloom—everything that had been contorted about the Ambience—could be set to rights if I consumed them. There would be no power for anyone but me, and I could use it to save the world.

But Sam's voice crept into my head, resonating through me from the Ambient light that persisted in my heart. *The Ambience gives life to Celuthia. When it wanes, life itself wanes. When it flourishes, we all flourish with it.* Bryn's face flashed into my mind, tortured by visions of this exact moment in a myriad of gruesome illusions.

If I followed this dark impulse, I might save Celuthia from the Gloom, but I would risk the slow decay of life itself. I would manifest Bryn's worst fears and break his heart. The connection between us glowed, our unique tether to each other, and I knew to the depths of my spirit that embracing this darkness would shatter it beyond repair. Despite the allure of the void, I shook my head.

"I can't take this power for myself," I said, my voice a chorus of screams and whispers. Derth's eyes locked on mine, and I felt the fear behind the void swimming there. "But I can use it to stop you."

I shielded the bond to Bryn and the small spark of my thread to the Ambience, the only pieces of myself that remained in the void that now obeyed me. It had no other choice.

My thoughts reverberated through the room like thunder, rippling across my link to the Pool, swallowed by the void. *He cannot have this power. Take it from him.* The void trembled, and from its depths came a sense of detached amusement that vanished a moment later.

As you command.

Derth's black eyes began to glow as the void retracted from him, his darkness channeling into me to make way for the light that remained in him. Derth screamed as my hands crushed the sides of his head.

"What are you doing?" Tears ran from his eyes, where the last vestiges of the void remained.

"Taking this power from you!" I yelled. My voice thundered with the voices of the spirits, the rumble of the void, and he flinched. My words were not entirely my own. "It is not for mortals to wield."

The void contracted, stretched thin by the pressure I placed on it. Derth's eyes brightened, fading to pale blue, and as the void retreated, I felt the vulnerable mind beneath. I flashed him a wicked grin, and plunged into it, as rough as he'd ever been with me.

We saw ourselves through each other's eyes. Shadows writhed beneath my translucent skin, and my hair lifted from my head in a phantom breeze. Gone was the malevolent, oppressive will of Derth the monster, avatar of the void, conduit for the Gloom. Now, I could feel him as I felt Bryn, and he was afraid.

More than his fear, I heard whispers, voices vying for his attention. He tried to resist me as I dove deeper into his mind. But this was mine to control, not his. And I *needed* to see what he was so afraid of.

A sliver of darkness remained within him, shrinking away as the void and I approached like an inky tidal wave. We grasped that root like a wilting weed, and as we pulled, we revealed Derth's spirit tucked beneath.

His face twisted with desperate anger and madness. "This power is *mine*! It would consume you, and then the Malachi will be free to plunge Celuthia into darkness!"

I hesitated with my hand on the root, his tugging like the buzzing of a gnat for all the good it did. "Is that who did this to you?"

"No one did this to me," he spat. "I wanted more power, so I took it."

"No," I replied, because I could feel the void's will pressing down on mine, testing me for weakness, waiting for the light of the Ambience to abate enough to wrest control from me. For that wall to crack so that it could consume that thread all the way to the Pool. "But it doesn't matter."

He screamed. "No!" I plunged beneath the root, and his memories were laid bare.

Flashes came to me, not of darkness, but of light. A bright garden, lines of trees around a gravel path, a gleam in the distance. The ocean, sparkling far below as he stood atop a hill, ship sails like fluffy white clouds. The touch of a large hand grasping his as they walked, chasing someone small. A woman with chestnut brown hair, smiling at him. Her blue eyes crinkled as she did, and her mouth formed a word.

Aethard.

Cold shock ran through me as I beheld that face. I knew it with every part of me, even in my connection to the Ambience. I'd dreamed of her, though her features had long since faded from memory. This was my mother. Why did he know her? Had Derth *killed* my mother?

"No," he whimpered as tears rolled down his cheeks. "Not her. Not again."

"What did you do to her?" I demanded, cold fury overtaking me as I shook him. As my voice thundered, a chorus of spirits flowing from the Pool straight into the void. "What did you do to my mother?"

CHAPTER FORTY-TWO

"No..." he muttered in horror. I tried to release him, to get away from this nightmare, but I was as bound as he was. A man with bright red hair held the little boy's hand, and he'd called that girl with auburn hair Little Flame...

Had that been the spirit of my father that aided me against Roglin? How could Derth know my parents?

Derth gasped as he looked at me, his eyes now the same color as the young boy in the memory. The last vestige of darkness inside him writhed as his spirit fought against it, trying to free itself. As he did, his body writhed, bones cracked, and his eyes opened wide as he trembled.

My skin prickled as my heart slammed in my chest. My mind hadn't caught up yet, but I could feel the weight of whatever revelation loomed over me.

He looked at his hands, one gnarled, as it had been, the other smoother, younger. He was looking down at me now, his body strong and steady, his hunch gone. He squinted, studying my face. "L-Lilaena? I thought you were dead."

A jolt ran through me when he said the name. A faded memory came to my mind, the man with fiery hair saying the same name to me, my mother leaning over his shoulder as they tucked me into bed at night. I'd forgotten how much love I'd felt when that word left their lips.

It bubbled up inside me now, along with the deep grief their loss had caused.

The void spread, trying to smother the small part of me that screamed to be released from the shadow. I yearned to step back into the light shining from Bryn's tether, away from this flash of my past that rekindled the humanity that screamed for me to dispel the darkness.

Another memory came to me of a boy, with pale blonde hair and bright blue eyes. Someone who'd played with me, someone who'd taught me how to look for frogs. My brother, Aethard. I searched Derth's face, seeing the features of that boy twisting back into the face of the monster that haunted my dreams. How could he have become... this? Is this what I would become if I gave myself to it?

"That's not possible," I muttered, denial sweeping through me. "You can't be."

His face crumpled, but he covered the pain with a sneer. "I am."

"H-how?"

He looked deep into my eyes, as if he could see the battle waging beneath my skin. Perhaps he could. A cruel smile twisted his mouth. "You want to hear our messy family history right now? I think you have more important concerns."

There was a *tug* on the void, from Derth. Aethard.

"How?"

Tug. "Our parents were King Demtrius's agents, his Ambient spies. He used them," the pain was back, lacing his words with vitriol, "and it was only a matter of time before he did the same with us. I tried to stop him, it went wrong. I thought you'd all died, and I was glad while I dragged my contorted body away from the palace. To hide, to forget, and to find a way to take the power I'd need to finish the job." *TUG.* I gasped as the void shifted, turning its attention to my... brother. "Roglin's ship was convenient."

A memory—my memory—stirred, of heat against my skin, my hair blown back as my mother screamed my name, and a hole opening in the floor beneath my feet before I splashed into the ocean. I'd dragged myself to that beach and cried myself to sleep, wondering where my mother was. But when I woke, it was all a blur.

"I remember that day," I said. "Someone sent me away from the fire. They opened the world to do it."

"*Of course* they saved *you*. Their baby, their Little Flame." *TUG.* "Give it back," he snarled, "before it eats you alive. I can put it to good use." He flashed me a feral smile. "I promise."

"Aethard," I whispered, clutching my hand to my chest above my heart, and I was surprised to find that seeing that familiar face contorted like Derth's hurt. Deep in my heart, something I hadn't known existed broke.

"*Give it to me!*"

I thrust my hand down the front of my bodice and pulled out the leather braid. And then I slid the Clinch onto his wrist and pulled it tight.

He grasped the leather, and his face paled. "What have you *done*?" He writhed, and I pulled the last shreds of the void free as the Ambience drained out of him. He hit the floor with a thud, just as the void roared to life, whole again, and the Ambient Pool within reach.

It redoubled its efforts to smash through that wall keeping it separate from my spark, from Bryn's tether. It whispered of the power I could obtain if I gave myself over to it and consumed the Ambience.

I cast about for anything that could help me, locked in place while I fought against the void. The walls were covered in shelves, packed tight with leather spines, and the charred chair was on its side next to the open door. Beyond that, the spire's interior walls gleamed white. And with Derth gone, and Aethard's influence suppressed, my mind was clear again. Bryn pushed in, but the connection flickered, maintained only by the spark I'd given him.

Lila! I can feel you, I'm coming! His feet pounded up a flight of spiral stairs. His desperation to find me matched mine, almost as great as my fear as my lungs burned to draw a breath. The void was suffocating me, burning through the last of my power to get that wall down. *Hold on, we can figh-*

He was gone, our link consumed by the thing inside me as my power failed. I looked at Aethard, at the bracelet on his wrist. This thing had given up its hold on him when he lost his connection to the Ambience. Did it need power to survive?

It no longer whispered to me of the power I would gain, only sought to control me and my connection to the Ambience. I took a deep breath, trying to think past the smothering darkness as Bryn burst into the room.

"Lila," he called, sliding to his knees the last couple of feet to where I crouched on the ground. I hadn't realized I was on my knees. "What is it? What can I do?" He glanced over his shoulder at Aethard, and then back to me.

I shook my head and cleared my throat. "I got the darkness out of him, but it's..." I groaned as it dug deeper, "it's in me. It's eating me alive." It hadn't been able to smash me to pieces, so now, it sought to change me—like Aethard—and once it had, I would open the way to the Pool. The world faded in and out as I struggled to maintain my sense of self.

"Don't give up," Bryn pleaded. "Let me help you." An influx of my power flowed from him, giving me the strength to lift my head from where it had sagged against Bryn's chest. For one moment, it helped. The next, the darkness increased. It consumed the power as fast as Bryn could give it to me, and my body shuddered.

I screeched and tried to pull away from Bryn. "Stop! It's getting worse!" Our connection was drawn into the void, darkening as it sought to control the power we shared. It was as vast as the Pool itself, and I reeled when I felt Bryn's spirit being drawn into the battle that waged inside me. "*Don't touch him!*"

The void recoiled, forced back by the command. And I shut Bryn out, as I'd shut him out so many times lately. To protect both of us.

Aethard stirred and groaned as Sam burst into the room. The old man looked haggard, and tears streamed down his face. But he stooped next to my brother and exchanged words I couldn't hear over the roaring in my ears.

"Please let me in," Bryn pleaded, kissing my forehead. The void spread again, and my vision narrowed until all I could see were Bryn's blue eyes. Their beauty struck me as they had the first time I'd seen them. My heart clenched. "I can help you."

"No," I croaked. "If you help me, you give it more power. It'll come for you next, or Sam, and I can't let that happen." My muscles creaked as the void pushed against them, trying to reorder them. Again, it offered me a way out; let down the wall I'd made around the Ambience, and it would let me remain as I was. "*No*," I croaked again, and my mind began to unravel under the weight of every one of my nightmares at once.

I can't let it out, I thought. My eyes fluttered, trying to close. I was so tired, I just wanted to sleep. To let Bryn hold me until I fell asleep. But the Ambient Pool was in danger, and if I let my guard down, it would follow my thread all the way there. *I can't let it in. I need to cut it off.*

Sam appeared in front of me and took my hand in his. "Lila, I'm here."

"I'm going to... keep you safe," I muttered. I turned my head and caught sight of Aethard sitting up, staring at me as if he couldn't decide what to make of me. Looking at his pale face, the shape of his nose and brow so much like mine, I wished I had time to talk to him, to see whether Derth was really gone, and we could move forward together. My head rocked back, and I gazed at Bryn. His face was a mask of pain, grief, and furious denial. He called my name, barked at Sam to help him, begged me for a way to save me. But he couldn't save me from this.

Now, I had to keep *him* safe.

It can't feed on my tie to the Ambience if it's gone, I thought, waiting a moment too long before realizing that Bryn couldn't hear me. *And since I can't ask the spirits for help...* I turned the last of my willpower on the void, and commanded, *Kill me.*

The nightmares ceased, the change it sought to make in me halted, and the void went still. It was the antithesis to the Ambience, but there was power in that. And that power was mine to control, Ambience or no. It fought against the command, even as it grasped my heart and ground it to a halt. *Thump thump.*

I collapsed in Bryn's arms. "Lila?!" he shouted. His face contorted in fear, but I smiled knowing that the void would die with me. "What did she do?" he asked. The air stirred as people moved around me, Aethard's face appeared above me, and Sam's rough, warm hands touched my face and my chest above my heart. *Thump, thump.*

"It's trapped," I whispered. The void howled as it withered, starved of the Ambience that it craved, still struggling to disobey.

You will cease to be, the whispers said. *Your spirit will disappear forever.*

Then we disappear together. With no power to fuel it, it couldn't manifest outside of me to search for a new host. My body was its tomb.

Thump... thump.

It battered at the walls of its tomb, violently trying to escape. My body twitched, tossed around from the impact, from the force of its death throes. Bryn cried out and clutched me tighter. Sam and Aethard argued in urgent tones, words that I didn't understand. My focus was directed inward, waiting, and watching to see that the darkness couldn't escape.

Thump...

The whispers called out, too faint to hear, but in them I heard a single voice, a single source beyond the darkness. I could almost feel it, like a shape in the fog that I couldn't identify. But my mind wandered. A different darkness bloomed, welcoming and calm.

"Lila," Bryn whispered. "Don't leave me. Please, I love you. You can't give up!"

Staring up at the place where I thought he was and unable to see through the darkness, I yearned to touch him, to hold him again. But I couldn't feel my body, and my arms wouldn't obey me.

...

I tried to say something, but I couldn't speak. I just hoped Bryn could hear me.

Goodbye.

He felt her slipping away. She wasn't fighting it, just giving in. Bryn couldn't accept it, couldn't believe it would end like this. That Derth had taken her from him, like he had in all his nightmares. But Derth was gone, replaced by the man in front of him, with pale blue eyes full of fear, and a face that was so like hers.

"I can't stop this," Sam insisted. His hands cupped her face, stark against her pale skin.

There must be something I can do, Bryn thought. She'd shut him out so that thing couldn't get him. But he could still feel a small sliver of her power inside him. Through it, he felt her body fading, and her spirit following close behind, choked by whatever she'd pulled out of Derth.

"We're stronger together," he whispered into her hair. "I can't let you go." Holding her tight, racked with sobs that felt like his body would crumble from the force of them tearing from him, he *pushed.* Pushed the Ambience to connect them, and when he felt its tenuous grasp on the dimming light inside her, he *pushed* it to take hold and bring her back. His body, mind, and spirit all trembled with the force that he placed on the spark she'd entrusted to him, ignoring the fragility of the connection they shared and her fear of him overwhelming her. He couldn't—*wouldn't*—let her slip away. He'd forged this bond before, and together they would be strong enough to bring her back. If the darkness got out, they'd be strong enough to take care of that, too. There was *nothing* they couldn't do together.

"Bryn," Sam said, "she did this for a reason. She told you not to do anything."

"I won't lose her!" Bryn screamed. He poured every ounce of his gifted strength into tearing down the wall between them, into unmaking what the spirits had done at her behest. *It doesn't matter,* he told himself when he felt her will in every part of that wall. *I can't let her go!* he railed at the Ambience that held him at bay. Her light winked out, and he screamed, body and soul. *Let me in!*

His spirit forged a radiant path through the darkness, and there, in the center of it all, gathering that darkness like a cloak, was Lila. Her spirit seemed so fragile, the darkness so intertwined with her, that he almost hesitated. But he could think of nothing but protecting her, wrenching her from this prison and shoving her back into her body.

So he grasped that spark that she'd given him, and he *pulled.*

We come.

CHAPTER FORTY-THREE

I'd never been afraid of the dark before.

But with the crushing black void swallowing me, with my inner light gone, I could certainly understand why so many people were.

My heart had stopped beating, I'd felt it. I'd felt the void losing its anchor in me as my body failed, as it forever lost that path to the Pool that it sought. I'd heard millions of whispers curse that loss, as if all the spirits it had consumed—broken and whole alike—had lost their way back, too. And I'd heard one voice beneath the rest as it sighed in frustration and disappointment.

But the whispers were fading, too, and I felt nothing but emptiness. There would be no finding my rest in the Pool with spirits of fallen Ambient. I'd stolen my chance of finding my parents again. And I would never again feel Bryn's spirit intertwining with mine. But I still had a grip on the void as I floated away from the world, and at least I could take satisfaction in that.

And then a spark appeared in the darkness, hurtling toward me like a falling star. I felt its warmth as it came closer, and then I heard my name.

"Lila!"

"Who..." I asked, though I had no voice, no body to speak through.

"It's not time." The voice evoked memories of arms holding me close, of the smell of woodsmoke and sunshine, and the feeling that I was never alone. "There is so much more that you must do."

"Who are you?" I asked. The light grew—"Lila!"—and bathed me in warmth.

"Someone who has watched over you your whole life, Little Flame." I had no eyes, but I could feel his broad smile, the flame-bright hair, and the hazel eyes. My father. "Now, you must watch over Celuthia, and bring balance back to its heart. The void was not meant to be wielded."

If I'd had hands, I would have raised them to block out the light. I felt the next words like a blow to my chest.

"I can't lose her!" Bryn.

My father's presence burned away in the light—my light—and Bryn's voice came again.

"Let me in!"

I recoiled, even as the remnant of my spirit yearned for his. If he forced me out of this void, would it consume the Ambience? Would we destroy everything?

The light slammed into me.

And the void came with me.

Darkness curled around me, and Ambient light radiated from Bryn. His eyes were prisms, his skin glowing like the sun, his hair lifting from his head. And that small spark of *me* inside him, it was a brilliant flame. The spirits surrounded him, stretching their hands to me, clutching me as they lifted me the rest of the way from the emptiness I'd been in.

Thump Thump.

"Lila," Bryn breathed, and his joy, relief, and *power* flowed into me. It was mine... but it was his, too.

The void pulsed toward him, across the bond that he'd forged. His mind intertwined with mine until my thoughts were his, and his were mine, and I couldn't tell where he ended and I began.

"No," I said. My voice was his voice, and the low rumble of the void. And then the world exploded.

Light and dark collided, but there was too much of the darkness, and it twisted the light as it grew and grew and grew. It condensed into a roiling mass, a cloud of darkness filled with flickering Ambient light. The air rushed out of my lungs. I gasped, but there was nothing to breathe. And the Ambience and void still danced around us, colliding over and over, pouring more chaotic energy into the cloud forming around us and through us.

I couldn't take a breath to tell him, so I thought, *Stop. You need to stop. Look at what you're doing!*

His beautiful face was a mask of horror that matched the horror he now felt, watching what we had wrought, and realizing that he couldn't stop the Ambience. He'd channeled it from the Pool, and he had no idea how to let it go.

I reached my hand out to him, a silent offering of support as he screamed inside our heads. And when they joined, I opened myself to him, sending my void-entwined spirit to meet his.

The reaction taking place before us was blinding, but we could not shut our eyes. All the potential of the Ambient Pool was pouring into its inverse, and the chaos of the resulting energy swelled, creating a vacuum in the room. The energy in the surrounding room drained away, books crumbled on the shelves, and Aethard and Sam were left to scramble out of the room.

The cloud spread beyond the walls. The opalescent glow disappeared. The cloud negated the Ambience everywhere it touched. Just like...

The Gloom, we thought. We were inside of a Gloom as it formed.

We were its catalyst. It hadn't been Derth, after all. It had been the collision of the void and the Ambience. We could see the smallest particles of each, laid bare by our connection to it. Light and dark collided over and over, releasing chaotic energy as they were annihilated.

Our bodies ached for air while a cloud condensed between us, retracted into a pinpoint light, and then exploded through us, burning through our bond. My body hurtled against the nearest wall with a sickening crunch, and I gasped as air filled the room again. Bryn hit the opposite wall and slid down, his eyes dazed and unseeing for too long as I stared, unable to move, to find out if he was alive. The explosion tore into the spire, prismatic light flashing through the crystal walls before they darkened as if covered in shade cast by the cloud it had been moments before. The bridge between us crumbled until the spark we'd shared, that Bryn had made his own, was separated by a chasm of darkness. My mind was lonely without his thoughts.

Sam stumbled into the room and locked eyes with me. I looked at Bryn, the only plea I could offer, and Sam understood. He limped to Bryn and knelt before him, blocking my view, but I continued to stare in their direction, watching Sam's spirit flare with Ambience, and then Bryn's coughing fit. His eyes refocused, directly on me, and his face crumpled. His lips formed my name, but I couldn't hear him. I couldn't hear anything through the pressure in my ears.

I didn't see Sam approach, but I felt the Ambience surround me, and then my ears popped, my mind cleared, and my joints and back filled with blinding agony. I closed my eyes against a stab of pain through my head, and my body drooped, suddenly too exhausted to hold itself upright against the wall.

"Lila," Bryn called. His gait was uneven, one footstep and then a shuffle, and then he was next to me, jostling me. I whimpered, the pain digging deeper into my bones.

A sob tore out of Bryn's throat, punching another hole in my heart. But it was beating, I was here, and the void was gone.

"Lila," he whispered. His fingers slid through mine. "Please, love,"

Warm callused hands touched my face, my shoulders, and each of my arms. The pain subsided, but I was left with a dull ache that jolted with every small movement. I managed to crack my eyes open as Aethard poked his head through the door to survey the scene.

"Lila, the Gloom, what happened?" Sam looked terrified, and even more haggard than before. Bryn leaned close, asking with a raised eyebrow whether he could move me.

I shook my head, not ready for more pain. "We did it." Sam's eyes widened in shock. "It was the Ambience and the void colliding, and we did it." My eyes darted to Bryn's face and away, toward my brother. "It wasn't Derth." When my eyes locked on his, I felt a shock of familiarity, seeing myself, and our father. More than that, I remembered him, and our childhood together.

The first time I'd used the Ambience had been to snatch the doll he'd taken from me out of his hand. He used to hold my hand as we walked through the palace grounds, telling me the names of the flowers growing amongst the trees. I remembered the time he'd squealed when our father threw him in the air, as I snuggled against our mother's chest.

Those lost years clicked into place, but I couldn't reconcile the love I'd felt in them with the man staring back at me. He didn't *look* like Derth anymore, but the deep well of pain and disdain in his ice-blue eyes remained. How could I be sure more of his dark impulses weren't waiting to be unleashed?

My eyes darted to the bracelet on his wrist. At least he wouldn't be able to use the Ambience against us. Not unless *I* decided to remove the bracelet. One small consolation in all this madness.

"Aethard," I said warily, the word almost a question.

"Lilaena." My given name was an uncertain accusation.

"Lila," Sam insisted. "What *happened?*"

I gave him the best description I could of all that I'd experienced, watching Aethard as I relayed what our father's spirit had told me. The only response was a slight narrowing of his eyes, and then he looked away to survey the dark crystal walls around us. When I'd finished, Sam's mouth opened and closed several times, trying to find words.

Bryn shifted next to me, but I couldn't look at him. I wasn't ready. Instead, I looked at Aethard.

"Are you..." I trailed off, not sure what I wanted to ask. Was he all right? Was he the man that haunted me, or the man my brother should have grown to be? I had no idea what I expected, and I could see that he didn't, either.

He seemed to understand my loss for words, perhaps seeing the struggle on my face. "I'm different," he said with a shrug and a frown. "But you can see that. Why?"

"Why what?"

"Why did you do this?" he whispered, glaring at the bracelet.

"There are a few reasons," I replied. "The most obvious being that Derth—you—were a monster who used and tortured people, and I wanted you to know how it felt to be powerless." His eyes darkened. "The simplest answer is that I couldn't get the void out of you without it. The most surprising is that I...couldn't stand to see you like that anymore."

His eyes shot to mine, widening. "What do you mean?"

"Even after everything, I have to wonder whether you could be redeemed."

Aethard's mouth twisted into a snarl. My heart twisted again. "You *must* be my long-lost sister, since you seem to have inherited our parents' arrogance. *Redeemed?* What makes you so certain that your point of view is the moral one?"

"You think your actions have been moral?" Bryn demanded, his voice thick with indignation. "You've tortured and murdered people."

"So have you," Aethard spat. "I was trying to survive, same as you. And now, I can't protect myself next time someone comes for me."

My lip curled. "Enslaving people isn't surviving. Even the Malachi doesn't justify going to such lengths."

He looked at his hands, the heated loathing cracking for a fraction of a second before he schooled his features into a mask of condescension. "You're playing with things that you don't understand, *little* sister."

I inhaled as I stared at Aethard. The Ambience strained and I found that my careful walls weren't enough. Something had changed in me, and I felt volatile, as if I'd regressed to that previous version of myself that had no grasp on her power. But as I marshalled my strength to rein it in, I realized that I had as much control as ever; the *Ambience* was stronger. And it felt much closer now, as if some of that potential had remained with me. "Then explain them to me."

He narrowed his eyes, and seemed to sense the danger he was in because his haughty attitude deflated a bit. "I can see that there's nothing I could say that would help me right now." He glanced at Bryn, and then his eyes locked on mine. "You took my Tether from me, the only thing that was still mine. I'm your prisoner, and I don't see much incentive to open up right now. You want to redeem me?" He sneered again. "Then take this thing off," he shook his wrist, "and let me go. You'll never see me again, I promise, and I'll find a quiet place to avoid the Malachi for the rest of my life."

I was already shaking my head before he finished. "I can't," I replied. "I have no idea what you'd do, or if you might hurt someone else."

"*You've taken everything from me!*" he roared, shooting to his feet. I scrambled slowly to my feet with difficulty, and Bryn was between us faster than I could track. "The Ambience, the void, *everything* that kept me safe!"

I frowned, confused. "The void wasn't keeping you safe," I said.

He closed his eyes and let out a bitter chuckle. "More that you can't understand."

"Then *explain* it," I insisted, gritting my teeth in frustration.

"You remember the veil I used to keep you calm?" Bryn bristled and I nodded. "Well, that was nothing compared to what the void did for me. I didn't have to go through the fear—the pain—of mourning our parents, of a life where I had nothing and no one. I made things happen. I had the power to make them happen. Now..." He grimaced as tears welled in his eyes. "I'm powerless, and all I have is pain."

I stepped past Bryn, the first flicker of empathy for my brother breaking through my frustration with his hostility. But when I reached out to place a consoling hand on his shoulder, he shrugged it off violently and stepped away.

"Don't touch me," he growled.

I held my hand up in surrender, my empathy swallowed by frustration again. "Fine." I turned to find Bryn directly behind me, and couldn't help but meet his gaze. My heart ached with the depth of my love for him, but the betrayal was just behind it, nestled next to the fear and distrust. I'd given myself to the void to keep us safe, to destroy it so that it couldn't destroy the Ambience. And he'd undone that. He'd taken my power as his own, and we'd created the Gloom.

It didn't matter that I couldn't hear his voice in my head; I could see the same emotions flickering across his face. Love, hurt, betrayal, fear, and behind all of that, the belief that he'd done the right thing. But I wasn't so sure, and I could tell from the surprise that flickered across his face that he'd noticed.

"If you won't let me go, what's your plan?" Aethard asked. I detached my gaze from Bryn's, and it was a relief to be out from under that weight. "Are you going to drag me around with you? Force me to live on your ship while you fight the evil forces of Vortheim?"

"I don't know," I answered. I considered a lifetime of forcing this angry man to stay at my side, always wondering whether he'd kill me in my sleep. It was exhausting and debilitating, and I didn't know if I had the strength for it.

Hunter's voice echoed from the base of the spire, and Bryn didn't spare me a glance before ducking through the door. Aethard watched him go, and then turned a mocking smile to me as if to ask what his problem was. I ignored him.

Hunter appeared, breathless, a few minutes later, with Bryn trailing behind. He didn't look my way, but I grasped his hand when he was close enough. There was so much to say, and this wasn't the time.

"Such a waste," Sam muttered, and I watched him sift through a pile of ash at the base of the nearest wall. The remains of all those books, blasted apart by the Gloom.

I opened my mouth to ask him what he meant, and then a wave of terror gripped my heart. I clutched my chest, afraid it would stop again, and then the sensation was gone. A glance around the room told me that everyone had been affected similarly.

"That's not good," Aethard grunted.

"The defenses?" I asked.

He grimaced. "I don't know. They aren't supposed to do...that."

"We need to stop them."

"Elders' luck to you," Aethard scoffed. "I haven't been able to do anything but redirect it, but it was never this strong, and I don't think I have as much leverage as I did." He lifted his wrist again to punctuate his point. Another wave pulsed out, stealing the breath from my lungs in a wave of terror. Aethard doubled over, panting.

He scowled at me. "Whatever you did is getting worse. Since you've destroyed everything of value here, we should leave."

Destroyed everything? I glanced at the ash on the ground, and realized that they must have held some trace of the Ambience. The

Gloom had swallowed it as it formed, just like the other cloud we'd encountered. I looked at the ceiling, wondering how many rooms, how many floors, had been affected.

"We need to find Colagh and Tanjiu, and get everyone out of here," Hunter said. He turned a hateful glare on Aethard. "How did you redirect it? Can you do it again?"

Aethard's withering stare was enough to dissuade us from that hope. "No. I can try, if my *sister* would like to remove the bracelet?"

"No," I said at the same time as Bryn. We shared a loaded glance.

"If you insist on finding someone before we flee, we should seek out the orbs higher in the spire," Aethard said. "I doubt even a Conduit like you could do anything to change what's happening now." He looked between Bryn and me, an evil grin spreading across his face. "Perhaps the two of you could have done something, but now...?" Bryn stiffened.

"Show us where it is," I said.

Bryn stepped closer to Aethard, who moved away from the rest of us, into the central chamber. Hunter shook his head once, to let me know he wasn't happy, and then followed. Sam took my hand and gave it a gentle squeeze as we filed in behind them.

"What am I going to do about him?" I asked him. I nodded in Aethard's direction where he'd stepped onto the staircase with Bryn on his heels.

"I don't know," he replied. "Let's focus on getting out of here first."

CHAPTER FORTY-FOUR

The entire spire was black like obsidian. The opalescent quality of
the walls was gone, and Ambient light flashed through the stone at
irregular intervals. The energy I'd sensed here was wild and angry. And
on every wall, where Aethard informed us scores of books had sat on
the shelves, we found more ash.

We emerged onto another level, dotted with many dusty tables and
chairs along the walls between several doors. Aethard led us to the
second door on the left and walked into the room beyond.

The room curved around, taking up half of this level, with floor-to-
ceiling shelves following the curve of the outer wall. The shelves were
lined with glass orbs identical to those we'd seen throughout the city,
and between the door where we stood and those glass orbs were
winding bookcases covered with more ash.

Bright light shone through the window, refracting from the orbs,
illuminating the scattered remnants of all these tomes that still floated
in the air. Most of the orbs held a dull red glow, the only points in the
vicinity that gave off any trace of Ambience outside of Sam and myself.
But a large section of them were dark, and I couldn't guess at what
could have done that if the Gloom hadn't. Aethard strode through the
room, leaving a trail of ash in his wake as he approached a shelf and
bent close. I followed behind, wondering what forgotten knowledge I

was trampling through.

Aethard quirked a brow at me when he glanced my way, and then pointed at an orb at eye level. I blinked in wonder as an image moved within, and as I focused on it, that image resolved into Colagh and Tanjiu, supporting each other as they limped through the city. Aethard gestured at the orb and a projection appeared above it, hovering in space. Colagh and Tanjiu stopped in their tracks and cowered with their hands above their heads. My blood ran cold at the pure terror on their faces.

"How do I stop it?" I asked. I watched as a dark cloud filled the adjacent orb, falling over Colagh and Tanjiu. It flashed once from within, and seemed to swirl around them like it was alive, trying to corral them in place.

Aethard shook his head. "You don't," he replied. "See that red color?" I nodded. "It wasn't like that before you made that Gloom. My guess is that it's interacting with the city's defenses, which will only get worse from here. You could redirect them for a time." He smirked and pointed to the shelf below, where I spotted the Salavans cowering inside the building we'd left them in, with a transformed Paerna still unconscious on the ground.

I growled at the twisted delight on his face, knowing that I couldn't risk *any* of us scattering throughout the city to chase after illusions. Aethard glanced at the bracelet on his wrist. "I spent weeks experimenting with all these things. It's possible I could find a better way... for a price." He held his arm aloft to show me the bracelet again. I seethed, starting to hate the gesture.

The energy from the orbs was chaotic; this was a nexus of power for the city, and with the hub spiraling out of control, that power was spiraling with it. My brow furrowed as the thought came into my head. Before the spirits had cut me off, I'd felt my connection to the Pool like a light, a tiny aperture that could be opened to let the Ambience flow through me. Now, it was a window thrown wide, more volatile than my power had been before.

I focused on Sam, watching him lean toward the shelf to frown and squint at the orbs, and when his power flashed, it was like inhaling the scent of a dusty tome, the smell of ink, and the feel of charcoal dragged across paper. Aethard was a howling wind behind a thick pane of glass, muted and tumultuous, as if his entire being was in turmoil. I imagined it was.

I hesitated before I turned to Bryn, not sure that I wanted to know what his energy felt like. But I felt his eyes on me, drawing me to return his gaze. The corner of his mouth quirked up when I did, and his eyes softened, his emotions locked behind a determination to show me love and understanding, and nothing else in this moment. Deeper within I felt a tiny mote of raw Ambience, what was left of the power I'd given him.

But it wasn't mine anymore; it was the feel of a drawn bowstring on his fingers, and the smell of warm leather. All his, and it was subdued, as if what he'd done for me—and the catastrophe we'd created—had diminished the light inside him. The tether between us was still there, but it wasn't strong enough for him to imbue me with his strength, or to join our minds and share our emotions. It wasn't strong enough for us to join our spirits.

Sam grumbled next to me, and I tore my eyes away from Bryn. "I don't know that there's much that can be done here. Not even you, Lila, would have the power to stop this. I think Aethard is correct in his assessment."

"Elders' eyes," I grumbled. "Do you know where they are?"

Aethard glared at me as he leaned forward, looking between the two orbs that still projected the images of our cowering allies. "Such clever devices," he mused. "Capable of projecting harrowing visions, sight into places far away, or a simple light." He cast a glance at the rows of dark orbs. "Pity those don't seem to be connected; I'd have loved to see what was on the other side."

"You used them to attack us?" I asked. My memories of a loving brother warred with my hatred for Derth and my growing distaste for this flippant man that had replaced him.

He gave me a sidelong glance. "Yes. These two are close," he said, tapping the glass orb with his finger. A musical peal like a small bell rang out, the other orbs resonating with the same note. "Between us and the docks." He chuckled as they took off running. "They've been stuck in the same loop for a while; they shouldn't be hard to find."

"At least we don't need to split up," I said. Sam cast a melancholy gaze over the destruction in the room, and I put a hand on his arm, taking in the destruction alongside him. I'd hoped to let him peruse some of this knowledge, perhaps find something about Conduits, or, in the wake of what Bryn and I had done, find whatever information the Vorthes had discovered about the Gloom.

We filed out of the room, Hunter leading the way down the stairs as Sam kept an eye on Aethard. Bryn took my hand, halting me inside the doorway, and I watched as he lifted it and brushed his lips across my knuckles. A small gesture, one he'd done countless times, but I felt the apology in the way it lingered a heartbeat longer than normal, in the way he screwed his eyes shut, as if holding in tears.

He looked up, and our eyes locked. There were so many things I wanted to say to him; I was so relieved he'd made it through the city, I was so unnerved by Aethard and the man he'd been, I'd seen my parents. Most of all, I wanted to tell him that I loved him, but that he'd broken my trust when he'd taken my choice away from me. And I was glad he'd done it because it meant I was here with him. And I hated that he'd done it, because I knew, if given the choice, I'd do the same to keep him here with me, even if it meant dooming the rest of the world in the process.

I didn't have the strength to face what kind of person that made me.

So, I settled for a smile, which he returned. We shared a loaded glance, knowing that things were different between us. But this wasn't the time, and when he let go of my hand, I followed behind.

I watched as he wound down ahead of me, his gaze never leaving Aethard—who was stiff with indignation and ignoring Hunter's many suspicious glances. I let out a long breath, wondering what in the Elders' names I was going to do about my brother if we got off this island alive.

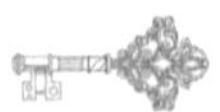

The short distance to Colagh and Tanjiu took a very long time. Assailed by nightmarish visions that layered over all the others just below the surface, I couldn't help but clutch my head and huddle in on myself every time a new wave of panic gripped my heart. It was coming more frequently, and far too often over the short distance that we ran. We stopped to battle illusions, clutching each other to keep from separating in the height of madness.

It was getting hard to discern what was real and what wasn't, and when we found Colagh and Tanjiu huddled at the base of a building, I almost didn't stop. But Aethard knew, could somehow see through it better than the rest even without Derth's power, and dragged the rest of us to a halt before we could pass them by.

"Why help us?" I asked with a faint glimmer of hope that my brother was showing signs of shucking the evil persona I'd freed him from.

That hope was dashed when he curled a lip in disgust at the whimpering Vorthes clinging to Sam and Bryn. "I don't want to be here any longer than we need to, and I know you. You'd drag us all over the city to search for them.

I clenched my fists but didn't say anything as I turned to Colagh. His eyes were wild, his hands clutching Bryn's collar, and his mouth opened and closed in small, rapid gasps. I shook his shoulder, and he recoiled. Tanjiu wasn't much better; they clutched Sam to their chest, like a parent sheltering a small child. I let out a bark of laughter at the absurd way that Sam's mouth fell open, and then cleared my throat when Hunter raised a quizzical brow my way.

Stop, or they'll think you've lost your mind, I thought.

But with Hunter helping Sam and Bryn hauling Colagh further along the street, we were moving again. The ground shifted, and I was thrust into the void, writhing in interminable darkness, and then I was back in my body. This time, Colagh and Tanjiu blinked, as if released from their nightmares with us.

"L-Lila?" Tanjiu asked. "What—?"

"We need to leave," I told them. "Before the defenses take hold again."

"Where is Derth?" Colagh demanded. I'd never seen him in such disarray, but he composed himself quickly. "Did you catch him?"

"I'll tell you everything that's happened once we're on the ship," I said, "but we need to go *now*." I moved aside and gestured to let them pass me. "Paerna is alive and with the people we rescued. We'll get him on the way."

They both perked up at their friend's name, and swallowed any other questions or protests they might have. We started to move again, faster this time as Hunter took the lead with the Vorthes close behind. Bryn lingered at the back of the group, between Aethard and me.

It was a short jog through deserted streets to find the house the Salavans were huddled in. The Vorthes ran to their unconscious friend and recoiled from what they found. Colagh whispered a few words to Tanjiu, their eyes wide, before waving his hands to lift Paerna from the ground with a gust of air. He remained aloft as the Vorthes led him out of the building ahead of the crowd of confused, half-starved people.

One woman in leather armor caught my arm before she followed the rest. "What happened to us?" she asked with an air of command belied by the wide-eyed look she gave Colagh, who had just summoned wind with the wave of his hand. "Where are we?"

There was too much to explain right now, so I told her, "The gift is real, and a man used it to control all of you, to bring you here. We stopped him, but we need to leave before things get worse."

"The waking nightmares?" she asked.

I nodded, and though she frowned, she didn't argue further, and helped me usher the other Salavans, all harrowed and thin, but able to walk. Hunter led them away in the direction of the Vorthes who turned down another alley with Paerna floating before them. Bryn hefted a man's arm over his shoulder to support the weight of an injured leg, and we set off, Aethard straggling behind.

I let everyone pass me to fall in beside him. He shot me a distrustful glare, and then focused his attention on the path ahead. "How long before we lose our minds completely?" I asked.

"Not long now," he replied, his eyes wide. He stumbled and caught himself, pulling away from my instinctual reach to steady him.

"What are you seeing?" I asked.

His nostrils flared and his mouth tightened into a thin line. When he looked at me this time, I saw genuine fear in his eyes, with no condescending attitude, no haughty disdain. Just a man who had seen

more than his share of horror. In that moment I saw past Derth to my
brother beneath. A victim, whether he'd invited the darkness or not.

Now, I was curious whether he had.

Aethard's shell of contempt slipped back into place. "What haunts
me is more than you could stomach, *little* sister," he replied. He
muttered to himself. "You wouldn't understand."

"I'd like to," I replied, "if you'd let me."

He grimaced. The silence between us stretched as we walked,
louder than the groans of the people ahead, trying to fight off the
encroaching aura of terror building around us, straining for release.
The orbs pulsed with the same red we'd seen in the spire, as if in
warning of whatever was about to be unleashed. I didn't want to be here
when it was.

We need to move faster, I thought, expecting Bryn's reply. But the
hollow in my chest was my only answer. "We need to move faster," I
called out. Bryn half-turned his head and nodded, and then he and Sam
urged the people to move faster, and Hunter picked up his pace at the
front of the line.

"I didn't ask for this," Aethard muttered. I glanced at him, not sure
I'd heard him until his eyes slid to mine. "The darkness, the void,
whatever that was. I didn't ask for it," he said again, his eyes meeting
mine. "But I used it. I knew what I was doing. I thought it was the only
way to survive, and maybe that wasn't all my idea, but *I* did those
things."

"Where did the darkness come from, then?" I asked.

"It doesn't matter," he said. "It's over, and I'm your prisoner now,
so what does it matter where it came from?"

"It matters because I want to know what happened to you," I
insisted. "How you could be the boy that I remember holding my hand
in the gardens, *and* the man that tortured me and tried to kill me."

"I'm not that boy anymore," he replied. "He died with our parents."

"I'd like to hear how that happened," I said, gently, because I could
see that I was one wrong word from him closing up again.

He huffed out an angry breath, the angry mask sliding over his
countenance. "This is hardly the time for a family chat," he said. "And I
don't think you've earned my whole sad history yet." He shook the

bracelet on his wrist, and I rolled my eyes, all sympathy and curiosity lost in the face of his arrogance. "I think I've made the price clear."

"Fine," I grumbled. The small speck of sympathy burned away from the anger and resentment he inspired. "Let's get out of here."

The arch in the wall came into view, and the moment I stepped through, the pall of fear and dread disappeared as if it had never existed. My shoulders sagged in relief, as did everyone else's. We still had to get through the fog, and hope whatever was happening on the other side of the wall behind us didn't spread, but, for this one moment, we were safe.

Pushing through my exhaustion, I strode past the Salavans as they sagged to the ground, and Hunter and Sam, who were talking to Colagh in hushed voices. I took a deep breath, inhaling the fishy odor of the kelp clinging to the shoreline at low tide, strangely soothing after the stale smell of dust I'd just left behind. I felt Bryn's approach before I heard him, his energy soothing as it enveloped me in the scent of tall pines.

"I saw you talking to Aethard," he said, his mouth twisting when he said the name. "Is everything all right?"

"No," I said with a chuckle devoid of humor. "It's not. I thought stopping Derth would give me closure. But now?" I glanced over my shoulder at Aethard, who'd set himself apart from the crowd. "It's a different problem. And there's Vortheim, and the Gloom, and... I can't explain it, but I feel it's all pulling me toward something. Like it's all on me to figure out."

"It's not," Bryn insisted. I shook my head, and he took my hands in his. A jolt went through my body from his touch, the spark in me recognizing the spark in him, subdued as it was. "I'm with you. Whether you decide to march to Vortheim or find a place where we can ignore the world's problems for the rest of our days, I'm with you."

"I know you are," I sighed. I released his hand and held mine out to the fog to push it aside before sending a gout of flame into the sky. "For now, let's settle for getting everyone off this Elders' cursed island."

CHAPTER FORTY-FIVE

Safely ensconced in the galley of the *Celerity*, we recounted all that had happened on the island to Captain Morrig. The people we'd rescued had been fed and were resting in borrowed berths, Paerna was recovering in the surgery, and Aethard was brooding at the far end of the table as everyone cast furtive glances his way.

Sam's brow furrowed as he wrote in one of his many notebooks, documenting every word I said, asking me to repeat my observations and sensations more than once.

He muttered to himself after I'd finished, and Colagh stood behind him at the table, peering at the scribbles unfolding beneath Sam's pencil.

"So, Derth is... dead?" the captain asked, brow scrunched in confusion.

I nodded hesitantly. "Yes, in a way," I replied. "But whatever changed Aethard was more than the void, I'm sure of it." I glanced at Aethard. "I don't think he did this to himself. He said as much, but more than that, I *felt* something in it, using it. And my..." I hesitated, gazing up into Captain Morrig's face, the only father I'd ever known, "father... told me the same. He told me to bring balance back to Celuthia. Whatever that means."

"So, our criminal was your brother," Colagh said. "All this time, the monster we sought was a young man corrupted by the void, so powerful that it created new Gloom clouds and almost destroyed one of the most powerful Ambient I've ever seen."

"He may have been corrupted," Bryn interjected, "but he controlled his actions. He admitted as much." Aethard glanced sidelong at us but said nothing.

"True," Tanjiu admitted, "and yet we were sent to capture him without knowing the extent of what we were chasing. If we'd put the bracelet on him, would we have unleashed the darkness on ourselves? Would it have done anything without your intervention?" There was a bitter taste to their energy that had been festering since Pearl's death.

"Remember, the Gloom only came when we counteracted the darkness," I said, pointing at Bryn and myself. "The combination of Ambience and void was to blame, not the darkness alone."

"Perhaps the Malachi didn't know the extent of what he sought," Sam suggested.

Colagh let out a short, angry bark of a laugh. "He knew." All eyes focused on him. Even Aethard turned to listen. "I was told that obtaining Derth was of paramount importance. And that it was possible that he would be difficult to contain, but what he carried would change the fate of Vortheim. I was a fool to hope that he could help us end the Gloom. And I am genuinely sorry to see that it was your brother caught up in my country's machinations."

"It was your Malachi that started all of this," Aethard said with a cruel smile. "The darkness? He's the one that gave it to me."

Colagh's face went blank, and then he shook his head once. A denial. "No, not even the Malachi is that powerful." His wide, pleading eyes sought mine. "It would have destroyed the Ambience if you hadn't destroyed it; there's no way he could be utilizing it, correct? We would have seen signs..."

"It *is* destructive," I replied carefully, "but when combined with the Ambience we channeled, it became..."

"The Gloom," Tanjiu whispered. They shook their head, their body stiff. "Did the Malachi... is the Malachi creating the Gloom?"

"I have known of the Ambience my whole life, studied it in school, and I have no idea what to make of this," Colagh said.

"If I understand this correctly," Sam drawled, turning between several pages as he spoke, "the Gloom is no more than the byproduct of two opposing forces colliding. The Ambience is a force of pure creation, and the Void is its entropic counterpart."

"That much we learned in school," Tanjiu said.

"Yes," Sam waved his hand in the air, "but they should not react to each other this way. They have existed in a balance since Celuthia's origin, as far as we know. Has the Gloom always been a problem in Vortheim? Do your history books go back that far?"

Colagh frowned. "We have much documentation about Vortheim's founding, as the first Malachi was the one who founded it. By all accounts, the first Gloom wasn't encountered until hundreds of years later."

"Ah!" Sam exclaimed. "Something must have changed in that time, to fundamentally change the nature of the Ambience and the Void. Something that allowed the Void to be wielded in the same way that the Ambience can be. I'd assumed that Derth's darkness was an affectation to inspire horror in his victims, but it was the perfect example of such a wielding. When those two opposites collided, the Gloom was formed. If that bond between you two hadn't broken, the Gloom may have grown infinitely larger, or been far more dangerous than it was."

"The Gloom existed before these two," Tanjiu protested. "Even if they made this Gloom, and the one before that, they couldn't possibly be responsible for the rest."

"Perhaps there are more like them," Sam offered. "Or, perhaps Vortheim is more volatile an environment than Trylia, since the Ambience is so diminished here."

The room fell silent, and my head spun with the implications of what we had done.

Colagh's face turned red as his Ambience flared red hot with rage. Betrayal was written all over his features and his posture, down to the fists clenched so tight that his skin over his knuckles turned white.

Aethard's smile widened. *He's enjoying this,* I thought, disgusted. "I didn't realize it at the time," he continued, "but the first seeds for the void were planted by him. Now that my memories are back," he grimaced, "I can see what he hid from me at the time. I may have been angry enough to try to murder our king—killing our parents in the process—but Junal of Vortheim was the one who twisted it into something darker. Something the void could latch onto, allowing it to take control of me."

Colagh began to shake, and the rest of us stood silent as the implications sank in.

Aethard chuckled. "The Junal I knew wouldn't have thought twice about leveraging the hope that his prodigious power could end the Gloom, to amass more political power. His father came to Trylia to end the war, but Junal wanted none of it. Why wouldn't he make himself a weapon to stall negotiations? He was darkness incarnate, like the thing that had a hold of me."

Tanjiu's mouth fell open in horror, but Colagh's deep frown was bitter. Angry resignation radiated through his vivid, roiling aura.

"You must admit, dear friend, that there is truth to what he says." Colagh placed a hand on their shoulder. "We both have felt uneasy since the current Malachi began his reign. For me, this confirms what my heart has been telling me. And I, for one, will not be going back. Neither should you, my friend. And we both know that Paerna can never return."

"Why?" I asked.

"He's been touched by the Gloom. They'll kill him on sight." He shrugged. "Your Trylians would likely do the same, but there are plenty of places to hide. Once he's recovered, we can make a quiet life here."

"I will stay, to help you care for him," Tanjiu said. "After Pearl, I don't want to abandon you."

"I don't like the idea of three Vorthe Tethers wandering around Trylia on their own," Hunter said. "How do we know they won't cause havoc?"

"We don't," I replied. A warm rush of Ambience brought a wave of instinct with it, perhaps from my father, perhaps from somewhere deeper, and I held a hand out to Colagh. "I want your word that you won't betray what you know about us, and that you won't harm the innocent with your power. I want a vow that you will give up your Tether if you break that word."

My hand glowed with fiery brilliance, reaching for Colagh and his power, a twin to my flame. When he extended his hand to clasp mine, our power intertwined. "I swear it," he replied, and the glow passed to him until we released our grasp. I did the same with Tanjiu, and then the light in my hand flared out.

"What was that?" Hunter asked. Bryn was staring at me with admiration, his energy flaring in tandem with mine.

"An Ambient pact," Sam said with a curious tilt to his head. "I've never seen one in person. How did you know to do that?"

I shook my head, as confused as Hunter. "I don't know. It felt like something I'd done before, but that's not true."

"Hmmm," Sam replied, "perhaps your father gave you more than a responsibility."

Aethard groaned. "Of course he did."

I chose to ignore his outburst and gazed instead at Colagh and Tanjiu. "Where will you go?" I asked.

"I don't know," Colagh admitted. "Perhaps somewhere close to First Port, so that we can keep an eye on the Gloom off the coast, and warn people if it comes near. Somewhere nearby, but remote enough to avoid curious gazes."

"I wish there was some way to get into Salvation," Sam muttered. "I wonder if there's anything there to learn about the Gloom."

"I told you I'd get you home," I reminded him. "Now we have another excuse to try. We'll get the Salavans home, and then we can head in that direction."

"And what about me?" Aethard asked. "Am I to follow you wherever you go? Or will you force a pact on me, too?"

I stared at him without responding. I'd wondered the same thing, but hadn't given it much thought with everything else that had to be done. Now that I was faced with the choice, I didn't know what to say. Could I commit to watching him for the rest of my life to ensure he never gave in to the darkness again?

"For now, you're with us," I told him. "We'll get you a horse in First Port, and when we're done in the north, we'll go to King's Port. After that," I shrugged, "we'll see."

Paerna finally awoke before sunset, disoriented, with no memory of what'd happened to him. Colagh and Tanjiu helped him to the berth deck to rest—avoiding mirrors until they could explain—leaving Bryn and me alone in the surgery to find our rest. We stood in awkward silence, but I couldn't think of a way to start a conversation. So much had changed in such a short amount of time, and I couldn't put into words all that I wanted to say.

Bryn broke the silence first. "Tell me what you're thinking," he said. "I can still read your face like I always could, but I feel like there's a hole inside me where you used to be. I can't stand not being able to feel you."

"I don't know how I am," I told him, my voice flat as I struggled to hold my conflicting emotions at bay. "I have a brother, and pieces of my childhood are coming back to me, but I'm still getting flashes of horrible visions when I close my eyes, and I'm not sure what's real. I met my father's spirit, and all he did was give me some cryptic message. And I have the same hole inside me that you have, because you tried to undo what I'd done." My anger was the first to emerge, and his face crumpled. "You took my choice from me, Bryn. And it cost us something so precious. I didn't realize how much I relied on that connection, how much it meant to me. But now that I can't feel you, that you *took part of my power*, I feel like part of me died."

"I'm sorry," he whispered. My heart ached at the pain on his face, the true remorse warring with righteous indignation. "I didn't want to lose you. You were dying!"

"That was my choice!" I retorted. "That darkness was hungry. It wanted to consume *everything*, and I didn't want to risk it getting loose. To go after Sam, or the Vorthes, or *you!* I don't blame you for the reason behind it, I love you for it. But you should have honored what I sacrificed, instead of sacrificing what we had."

"If you'd died, we wouldn't have had it anymore," he shouted, his face now flush with anger, too. "Without you, that connection didn't matter! Would you have sat and watched if it was me? If I decided to sacrifice myself to save everyone, would you sit by and accept it?"

I blinked a few times, my anger a beast clawing at my hold on the Ambience. That window cracked open, and my skin started to glow. "*No.*"

"I know," he said. He strode the few steps separating us and grasped my hand, holding my ring up between us. "I know this wasn't an idle promise. I know that you love me, and you would fight against the Ambience itself to save *my* life. So don't tell me that I was wrong to defy your wishes, because you would have done the same to me."

"No," I began, but he tucked a finger under my chin as he closed the rest of the distance between us, so that I was looking up into his face. His breath fluttered the wild strands of my hair hanging around my face as he interrupted me.

"You *would* have," he insisted. "Because you are strong and fierce, and you never give up without fighting for what you believe in. That's why we came here, hunting a man who was wreaking havoc on the continent. That's why we're together, because you fought to stay alive when Aethard was Derth, torturing you to death on that ship. And because you fought for *me*, when my uncle could have killed me. Because you love me."

"I do," I whispered. He crushed his lips against mine, and I didn't have to hear what he was thinking to know that he needed to feel me as much as I needed to feel him. I leaned into the kiss, wrapping one arm around his shoulders while the other grasped the hair at the back of his head. His arms wound around me to pull me flush against him.

I thought I lost you, I thought, but there was no reply. He couldn't hear me, and I sobbed, mourning that lost connection, hoping we wouldn't lose each other without it.

"I almost lost you," Bryn murmured, echoing my thought. "It felt like my heart was going to stop when yours did," he said. "I will always choose you over everything, even if it means the world will shatter around us. Because I know that we can put it back together. I can't..." he shook his head, "can't lose you."

"You won't," I breathed. Because despite everything that had changed between us, one thing hadn't. I loved him, and there was no doubt in my mind that he loved me. "You are my home." I touched my forehead to his, staring into his cobalt eyes. There was a ring around his pupils now, a flash of Ambient light that flared when his gaze met mine. "Whatever comes next, we'll face it together."

EPILOGUE

The Silver Peaks loomed high above us as we emerged from beneath the trees at the northern edge of Esteweld Forest. It had been months since our encounter on the island, taking a few weeks during a harsh winter storm to recover in First Port. The Vorthes stayed for a short time, and then left to find their own way on the outskirts where Paerna wouldn't be seen. When the weather finally broke, we hired a few wagons for the Salavans, retrieved Raven and the other horses from the stables, and headed west toward Salava.

Two weeks ago, we'd delivered the residents of Salava home to their families. It'd been a tear-filled and heartwarming event, individual reunions becoming a city-wide celebration that coincided with the spring solstice. After several days enjoying the hospitality and gratitude of the town—while Aethard stood apart from the crowd—we'd set off to the northeast, following Sam's directions toward Salvation with bags full of provisions for a long journey.

The sun sat at its apex in the pale blue sky as we found enough space to corral the horses and eat a hasty meal at the northern edge of Esteweld forest. The ground was littered with stones the same dull grey as the mountain visible through the trees.

I joined Bryn as he brushed the horses and picked their hooves clean of rocks and other debris, sharing a shy smile with him when he looked up. As I grabbed a brush for Raven, I saw a flash of memory; my mother's hand covered mine as she showed me how to brush our horse for the first time while I balanced on a stool in the barn. I recalled the smell of warm hay and the pride I'd felt when she told me what a good job I'd done.

The madness I'd almost succumbed to had faded into the realm of actual nightmares, but the flashes of true memory still took me by surprise.

Raven nudged my shoulder as I approached. When I didn't give her a scratch, she picked at my braid with her teeth. The soft fur of her nose brushed against my cheek, and I laughed.

"I missed that sound," Bryn said as he chuckled. He looked up from Badger's hoof with a wide smile on his face. "I haven't heard you laugh in months. Not like that."

"There's been a lot on my mind," I replied as I scratched behind Raven's ears. "But I'm glad we're here. I don't think I've ever seen Sam so excited."

Bryn glanced in the direction of our friend, who had his nose buried in one of his notebooks. "I'm glad you're happy," he said, trying to mask the pain he felt. Throughout these long months, our relationship still held a bitter edge that it hadn't before; it was something I'd been trying to fix, to put aside my resentment. And we both knew that I hadn't been able to.

I patted Raven's neck before moving away, and reached out to grab Bryn's hand when he dropped Badger's hoof. He looked up into my eyes, and I cupped his cheek.

"I *am* happy," I said. "We survived and we're together. No matter what's happened, I know I have you."

Bryn kissed my wrist. "You *always* have me."

After our meal we followed Sam out of the trees to stand at the base of the massive edifice looming high in the sky. His hands skimmed the base of the mountain. "This is the spot, I'm sure of it," he said, trying as hard to reassure himself as he was us. It looked like nothing more than a solid wall of rock.

With my senses enhanced as they'd been since the island, I could feel that this wasn't an ordinary mountainside. There was a slab set into the otherwise solid mountain, acting as a doorway that would be impossible to move without the Ambience.

There were echoes of countless touches of different Ambient over the centuries. Most of them were as old as Sam or more, and there were even a few traces of his energy long-faded within. "I can feel you in this place," I told him. His fingers clutched his notebook tight. "The entrance is covered," I placed my hand in the center of the slab, "and every time someone opened it, they left a trace of their energy behind. Some are recent." I smiled at him. "I think someone's living in there."

His face lit up with excitement and anxiety. "It feels strange to be here again after all these years."

I smiled. *It's so nice to see him like this,* I thought. I waited a beat, but there was no response, as usual. My smile faltered. *I keep forgetting Bryn's not listening.*

In the months since our connection had dulled, I'd mourned its loss almost constantly. To have someone know my mind without having to voice my thoughts had been a gift. It was so much harder to communicate out loud, when my mouth twisted what I tried to say into a garbled mess that often didn't convey what I wanted it to. I'd tried to fix it, to form a new bond like I had after our battle with Roglin, but something had changed. Before, it felt like bringing two halves of a whole together, as if there'd been a void in my spirit that his fit perfectly.

Now, our energies felt complete on their own, and it wasn't the same.

Bryn noticed my inner turmoil, as he usually did, and flashed me a wan smile. I wished I could hear what he was thinking. But, since then the resentment would be laid bare without the filter, perhaps it was for the best. I did my best to smile back, but I could see that it didn't reassure him.

I forced my thoughts back to the mountain in front of me as Sam's power probed the granite and schist alongside mine. He'd started to show his age in Stalth after our encounters with the void, but I kept my face even as I realized how weak his power had become. Even in the months since we'd left the island, he'd diminished.

"I think I can get it open," I told him. "Stand back."

Aethard snorted, and I rolled my eyes. I'd hoped we could make time to talk somewhere along the journey west, but he'd remained aloof, only interacting with us when necessary, or when he found it necessary to make a snide comment. I put him out of my mind as my power slid into the rock, feeling the edges of the slab and digging in like fingers digging into soft dirt. It shifted as I pulled, a host of ethereal spirits pulling with me, and the slab began to shift. But the energy imbued into it felt like it was fighting to stay in place, and the miniscule ground I gained was taken back.

"It's not letting me move it," I grunted.

"Not letting you?" Hunter said. "A piece of rock isn't *letting you* move it?"

"Likely a defense mechanism," Sam replied. I shuddered. "Perhaps it will only open for certain individuals."

I huffed out a breath, pulling harder, but only succeeded in tiring faster. I released the slab and stood back, hands planted on my hips as I glared at the mountain, frustrated. *We've come all this way, I promised Sam I would help him, and I can't move this cursed rock!*

My frustration flared into anger, but it didn't feel entirely my own. As a Conduit, Sam had taught me that my emotions had always influenced the Ambience. Now, after what Bryn had done to bring me back, it was as if the Ambience had found a new home in my spirit. My power was more volatile—like my emotional state—but I was in control of it. And the spirits resented being rebuffed by whatever was keeping this entrance shut.

Letting my anger flare bright with theirs was easy; after all we'd been through, I had a deep well of lingering resentment to pull from. Everything that had happened with Derth, the nightmares fueled by visions brought on by the island, Aethard's insistence on alienating all of us, and worst of all, the bitter regret I felt about Bryn's betrayal all stoked my anger higher and higher. I felt like a volcano about to erupt, and I focused that into the Ambience as I let it burst free.

So violent was my outburst that the spirits were given visible form. Translucent and glowing like fiery embers that heated the slab of rock as it slowly slid forward until it came free of its moorings amid a shower of pebbles torn from the mountain around it. With a guttural shout I thrust the slab aside, leaving a long circular tunnel visible where it had once stood.

I closed my eyes, letting the Ambience burn through me in a cathartic wave of rage that I'd suppressed for months. My burning spirits crowded around me like a wall of flames, ready and eager to unleash my wrath while my blood pounded in my ears with the beat of my heart. There was something so alluring about this power, more so than the void, more than the power Bryn and I could command, because it was all *mine.* I didn't need to rely on anyone but myself as long as I was willing to embrace my anger.

"Lila?" A voice called to me from a distance. It lanced through me over the pounding heartbeat in my ears and the roar of whispers from the spirits. My eyes shot open to see Bryn standing before me, outside the ring of translucent flames. He wore a mask of concern, and his eyes held mine. He reached out a hand as I opened my mouth to stop him, terrified that he would be scorched by the heat dancing between us, but he passed through unharmed as if it didn't exist.

He didn't say anything more, but I saw my anger reflected in his eyes, and I remembered that he felt the same as I did. The love and understanding in his gaze doused my anger and their flames, and I shuddered as they fled in the wake of my love for the man that would brave the blaze of my anger to remind me that I was loved.

I took the hand still reaching for me and brought it to my lips. He closed his eyes with a sigh of relief and pulled me into his warm embrace. Sam moved past us, toward the tunnel, his eyes full of reverence and trepidation.

We gathered the horses, tying Sam's Whiskey to Badger's lead, and followed Sam into the close tunnel. The space was just big enough to allow the horses to pass single file. The walls showed no tool marks, too smooth and perfectly cylindrical to be natural. They'd been shaped by the Ambience, I was sure, but I couldn't tell how long ago because of the precision with which they'd been created. Orbs affixed to the wall on either side glowed along the length of the tunnel, their light mimicking the pinpoint of natural light at the other end. I half-expected them to glow red, but they remained the same.

The trip through the tunnel was over soon, and I stepped out beneath a rock shelf looming overhead. Boulders cut off all but one path winding through the mountain that blocked our view of anything beyond.

Sam looked around with a worried frown when he emerged from the tunnel. "What's wrong, Sam?" I asked. "It's not what you remember?"

He shook his head. "No. I didn't anticipate the amount of damage this far from the city itself. I was in a bit of a rush the last time I left the valley."

"What used to be here?" Hunter asked.

Sam sighed, and then pointed at the boulders, some of which were as tall as the trees we'd passed in the heart of the forest that stretched up into the sky like mountains themselves. "These rocks used to be an arbor that one of our masons carved. A forest of stone trees to mirror the forest on the other side of the mountain, arranged in columns to usher visitors through to the city. They were so intricate that they could have been mistaken for actual petrified trees."

We followed the curve of the mountain as it diminished in size. Tufts of lichen and scrubby underbrush thrived in the scree all around us. Eventually the mountainous terrain gave way to another evergreen forest, with waterfalls feeding creeks that fed into a larger river. The ground sloped down along our path, and the river fell over many drops, spraying water into the air in a constant mist to our left.

The beauty of our surroundings astounded me, and I understood why Sam had chosen his new home in a place that so closely resembled this hidden refuge. Bryn's face glowed with delight as he looked around. Splendor like this spoke to his soul in the same way that the ocean spoke to mine, and my heart soared to see him enjoying the beauty as I was.

He suddenly tensed and scanned the area. As he did, I noticed that the flow of Ambience had changed, rippling from behind the boulders at the same moment that Bryn's head snapped in that direction, hearing something too soft for the rest of us to hear.

Bryn's entire body froze, not standing ready for an attack but coated in a foreign Ambient power that locked his limbs in place. My foot left the ground, and then all my muscles froze. I didn't fall, but hung in the air, no matter how much I willed my foot to touch the ground.

Materializing out of thin air from around the far side of the nearest boulder, a tall man wearing a cloak of slate grey glared at our group. His features were severe, and he stood as if ready to attack, though he bore no weapon. His striking brown eyes narrowed as he scanned each of us in turn, and then his attention honed in on me. Like burrowing insects his power dug into my mind, trying to wrest information from me.

But I'd been violated like this too many times, and I would not let it happen again. Anger burst out of me in a shockwave that rocked the man onto his heels. He cocked his head to the side, and his eyebrows raised in surprise before he regained control of his features.

The ground cracked beneath his feet when my power erupted in a gout of white-hot flame. A deluge of water poured from his outstretched hands to douse the flame closest to him. The flames subsided, the ground left scorched and cracked as I struggled to break free of his hold. My toe twitched as he strolled closer, still glaring, until he was mere inches away.

"Who are you?" he asked. He sounded curious, unconcerned, as he waved a hand near my face to free my mouth of his control to speak.

"Release us, and I'll answer your question," I snarled. The corner of his mouth ticked up in a condescending smile.

Sam mumbled urgently, unable to move his mouth until the man glanced in his direction. "I long for Salvation, body and soul," Sam gasped. The man peered at him, his eyes wide with shock as he lowered his hood. Pale blonde hair was pulled back from his severe, angular face, tied at the back of his neck. The stones shifted from the other side of the boulder, and another person appeared. The same facial structure—though softer—and hair color, but her gaze was suspicious where the man's had grown curious.

Both regarded Sam for a long moment before they bowed deeply in response. As one, they replied, "Salvation you shall have."

"Who are you?" the woman asked.

Sam replied cautiously. "My name is Samuel. I've been away from home for a very long time, and I wish to return. And show my friends the place where I was born."

"That may be," the woman answered, "but there is more to you than meets the eye. This woman," she said, turning her gaze in my direction, "contains great strength."

"I swear on my life, we mean you no harm. If you could release my companions, I would be most grateful," Sam said.

Pine needles rustled behind me, and I watched Bryn flex his fingers when he was released. The blonde man's energy still held tight to me, though, and my anger flared, pushing it back a bit further. My fingers twitched, and the man's eyes shot to them. Aethard walked into my field of vision. A mocking smile twitched on his lips before Bryn pushed him toward Hunter, frowning when he noticed my continued restraint.

"Let her go," Bryn growled, putting himself between the strangers and me. My power burned away more of the violating Ambience. My hand flexed in an echo of Bryn's movement before the man's eyes ticked to Bryn.

"We do not allow visitors," he said imperiously. "You may know our key, but we don't know *you*. You will be watched, and if any of you-" his warning gaze cut to me, and then to Sam, "-do anything to the detriment of our community and its people, you will be stripped of your power and held in a cell until you forget what the sun feels like."

My restraint fell away all at once. I straightened and returned the strangers' accusatory stares. "My name is Lila, and this is Sam, Bryn, Hunter, and Aethard. We're here to bring our friend home." I gestured to Sam. "We aren't here to harm anyone, you have our word. But if you try to pry into my thoughts again, I *will* defend myself."

They scrutinized us for a long moment, and then the woman stepped forward. "As the two Ambient in your party, the others are your charge and your responsibility," she said to Sam and me. I shared a look with Aethard, who tugged the sleeve of his shirt over the bracelet encircling his wrist. "Any wrongdoing on their part shall be rectified by you, according to our laws."

"Agreed," Sam replied, "though there will be nothing to worry about, we assure you."

The man held out his hand to Sam, all trace of cold suspicion melted by a warm smile. "My name is Aydan, and this is my sister Nadya." Nadya bowed her head, still aloof. "We will take you to Salvation to see the council, but please do not use the Ambience until you have been cleared to do so. We have a long history of grief at the hands of outsiders, and I would dislike being forced to defend my city."

"We understand," Sam said, and the rest of us nodded in response. Aydan walked ahead while we fell in line behind him, with Nadya trailing behind.

"My people are here," Sam whispered. "The Ambient are alive." Happiness rolled off him in waves. It was infectious, and my unease was no match for the hope it inspired in me.

We came around the edge of the mountain, and the basin of the valley was laid before us, nestled in the arms of snow-capped mountains. A vast ocean of green grass covered the sloping trail downhill, with islands of wildflowers in every color imaginable. A gentle breeze carried an overwhelming floral scent up the hill.

Large green fields sat between irrigation channels that sparkled like flowing sapphires beyond the wild growth. And, glowing like a beacon, a massive white spire rose from ordered streets of a city large enough to rival King's Port.

Sam gasped as tears rolled down his cheeks. "Welcome to Salvation."

ACKNOWLEDGMENTS

I am so grateful that I was able to add another story to this series. First, I will always thank my husband, Quinn Brentson, for helping me through the highs and lows, offering me encouragement and talking through the details with me.

To my kids, Carter, Kaylee, and Ellie, thank you for your excitement and your belief in me. Thank you for tolerating my hours at the computer.

To my parents, Holly and Tim Fisher, thank you for showing me that I can accomplish whatever I set out to do. To my brother, Alex, my sister, Rhiannon, and my in-laws Paul and Sherrie, thank you all for being enthusiastic supporters in all stages.

For everyone that helped me to make this book so much better than I thought it could be. Woody Johns of Copper Coin Editing, you are a beacon of reasonable suggestions and the best constructive criticism that I've ever known. To my beta readers, Trinity Cunningham, Paul Brentson, Sherrie Brentson, Shari Lane, Beth Waymire, Rhiannon Brentson, Anastasia Dumarque, Jamie Strube, and Katie Zeliger, your feedback was invaluable.

Once again, Marybeth Mondok, my cover is beautiful, and the scene breaks are exactly what I wanted. My character art, my short story covers, it's all amazing.

Finally, thank YOU for reading this book. Thank you for taking a chance on an independent author's dreams. I hope you'll continue with me as these characters' stories unfold.

Extras

The Story Continues in

FACADE OF SANCTUARY

Book 3 of the Ambience Series

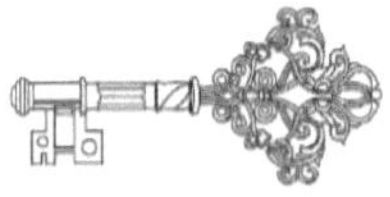

Coming Soon!

DANA C BRENTSON has been enjoying fantasy storytelling since she was small, whether in books, movies, or video games. As an adult, she began to create her own stories, which blossomed when she started to explore tabletop gaming.

Find out more about her and her other works by subscribing to her newsletter at www.dcbrentson.com

If you enjoyed
PROVENANCE OF POWER
Check Out
SALVATION'S FALL
The Ambient Series: Sam
By Dana C Brentson

Sparks flew all around, flames dancing for seconds before fluttering in a gust of wind. Laughter and shouts of exasperation echoed off the stone edifice of the white spire glinting in the sunlight, and Sam smiled to himself.

The children took to his lessons better than he thought possible, already manipulating the elements faster than he had at their age. They freely called upon the spirits that tethered them to the Ambient Pool at the heart of their world, and those spirits granted them access to it and allowed them to alter the fabric of reality as they wanted. A small hand grabbed his and shook it with the unrelenting fervor of youth.

"Mister Sam! There's someone here for you!"

"Master Samuel?" a timid voice called. Sam turned to find one of the council's messengers standing in the path leading into the heart of the city.

"Are they back?" Sam asked, eager to hear the news of his parent's return. In these times of peril, with Ellen's forces hunting the denizens of Salvation, it had become a sacred duty for his father and mother to help protect their home and its people. They were in charge of security, after all.

"Yessir," the young man replied with a deferential nod. "Just walked through the gates and asked after you."

Sam turned to the children under his tutelage. "The lesson is over for the day." He clapped his hands together as the children yelled their excitement and scattered, skipping and laughing in the afternoon sun.

Sam turned and followed the messenger as he wound his way through the city, feet crunching along the gravel path from the Spire at its heart to the council chamber. The sun warmed his face and helped to dispel the anxiety building in his gut. His parents had been gone for a week trying to locate Ellen and the children she twisted into living weapons. He took another glance over his shoulder and gave silent thanks for his students' safety.

The squat dark stone building that served as the hub of government for their community loomed ahead. Several people lined the cobbled stoop, and turned at the sound of approaching footsteps. Among them Sam spotted the tall, muscular frame of his father, his hard blue eyes breaking their stern gaze for the briefest of smiles at his son. Next to his father, his mother's long blonde mane shone in the blazing light of the afternoon sun, liberal streaks of gray glinting like silver.

Her warm brown eyes found his and a radiant smile broke out, transforming her worried countenance into the carefree woman he had clung to as a babe. She stepped down and stood on tiptoe to kiss his cheek. Diminutive in stature, she had always seemed a giant to Sam; her intellect and compassion lent her the presence of someone mighty. Even as he folded his arms around her and tucked her head beneath his chin, her words made him feel a child again.

"My Sammy, how I've missed you." She pulled back from his embrace, beaming up at him. "How are the children?"

"Excelling. Every day they surprise me."

The doors to the chamber swung open on creaking hinges, summoning the attention of all those in attendance, and everyone filed into the rectangular building in the direction of the council at the far end. Sam's father stepped forward to lead their patrol as the doors swung closed behind them. Orbs set high in the walls cast light mimicking the sun, and their shadows danced behind the congregation as they passed rows of chairs. A myriad of purposeful footfalls pounded the raised wooden floor of the room as if a frenetic drum beat were announcing their presence.

A younger member of the patrol stumbled, catching his foot on a chair. Sam stopped to lend him a hand, grasping the man's arm at the elbow. Sweat beaded his brow and dampened his fringe of dark hair. Sam thought he felt a tremor pass through the man as he pulled his arm free and righted himself, but the council began to speak and Sam's attention wandered.

"She's moving again. We found bodies from the last patrol and several dozen children, but no sign of where she fled to." His father's voice boomed, echoing back through the room.

Sam placed a hand on his mother's shoulder as he peered over it at the council. She shivered, and Sam's brow furrowed in concern. Her shirt felt damp to his touch, her hand clammy when she reached up to pat his. Concerned, he looked to his father, finding sweat trickling down the back of his neck. As another council member began to speak, Sam's head swiveled back to the young man. He stood stooped, his face ashen and body trembling. Sam removed his hand from his mother's shoulder and moved to the fore of the group to speak with his father.

"Master Samuel, do you have something to say?" Dorian, a junior member of the council spoke up over the voice of his superior as Sam craned his neck to look at his father's face. Another tremor shook the large man, and his gaze locked onto his son's. Sam's eyes widened in panic as his father uttered one word and then reached out in an explosive movement toward the council.

"Run!"

Thank You

Thank you so much for being a part of this story, for continuing Lila's journey. If you enjoyed *Provenance Of Power,* please consider leaving a review on Amazon or Goodreads. For independent authors like me these reviews are extremely helpful for getting our work into more reader's hands. If you can't review on either of these sites, please consider leaving a review on social media.

Again, thank you so much for reading. I couldn't keep writing if it weren't for people like you.

With love and gratitude,
Dana